Malevolent KARMA

Norman MacRitchie Reeley

All Rights Reserved.

No part of this publication may be reproduced or transmitted by any means, electronic, mechanical, photocopy or otherwise, without the prior permission of the author. This is a work of fiction, and except in the case of historical record, the names, characters, and incidents are either the product of the author's imagination, or are used fictitiously. Any resemblance to actual persons, living or dead, business establishments, events, or locales is entirely coincidental.

Copyright © Norman MacRitchie Reeley 2012
Second Edition 2014
Norman MacRitchie Reeley has asserted his moral rights.

Norman MacRitchie Reeley
All rights reserved.
ISBN -13: 1495323874
ISBN-10: 1495323870

A CIP Catalogue record of this book is available from the British Library

First Paperback Edition 2013
This (Second) Paperback Edition 2014
normanreeley@gmail.com

Malevolent Karma

Contents

Prologue	...09
Book One: The Chronicles of Jonathan Amersbey	...11
Book Two: Alistair MacLeod's Story	...146
Book Three: In Mitigation of Iñaki Anton	...215
Book Four: Convergence	...393
Epilogue	...453
The Author	...455
Praise for Malevolent Karma	...456

Malevolent
'Having an evil or harmful influence'

Karma
'The total effect of a person's actions and conduct during the successive phases of the person's existence, regarded as determining the person's destiny'

1985, the miners are on strike, Northern Ireland is aflame and the Cold War is at its height. NATO is about to launch the biggest ever, Europe-wide, Soviet attack war simulation. HMS Resolution, GB´s Polaris nuclear ballistic missile submarine, has a key role in the War Games.
One year after the Brighton Bombings, the Provisional IRA and ETA the Basque terrorist organisation have an opportunity for another spectacular.

The convergence and crossing of the life paths of three young boys, born on the same day but thousands of miles apart, provides the conduit for a Provisional IRA attack with World Wide implications.

Was the destiny of these three boys influenced, or somehow pre-determined by a higher force?

Malevolent Karma

Acknowledgements:

My grateful thanks go to both Allan Dignan and Alan Carr, PR Officers at HMNB Clyde, Scotland, and the late Tony Pithers for their valuable insights and technical advice on Royal Navy matters.

I would also like to extend gratitude to the magnificent young officers and men who manned the Royal Navy Polaris submarine fleet in the nineteen eighties; it was a pleasure to know you and serve you up at Whistlefield, and you provided, albeit unknowingly, the background for this novel.

My own family has my thanks for their inadvertent contribution to the story; I hope they forgive me if they have at times felt like slaves!

My thanks to the friends who encouraged me to put pen to paper although they were promoting a different story ...maybe next time folks!

Finally, Gina, who unfailingly encouraged me and has had to put up with a year of completely disrupted routines, frustrations and hours when my brain was operating in Scotland, Ireland, England or in the Basque country.

Finally, finally... for the host of friends (and all of my readers are my friends), who have enjoyed reading the first edition, especially to those who have written to me expressing their opinions. I have taken on board all comments in the preparation of this second edition.

My grateful thanks to all of you.
Norman MacRitchie Reeley, October 2012 and 2014.

Norman MacRitchie Reeley

[Type text]

[Type text]

PROLOGUE

"To himself everyone is immortal; he may know that he is going to die, but he can never know that he is dead." ~Samuel Butler

He did not know who killed him. He was not to know, why, when, or even how he died. There was no previous indication of life-threatening issues. There was no hint of danger, nothing out of the ordinary, as he lived his normal routines of life in the weeks, days, minutes and even seconds before he was removed from the face of the earth as a living being. On reflection, it was a good way to go. He was there in body spirit and soul – a conventional human being – and in a microsecond POUF! The man no longer existed.

As I write this, a sudden window of childhood memory flashes into my thoughts. It is one of us all stalking our friends who are the Indians, and our gang of cowboys whooping with glee as we killed the last of the Apaches, who fell dramatically into the heather and bracken of the battlefield. The Indians definitely knew they were dead, because *Bang-Bang* in your face, meant you were!

Most victims …of old age, cancer, heart disease, or the myriad of other reasons to depart this life, have some time to prepare, receive the love and sympathy of family and friends. They have time and opportunity to reflect on the meaning of life and their own mortality. They are able to write their last Will and Testament, and make peace with themselves and their God. Some go willingly; others with terror in their eyes until the light extinguishes from within, and without.

This man, this human being, was denied such dignity: the experience, the understanding, and the sensations. He missed the joys and regrets of memories, the pain, the suffering, the mental relief, or the anguish, of knowing he was going to die.

He had no idea of his imminent departure from this life.

Norman MacRitchie Reeley

Book One

The Chronicle of Jonathan Amersbey

"A woman's hopes are woven of sunbeams; a shadow annihilates them."
~George Eliot

Chapter 1: 1964 Alicia

Alicia Vickery would have been described as an archetypal English beauty. Long, luxuriant, natural blonde hair, that cascaded over a graceful neck, with an almost translucent hint of blush in her complexion. The brilliant azure blue eyes brimmed with the energy and enthusiasm of a healthy, assured, fun-loving girl. She was elegantly tall, with a high firm-breasted, slim figure and an assured feminine poise, which since thirteen years old, had turned heads, male and female.

Alicia´s family background and class, whilst not in the aristocratic ranks, had enough wealth to trust fund a first-class girls´ school education and her subsequent reading of Fine Arts at Oxford. She had prepared well for high naval society, and her own secret ambition was to become the wife of the First Sea Lord, as her antecedent heroine, her great grandmother Grace had been.

The young Grace Vickery was in China during the Boxer rebellion, and is said to have had the elegance, the poise and steely backbone expected of high rank. It was a surprise to no one when, during the uprising, she shot and killed two would-be rapist rebels in her quarters. Most of the other spouses would have been paralysed with fear; indeed many suffered just that, when the news did its rounds in the Cantonment.

At university, Alicia didn´t exactly rebel, but rather abandoned the reserve and restrictions imposed at Rosedean Girls' School. She quickly shed her Girls-school reticence and positively revelled in her newfound liberation. Parties were `de rigueur´ and the odd joint smoked, followed by uninhibited sexual liberation that verged almost on nymphomania. She did however, leave enough time for study, and came out with a 2:1 in Fine Arts Restoration. When Alicia returned home for what was supposed to be a short break after a year of post graduation work in Florence, her father, Commander Charles Vickery, was in post at Devonport Naval Base.

Alicia did not want for attention from the hundreds of young officers around Devonport and was in demand almost as soon as the train pulled into the station. Her natural beauty, now enhanced by a spectacular golden tan, indicated that most of her post-graduation research had been conducted away from the gloomy art restoration workshops around the Uffizi Gallery. No ...for the past year, Alicia had committed herself more to the sybaritic arts of the artistic and bohemian set in the delightful Tuscan City, and the nearby beaches of the Riviera Toscana.

The frenetic round of artists' exhibition-openings, obligatory parties and beautiful young Italian lovers had finally jaded. By the art of seduction, willingly received, she convinced one of her mentor professors that she was worth a merit on her post-graduation thesis. With her academic award in her suitcase, Alicia returned home at a loose end, and quite convinced that the stuffy, debutante-riddled art-world was too restrictive for her character. At one of the formal dances on the base, she found herself staring at a fantastically good-looking young officer who was engaged in conversation with a very attractive dark-haired girl of her own age.

Something clicked in her mind and, when he caught her eye. She sent him a dazzling Alicia smile, which appeared to discomfort him, sending a red flush up his face. Alicia decided to go in with a full broadside and, walking between them, boldly asked him to dance. The girl fired off a missile of `piss off´ eye contact, but Alicia stood her ground until Lieutenant Gorgeous shrugged his shoulders and said, "I´ll be back in a minute Audrey," and took her by the arm onto the dance floor.

The Royal Marine Band was playing 'Moon River', surprisingly well sung by the young, boyish, Sinatra-style crooner. After a little awkward, *"I´m Simon Amersbey,"* and, *"I´m Alicia Vickery"* introduction, she snuggled into him to enjoy the dance. The floor was crowded and when `Moon River´ came to an end, she held on to him, until the band melted into `Cry me a River´. He didn´t resist and Alicia stared down the girl, Audrey, who was still at the edge of the dance floor awaiting his return.

They moved around the floor, easily and completely as one, engrossed in each other, breathing each other in, the scent of her perfume, mingling into his slightly sweaty, masculine smells. This time, when the music ended, she steered him to the opposite side of the room but in any case, he was in no hurry to break apart. He held her firm and close, enough for her to feel his manhood against her thigh. As they chatted, she was deliberately chafing her thigh against his erection.

He was obviously becoming flustered at this attention, but also enjoying the experience. "Do you mind if we loosen up a bit?" he asked, "It´s getting very hot in this damn uniform."

"Lieutenant Amersbey, would you be asking this of a Lady in the Tropics? If so I think you had better insist on Arctic patrol."

"No my Lady, I will just have to do my duty, and suffer the heat." Looking down at her, he asked, "You´re a very interesting and attractive girl Miss Vickery, are you by chance related to the Captain Vickery at the Submarine School?"

Mischievously, and in a mock Georgian accent, Alicia replied, "Wal naow ma dear Mister Amersbey, do ah look like a poor navy gal?"

He replied in equal measure, "Wal ya know Missy Alicia, ah jus´ don´ wanna be gitin´ ma nuts sliced off ba´ the good Captain."

"Don´ ya´ think a sully thang like tha´," Mister Amersbey, "Ah´m a big gal of independence, an´ ma daddy no gonna cut na´ balls unless ah´ ask him to." At that they laughed, and danced, and drank until the catering crew began sweeping the Mess floor.

It was prudent to book into the local Travel Lodge, and fortified by a bottle of brandy brought from the Wardroom, Alicia proceeded to give Lieutenant Amersbey the best sex in his entire life; the touches of seduction and sensuality productively inculcated during her year in Florence.

Chapter 2: A perfect couple

Simon Amersbey was unusually tall and dark for a young Royal Naval officer, and very, very handsome in a Latino sort of way. Lieutenant Amersbey was an admirable catch for any ambitious filly with a high office future in mind, and to be altogether candid, Alicia was the perfect partner for him, as he was no slouch in the self-promotion stakes either.

It should not be suggested that Alicia did not actually love Simon, when they married ...that would be most unfair, but the suggestion made its rounds nevertheless. The disappointed mothers of possible suitable spouses for this young officer consoled themselves in speculating about exactly who was his father... surely he was not an Englishman?

It was the wedding of the year in the high echelons of the Royal Navy Devonport milieu. The deliriously happy couple revelled in the attention of the two-hundred guests, which included the participation of two Admirals, one Vice Admiral, and some VIP Ministry of Defence officials... all personal friends of Captain Vickery, the bride's father. The future burned very bright for the newlyweds, as they jetted off to Barbados on their honeymoon.

Back in Portsmouth, they were the perfect young couple. They became active in all the social events in the Mess, very vibrant, very entertaining and effervescent....yes that is the word....effervescent! They instilled genuine sparkle in the dullest obligatory social function and, in consequence, were admired and despised in equal measure.

Alicia had still not made up her mind about what kind of job she wanted to do. In fact, her options were limited as Simon's career was the priority; her own career would have to be built around the exigencies of the Service. Instead, Alicia threw herself into the officers' ladies round of charity events and social work with the families of 'below decks' ratings. She was especially attentive and energetic in the charities and causes favoured by the current commodore's wife and became, in fact, a very good friend and companion to the rather lonely, timid woman.

Life was good for them, and on the grounds that is was better to wait for some advancement in Simon's career, they had delayed the expense and tribulations of buying a house with the accompanying responsibility it brought. They opted to live in the neat semi-detached officers' quarters in Devonport.

Alicia finally opted to take a job in the Royal Navy Public Relations Unit in Dartmouth. She was more than suitable for this type of work; her good looks and poise were important assets in the PR world. She found that she was enjoying her work, varied and interesting as it was. She also continued in her voluntary family support work. It never failed to amaze her, how some of these people lived!

Before the marriage, Captain Vickery had made discreet enquiries into his future son-in-law's training and career to date. Confidentially, he was told that the young Simon was too egoistic to make a good officer. He was competent, but had no empathy with the men under his control... a bit arrogant, and thought only of himself. This corresponded with Vickery's own opinion but his daughter was evidently so much in love with the man, he did nothing about it except to discuss the matter with his wife Helena.

She was appalled and angry; "You forget your own officer-training Charles, you were a bloody tearaway!" The Captain said nothing of this to his daughter, but he resolved he would not interfere in Simon's progress in the Navy; he would have to prove his merit first. The truth was that the two men maintained a cool relationship. Simon was rather resentful that his father-in-law would not use his influence, and pull a few career strings. After all, he was his son-in-law and family should surely come first?

Alicia was always a little scatterbrained and forgetful in her routine of taking the contraceptive pill, sometimes deliberately not taking it, as it made her feel nauseous. Inevitably, she fell pregnant. It was not planned, and she and Simon shared mixed feelings about the prospect of having a child when they were not really prepared for one. His career was only just getting off the ground, and they were not settled in a permanent house yet. The pregnancy itself was normal and healthy, but Alicia found pregnancy a difficult condition to bear. Almost from the start, she couldn't bear to have sex with Simon. Their lovemaking had been spectacular, and now she became irritable and moody, her ankles swelled up and she became constipated and heavy, bloated with the child within her womb. The heavy, thundery August of her eighth month, with the baby moving and kicking inside her, disturbed her sleep.

The young lieutenant was on a destroyer in the North Sea, when a beautiful baby girl was born on the seventeenth of September, three weeks premature, and after a long and hard labour for the mother. Alicia insisted on naming her daughter Francesca, over the mild objections of Simon, who wanted a traditional English name like Elizabeth, his late mother's name.

Francesca was an ideal child, the waking, sleeping, feeding, burping routines going like clockwork. The baby seldom cried, and usually lay gurgling happily in her pram. Simon was enchanted by his daughter; this little creature, part of his genes, but he felt a bit left out of it now, just a touch jealous of the time and attention the baby was absorbing.

Alicia quickly recovered from her pregnancy blues, regained her figure and health and positively revelled in the attention and admiration of the other wives. The only cloud was that she almost felt sick at the thought of making love again with Simon. She couldn't understand it, after years of sexual inhibition, she had completely lost her libido. The thought that she might become frigid, terrified her, but she just could not face sex and had closed the door for many months, refusing on the grounds of some continuing woman's problem.

Simon began spending more and more time in the Officers Wardroom, partying and drinking with his old unattached friends, those who were still at Devonport. He was coming home at all hours of the night, usually very drunk, which ignited frequent heated arguments. Rumours of infidelity were in the air and being gossiped about in Navy wives' circles.

The perfect couple were drifting apart, but neither of the two seemed inclined to make the extra effort to recover their relationship.

Chapter3: Death in the family

Tragedy struck the family. Captain Vickery had a fatal stroke whilst at his office. It was completely unexpected. He had always looked after his health and kept supremely fit. Alicia and her mother were devastated with grief. The bottom had fallen out of their world. He was the rock that they leaned on, depended on for all their emotional stability, and they had both loved him dearly. They could not imagine him not being around.

The Flag Officer funeral passed as if in a horrible dream. Tradition demands of Military wives to hold back their emotions, and maintain discipline. This only fortified the private nightmare that Alicia and her mother were unable to escape. Simon was given a month´s leave, and took care of all the Legal and other administrative arrangements. He arranged for a nanny to look after the baby; however, the baby seemed to sense the drama and tragedy around her and fretted so much that Alicia asked her to leave. It was the best decision for all. Alicia and her mother, who chose to stay for a few weeks to help, were, in a way, forced to come out of their grief, helped along by the innocence and baby antics of the little Francesca.

Simon did all he could to help, but again had a feeling of being an outsider in his own home. Alicia didn´t seem to want his love and tenderness, and insisted that the baby slept in her crib beside the bed.

A month passed. Helena, Alicia´s mother, made the decision to return to Scotland, where she had been raised, and where most of her old friends still lived. The desolation of death, and uncertainty about her future gave way to a determination to begin rebuilding her independent life. The relationship of shared grief with Alicia had all but passed, and the two women were, at times, barely on speaking terms.

Simon was given a new posting, a step up the ladder, as Lieutenant on a small Mine Countermeasure Vessel operating in the Mediterranean. He was a little concerned about accepting, but knew that if he turned it down on compassionate grounds, it could be a long time before he gained any promotion. Alicia was frankly happy to see him off for a while, at least until she had recovered from having the baby, and the death of her father.

Lieutenant Amersbey was at sea for seven months, before he got his first home leave. During this period, Alicia had recovered much of her old spirit, and doted on her child. She was missing Simon. The old adage that, `absence makes the heart grow fonder´, seemed very much to apply in her situation. She discussed this over the telephone with her mother, who confirmed that this was very much the case with Navy wives.

"When your father was away, the first few weeks were great. I had time for myself, no routines etcetera but, later on, the loneliness, the need for male company, and of course the physical needs of each other got stronger." She warned, "For God´s sake Alicia, don´t get involved with another man just because you´re lonely!"

"Bloody hell, mother, one´s quite enough, thank you!"

Simon returned home on leave. It was almost as if the tensions between them before he left had not occurred. She had decorated the front door of the house with 'welcome home hero' and bunting, much to his surprise and embarrassment, and he delighted in seeing, and holding high, his beautiful, now one-year-old daughter.

Babysitter arranged, they went down to a little Italian Restaurant in Portsmouth for a romantic meal, helped down by two bottles of a good Barossa. This time however, although on the whole pleasant, at times there were awkward silences, just a little unspoken tension, as though they were still feeling around, not wanting to spoil the 'hero's homecoming.

After paying off the Babysitter, Alicia went upstairs to check on Francesca, whilst Simon poured himself a large duty-free Armagnac, and sat in front of the fire, reflecting upon the evening. He couldn't understand it, the undercurrent of tautness that he felt existed between them. He was home after almost seven months and had been looking forward to this day for weeks. His beautiful wife was upstairs and probably waiting for him, but he, and she, had changed. After reminiscing a bit over past times, he downed the rest of his nightcap, and went upstairs.

Alicia was already in bed, and to her dismay, felt this old nervousness coming over her again. Her mother had not too subtly reminded her of her marital duties to her returning husband, and she actually wanted to get back to normal with Simon, but something was holding her back. Their lovemaking therefore, had a perfunctory duty about it, with relief being the most important sensation for them both when Simon ejaculated. He had not bothered to ensure she had any degree of satisfaction.

Afterwards, each of them lay awake, without speaking and sleep came fitfully for both of them. After a few days of this, unconscious sparring, an anxious Alicia, telephoned her mother for advice. Her mother listened quietly to her daughter's dilemma before interrupting, "Alicia darling, you have to work at it ...marriage, I mean. Do you think your father and I had roses and cream for our thirty-six years together? I can tell you now; he was bloody difficult at times, especially when he came home after a tour on his Ship.

"Aboard they are living in a different, all male, macho world. They are used to being obeyed, if they want a cup of tea on the Bridge, they send for one, and a little Mess Steward brings it up. My God, when he was on the submarines, he even came home smelling of other men! It takes them a while to adjust to home life again. Meanwhile it is our job to bring them back down to earth. Candidly, it is you who will have to take the initiative, you´ve got to give him what all men most desire from their wives; what they have been dreaming about at sea, remember he has not had sex for a long time."

"Mother! I´ve never heard you talking this way before!"

"Alicia, do you think your father and I never had sex?"

"I never thought about it frankly, mother."

"Well it´s not me who has the problem at this moment in time, but I can assure you, your grandmother put me right in this respect, so get to it my girl, or your action man will be looking around for someone else, and fast!"

Alicia responded with little enthusiasm; "I´ll try, mother, I promise you, I´ll try." Still, she could not imagine her mother and father indulging in home pornography!

Mother was right, she thought, he is the one who has to endure whatever danger the Navy places him in, and she knew it was good advice. After all she belonged to five generations of Royal Navy Officers and knew the role that wives were expected to play. It was not that long ago that they were so hungry for each other she thought that maybe they were abnormally charged!

This time, she set about it in a more cold-blooded way. No candlelight romantic dinner or other distractions, just good old fashion sex, and if she could not reach orgasm, she would fake it!

She took charge; he a little wary at the turn around in attitude, but when she began working on him in the way she used to do, the response was immediate. She allowed him the ecstasy of coming in her mouth, and resting, before beginning once again. The second time around, he was more in control, and responded orally with her until she cried out in a shuddering un-faked orgasm.

They changed angles, positions, she on top, then he, front, back, and climaxed together almost in exaltation of relief and ecstasy.

Falling back on the pillow, he said, "Bloody hell! That was good!" They fell asleep, embraced in each other's arms, until Francesca let them know it was time for her breakfast!

Chapter4: Promotion!

The rest of his leave passed in a whirlwind. With only four days left, he got an urgent phone call to attend an interview with the RN Personnel (Officer Deployment) Office, at ten o'clock the following morning.

He presented himself next morning, in full uniform as required. He was ushered into the office of the Commodore Personnel by a chief petty officer. Captain Anthony Pithers had been a personal friend of his late father-in-law, Captain Vickery, and thought Vickery had been just a bit too critical of his young son-in-law.

The captain stood, returned Simon's salute, and then shook his hand warmly "How is Alicia?" He enquired, "I've been meaning to call, but never had the time, I'm afraid." It's almost a year since Vickery died, what a tragedy!" Simon murmured the expected social exchange, wondering why he was there, when the captain intervened in his thoughts.

Formally, he stated, "Lieutenant Amersbey, I have been studying your file. I have an emergency on my hands. One of our minesweepers, HMS Rothesay, had been undergoing a refit and upgrade to the new Mine Countermeasure Class in Glasgow, and is due to begin sea trials next month… five weeks to be precise. You are currently on Dundee, one of her sister-ships, so you know the type… old, but reliable."

He explained, "My problem is that the captain of Rothesay fell down a crevice or something in the Alps, and has a compound fracture on his leg. He'll be out of action for at least six months. I need a `fill in´ commander to see the ship through its sea trials. You would have the rank of Acting Lieutenant Commander, but on successful completion of the tour, this would become a permanent promotion."

Consulting a file, he went on. "The first officer, Lieutenant Barclay has been with Rothesay four years, but is considered as being too close to the men to take over. You will have an excellent chief engineer, John Scobie, who'll keep your engines ticking over. The rest of the officers and crew are from the established complement and a sprinkling of new hands. You will also have some American technicians to sort out anticipated teething troubles with the new radar systems."

The captain asked, "Do you have any questions?"

"When do I leave, Sir?" Simon immediately responded. *Christ, my first command, he thought, wait 'till Alicia hears the news!*

"Not so fast Amersbey; there´s some pretty complex radar and weapons systems stuff being installed on the ship. You'll have to go over to Lockheed Martin in San Diego for a four-week crash course. You will have to leave on Thursday; the CPO in the Travel Section will give you your travel schedule." The captain stood up, "Good luck Lieutenant Commander", and shook hands with Simon.

They both saluted, Simon about-turned, and left the room with a barely suppressed smile on his face.

Alicia was over the moon, lieutenant commander at twenty-nine! Her friends would be green eyed with envy! "Yes!" She exclaimed, and rewarded him in her appropriate way.

San Diego proved to be both intensive and exhausting, giving Simon no time to relax and enjoy the attention of the young American secretaries, who were intrigued by the extremely handsome Royal Navy officer.

Returning to Portsmouth, and much to Alicia´s annoyance, he had only forty-eight hours leave before he flew up to Glasgow to join HMS Rothesay.

Chapter 5: Yarrow's Shipyard, Glasgow

Glasgow was cold, damp and foggy, and darkness was already approaching at four o'clock. Simon felt jaded and jet-lagged in the taxi to the shipyard, and fought to contain his focus, as he studied his orders.

Yarrow's Shipbuilders was buzzing with activity over a variety of naval vessels, in various stages of construction. He had to wait for ten minutes at the gatehouse, before the navy agent came to collect him. By this time, darkness was almost complete, and the yard was lit up with arc lights. Two thousand men were labouring to a cacophonic din of noise from grinders, jackhammers, lightning flashes from welders, all assaulting his already reeling senses.

Simon was led through the chaos to the Shore Captain's Office, and offered a cup of tea. He was then informed that HMS Rothesay would not be able to sail for at least another three weeks. There had been a series of unofficial strikes by different unions, and, although they were now operating on twenty-four hour shifts, the Project was still way behind schedule. The Admiralty had been informed on the situation, and his orders were to take command of the ship, and prepare as best as he could for the signing off from the yard. Meanwhile he would be billeted in a small hotel, within walking distance of the shipyard.

After tea and a familiarisation of the current situation, he was escorted to the dock, where HMS Rothesay was tied up. Lines of tangled hoses and electricity cables snaked over decks swarming with shipyard workers. Simon was surprised to note that there did not appear to be a naval watch on the gangway; in fact, the only sailors he could see were a chief petty officer and a couple of able seamen, checking and loading supplies at the stern. Excusing himself, and declining an offer from the agent of a drink later, he walked up the gangway, squeezing through various groups of workers, and along to the stern of the ship.

The CPO and AB´s stood to attention as he approached, and he said, "Please stand easy." Addressing the chief, he asked, "Who is the officer of the day just now, and why is there no one on the gangway?"

"Lieutenant Barclay has not posted a Watch, Sir, it´s pointless when all these guys are going back and forth all day."

"That´s precisely why there should be a guard, chief!" He snapped. "These guys, as you term them, will be stealing everything that´s not screwed down. They would be off with that Bofors four-inch gun, if they could lift it!"

"Yes Sir," a chastened CPO admitted.

"Who is the officer in charge as of now?" Simon asked.

"Lieutenant Barclay is the first officer Sir, but he has gone into town today, Sir."

"Are there no officers on board chief? Is no one in charge of this ship?

"Well, Lieutenant Hanson is in the operations room, working with the Americans on the radar, and I think Lieutenant Scobie, he´s the engineer, is down in the engine room."

Simon wiped a hand over his eyes, and asked the CPO to show him to the captain´s quarters.

"I´ll do that Sir, but you won´t be able to use it, they`re still building it! The officers´ wardroom is okay though; Lieutenant Barclay made them finish that as a priority." This was said with an undisguised smile exchanged between the four in the work party.

"Fine, take me to the wardroom, so as I can dump my bag please," Simon said this with an unfortunate note of resignation. Exhaustion was beginning to take over his brain, at precisely the time he needed to be alert.

The wardroom, indeed, seemed to be the only habitable place on the minesweeper. Simon had a look around the ship and encountered chaos, wiring exposed, plumbing unconnected, holes in the decks, sparks from welders on the superstructure. Dejectedly, he thought, *this will not be easy; it´ll take months to sort this out.* In the operations room, there was a heated exchange going on between an American, a civilian technician and a young officer in Navy blues.

They only stopped when Simon intervened, "Lieutenant Hanson?"

The officer turned away from the others, and still visibly angry, asked; "Are you the new captain, Sir?"

"Yes, I'm Lieutenant Commander Amersbey, and extended his hand. The answering handshake was perfunctory, weak, surprising Simon a little. "You have a problem here lieutenant?"

"More of a disaster Captain; these so-called experts can't get a damn thing to work in here. I was Operations Officer on this ship before these people ruined it. There was bugger all wrong with the old Marconi radar, now we've got this American muck!"

"That's a bit unfair Sir," interrupted the American. "We shipped the entire package over here, complete and now your officer is blaming us for parts being missing! This stuff is valuable, and Top Secret, but it's lying around the fucking deck in bits! By the way, I'm John Sumner, from Lockheed."

Simon returned the handshake, this time firm and strong.

Turning to the other civilian, he asked; "And you are?"

"The man in the middle; Alec Donaldson, I'm Ministry of Defence, Radar." Again, he encountered a firm handshake.

"Forgive me gentlemen, but, is this not a shipyard problem?" Simon asked.

"I wish it were," answered Donaldson, but I'm sorry to say that this is a direct contract between Lockheed and the MOD. Sumner has a point though. We shouldn't be leaving this stuff lying around."

"Mister Sumner, you are the man in control here. Can you get all the bits over from the States, by yesterday?" Out of the corner of his eye, he could see Hanson visibly angry that he was taking over his role.

"It's already on the way, Captain. All I was asking of your buddies was effective security, in case the Ruskies get enough damn parts to build their own!"

"I will guarantee that Sumner. There will be a seaman in this room, twenty-four hours a day, until we sail!" Turning to the lieutenant, he ordered, "Lieutenant Hanson, get it organised."

"Sir, we don't have sleeping quarters on board."

"Who in the hell said anything about sleeping, Hanson? I am ordering you to organise a Watch, twenty-four hours a day on this ship, as of now!"

Hanson angrily protested, "The first officer is Lieutenant Barclay, Sir. It's his job to organise the Watch."

Furious that his junior officer was questioning an order in front of civilians, Simon grated, "Lieutenant Hanson, do not question my orders, just carry them out, is that clear?"

"Yes Sir!" Hanson turned about, and stomped out.

The two civilians were looking embarrassed, and Simon apologised for the incident, but was inwardly furious with the absolute lack of order and discipline on Rothesay.

It was nine o'clock, before a dog-tired Simon could leave his command, reasonably satisfied it was secure, with a CPO responsible for a night Watch. After explaining the situation to a shipyard manager, he had also secured the services of a yard security guard on the dock itself.

There was still no sign of the Lieutenant Barclay.

Although deadbeat, Simon felt hungry enough to stop at the appropriately named Admiralty Arms Bar, on the way to his hotel. He entered the lounge bar, ordered a pint of McEwan's, a cheese sandwich and some crisps, and sat in the corner. He leaned back against the partition wall, as he awaited his sandwich, trying hard to relax, to ease the tension in his head and shoulders. Being a Tuesday evening the lounge was quiet, with only a young couple sitting at the bar talking to the barmaid.

All at once, he became aware of Lieutenant Hanson's voice, sounding through the partition, which backed onto the public bar. He strained to hear without drawing attention to himself, and could just make out some of the conversation.

"John, you should have been given the command. Christ you know the Rothesay inside out. It´s ridiculous, he's just a fucking wanker, with his hand inside some Admiral's fly."

Unknown voice: "Too fucking true it should have been mine! I've worked my arse off on Rothesay for four years. The bastards! What else did he say?"

"Not much John, he was going on about the Watch not being mounted, but he was asking questions about you also. Where in the hell were you today, anyway?" The voice replied.

"What´s the point of mounting a Watch, when there´s still a hundred shipyard guys walking on and off the bloody ship. I bet they down tools tomorrow, when we start to ask them to open their bags. Christ, that will be a laugh; Captain know-fucking-all having to negotiate with these Union Bolsheviks." He changed the subject, "Jesus, what a ride I had today with Chris; her man was in Edinburgh all day. By Christ, am I'm going to miss her."

"Maybe we can lose some more parts?" Hanson suggested, "Get you another few weeks shagging time."

"Not a good idea, Hanson, that bastard will be counting the spoons from now on! No, take it easy, it's going to be long and hard sea trials for our young captain, once we get underway."

Simon had no doubt who's was the unknown voice and got the picture; he thought to himself, *Shit, that's all I need on my first fucking command, two key officers against me….shit!* The day suddenly caught up with him, and he slipped out the bar, turned up the collar of his coat, and walked through the bitter darkness to his hotel. Thankfully, his bedroom was warm to the point of being stuffy, and he had to open the window for some fresh air. He ran a bath, and whilst it was filling, took of his clothes whilst watching the late news on the wall mounted TV.

'There were riots in Derry again, Catholics trying to kill Protestants and vice versa, with the Army having to restore order. Fifty-one police officers injured four of them in a serious condition.' *Good God, he thought, these people are still living in the seventeenth century.* 'Mods and Rockers are planning a weekend of mayhem in Brighton.' *A bit of National Service would maybe sort out their problems,* he commented half-aloud to himself, and eased his body down into the luxury of his bath.

He awoke with a start, with the bathwater now tepid. *Damn it! I wanted to have a look over some of the ship's papers.* Instead, he slipped into bed, and watched the Avengers. Diana Rigg and Honor Blackman were kicking the hell out of a huge, ugly, muscular Russian spy.

Again, he drifted off and was awakened by the snow effect television telling him the Avengers were not that exciting.

Simon was dressed and down for breakfast at six thirty, aware that the day shift began in the shipyard at seven thirty. He was surprised to see the American, John Sumner, who waved him over to his table.

"Morning, Commander; sleep well? How's your day been so far?"

"Morning Sumner, considering I'm just out of my bed, fine, but I feel it's going to go downhill from now on."

"You'll be okay. Your boys just need a bit of a kick up their backsides, that's all. Are you aware that I'm coming on the sea trials with you? That's if the damn shipyard can get around to finishing the bloody ship."

"I knew one of the Lockheed boys was coming to do the calibrations, but didn't know it was you." Simon was secretly pleased, he was sure he could get on with this man.

Pulling a face, Sumner continued, "Well, it's going to be me, and I'm not a happy bunny! I'm not good on these little boats, and it's winter out there!"

"Ship, Sumner, not boat, Simon corrected. I´ll try to make you as comfortable as possible. You can share my cabin. Besides, it should only be a week or two, all going well. But firstly, I´ve got to get my crew into condition."

"That´s a job and a half," Sumner added as they finished their tea. "Good God, Commander is there no decent coffee in this country?" "I´ll give you a lift down to the yard."

Chapter 6: Confrontation!

Simon convened a meeting of all his officers at ten o´clock in the wardroom, after first touring the ship with the duty officer, a young sub lieutenant new to the ship. He took copious notes as they threaded their way through the plumbers, joiners, electricians, and other tradesmen labouring to finish the ship. He had made a point of introducing himself to the shipyard Project Manager, and to the trade´s supervisors, and asked them to keep him informed if they encountered problems. He mentally made a firm deadline of three weeks to set sail on the trials. His officers and crew would be ready, even if Rothesay wasn´t.

Somehow, he wasn´t surprised to find Lieutenant Barclay absent when he entered the Wardroom at ten o´clock for the assembly. He was seething inside, but remained calm as he introduced himself. He then voiced his displeasure at the lack of Royal Navy professionalism on board HMS Rothesay.

Lieutenant Hanson asked permission to speak, and when Simon granted it, he began complaining about the difficulties with so many yard workers around. "No excuse," snapped

Simon. "How many of you have been on basic discipline and fitness training?" No one answered, with a few looking embarrassed. "I thought so," said Simon, "that's first priority, as from now!"

He asked each officer in turn to introduce themselves, and explain a little of their background experience. Just at this point, the door opened, and another officer walked in, and sat down. "And you are...? Asked Simon quietly, aware of the heightened tension in the wardroom.

The newcomer answered, "Lieutenant John Barclay"

"STAND UP LIEUTENANT, WHEN YOU ADDRESS A SENIOR OFFICER!" bellowed Simon.

Some of the junior officers visibly jumped with fright, and a silence seemed to fall over the entire ship. Even the jackhammers had stopped.

Barclay got to his feet lazily, looking around to see if he had any support. No one looked at him, as he said, "Lieutenant Barclay, Sir."

"Lieutenant Barclay, you are the First Officer on HMS Rothesay, are you not? This was calmly asked of Barclay.

"Yes, I am, and have been for four years," was the reply, said with a slightly bored, arrogant tone.

Simon roared, "BEHAVE AS IF YOU ARE THEN! You are late for duty, what is your explanation?" Again, there was a stunned silence, with the officers exchanging looks.

This time Barclay responded, "I'm sorry Sir, I overslept."

"I repeat Lieutenant Barclay, I expect you, above all officers on HMS Rothesay to behave and maintain discipline befitting Royal Navy standards, and to show an exemplary example to the more junior officers and crew. You will attend a private meeting with me at twelve o'clock, here in the wardroom. You are dismissed!"

Barclay, furious, humiliated and embarrassed at his defeat, looked around, made to say something but thought better of it. He stormed out, slamming the door behind him.

Simon was tempted to bring him back again for a further reprimand, but decided he had scored an important victory. He was fully aware, though, that Barclay was going to be a formidable foe. He was obviously carrying an enormous chip on his shoulder at being passed over for command of HMS Rothesay, and it was unfortunate that Simon was going to be the target for his bile.

Simon thought through his tactics for his interview with his first officer. His anger was prompting him to slap him down with a charge of insubordination, but his brain forced him into thinking more of the reality of the situation. Barclay knew the ship, inside and out. He had commanded most of the men as deputy to the injured Captain, therefore knew their strengths and weaknesses. Undoubtedly, Barclay was angry and disappointed that the Admiralty had passed him over and promoted a younger, less experienced officer.

Simon fully understood his disillusion, but the Navy had their reasons, and one had to accept it as such. It would certainly be better to try getting him to cooperate, but difficult, given their initial contact. He would then proceed on a conciliatory approach, and appeal to the man's sense of duty to the Service.

Simon had the wardroom cleared of the officers, and arranged a pot of tea and a plate of biscuits with the Wardroom Steward.

Lieutenant Barclay entered precisely on twelve. Simon was hatless, and therefore they didn't exchange salutes, only a tense "Sir" and "Lieutenant" greeting. Simon ushered him to a table, and began. "Lieutenant Barclay, let's keep this off the record, agreed?" Barclay nodded his affirmation, and Simon continued. "I'll get right to the point then. As you know Lieutenant Commander Martin has broken his leg, badly it seems. He will be returning to HMS Rothesay when he regains fitness."

He continued, "You and I have been placed by higher authority to work together and bring Rothesay back up to fighting condition. We will have to all intents and purposes, a new ship, more capable than before, with the ability to find and sink submarines, as well as the old minesweeping functions." Changing his tone a little, Simon appealed to his first officer, "We have to learn to use the new equipment, and train the men in using it effectively, in as short a time as possible. I am asking your full cooperation in assisting me to bring this about."

"You said that this was off the record?" Simon´s heart sank, when he detected the menace in Barclay´s voice, but he nodded, yes. "Well that was a fine rally to the flag speech, Captain. Let me tell you that I have worked damn hard on this ship for four years... I ran the bloody ship! This command was mine, and you have stolen from me!" Barclay continued spewing his venom, "I have no idea why you are here, but I know how. I was late this morning because I was waiting to hear from a mate of mine in Personnel in Portsmouth. Unfortunately my mate is not so far up the pecking order as your mate, Captain Personnel himself, who, just conveniently was best friend to your wife´s dead father, the famous Captain Vickery!" He spat out, "Now, Captain, what chance as an ordinary, hard-working up-from-the-ranks lieutenant in the face of the Big Guns?"

White with anger, Simon retorted, "You could not be farther from the truth, Barclay, but I´m not here to talk about my family connections. I was hoping for some cooperation and assistance from you – too much to ask for I gather, but I will insist that you carry out your duties according to Royal Navy regulations, or I will remove you from your current position!"

Sneering openly, Barclay retorted, "Oh no you will not, Captain. While we are being frank, I know you can´t just phone up your uncle or whatever, and replace me. No, this is your first command, you can´t afford a controversy of a disciplinary action against me. You´re stuck with me, unless it´s me who asks for the transfer, so let´s cut the crap. I will follow your orders and carry out my duties, according to the regulations, but don´t expect any favours."

Simon angrily responded, "At least now we understand each other lieutenant. I warn you not to underestimate me. I´ll be watching, and if there is evidence you are working against me, as commanding officer of this ship, I´ll go all the way to destroy you!"

Smiling, Barclay answered, "I´m not frightened Captain. I know my job. You´re the new boy here and I'll be watching you and that´s much more important when it comes to questions of competence! Is there anything else you wish to discuss, on or off the record ...Sir? I would like to get back to my duties, Sir."

This man´s arrogance is breathtaking, thought Simon, but instead of risking further conflict, he curtly dismissed Barclay from his presence.

The shipyard work seemed to gather a new urgency, now that a commander was on board the Rothesay. Order and training had been restored, and morale among the officers and men improved. Simon went out of his way to avoid conflict with his first officer, and Barclay was carrying out his duties to the mark.

A clique had formed around Barclay and Hanson, which predated Simon´s appointment as commanding officer. He could do nothing about this but was relieved that the two other key officers on Rothesay, John Scobie the chief engineer, and George Norris, the weapons officer stayed out of Barclay´s circle.

Finally, after a further five weeks, HMS Rothesay was signed off for her sea trials. A small team of Yarrow´s technicians were coming to fix any small problems, and the ubiquitous American, John Sumner was representing Lockheed Martin, the radar, sonar and weapons systems manufacturer.

Two nights before the sailing, Simon organised a reunion for the crew, except those unfortunate to be on the Watch. It was held at the Admiralty Arms and paid out of 'company' Mess funds. The night proved to be celebratory, rather than drunken, with the only sour note coming when a pretty inebriated John Sumner called Barclay 'arsehole of the year', sparking off a 'Yank prick of the century' response.

John Scobie was at the fore in calming things down before things got out of hand, but again Simon was left with a sour taste of bad omens; trouble was always just around the corner.

Simon had not been able to go home since he had taken command. He didn´t trust his second in command, and Barclay himself didn´t take any leave although he was entitled to several days off-duty. It was like a game of cat and mouse, Barclay always looking for an opening.

In recompense, Simon had been calling home regularly but, oddly, Alicia had been sounding a little reticent; there was little warmth for him in her voice, which he put down to her missing him again.

Acting Lieutenant Commander Amersbey's last night in his hotel room was sleepless. Unaccountably, all the pressures of the last few weeks, and the worries that something might go wrong during the sea trials, suddenly crashed into his head. His brain refused to unwind; flashes of bright white lights, alternating with blood-red images refused him peace. The nerves were causing havoc in his stomach. Twice he had to get up to the toilet, the last visit with such urgency, that he almost fouled the bed. He awoke early; the chill and darkness reflected his edginess, his discomfiture.

Tongue coated in fur, sour spittle in his mouth, and a troubling acidity in his stomach, only reinforced his mood of anxiety. As he shaved, he studied himself in the mirror, honestly. *Do you have the ability; are you capable of leading these men into a war; do you the balls for this Simon?* At this moment, I don't know, he confessed to the mirror. Then, as if reawakening afresh, he spoke aloud to his image... "What in the fuck am I thinking? Jesus I'm going mad! Get a grip; this is the best day of my career! It's my ship! Yes!" he shouted, as he punched the air.

He ran the shower hot, and then cascaded freezing cold water until he was almost shivering. Towelled dry and glowing, he went downstairs to breakfast with Sumner, now in a buoyant mood.

Chapter 7: Sea Trials

"Bear off forrard, let go aft, steer one-point-five into the channel. Ahead slow!" Lieutenant Commander (Acting) Amersbey's quiet orders, were relayed by the sub-lieutenant on the Bridge. In his pride, Simon's heart was swelling in his chest almost up to bursting point. It was a beautiful, bright, frosty morning, with a scattering of cumulus over an otherwise clear-blue sky. The winter sun was peering out from behind the shipyard sheds, giving way to rows of tenements, as HMS Rothesay slowly made her way downstream on the River Clyde, a lazy trail of smoke leaving a trace behind them.

Soon, they were passing Clydebank's Rothesay Dock, and John Brown's Shipyard, where the colossus of Queen Elizabeth 2, was towering over the yard and the river, green fields on one side, in stark contrast with the heavy industry on the other. Simon was anxiously asking for reports from all lookout stations, and the engine room, unnecessarily so, as the high tide had turned and was sweeping them downstream at four knots, with only a controlling propeller speed to maintain direction away from the mudflats below the Erskine Bridge towering high above them.

Now that that industry had been left behind, he marvelled in the day, looking over to the right at the Kilpatrick Hills, the extinct volcano with Dumbarton Castle perched on top, and the start of the Southern Highlands beyond.

His nerves began to flutter, as Rothesay approached the entrance to the Gareloch, where his first docking procedure would take place at the Faslane Nuclear Submarine Base, and under the critical eyes of Commodore Clyde himself. There was an increase in vibration when Simon gave the orders to increase engine speed, as they changed tack to enter Rhu Narrows, where the still outgoing tide rushed through. There was a heart palpitation when he had to order more revs against the strong current.

He had an uneasy feeling that the response time from his orders was greater than he expected, but he was new to the ship, and it passed.

Up ahead to starboard, an enormous and menacing black cigar shaped Polaris ballistic missile submarine sat uncomfortably alongside the grey painted buildings of Faslane.

The whole Base sat incongruently amidst a beautiful landscape of mountains and sea loch, dazzling in the winter sun. Simon concentrated on bringing the warship into the dock, which was effected perfectly, much to the relief of most, if not all on the bridge.

Simon reported to the Commodore Clyde Office, and received his orders, which included a submarine detection exercise as part of HMS Rothesay´s sea trials. This would take place within a week in the deep-water testing zone in Loch Fyne. Meanwhile, the commodore, and a few other senior officers, requested a tour of Rothesay, to familiarise themselves with the new Lockheed systems, instigating a little panic aboard.

The VIP's were piped aboard, to be welcome by Lieutenant Barclay as the watch officer. Simon stood slightly to the as the commander of the ship. The commodore gave Simon a warm greeting and asked after the health of Alicia. Simon was mystified as to who he was and, taken by surprise, could only croak, "Fine Sir," in reply.

Lieutenant Barclay's face mirrored thunder.

In the event, the tour was restricted to the points of the commodore's interest, during which John Sumner, George Norris, and Hanson were subjected to a barrage of questions. Hanson made a good account of his knowledge of his subject, but reserved his opinion on the effectiveness of the radar and sonar, until properly calibrated and tested. Weapons Officer Norris made the same comment on his area of expertise.

The commodore thanked Simon, wishing him good luck with the trials. He was piped ashore to the salutes of Simon and his officers.

As Simon, feeling pleased with himself, watched the VIP's walk away along the dock, he was startled when Barclay whispered in his ear, "I hope the commodore is just as pleased with you at the end of the trials!"

Simon stared at him, before asking, "Do you know something that I don't know, lieutenant? I'll remind you once again of your duty to the Royal Navy, if it's still beyond you to show loyalty to me!" Barclay just shrugged his shoulders, and with a slight smile, saluted, and turned away.

Lieutenant Scobie later reported to Simon, that he was a little concerned with the starboard engine; there seemed to be a bit too much vibration, hopefully it would disappear at higher revolutions.

Simon used this opportunity to voice his concern about the engine response concerns he experienced, but Scobie explained that Rothesay had always behaved in this way. "Part of the old girl's temperament Sir. The engines have been overhauled, not replaced, but you'll get used to it in time."

Sumner invited Simon to dinner at a little Italian restaurant in nearby Garelochhead. Accompanied by two other Americans working for Lockheed Martin in the Base, they enjoyed an excellent authentic Italian meal, but it was the proprietor, an enthusiastic, slightly mad character, dancing with all the ladies present and rendering a bad version of 'O sole mio' and other classics that stole the show.

Such was the fun, that Simon forgot his troubles and drank too many flaming Zambucas, on top of the three bottles of Chianti they had already consumed.

Chapter 8: Alicia's Bombshell

Back on board and waking before dawn, Simon regretted the night before, and had to resort to a couple of aspirins and mugs of strong coffee to clear the fuzz in his head. They were due to cast off at ten o'clock, taking advantage of the outgoing tide.

He went back ashore to receive his written orders and decided to telephone Alicia from the privacy of a booth in the officers' wardroom. He almost instantly lamented his phone call, when Alicia answered with the news she was pregnant again. She was tearful, and upset, and more than a little paranoiac about how she had suffered so much with Francesca, and insisted she was not ready for another. Simon tried to reason with her, about how happy they were with little Francesca, but to little avail; she would not be consoled. It is almost impossible to achieve empathy on a telephone, with someone four hundred miles away, and it left Simon drained and depressed.

He finally made the excuse that the ship was waiting for him, and promised to telephone the first chance he could. Walking back to the ship, he tried to concentrate on the job in hand, the sea trials. *Shit, I'll need to get a grip here*, he chided himself, but his thoughts kept wandering back to Alicia. Aboard once again, he had satisfaction of noting that HMS Rothesay was ready to put to sea, given that carpenters were still finishing off the AB´s quarters.

Back on the bridge, he instructed Barclay to take control, which he did with ease and confidence, despite a strong westerly blowing in from the Atlantic, imparting a heavy chop to the loch surface. As the ship exited the Narrows into the Firth of Clyde, the full force of what was now a gale force wind was causing the minesweeper to pitch and heel over. The helmsman fought the wheel to bring the ship into the teeth of the wind. Barclay, with his calm regular commands maintained complete control.

Over the next three days, they went up and down the Firth of Clyde, and around the Island of Bute, calibrating radar and the sonar. The CPO´s bore down on the crew training in their sea duties; testing everything before going out into the open sea. Sumner was in a foul mood, as was Lieutenant Hanson; they were having problems with the new Lockheed equipment. HMS Rothesay was due at Strachur, on Loch Fyne in two days to rendezvous, and begin testing with the submarine. Simon furiously told them to stop arguing and resolve the issues.

The weather was deteriorating, and Simon decided to head for Loch Fyne, rather than be caught out in a busy fishing and shipping area without an efficient radar system in service. By the time they got into Loch Fyne, the gale was blowing storm force seven, with rain and visibility down to five-hundred yards. The small ship was rolling and pitching all at once, freezing spray drenching the bridge. Sumner and all of the shipyard technicians were in their temporary bunks. Even old hands were green. Testing was impossible; therefore, Simon radioed Faslane that he was putting in to

Tarbert to ride out the storm. Permission was granted, and they would advise the submarine that a delay was necessary on the rendezvous.

In the end, the storm sat over the Kintyre Peninsula for a further four days. There was no alternative but to allow the Yarrow technicians to leave the ship for the weekend, conditions aboard being too bad for civilians. Simon fretted; a week had been lost, and to all intents and purposes, they were no farther forward on the Sea Trials. Chief Engineer Scobie was worried about his starboard engine. During the storm, enormous pressure had been place on the engines and the vibrations had intensified. He still had not found the cause of the vibration, but now suspected that the starboard shaft might be out of line. If that was the case, the trials would be over and they would have to return to dry dock to fit a new one.

With all of this on his mind, Simon discounted telephoning Alicia. It would only add to his pressure, and at the moment he had enough. In the back of his mind, he worried about Barclay. His deputy was too quiet, saying nothing, but carrying out his duties to the letter ...but no more. Simon was sure he was up to something… but what?

The weather finally abated, and HMS Rothesay cast off for her rendezvous with the submarine at Strachur. Chief Engineer Scobie asked for a full ahead run up the Loch, to assess his troubled engines. Simon ordered a gradual increase in speed to full ahead, and at first, there was only a slight tremble and vibration. Scobie asked full power from zero knots, and when the minesweeper got up to twenty knots, the vibrations were being felt throughout the ship to be followed by a jolting bang. The ship lost power. The chief engineer didn´t need to inform the captain that the trials were over for now, until the damaged engine could be replaced.

"Bad luck, captain," Barclay said with a smile and a shrug, "there´s always another time."

This led Simon to wonder if Barclay had anything to do with it. *Christ, I'm getting paranoiac now,* he thought. Scobie reported that they still had half-power available and could make it back to port.

Simon reported to the Commodore Clyde Office, and received instructions to head over to Greenock, on the Clyde, where damage would be assessed and repaired, or a new engine fitted.

It was a despondent Lieutenant Commander Simon Amersbey and his ship's complement that limped back through the Kyles of Bute and over the Firth to the dry dock at Greenock. John Sumner announced that if it was going to be dry-docked for more than a week, there was nothing he could do here, he would fly home to San Diego and see his family.

HMS Rothesay was in dry dock for five weeks. The fault, as John Scobie had suspected, was found in the main shaft, which had finally sheared, an extremely unusual event. It was even more unusual when the engineers discovered traces of tiny ball bearings, foreign to their situation. No one could explain how they came to be there. The propeller on that shaft would also have to be rebalanced, after the shock of the shaft fracture.

Sabotage was suspected, and a team of investigators from the Royal Navy Special Investigation Branch came over from Faslane to interview the officers and crew. The questioning was thorough, and lasted almost a whole week.

The engine room ratings were naturally under suspicion as to how ball bearings found their way into a propeller shaft. John Scobie vigorously defended his team, but could not offer a reasonable explanation either. Simon felt tempted to point a finger in the direction of Barclay, but had absolutely no evidence to that effect. It was unlikely, that Barclay could have accessed the engine room without arousing suspicion, but who did it?

The Special Branch left the ship with the matter unresolved, and the focus of the investigation turned to Yarrows shipyard. *Not an auspicious start to my command,* Simon gloomily thought to himself.

Barclay himself showed no signs of concern, "After all, I´m not the captain," smiling to himself with satisfaction. "This is only the beginning."

There was nothing to do but to await the repairs; therefore the ship´s company was given leave to return home for seven days.

The captain did not take his leave; he was terrified something else would happen if he was away. This feeling increased when Barclay returned after only three days in Glasgow, announcing to everyone in the wardroom that he was bored.

Simon instead telephoned Alicia, to see if she felt well enough to come up and visit her mother in Helensburgh, just across the Clyde from the dry dock in Greenock. Alicia wasn´t in any better state of mind, and brutally stated that her mother was the last person she needed right now, with all her advice and nagging. She maintained a barrage of complaints about her morning sickness, headaches, general ill health, also, she was down in Devonport, alone, to look after Francesca.

Simon tried to pacify her... *It will soon pass*, to be floored by, "What in the fuck do men know about being pregnant? You have the fun, and we get screwed twice over!" He tentatively suggested a termination, to be told, "You arrogant bastard, don´t you dare suggest that to me!"

Suitably chastened, and distinctly unhappy about his impotence in the situation, he thought, *Bloody hell, this is all I need, on top of Barclay trying to bury me!* No, she would have to deal with it herself, that´s what Navy wives do! Nevertheless, he was ill at ease. He was at a loss about why she couldn´t keep up with her contraception regime; this was another unplanned pregnancy!

Next day came bright, but breezy, and after ensuring that Barclay was away from the ship, he took a ferry over to Helensburgh, to have a talk with his mother-in-law. He walked up the hill from the pier, and along by the park to her cottage. To his dismay, she was not at home. He cursed himself for not telephoning in advance.

A neighbour, after having observed him through her net curtains, informed him that Mrs Vickery was away with a friend for a week to Arran; could she help? Simon thanked her, but said no, he´d phone her next week sometime.

Chapter 9: Old friends reunite

Simon was at a loss at what to do next. He needed a day away from his command and didn´t wish to return to Greenock so soon in the day. He walked back down Sinclair Street to the sea front, admiring the view across the river to the hills above Greenock and Port Glasgow, and over to the right, the Roseneath Peninsular, with the painted white houses of Kilcreggan and Dunoon reflected in the sun.

Feeling refreshed and a bit more positive he entered the Imperial Bar, with the intention of having a pint and a Pub Lunch. As he entered the bar, he was startled to hear a shout, "Simon! Over here!" Simon recognised the voice immediately. Andrew Randolph, `Randy ' to everyone who knew him, was one of Simon's close friends at Dartmouth College, and later in Devonport before their career's took them in different directions. Simon remembered that Randy had gone into the Submarine Service, hence his presence here in Helensburgh.

They greeted, and embraced like brothers, effusively and heartily. Randy introduced him to the others at the table, "This is Simon, or just `Simple´ as we called him; Simon, meet Ken Samson, Janice, his lucky wife, and Gina…something; Simonelli, as in ice cream, friend of Janice. Come on sit yourself down, it's great to see you! What are you doing here?"

Simon was delighted to meet his old friend; someone he could relax and laugh with; he had been rather lonely recently since John Sumner left for the States. Randy was Lieutenant Weapons Officer, and Ken the Communications Officer on HMS Revenge, the Polaris `bomber´ submarine Simon had seen in Faslane a few weeks ago. They were due to start a six-month underwater patrol in a few day´s time. They swapped stories and laughed at each other's jokes, directed at the Navy, and one pint merged into another until Randy, looking at the clock above the bar, exclaimed, "Christ, I need to get moving! I'm meeting Audrey in the Rosslea in ten minutes! Simon, come on, Audrey would love to see you!"

Simon looked down, a little boyish and embarrassed, and made the excuse he had better get back to his ship. He´d been going out with Audrey before he met Alicia, and there had been bad feeling between the two women ever since. Randy was insistent, "Come on! You two also! I´ve got the place cards and flowers in the car for the Ladies Dinner tonight."

"Why not?" Gina enthused; "we could all have a bite to eat there."

The others agreed, and Simon, just a little reluctantly, was forced to concede. He was enjoying the cheery company, after so much stress in his recent life. They were five minutes late when they turned into the drive of the Rosslea Hotel. Simon marvelled at the setting; the sea opened up before them; the Sailing Club just over to the left, and an old classic wooden America´s Cup Yacht anchored in front of the hotel.

Audrey was waiting for them in the bar, sitting at a table by a window overlooking the panorama. It was quiet, most of the business crowd having finished lunch, and back at work. Randy and the others went in ahead, obscuring Simon from her view, until he said, "I've a surprise for you darling!"

"Simon! She exclaimed, I don't believe it! She embraced him tightly and gave him an affectionate kiss, which he returned thankfully. Simon's apprehensiveness disappeared immediately with the genuine warmth of the greeting. "You're supposed to be in the Med, or was it the Gulf?"

"I was, but now, as you can see, I'm here, enjoying the lovely Scottish weather," he joked.

Randy butted in. "The lucky bastard got his first command... Mind you Audrey, he's blown the bugger's engine! Always the speed merchant, old habits never die do they? ...Have you spoken to Ronnie yet, Audrey?"

"No, he's through in the function room organizing the tables," replied Audrey. "We'll talk to him after a bit of lunch. I'm famished!"

The waitress came over and they ordered a bottle of Moët, to raise a toast to Simon's Command, and a happy reunion, as the excuse. They all ordered food from the Table D'hôte Menu, the Special Steak and Kidney Pie for the men, whilst the women went for fish or salad.

The lunch was one of the happiest Simon had enjoyed for a very long time. Good food, great company, and a plentiful supply of wine had conversation and laughter flowing around the table. The singles present, Simon and Gina, eased into a comfortable easy relationship, balancing the two married couples.

The manager, Ronnie MacDonachie, appeared at their table, and offered them another bottle of Champagne, which was declined because the women did not want to begin their evening dinner surrounded by drunken sailors. After dinner was no problem, as they had plans for them!

Simon and Gina felt a little out of the conversation, which had turned to the organisation for the Ladies Dinner, and other incidentals. They conversed between themselves, mainly talking about Gina´s life. Simon had been studying her surreptitiously throughout. Her dark Italian looks betrayed her origins. She held her head high, chin up, which added inches to a small but voluptuous body. Her black hair was long, luxurious and waved. Carefully tended black arches and lustrous eyelashes on her flawless, olive skin accentuated dark-brown pupils and the crystalline whites of her eyes. Her outstanding feature however, was her sparkling personality and easy, spontaneous humour.

"You are Italian?" Simon asked somewhat unnecessarily.

"No I´m Scottish – can´t you tell by my accent? She laughed and went on. "After the First World War, my grandparents emigrated from Tuscany, and settled in Scotland, therefore, I´m second generation Scottish. My dad was born in Greenock, where your ship is now."

"What are you doing in Helensburgh? Simon enquired."

"Simonelli´s are quite famous in the area. We have Fish and Chip Shops, Ice Cream Parlours, Italian Delicatessens, and a Wholesale Catering Supplies business. I run the delicatessen in Helensburgh. I also do the company PR and advertising. We´re a mini Mafia, so watch out! I could have you liquidated," she laughed.

As Simon was contemplating all this, Audrey turned to them and suggested, "Why don´t you two join us tonight? One of the couples has dropped out, you can take their places."

Gina instantly declared, "I´m game! What about you, Simon?"

Simon said, "I´d love to, but I think it´s an evening for Revenge officers and their partners, is it not? Besides, I´d better get back to my ship." Randy butted in.

"Simon we´d love you to come, there are always other Navy guests from the Base. I promise you´ll not be out of place. Have you got your Watch Officers posted?"

"Yes, the bloody Ship´s in dry dock!"

"Well, it´s not going anywhere is it?" They all laughed.

Malevolent Karma

Audrey intervened again. "Please Simon... Look, Gina is looking miserable!"

Gina had gone quiet but embarrassed, she joked, "If the Prince won´t take Cinderella to the Ball, she´ll just have to stay back and clean the kitchen."

"I don´t have my dress uniform here, so I´d have to go back over to Greenock," Simon complained half-heartedly.

"I´ll lend you my Tuxedo, interrupted Ken, you´re about the same Hunk proportions as I am." Sounds of derision erupted from the women.

"That's settled!" Audrey exclaimed and, looking pointedly at Gina, added, "You can stay with us overnight if necessary."

"That´s fine, but I´d rather go over on the ferry, and pick up my uniform, if you don´t mind. If I leave now, I´ll be back by seven-thirty, is that okay?"

"Promise you´ll come back?" Gina asked then, a little embarrassed, added in a little girl, plaintive voice, "I don´t want to get dollied up, if I´m going to be left cleaning the kitchen."

"I´ll be back, Cinderella, he laughed, a Royal Navy Officer always stands by his word." Andy offered to run him to the Pier, and come back for the girls, but instead, they all stood up, paid the bill, and hurried out to the cars.

Simon just made the ferry and jumped aboard as it was leaving the Pier. On the way over, he reflected on the day. He'd had a wonderful time ...what a nice, cheerful crowd: and Gina? He knew he was entering dangerous territory. She really was an attractive girl, but nothing was happening between them. They were only partners for the evening.

He went straight to the ship and, satisfied that all was in order, informed the Duty Officer that he would be away for the night but, in emergency, could be reached at the Rosslea Hotel, where he intended staying. Showering, and shaving quickly, he packed his Dress uniform, now with the Commander stripe, and took a taxi back to the ferry once again. He was in his room at the Rosslea at a little after seven o´clock. He showered again; shaved, dressed carefully and groomed until he was satisfied he looked good.

They had agreed to meet in the Bar at seven-forty, and Gina arrived with the Samsons just in front of the Randy and Audrey. They posed for the Official photographer; the event would be reported in the Faslane News, the Base´s internal newspaper. The Ladies looked spectacular in their formal evening dresses and best jewellery, but the men no less so in their full dress uniforms, Medals and Insignia gleaming.

The Officers' Ladies' Dinner, a semi-formal affair, was held just before a submarine left on an extended patrol, as a pleasant leave-taking evening. As well as the formal Dinner, there were light-hearted speeches and toasts and, at times, dancing. If a superior ranking officer is invited, he would normally make a speech, and propose a toast to the Submarine and its Company. Randy was the Social Secretary on HMS Revenge, and hurried off to arrange a welcoming party with Audrey, taking Andy and Janice with them.

"We´d better hang back a bit, it´s not our show, Simon suggested. Would you like a drink?" he asked, suddenly feeling a little nervous.

Gina, observing this, put on a shy, girlish voice, "Sex-on-the-beach, please." Simon laughed aloud, causing a few guests to turn and stare. "Okay, you´re on, but before that, we´ll have some champagne," he said, taking two flutes from a passing waiter.

They chatted, and circulated with other guests. Gina was known to quite a few of the women, and Simon was pleased that she could hold her own in the largely social chit chat until the Maitre D'hôtel announced, "Ladies and Gentlemen, Dinner is Served!" Holding back, they checked their table places, and were pleased that they were seated beside their friends, alongside the VIP guests´ table.

The entire company stood, as the Commodore Clyde, and the rest of the VIP´s entered the room and took their places. The Commodore motioned for the company to be seated. Ken Samson stood, said a short Grace, and the dinner was served.

The food and wine were excellent. The company relaxed with much cross-table chattering and conversations going on in the room. Finally, coffee was served; a Vintage Port was passed around, and liqueurs served to the ladies. Ken Samson once again rapped on a glass with a spoon, and announced the toast to the Queen; the Company rose to their feet, and in unison, raised their glasses. "The QUEEN," resounded around the room from eighty-four voices. Permission to smoke was given, and the guests sat back in anticipation of the speeches, of which only one would be of a serious nature.

A series of hilarious discourses followed, until it was the turn of the senior officer present, Commodore Sir William Caruthers, to propose a toast to the Ladies. He began on a slightly serious note: how necessary the Submarine Service and Britain´s Nuclear deterrent in particular were, in helping to maintain world peace, in face of the still belligerent Soviet Union threats and received loud applause from the company.

On a lighter note, he recounted his life as a young Officer, and the scrapes he got into when he was courting his wife, who was sitting beside him displaying faux embarrassment. His finishing line and Toast to the Ladies was, as Navy tradition demands. "Gentlemen, be upstanding and raise your glasses... To our wives and sweethearts; may they never meet." He sat down to an enthusiastic applause.

The Band then began to play, and a few of the more confident couples followed the Commodore and his wife in the first waltz of the evening. Less formal dances followed later, with the band livening this up by giving passable renditions of various Elvis Pressley, Beatles and Rolling Stones hits.

It finished as intended, as a wonderful party night: a farewell to wives and sweethearts. When the company stood for 'God Save the Queen' followed by 'Auld Lang Syne' there was much emotion hanging in the air, with not a few tears in the ladies' eyes. Their men-folk would be out of touch, under a dark, freezing North Atlantic for six months or so.

The three couples retired to the bar for a final nightcap, winding down and laughing at the night's speeches and the Commodore's efforts to do the Twist. At last, it was two in the morning, the Bar was closing, and taxis called to take them back into Helensburgh.

Audrey suggested that they shared a taxi with the Samsons, as they lived close to each other on the officers' quarters. They said their boozy goodnights and left. Simon ran upstairs for his coat and a few moments later, he and Gina were ensconced in the taxi, on the short journey into Helensburgh. Once again, an awkward nervousness surfaced between them, each one wondering what the next step should be.

Gina lived in an apartment above her delicatessen in Colquhoun Square, and five minutes later, they were standing outside the door as she fished for her keys. Would you like to come up for a moment? She asked, and with a nod and a smile, Simon paid off the driver.

Once inside the apartment, he took her in his arms, and found her mouth with a hunger. She immediately responded, her tongue seeking his, her hand reaching down for his erection. After a few minutes of indulgence in exploratory caressing, she led him to the bedroom, both casting off clothes; so elegant before, they were now scattered in a line towards the bed.

Their lust was mutual, but slow and careful, each giving and taking, tasting and teasing, until the need overcame them to plunge into a glorious ecstasy of simultaneous climax, clinging together as if their very lives depended on it. A silence descended; nothing was said between them and they clung together as they fell into a comatose sleep.

The ringing telephone woke him. He had a clanging bells hangover, and at first did not know where he was.

Remembering, he realised that Gina was not beside him, and he picked up the phone without thinking. "Awake at last, sleepy head?" Gina´s voice asked.

"Just, you woke me up! Where are you?"

"I´m downstairs at work, some of us have to! When you´re dressed, come down and get some breakfast, okay?

"Fine by me," he replied, "I´ll wake up first though! See you in about twenty minutes."

Simon found the bathroom. Gina had thoughtfully laid out a new toothbrush, and a ladyshave outfit, which he used to scratch at his stubble. A hot, then freezing shower, eased his hangover, and he towelled himself dry surrounded by and smelling the femininity of her bathroom accessories.

Retrieving his dress uniform, which she had hung up to ease the creases of its night on the bedroom floor, he dressed, feeling relaxed and at ease. He frowned to himself when he thought about Alicia momentarily, but put his conscience to the side; it was only a one-night stand, after all. He bounded downstairs. Out in the fresh air, the square was busy with people going about their business. He held the door of the delicatessen open, allowing two women to enter before him.

The shop was decorated in the style more of Paris than Rome, very pleasant with etched glass displays, scrolled mirrors of seemingly acres of greenery. The coffee shop area was busy, but he spotted Gina sitting at a corner table beside the cash register. As he approached, she stood up, "Hmm, you look better than I thought you would, she said as a greeting and gave him a light kiss on the cheek. What would you like for breakfast?"

"I would love a bacon roll, if you do them, and a cup of black coffee, thanks."

"Irene," she called to a harassed-looking middle-aged waitress, "can you bring a bacon roll and black coffee for him, and an espresso for me please."

Irene answered, "Okay," and went about her work.

"Enjoy last night?" Gina asked with a provocative smile.

"Wonderful night... really enjoyed the dinner. The dancing was a little shaky, you´ll have to brush up on the Rock ´n Roll!" Simon teasingly replied.

"Nothing more ...something after the dancing?"

"Can´t remember a thing," he said with a puzzled expression. She smacked him on the head, and they both laughed. She became serious.

"Look Simon, don´t worry, I know you´re married; I´m not after a serious relationship. I like you a lot and I´m happy if we could see each other now and again." He addressed her seriously...

"Gina, not only am I married, but my wife is expecting another baby. I will be in this area only for another week or so. Last night was wonderful, you are a lovely girl and I´d love to see you again, but we both know it would be a mistake."

"Listen Simon, please don´t say no, I´m a big girl, I don´t need commitment, just one more time, please." She put her hand on his arm.

At this precise moment, an elderly lady came up to the table and looking at Simon said, "Hello officer! I thought it was you; you do look wonderful in your Dress Uniform; my Henry was so handsome in his." Sadly she added, "He was in the submarines also you know, but he passed away two years ago." Simon looked askance at the woman.

"I´m sorry, do I know you?"

"I spoke to you yesterday! You were looking for Mrs Vickery, remember?"

"Oh, I´m sorry, my mind was away for a moment, of course I do, you´re her neighbour. *Shit! He thought to himself, this is all I need right now!*

"I just wanted to say hello, I´ll leave you to your business," she added, looking pointedly at Gina, who had surreptitiously removed her hand from Simon´s arm. Gina noticed his fear.

"For God´s sake Simon, don´t worry, we´re simply old friends having a cup of coffee together."

"If only," Simon replied grimly. "Gina, this is a small town, everyone knows everything, my mother-in-law will know about this within half-an-hour, and she's on Arran!" His breakfast arrived then, and he ate it gloomily, as Gina attended to some paperwork, leaving him to his thoughts. After another cup of coffee, his humour returned a little. "Listen, you mentioned that your family own businesses in Greenock and the coast, right?"

Catching on, Gina replied, "Yes, and I've got a meeting in Largs on Tuesday. Can we meet?"

"Good, that would suit me, my ship should be ready to sail next weekend. I'll phone you on Monday, is that okay? I'd better get moving now and get back over. I've left my coat in the flat."

She suggested, "I'll go upstairs first. Wait five minutes and come up, just in case the old busybody is still around."

After she left, he got up, went to pay his bill, and was told that Miss Simonelli had attended to it. He opened the door and then, feeling conspicuous in his uniform, did an entire walk around the square checking for old `busybodies´ before going upstairs to the apartment. He knocked and entered, and Gina said, "I was beginning to think you weren't coming back for this." She was standing behind door, dwarfed in his coat. She turned her back on him then, teasingly, turned around to face him, slowly opening the coat to show her nakedness. He experienced an instant erection, responding to her provocation.

"My God, you're bloody sexy."

This time it was pure sex, urgent and demanding, until both were sated. As they were recovering the telephone rang, and Gina answered; after listening for a few minutes, she said, "Right, okay I'll come down."

"Got to go my sailor boy, I'm needed downstairs. Look, phone me anytime, but I'll see you on Tuesday." She dressed hurriedly, sorted her face, "Just pull the door shut," she said, and blew him a kiss as she left.

Simon lay a while, thinking ...*a remarkable girl ...why not, and it's only until next weekend*. He dressed, used the bathroom, pulled on his coat over his uniform and, checking his watch, ran down the stairs and cut down Colquhoun Street to the sea front. He was smiling to himself, as he ran over in his mind the past twenty-four hours... *Christ, I almost forgot my bloody clothes in the Hotel! Bloody hell; I'd better get my act together and concentrate a bit better.*

The day was cloudy, with a cold wind coming off the sea, *probably squally later he thought*, but feeling relaxed and cheerful, decided to walk along the promenade to the hotel in Rhu. He was striding along at a brisk pace, just passing, and admiring an Art Deco house built for a rich Glasgow merchant, when his thoughts were interrupted by a car horn drawing his attention. Randy and Ken were waving to him.

"Want a lift sailor?" Randy called.

It was only half a mile to go, but Simon was grateful to see his friends. He had been contemplating phoning Randy from the hotel, to say his thanks and goodbyes. They were going to the Rosslea to settle the Bill for the evening, and then off to the Revenge to begin their duties.

Laughter and leg pulling with Simon being the victim filled the time right up to the Reception of the hotel. Simon went upstairs to change back into civilian clothes, and packed. When he descended the stairs, Randy and Ken were disputing the bar bill with Ronnie MacDonachie, but finally had to concede. Submariners drink a lot at these events; after all, they would be without alcohol for the next six months!

Simon settled his account for the room, ruefully thinking that his head had never touched the pillow. He offered to buy his friends a farewell drink, but was declined; they were about to go on duty.

The friends made a heartfelt farewell; Simon was almost emotional. Thanks to them, he had shed the tensions of commanding HMS Rothesay, with all its associated problems. They promised to be in touch when HMS Revenge returned in six months – meanwhile, Good Luck!

He walked back along the shore to Helensburgh and caught the ferry over to Greenock. He was back on board Rothesay at three o´clock.

Chapter 10: Sabotage!

Lieutenant Barclay was by the gangway, bringing the ebullient Lieutenant Commander Amersbey back down to earth. Barclay reported that the navigating officer had gone down with acute appendicitis, and was unlikely to be fit for duty. He asked Simon, "Do you want a replacement, or should we make do with Sub Lieutenant Wilson?"

Simon answered: "Normally the sub-lieutenant would be the natural choice, but Wilson is just out of Navy College, and we´re going to be testing on the West Coast. With all the winds, tides and skerries out there, I think we should ask for a replacement."

Barclay agreed, and went on, "Bye the way, your friend, Sumner is not coming back; Lockheed are sending over a replacement, he should be here on Friday."

"Damn it!" Simon interposed, "that´s just twenty four hours before we´re due to sail; that´s hardly time for him to get to know the ship. What´s the position on the repairs, anyway; is there any news from the dockyard?"

Barclay: "I think you´d better speak to the Chief, he´s been looking for you all day."

"I´ll do that right away, he´s down below?"

"Where he always is!" Barclay said this with a touch of distaste.

Scobie, the Chief Engineer rarely mixed with the other officers, and only appeared in the wardroom at mealtimes.

Simon dropped off his bag in his cabin, and went down the ladders to the Engine Room.

Scobie was talking to one of his stokers, but interrupted his conversation as soon as he saw Simon. "Captain, I´ve been looking for you. Come into my cubby hole." They both squeezed into his tiny office under the ladder that Simon had just descended.

Simon noticed a fold down cot, which restricted space even more; Scobie then closed the door, making Simon feel almost claustrophobic.

"What´s the position on the repairs, John," Simon asked.

His Chief Engineer replied, "The new shaft has been installed, and we´re expecting the propeller back any day now, so we should be floating again by Wednesday; but that was not the reason I was looking for you. This business of the broken shaft; it was definitely a sabotage Captain, and none of my boy´s would do a thing like that. I know them, and I would trust them with my life."

"I accept that Chief, but who else would have access to the Engine Room, without one of your stokers seeing him?"

"I´ve been racking my brains Captain; remember I reported to you a slight vibration in the port engine, when we were still in the river?

"Yes, go on," Simon answered, intrigued.

"I reckon that the bastard put the ball barings into the shaft inspection aperture when we were still in Glasgow."

"Well that could be any of a hundred men in the yard."

"Captain, this kind of thing doesn´t happen in the shipyards now. It´s not the nineteen thirties; there are no German saboteurs, or Communist agents any more. These guys´ take a lot of pride in their work…Clyde built and all that. No, I think you have a problem on-board. I asked my boy´s if anyone was poking around when we still on the dock. Lieutenant Hanson was down here on several occasions when I was ashore."

Simon checked again that the door was closed. "Chief That's a serious charge your making against a fellow officer. I can't believe that Lieutenant Hanson would sabotage his own ship... for what reason? What would he want down here?"

Scobie answered: "He said he was checking out the magnetism levels throughout the ship, which the CPO found a bit strange. They were having problems with the installation, so he didn't question him. However, all this goes back to before you joined the Rothesay Captain. When Lieutenant Barclay was passed over for command, he was incandescent with rage, and he let it be known quite forcibly in the officers' wardroom."

Scobie continued: "Remember he was first officer for almost four years and in temporary command at this time. Lieutenant Hanson is his mate, and between them they were almost promoting a mutiny, or at least they wanted the all the officers to sign a petition on his behalf."

Simon was astonished, "But that's crazy, did he think the Admiralty would bow to this? It almost mounts to mutiny!"

"Quite!" Scobie interjected: "I was the one who put a stop to it. There was a meeting in the wardroom; I reminded him of his position as senior officer. I told them exactly what I thought of them, and their brainless idea. Barclay was so angry and belligerent, he and I almost came to blows. After that, he more or less went on strike and neglected his duties to the extent that there was no discipline or control until you came on board."

"Christ, what fools; Simon said, they would never have got off with it! But why sabotage the ship?"

"Not the ship as such ... me! I am the target; if my engines fail, the blame falls on me, and I get it in the neck. The Navy's Special Branch is convinced that one of my stokers must have done it. These little ball barings are of a type used in precision engineering, like those in Radar calibration discs. John Sumner was complaining some of his parts had gone missing, we can ask him if ball barings had also disappeared."

"Sumner is not coming back to the ship, Chief, and it´s still a long way from proving Hanson put them into the shaft."

"That´s true, Captain, but you should watch your back; I will not have any of them near the Engine Room from now on. I´m even sleeping down here now!"

"Thanks Chief," Simon sighed, "not the ideal conditions to be carrying out sea trials though."

Chapter 11:"Hell hath no fury... "

In his cabin later, Simon thought about Gina, and the complications that this was going to enter into his life if he continued to see her. His conscious per se wasn´t too bothered; he´d had a few one-night stands in his ports of call. She was too close to his mother-in-law, and he recognised that he was really was very attracted to her. Getting out now, before it all got serious was the best option; a clean break.

He sat down and composed an affectionate letter to her, setting out his thoughts, and ending that it would be unfair for them to meet again. Sealing, and affixing a stamp, he called for a junior steward to run to the post office, ensuring she would receive the letter by Saturday.

Going ashore to a call box, Simon then telephoned Alicia. When she answered, she wasn´t so hysterical this time, but he recognised by the frigid tone in her voice that she was still unhappy. He described meeting the Randolph's, and how they had enjoyed their lunch together, but then he decided not to mention the ladies´ dinner. He knew she would accuse him of having all the fun, whilst she sat at home bearing his children.

She was interested enough to ask after "that bitch Audrey", and how she looked. "I bet she doesn't look like me, fat and ugly."

"Come on Alicia, Audrey really is a nice woman, and after all, you won the prize…me!"

"Call that a prize? More like a booby!" she snorted.

Simon could see where this was going, and made an excuse that there were people waiting in line for the telephone. He said his "goodbye darling," and put the receiver in its cradle.

The weekend went by quickly. The crew had returned to HMS Rothesay, and the usual routines were re-established. There was a mood of buoyant expectation; they would soon be at sea again.

A further visit from the Faslane SIB Police, to re-interview the engine room stokers, almost went badly wrong, with tempers flaring. A furious Chief Engineer Scobie, had to be restrained by the captain from coming out with his accusations to an almost jaunty Lieutenant Barclay.

Simon had all but put Gina out of his mind, as he concentrated on the new orders he had received from Clyde HQ at Faslane.

The submarine exercise was put on hold with a tentative three-week schedule, until HMS Rothesay had completed her trials and everything was operational. After engine proving, he was to proceed to the Royal Navy Installation at Stornaway, in the Hebrides, and base the ship there until the sea trials program was completed.

Shortly after noon on Tuesday, the OOD, Lieutenant Hanson, called him to the bridge. "There's a young lady in a sports car was at the dockyard gates asking to see you. Dock Security wants to know if they should let her through."

Simon tried not to panic. "Shit, the bitch! She knows better than to do this!" Aloud he answered: "No, this is a private matter; tell them I'll come down in five minutes."

"As you say Sir;" a smug looking Hanson replied, and conveyed the message to dockyard security.

Simon quickly changed into civilian clothes, and in the passing, told Hanson he would be back in an hour.

Gina was standing alongside her flaming red Triumph TR6 Sports; hair tied up in a fashionable cobalt blue scarf, chatting to a security guard when Simon saw her.

He was furious, but had to admit she looked fabulous. The day was freezing cold, but sunny, and she was dressed in a white ski outfit. The hood of the car was down. She could have been in St Moritz.

Shit! He said to himself; *more bloody complications.* As he marched up, he dressed his mouth into a smile: "Hi Gina, this is a nice surprise! You look great ... didn´t you get my letter?"

She broke off her conversation with the guard, "Yes, darling, but I have something for you before you go. Can we go somewhere?"

"I´ve got an hour darling, is that okay?"

"That´s super!" she laughed happily; "Hop in; we´ll go for a drive."

The engine fired up with a throaty growl, and she turned the car around. Gunning the accelerator, the Triumph shot off down the road where she took the road for Skelmorlie on the coast. The wind was roaring over the windscreen, and it was too noisy to talk. Simon was quickly chilled to the bone, and he asked her to turn up the heating. Gina was driving fast on the winding coast road, overtaking recklessly, at times risking a crash.

He was uneasy; she was up to something, but what was a mystery, and he felt inhibited in trying to ask over the wind and bellow of the engine.

After fifteen minutes she turned into a pub car park, and he was able to ask her through his frozen face; "Why are we here Gina, what´s going on?"

"Simon, trust me; I want you to meet someone, that´s all. Stay here, I´ll be back in a moment."

Mystified, Simon did as he was told, still uneasy in his stomach. He got out of the car to walk around and bring some heat into his body.

After a few minutes, she came out of the bar with two men, and smilingly introduced them: "Simon, this is Franco and Vito; they are my brothers."

Simon put out his hand to shake Vito's hand, but received a tremendous punch to his face in return. He staggered back, unable to defend himself. The two brothers, proceeded to kick and punch him to the ground, and finished with a gob-spittle to his bleeding face, before standing back.

Gina, who had been standing calmly watching the beating, smiled into his face; "I told you I could have you liquidated. I am not a fucking whore, to be dumped when you've finished playing with me!"

Vito added, "Don't show your face anywhere within a fucking mile of my sister, do you understand?"

Simon was too distressed, dazed and bleeding to do anything else than nod his head. Blood was pouring from his nose, and he had a cut over his eye, as well as grazes on his face, where he had scraped it on the tarmac.

The three siblings turned and went back into the bar.

Simon picked himself up, and staggered over to the grass verge, mind in a turmoil. *Jesus Christ, what did I do to deserve this? What a bitch! She came on to me, as much as I did, if not more.* He was thinking of the morning in the flat, before he left.

Eventually, he gained control of his legs and stood up, wiped most of the blood from his face, and slowly gathered his wits around him. He walked into the village, conscious of the stares from the few people he encountered, and found a telephone box.

Looking in the mirror, he realised with horror what he looked like. His nose had stopped bleeding, but was swollen and grazed; his right eye was ballooning, and he had cuts and scrapes to his face. His trousers and jacket were torn; he looked like a drunk after a pub fight.

"*Christ Almighty! What am I going to say on the ship?*"

He found a taxi number pasted by the telephone, and ordered one to come immediately.

The taxi arrived after twenty minutes, and as Simon entered the driver asked, "What happened to you mate? Been screwing someone´s missus? Where to, Inverclyde Hospital? Might be a good idea; that nose of yours might be broken, if you ask me."

Holding his handkerchief to his nose, Simon asked him to take him back to the dockyard. On the road back, he still could not believe what had happened to him. *Why did she do that?* He kept repeating to himself.

Arriving back, he had only been away from the ship for an hour and a half.

His appearance on the gangway caused much consternation among the Watch. The ODD, still Lieutenant Hanson, was called from the Bridge, and the medical orderly summoned.

Simon was taken down to the sick bay, where he was patched up and stitched over his eye.

The medic pinched his nose to test if it was broken, which brought a gasp of agony, and tears to Simon´s eyes, and concluded, "I don´t think it´s broken Sir, I´ve seen plenty of this at our school with the rugby. It might remain a bit bent though, and that eye is going to shine for a week at least."

Hanson came down to the sick bay, during all this, accompanied by First Officer Barclay.

Barclay could hardly suppress his smile, as he asked his captain what had happened to him. "As you know, it´s got to be recorded in the ship´s log Sir. Have you reported this to the police? Were you robbed, Sir? My God! What is the world coming to… and in broad daylight!"

Simon was exhausted and still in shock from his beating. "Lieutenant Barclay, we can do the formalities later, if you please; I´ll give a full statement for entering in the log later. I don´t want the police involved thank you. Can you please leave me alone now, I am tired, and would like to rest."

He spent the night in the sick bay, exhausted, and aching all over. The orderly gave him a strong sedative, which helped him sleep, but as he was drifting in unconsciousness, *Why?* was the thought spinning through his head.

Next morning, Simon resumed command from Barclay. He was aching all over, but his nose and eye was giving him the most trouble. When he was shaving, he almost recoiled from his image in the mirror. His thoughts drifted on to Gina; *A crazy, dangerous woman.*
He kept to his cabin all day, except for the odd spell of fresh air on the bridge, avoiding the eyes of the seamen on duty. He gave a statement to the ODD for inclusion in the ship´s log. He had tripped over the seatbelt in the car, and had fallen, head first, onto the road.

The news had spread like wildfire throughout the ship, with an unusual number of the crew, appearing around the bridge carrying out maintenance work. The speculation centred on a mystery attractive young woman in a red sports car, confirmed by Lieutenant Hanson´s version of events.
Next day Simon had a progress meeting with Lieutenant Scobie, who confirmed the shaft and propeller had been re-installed. Simon gave his approval for signing off the work with dockyard.
With a certain amount of relief, Simon gave the order for the dry dock to be flooded. The roar of the water entering was like music to his ears. A few hours went by, HMS Rothesay was afloat again, and eased into a berth alongside the quay.

The new temporary Navigator reported for duty, seconded from one of the patrol boats at Faslane, and the replacement for Sumner from Lockheed, arrived shortly after, a day earlier than expected.

The Lockheed replacement was the archetypal young Ivy League American, brash, crew cut, and very sure of him-self. "I´m Mackenzie Harper," he announced, introducing himself to the captain. He then asked accurately, "Woman trouble captain?"

This brought stifled mirth to the bridge party, of which Simon had to ignore.

Harper then went on to depreciate the` little boat´ he was now on. "My last job was on Nimitz; it´s the biggest aircraft carrier in the entire U.S. Navy."

Simon reposted sourly: "Sorry about the inconvenience Mr Harper, but if your efficiency matches your humour, you won´t be aboard this ship too long."

Simon radioed Clyde Fleet HQ, for permission to cast off early next morning. Weather conditions were favourable, and he wanted to get back to sea.

As they were awaiting confirmation, the ominous black hulk of the Polaris ballistic missile submarine HMS Revenge, appeared out of the Rhu channel accompanied by her escorts, to begin her six-month patrol deep under the North Atlantic.

Simon thought of Randy and Ken encased in the giant cigar tube, and out of touch with their wives. Would they need to fire off their missiles? The Soviets had been rattling their cage again, but it was doubtful if Harold Wilson had the guts to stand up to them.

The signal came in from Faslane: "Permission granted, leave on the high tide, 0645 hours! Good Luck Rothesay!" Simon heaved a sigh of relief, now desperate to get the sea trials over and done with.

Chapter 12: The storm

It was still dark, but a clear frosty night, when Rothesay slipped her moorings, and on half power, headed down into the Firth of Clyde, taking a course that would skirt Arran and round the Mull of Kintyre. Simon refused John Scobie´s

Malevolent Karma

request to give her a run on full revolutions to test the new shaft. This had induced a terror in Simon's gut, fearing another breakdown before they could make progress on their sea trials mission.

The American technician proved to be efficient, and made progress with Hanson on the calibration of the radar and weapons systems. The basic sonar system was functioning well, but between them, they were still having problems calibrating the new, more sophisticated submarine detection equipment.

The first night at sea HMS Rothesay anchored off Tobermory. Simon, still aching all over and alone in his cabin, allowed himself a little satisfaction. He had found the American insufferable, with his continuous boasting, and had banished him to a bunk in the officer's quarters.

The forecast was still unusually fine, and he knew they would be able to enjoy the magnificent scenery of the Barra Sound, and Inner Minch as they approached Stornaway, their destination and base for the actual proving and training exercises..

For three weeks, HMS Rothesay tested, manoeuvred and trained in the new technology. They traversed the Outer Minch, and Inner Minch, guns firing at the Benbecula Range, and missiles into the Atlantic. Dummy mines were dropped and and then retrieved, and imaginary submarines electronically detected and sank with practice depth charges. The weather was variable but they did not encounter any of the storms, normal at this time of the year.

MacKenzie Harper left the ship, much to everyone's relief. They had finally found the problem on the submarine detection system, and Hanson had learned how to correct and recalibrate the new sonar.

The ship's company had trained and worked hard on the trials, and Simon ordered three days rotational leave for the officers and crew, as a `well done´ bonus

John Scobie had relations on the Island of Uist, and he went ashore after first posting a twenty-four hour guard on his precious engine room. No one, excepting for the captain, was to be allowed to enter unaccompanied.

Lieutenants Barclay and Hanson took a ferry over to Skye, ostensibly to do a little hill walking.

Simon stayed on board himself, still a little nervous. His injuries had healed well, except for a scar above his eye. He received new orders: He was to proceed to Loch Fyne, carry out a week´s detection and attack practice, and coordination exercise with HMS Warrior, a Hunter Killer Class Submarine. After completing the exercise, he was to command the ship down to its home base of Portsmouth.

Simon didn´t want to speculate on his future, but being realistic, the sea trials had not gone well, and although the engine problem was out of his control, the captain retains full responsibility for all that happens on under his command. He turned his thoughts to Alicia, and admitted to himself, he had work to do there also, to recuperate their relationship. Gina was a bad memory, a stupid dalliance that had turned out to be a painful nightmare.

Suddenly, as happens with a frequency in this area, the weather changed. Ferries in the Minches were cancelled, and Scobie, Barclay and Hanson were fortunate to get back to the ship in time for sailing.

Simon was now anxious to finish the mission, and he over-ruled the suggestions of Barclay, and the navigation officer to postpone sailing. Mine Counter Vessels were designed, and built to sail in all weathers, but the Minch is notorious for the ferocious tidal currents and wind shifts, which have helped to earn its reputation as being a graveyard for ships over the centuries.

The ship cast off, but just outside the port of Stornaway, and out of the shelter of the land, they encountered the full force of the gale sweeping in from the Atlantic. Rothesay was being battered on the starboard side by the wind, and twenty-foot waves were foaming over the ship's bow, spraying over the bridge windows.

No worse than Loch Fyne was, thought Simon, but visibility was falling as fast as the barometer. The ship was closed-up watertight; the lookout crew sheltering in whatever corners or bulkheads they could find as HMS Rothesay bucked and dived into the swell.

The wind increased to a force eight gale, and a sudden squall cut out all visibility, leaving them relying on the radar to keep them on course. The barometer was still falling, and a nervous Barclay advised Simon that they should head for Skye, and sit out what was evidently building into a ferocious storm.

Simon reluctantly agreed, and ordered a change of course for Portree, where they could shelter, and ride out the storm.

The ship plowed on, the wind shifting this way, then the other. The Helmsman was having great difficulty in steering a steady course. The converging currents pitching, and tossing Rothesay as if it was a toy; everyone braced against bulkheads or whatever they could find. The navigator was fretfully continuing checking and rechecking sonar readings, charts and the gyroscope, swinging in its binnacle.

Simon, holding on, his knuckles white, was trying to maintain an outward calm, but inside his stomach was betraying his fear. He had never sailed in these conditions before, in such a small ship. In the troughs, the waves were now towering over Rothesay, and visibility fell to two hundred yards. The lookouts were anxiously peering into the thrashing rain when darkness fell over the ship, like a cover over fearful children.

Now they were relying on the radar and sonar readings being called out continually by the CPO. Hanson went down to the operations room to supervise; at last, to the relief of everyone, they were inside the sound of Raasay, still in the grip of the storm, but noticeably less violent.

The lookouts still could not visually make contact with the land, although the radar showed that it was no more than a mile to starboard. Another half hour passed, Rothesay was groping through the dark, guided by the unseen radar beams, when there was a shout from a lookout; "Lights ahead on the Starboard beam!"

The relief was palpable; even in the Sound, the wind and currents were at odds, but at least the sea was no longer towering above in the troughs.

Simon instructed the navigator to check his bearings for entering Portree harbour, just as another heavy squall hit the ship, wiping out visibility again. He called down to the engine room, "Slow ahead, steady", but the helmsman advised they were going backwards on the tide!

Simon adjusted his orders, "Increase to half ahead, but prepare to reduce revs."

Suddenly, the sonar screens blanked out, and then relit, but the CPO warned, "Something odd Captain, the readings have changed; sonar was showing five fathoms, now it´s fifteen!"

"Call Lieutenant Hanson, get him to check it out," Simon instructed, as they proceeded forward, fighting the wind and tide.

The harbour lights were just visible through the storm, the navigator suddenly called, "Captain! Fifteen fathoms is not possible here, the sonar is wrong!"

Simon reacted, "Engine room, full astern!" just as the horrible, sickening crunching of hull on rocks sounded, and everyone not holding on, was thrown to the floor.

Chapter 13: The Homecoming

Early in her pregnancy, Alicia had to give up her job in Public Relations at the Naval Base. She was simply to unwell to continue, which added to the frustration and depression she already felt. Gradually, she also withdrew from the charity and social work she had been so involved in, and entered a stage of her life she had never before experienced; a feeling of being alone in the world, of being unwanted. Her friends no longer called as often; her mother was in Scotland, and the independent Alicia hated her continuing advice and exhortations to "snap out of it!"

"My God, Simon, what are you doing here?" Alicia, opening the door to the doorbell, appeared far from her best. She looked tired and haggard; her normally well cared for long blonde hair tied back carelessly. Alicia´s usual stylish dress of elegance now substituted by an old housecoat over her pyjamas, although it was almost noon.

Simon, visibly shocked by her appearance, recovered, "Is this the way you address your husband, just back from navy manoeuvres?"

Still surprised by his sudden appearance on the doorstep, Alicia apologised, "I´m sorry darling, but what are you doing here? What´s happened?"

"Nothing, darling, I applied for compassionate leave, that´s all. Aren´t you pleased to see me?"

"Of course I am, Simon, but I know it´s not that simple. Why didn´t you telephone and let me know you´re coming?

"I only wanted to surprise you, that´s all."

"Well you´ve certainly succeeded on that, giving him a brief hug and perfunctory kiss as she led him into the kitchen. Want some tea?"

"I wouldn´t mind a better welcome first, he answered. Bloody hell Alicia, I haven´t slept for twenty eight hours."

He had notice the pronounced five month bulge on her belly, as soon as she had opened the door; and now he knew that relations were going to be a little tricky between them.

"Simon, I´ve been up all night, half of it on my knees over the toilet, so I´m not in the mood for welcome home hero scenes." There was an added sharpness to her voice, which confirmed his thoughts.

I´m going to have to be careful here, he thought.

"Why don´t you go upstairs, and refresh, while the tea is brewing," she suggested.

He did as he was told, and was shocked to see the condition of the house as he passed; first the lounge, the bedrooms, and then the bathroom, which still had a smell of vomit lingering. *Christ almighty, she´s really letting things go this time.*

He thought of having a quick, badly needed shower, but upon opening the door of the cubicle, thought better of it. Instead, he stripped to the waist, wiped out the basin, and washed under a cold stream of water, splashing over his chest and shoulders. Thus refreshed, he went through to the bedroom, and picked a navy blue polo from his drawer, putting it on as he descended the stairs

Alicia was sitting at the kitchen table, holding her mug of tea between both hands. She didn´t look up as he entered, and, to his astonishment, there was a cigarette burning in an ashtray beside her elbow.

He poured his tea into an old Royal Lifeboat Association mug, and said, "Alicia, what in the hell´s going on? You´ve never smoked before in your life, and now, with the baby due, you´ve started? Look at you, you´ve let yourself go old girl."

"So Captain Hero knows all about babies and women´s health? Does he also know that the fucking pills they gave me to calm my nerves make me want to throw up all day? You know nothing Simon!"

"Christ Alicia, calm down; I didn´t come all this way home to argue with you; I´m here to help as best I can."

"I'm here to help as best I can" she mimicked. "I'll calm down when you tell me why you're really here! Have you stuck it into one of the Scottish shags, and got a dose? You forget Simon, I'm Royal Navy through and through ...if every matelot got leave for babies, the ships WOULD NEVER LEAVE THE FUCKING HARBOURS!" she screamed, "NOW, TELL ME WHY YOU ARE HOME!"

Shocked and completely off guard, Simon told her about the grounding of HMS Rothesay on Skye.

She looked straight at him; absolute venom in her eyes and hissed, "I knew it! As soon as I saw you at the door, I knew. Not only has Simon fucked me up; he's fucked up his career also! IT'S A DOUBLE FUCK UP! She scattered the mug of tea, and her ashtray hit the cooker as she fled upstairs, slamming doors on the way.

A debilitating weariness flooded over Simon. The result of the battering that his emotions and self-esteem had taken within the space of forty-eight hours. He sank down onto a kitchen stool, head bowed, and hands over his eyes, and began to weep uncontrollably.

Upstairs, Alicia was also weeping, but more in anger and frustration. "Here am I, with a baby in my body I don't want, and a useless arsehole downstairs whose just fucked up our future. Thank God my father is not around to see this!"

A silence settled over the house, until eventually Simon regained control of his emotions, washed his face in the kitchen sink and went upstairs.

He knocked quietly on the bedroom door, but there was no answer. He entered, and Alicia was lying down, face to the wall. "Alicia, please; I can rebuild my career, it wasn't my fault,"
There was no answer, so he sat on the bed, and put his hand on her shoulder.

"Don't touch me, Simon. I don't want to know; do what you want to do."

He thought of his daughter: "Alicia, where's Francesca?"

"She went up with my mother to Scotland for a week or two."

"I went to see your mother, but she was on holiday."

"I know, Simon; she told me … and she also told me about the Ladies Dinner you forgot to tell me about."

Drawing in his breath, he said, "It wasn't important and you were already upset when I phoned."

Bitterly she responded, "When the cat's away...."

He changed the subject back to his daughter, "Is Francesca alright?" he enquired.

Wearily, Alicia replied: Yes, Simon, she's fine; it's me that's not alright. My mother offered to look after her for a couple of weeks, until I can get my strength back."

"Oh I see. I thought she might be at the nursery."

"Simon, would you please leave me alone now, I would like to sleep."

"Alicia, I'm really very sorry." He patted his wife's shoulder again, and quietly left the room, closing the door behind his homecoming.

Simon was summoned to HMNB Clyde, as the principal witness in the Official Enquiry into the grounding of HMS Rothesay.

Eventually, the verdict exonerated him of the grounding of the ship, but received a reprimand for needlessly endangering his ship and his crew by putting to sea in exceptional storm conditions.

The mystery of the sonar and radar failure went unexplained. The Board opined that probably teething troubles in the new installation led to the breakdown in the equipment.

Chapter 14: Jonathan

There is widely respected theory that a baby bonds with its mother whilst still in the womb. Alicia´s problems during the gestation of her son would provide some more evidence of this, in her failure to bond with her baby Jonathan.

It wasn´t that she blamed him *per se* for him being born, but their marriage and had being going through a rocky time lately, and she didn´t feel ready for another child at this moment in time. It was a mistake, they both realised; a drunken party; a forgotten pill, and there she was considering an abortion, but in her conscience could not let her carry it out.

As the biological mother, Alicia felt guilty, and sorry for the child, but admitted to herself that she really didn´t *like* him.

The baby Jonathan had all the features of a miniature Simon; he would be very good looking when he was a man, but he seemed to be constantly crying, and never sleeping enough, therefore he always had a pinched, distressed look about him. He was so different from his elder sister, Francesca, who had been born with a halo of happiness around her, always contented, gurgling sweetly when a friend or neighbour poked her face into the pram, and sleeping as if connected to an alarm clock.

Simon was away on a weapons course in the USA for most of the first year, so there was no one to help with the night shifts, therefore Alicia became more and more depressed and tired.

When he was home on leave, there was a frisson of tension between him and Alicia, and his son became a kind of scapegoat for both of them.

Their son Jonathan therefore had a difficult early childhood, not receiving the attention, love, affection and personal development he needed and craved. He yearned for the attention, and love from his parents, but felt alone and unwanted in comparison with his sister; in truth, he was in fact unloved.

At the earliest possible entry date, the boy was sent to St Martin´s Preparatory Boarding School much favoured by the military and diplomatic elite. This school had a very good reputation for rigorous discipline, ideal preparation for the future leaders of the diplomatic corps and Britain´s military establishment.

In his first term as a new boy, he suffered merciless bullying and abuse from the older boys, which seemed to go unnoticed by the House Matron.

Miss Harper was a cold, soulless ex-nun who nevertheless maintained an orderly and disciplined House under her control. Any boy, bedwetting, crying in his sleep, or found playing with his twinkle, would face the wrath of a sexually repressed, God-fearing woman, and an ice-cold bath to remind him of his responsibilities.

Jonathan suffered his share of this punishment. He was homesick, frightened, and endured horrible nightmares in his first year. He was prone to wetting his bed during these dreams, much to the fury of the Matron.

His parent´s almost never visited, and on his term vacations at home, which would coincide with Francesca´s, he received little interest or attention.

Academically through his own indolence, he was in the lower quartile. He took no interest in sport or the extracurricular activities of the school, other than those of which were obligatory.

In this environment, Jonathan passed his most formative years, growing more and more introverted and uncommunicative as time went by.

Malevolent Karma

Chapter 15: The Persian Gulf

Simon´s career stalled after the HMS Rothesay grounding, but finally, he made Lieutenant Commander, and was posted as Executive Officer on HMS Greystoke, a Type 42 Destroyer bound for a tour of duty in the Persian Gulf.

He settled into his duties quickly, without undue problems. The captain was an ascetic character, who maintained a distance from his officers and other ranks. A strict disciplinarian, he ran a tight ship regime, and expected his officers to follow suit.

Great Britain was not officially involved in the Iran-Iraq war, but followed the Americans in leaning support towards the Iraq side.
Patrolling in the Gulf was more about maintaining a watchful vigilance. It was a boring routine, rather than active war. HMS Greystoke settled into the daily chores of training, more training, cleaning and constant routine patrolling. In five months, they had not one single incident to attend to other than one able seaman having to be air-lifted off the ship for an appendix operation.

In, and around the Straits of Hormuz, Iranian Revolutionary Guards Fast Craft Torpedo boats were a common enough sight on the radar, as they harassed and attacked tankers carrying oil from the Iraqi oilfields.
They never menaced the British or American warships, although at times playing cat and mouse games, just out of a threatening range.

It was Simon´s watch, the Dog watch, between four and six in the afternoon. The sun was still blindingly hot, dazzling off a lazy swell, humidity in the high ninety´s. The destroyer was patrolling in international waters, about three miles outside of Iranian waters.

Two IPS-16 Pey-Kaap fast craft appeared on the radar screens running parallel to the ship; in a seemingly innocent manoeuvre, they changed direction to a tack converging with the destroyer.

The sub-operations officer pointed this out to Simon, saying that they would converge in about ten minutes on this tack. "Shall we give them a buzz on the radio Sir?"

Simon answered quickly, "No we´re fine as we are; they´re only playing games again."

Simon looked at the radar screen, and then went outside as the Iranian craft sped into view. The seaman on the wheel stared stonily ahead, and after a few minutes Sub-Ops nervously asked, "Shouldn´t we sound Action Stations, or change our course Sir?"

"Good God no, Sullivan, the skipper is having his kip, they´re only playing about … you´ll get used to it."

They continued to watch the Iranians, who were at this time running parallel to the Greystoke.

Tension on the bridge was palpable, sweat dripping off the helmsman nose as he kept a steady course. Simon himself began to feel uneasy, but although perspiration was pouring out of his back, he maintained a cool facade, saying nothing.

Suddenly, the two fast craft, turned, and accelerated directly towards the destroyer.

"Sir!" The sub-lieutenant yelled, "they´ll be in range in a couple of minutes!"

Simon found himself completely paralysed, frozen in time. His brain closed down, his legs turned to water, and his bowels almost emptied. Finally, it registered that the sub lieutenant was shouting at him! "Sound action stations!" he screamed, appalled at what had occurred.

Officers and sailors were running to their battle stations, pulling on their fire protection gear, but just as the captain stumbled onto the bridge the Iranians separated and sped past, one in front of the bow whilst the other passed by the stern, and away, Revolutionary Guards waving and jeering in the wake from their boats.

"Good God!" The captain shouted, "how in the hell did they get so close! Were you all bloody sleeping?" He glared at Simon, as he grabbed at the microphone. "No firing until I give the order!" He shouted into the tannoy, "Maintain action stations!"

White with anger he demanded, "What in the hell happened here? They could have bloody sunk us with a torpedo!" Glaring around the bridge he demanded: "Did no one notice them, or did they just pop out of the bloody sea? I want answers!"

The blood had completely vacated Simon's face, his knees still felt unable to hold his weight, and he wanted desperately to pee. He had to grip a stanchion to control his trembling. Finally, recovering some composure, Simon answered, "It was my responsibility captain, I assessed they were playing their usual games, and, as you can see, I was correct in my judgment."

The captain looked at him, eyes blazing, and then strangely, said nothing more about the subject. He began giving quiet orders about the ship, and observing the Iranian fast craft until they were out of visual sight, then a further five minutes watching the radar.

"Lieutenant Gilroy, to the bridge" he announced over the tannoy. When Gilroy arrived on the bridge, the captain instructed him to take over control of the ship. "Maintain action stations, and call me immediately if the Iranians come back." Turning to Simon, he ordered: "Lieutenant Amersbey, report to my quarters!"

"Yes Sir", he managed to respond, and followed the captain into his quarters.

"What happened here lieutenant? I want a full explanation!" demanded a still furious captain.

Ramrod straight, and staring at a point above his captain's head, Simon responded, "Sorry Sir, I thought they were playing their usual silly games with us; correctly, as it turned out they turned away from us. On reflection, however, maybe I should have brought us up to battle stations a little sooner."

"Correct my arse!" The captain furiously interrupted. "You put this ship, and its crew into a dangerous situation, and I want to know why!"

"Sir, I simply misjudged the ranges, they came on much faster than I thought."

"Did you panic Amersbey? Did you freeze up?"

"No Sir, I was in control all of the time; just as I said; it was a misjudgement of the speed and range."

The captain stared at him, until Simon´s cheeks began to redden.

"Listen, Amersbey, despite reports to the contrary, I have always had faith in your abilities; you´re a competent officer, but I will not have an officer on my ship, that I cannot rely on in a war situation; do you understand?"

"Sir, please, I admit to a misjudgement on my part, I can assure you that it will not happen again." Simon was pleading for his naval career now.

"Nevertheless this was a serious lapse of judgment on your part. I will have to interview the others on the bridge as to what went wrong."

"Sir, I only want to restate that you can have confidence in me."

"Dismiss, Lieutenant; Gilmore will take over your watch now."

When action stations had sounded, the experienced hands had been stunned to see the Iranian fast boats so close to the destroyer. In consequence, Simon was the subject of stares and whispers from the men, as he made his way down to the officers´ wardroom.

He asked for a strong mug of coffee laced with rum. He was sipping this, pretending to read the notice board, when his hands began to tremble uncontrollably, his knees felt like jelly; he had to sit down at a table to regain composure. He knew he was in real trouble; this could quite easily turn into a court martial case. It all depended on his commanding officer, the captain. He accepted to himself, that he had bottled it. This had been his first potential enemy action, and, despite all his experience and training, he had experienced sheer and utter terror during the entire incident. Even now, his nerves were fragmented.

When the klaxon sounded the all clear, he almost jumped out of his seat. *Jesus Christ! what's happening to me?*. He went along the passage to his cabin, and showered before lying down on his bunk, reflecting, and afraid. He contemplated missing dinner, but realised that would be taken as a sign of admission of guilt and cowardliness.

In the event, there were only four other officers in the mess at dinner. The mood was subdued, no one meeting his eye, with awkward silences; only the hum of the generators disturbing the tension. The ambiance in the wardroom almost jarred Simon into screaming; *Are you all so fucking perfect that you don't ever make a mistake?*

When he was finished his dinner the wardroom steward whispered in his ear, "Captain sends his compliments, and can you join him in his cabin, Sir."

"Thank you Tommy," he replied, legs again jellying thinking, *Well, this is it; your future in the next five minutes.*

Simon made his way along the steel, painted passageway, and through the watertight bulkhead, to go up to the captains quarters, behind the bridge. He had a sudden, vital need to pee, and diverted into the officers heads, finding blessed relief from his bladder, but doing nothing to damper the panic rising again through his stomach. He took an extra minute to compose himself; splashing his face in cold water, carefully drying and checking his appearance. Breathing deeply, thinking again, *Here goes*, and ran up the ladder to the captains´ cabin. He knocked, and waited; normally he would have entered, as was the custom.

"Enter," came back the command. The captain, dressed in his blues, was sitting by his table, finishing his rice pudding.

He looked up and said, "Sit down Amersbey," indicating with a nod of his head the spare chair.

The cabin was stifling, despite the fans on the ceiling spinning full blast, only making a current of turgid, hot, humid air move around a bit.

The captain finally finished his meal as Simon began to feel the sweat on his back, and looked up, directly into Simon´s eyes, and said, "Listen Lieutenant, our job is not easy out here in the Gulf. We have very restrictive and strict rules of engagement acting as unofficial policemen in a war that´s none of our damn business, except that is, we need the oil to continue to flow uninterrupted."

The captain was communicating in an understanding tone; Simon was thinking, *Maybe I´m okay after all.*

He continued, "I´ve finished my preliminary investigation into today´s incident. I have interviewed everyone who was on the bridge, chief petty officer on the operations radar, and the lookouts who were on duty."

His tone and eyes hardened, "I am now satisfied that you had adequate forewarning from the ops-officer of the unfolding situation. He stated, that, in fact he had suggested, altering course to avoid convergence, and that you seemed to `be in another world´, when the Iranians changed tack and came directly for the ship."

"Sir, I…"

"Don´t interrupt me lieutenant! I have heard your version of the events, and, given the evidence presented to me, and what I saw with my own eyes, your action, or inaction in this case, put the safety of this ship and its crew in deadly peril."

He continued, still in a tone of severity: "I have checked over your record, and have noted that, aside from the minesweeper incident early in your career, nothing like this has happened before, or at least is not noted. I have no desire to oversee the destruction of your career, but my first duty is to ensure the safety of this ship and its crew, and that its fighting ability is not compromised." Pausing as if to gather breathe the captain re-iterated, "I must have absolute confidence in my officers and men, and you, as the First Officer of HMS Greystoke, have broken my faith in your ability to cope in a crisis situation."

Simon, appalled, and running with perspiration, again tried to interrupt the captain, "Sir…"

"DO NOT INTERRUPT ME AGAIN, Amersbey!

Simon stared down at the deck, and knew he was dead in the water.

The captain, satisfied that his executive officer was listening, went on, "I am requesting a transfer for you immediately. Our helicopter is going over to Bahrain in the morning, dropping off mail and our report bags; you will have a seat on it. You will report to the Naval Attaché at the Embassy, for further instructions; meanwhile, for tonight you are confined to your quarters." Gravely he continued: "The ship´s log has been written up, with the events recorded, and I have no option but to recommend an official enquiry; do we understand each other, Lieutenant?"

Simon was perfectly aware that an official enquiry would almost certainly lead to a court martial and the bitterness flooded into his mouth as he replied, "Yes Sir, but I….."

"I don´t want to hear it lieutenant, you may go and pack."

"Thank you, Sir," and he held out his hand. The captain just shook his head, and refused to take it.

He just made it to the ship´s rail, when he exploded his bile and vomit into the sea, heaving, and retching until there was nothing left. A sailor, on the bridge asked him if he was okay; did he need the medical orderly?

Simon shook his head in no, "I´ll be fine in a moment." He made his way, unsteadily, aft to the stern of the darkened destroyer neither noticing, nor responding, to the greetings of the men on the watch.

Looking over the stern, the shame came flooding into his head. *Jesus Christ, the whole bloody ship knows by now; what a fucking cock-up! One mistake and you're entire life fucked!* He thought of Alicia; they were married in name only. She had found out about his affair in Scotland, and now this; she would not forgive him in his spinelessness, as she would judge it.

He began to weep uncontrollably, staring down into the sea. The same sea he had loved since he was a boy, with dreams, now impossible to fulfil.

The destroyer was slicing through the swell, the engines vibrating throughout the hull; the pounding propellers were churning the sea into a vortex of phosphorous foam.

His mind racing, and in turmoil; he suddenly thought, *why not?* Once more, his legs jellied, and he had to grip the rail with both hands, but realised there was no other way, *God give me courage!* He half bent and slipped head first over the rail into the raging torrent of the wake, and into oblivion.

No one actually saw him fall. One minute he was there, looking over the stern, and the next minute he had gone. Half an hour passed. An able seaman on the Port watch was mystified; Simon hadn´t passed him on the gangway up the deck. However, he had the presence of mind to call the ODD, and told him his concerns.

The lieutenant immediately informed the captain, and ordered a quick search of the entire ship. The man overboard alarm sounded, and the destroyer swung around to search the sea; an impossible task as it turned out.

Chapter 16: St Martin's

By the age of eleven, Jonathan had finally adapted to his environment, and had learned discipline and importantly, to outwardly suppress his feelings. Introverted and timid, kept his own council. Now eleven years old, he had been unable to forge a close friendship with anyone until a new boy arrived at the school.

Mark Masterton was an altogether different character. Son of an Army Major stationed in Germany, He was tall and well built for his age, rebellious, loud, and abrasive. He had no fear in the face of any authority. Despite the obvious differences in character, Mark took a liking to the lonely Jonathan, and soon became his friend and protector.

He introduced Jonathan into the arts of smoking, shoplifting in the village, and the general small acts of vandalism for fun that infuriate the adult authorities alike. He was adept at not being found out, and instilled upon the younger boy the brother-hood of *omerta*, and the art of pointing blame in the direction of other innocent boys at the school. Throughout the school year, they became inseparable, and for the first time in his life, Jonathan had a real friend and companion.

Jonathan's parents allowed him to go to Mark's home in Germany during the Easter recess, where he enjoyed the more relaxed and easy attitude in the Masterton home.

The major, a strict disciplinarian in his command, doted on his son, allowing a much less stringent attitude at home. It appeared to Jonathan, Mark could do as he liked, enjoying the liberation and freedom of the Masterton household.

On returning to St Martin's, the boys continued to have fun, and soon they were in trouble again. They were confined to school for being repeatedly late for supper, and showing dissent to the Prefects. Mark and Jonathan decided to take their revenge on the school by destroying some of the showers in the House bathrooms.

A furious Principal assembled the whole school, and demanded the culprits own up; but no one accepted the blame although Jonathan was quaking in his shoes. Everyone, including the Principal, knew who was guilty, but there was no evidence, an in consequence the whole school was restricted to quarters for two weeks. Additionally, the Head and his Deputy caned all thirty-two boys in Jonathan´s House.

Reprisals came a few days later, when during inspection, the Matron found urine and excreta under Jonathan and Mark´s bed sheets. This time the Principal had his evidence of guilt, and despite their protestations of innocence, he publicly thrashed them until they were raw, weeping and humiliated.

Hands and bottoms had burning welts; their heads were full of resentment, humiliation and injustice, but there was going to be a reckoning for their enemies.

Chapter 17: A Navy funeral

A few days later, the Principal called Jonathan into his office. He still had the effects of the punishment on his bottom, and made his way there with some trepidation.

Jonathan was surprised to see his grandmother in the room; she had never visited him at school before.

In the presence of the Principle and the school nurse, his grandmother gently told him his father had an accident, and was dead.

Jonathan was aware of the adults watching him closely, but he seemed unable to react, other than say "Oh, poor father."

"Are you all right Jonathan?" asked his grandmother.

"Yes, perfectly," he replied, "does this mean that I have to go home?"

"Yes, of course Jonathan, your mother is very upset, and wants to see you." His grandmother continued: "There will be a grand Royal Navy funeral, with a parade of officers and sailors there, so you will have to be very, very brave."

"Can I say goodbye to my friend Mark, Sir?" he addressed the Principal.

The Principal replied, "No, that won´t be possible, Jonathan, Mark is in class, and you will need to catch the 12.30pm train. Matron has already packed your things; we´ll see you back at school shortly."

With that, Jonathan and his grandmother were ushered out to the waiting taxi to take them to the station just in time to catch the 12.30 train to Devonport.

On the journey down home, Jonathan tried to wrestle with his thoughts. He knew the significance of what had happened, but bewildered by his own feelings. His father had been absent from his life for so long; he had always been distant and aloof, and Jonathan couldn´t even picture his face at this moment.

At home, his mother hugged him, and told him that his father had fallen from his ship whist at sea. She emphasised that was very important for him to be very brave, just as his father had been.

It was like a dark, silence had settled over the house, the curtains closed, the adults were coming and going, all dressed in black and speaking in subdued voices. The stifling silence only broken by the ticking of the old mariner timepiece standing in the hall.

Francesca was there, and much more upset than he was. She was clinging to her mother, her tear driven face a stark contrast to her normal bouncy, self assured self.

Jonathan remembered afterwards the Marine Band playing solemn music, and lines of officers and sailors marching in slow time. His mother and grandmother were dressed all in black, with veils over their faces. The Royal Navy Chaplain conducted a Service of Remembrance for his father. Jonathan felt somehow detached from everything, as if he was standing on the sidelines looking in at an important event he could not understand. The boy, still his confusion of emotions trapped deep down within his mind, really wanted to be with his friend Mark at school.

 Alicia Amersbey, was, as often is the case in the various branches of the Armed Services, from a long line of Royal Naval family tradition, going back several centuries, and knew how to conduct herself with stoical dignity in the aftermath of the tragedy.

 Many of the official, and unofficial mourners at the full dress Royal Navy Memorial Service, commented at her remarkable composure under the circumstances …. The bitches had murmured, with some admiration at the reception, "In your face dignified hauteur; after all, he wasn´t actually killed in action, if you know what I mean…." "My Rodney said there would be an enquiry, it seems that he was up for a court martial!"

Chapter 18: Tantrums!

A few days later, Alicia and her mother drove Jonathan back to St Martin´s, and on the way dropping Francesca off at the station to take her back to her school. As she drove, Alicia explained to her son that she was going up to Scotland with grandmother for a little holiday, but she would be back in a week or two, so he must be on his best behaviour at school.

Principal James had asked to see Alicia as soon as they had arrived, and she and her mother were ushered into his study.

Jonathan, waiting outside on the bench seat, actually felt he was at home….his home, not the one down in Portsmouth.

After about half an hour, the Principal called Jonathan into the study. His mother stared at him with a furious expression, whilst his grandmother was studiously staring out of the window.

Alicia began, "Jonathan, Dr James has been giving us a report on your studies and behaviour this year, and your friendship with Mark Masterton. If we had any idea what was going on, we would never have let you go to Germany with him. Holding out what appeared to be an Academic Report, she angrily continued: "This too much, you will behave and put your very best efforts into your studies…are you paying attention Jonathan?"

"Yes mother" was all he could meekly reply.

"Jonathan, the Principal gently intervened, Mark Masterton has been a bad influence on you. He´s been in serious trouble with the police in the village, and I have had to expel him from school. His mother came for him yesterday and he is on his way back home to Germany."

It seemed to take a few minutes, but it was seconds, and something appeared to explode deep in the boy´s soul. All the pent up frustration, loneliness, the suppressed anger; the denegation of love and affection from his parents; all this erupted in tremendous "NOOOOO! …MOTHER, NO!

YOU CAN'T DO THIS TO ME! I WILL NOT STAY HERE! I HATE THIS PLACE!" A flood of tears cascaded from his eyes, and pointing his finger at the Principal he screamed, "MUMMY HE'S A PERVERT! HE TOUCHED MY WINKLE WHEN HE CANED ME!"

A stunned silence lasted all of two seconds before the Principal, enraged and white with fury, roared, "YOU LYING, FILTHY LITTLE BUGGER! THAT'S AN ABSOLUTE LIE! TAKE IT BACK THIS MINUTE!"

A very shaken and livid Alicia joined in the fray. "JONATHAN, STOP THIS! STOP IT THIS VERY INSTANT! YOU WILL APOLOGISE TO Dr JAMES, RIGHT NOW! ...GO ON, NOW!

Instead, Jonathan grabbed a heavy glass paperweight from the desk and hurled it through the window, narrowly missing a stunned and aghast Grandmother, transfixed to the spot by the scene unfolding in front of her.

"MY GOD, CONTROL YOUR CHILD", bellowed the Principal, yanking the door open to shout "NURSE, GET IN HERE!"

The two women, joined by the school nurse, struggled and finally subdued the boy, who had passed onto being hysterical.

The Hall, by this time had filled up with on-looking teachers and pupils, until the Principal once again roared, "GET BACK TO YOUR CLASSES!" He then addressed Alicia. "I think it's better for all, if you take your son back home and discuss his future." He went on, "He will not be welcome back to this school. I will send his Academic Report, such as it, is to your home. Now, Good Day to you!" With that, he slammed the door on them and stalked away.

The journey home to Devon was carried out in a strained silence, all three still in a state of shock, and with their own thoughts in turmoil.

Jonathan went straight upstairs to bed, after a tearful apology to his mother and grandmother, falling into a deep sleep almost immediately his head touched the pillow.

In the kitchen, Alicia prepared a light omelette for the two of them, as they shared a bottle of Cabernet, and discussed Jonathan and the scene at the school.

Her mother was anxious to get home to her cats in Scotland, who´d been left in the care of a neighbour. She had had enough drama with the funeral and now this! However, after another bottle was opened, the two women began a long overdue heart-to-heart talk.

"You know Alicia, you were always a stuck up, stubborn little bitch. You have no idea the rows I had with your father over you. He and Grandpapa absolutely worshipped the ground you stood on, and between them they made certain you got everything you wished for. They ruined you, and so between them you have turned out the selfish uncaring person you are."

"Mother, please, don´t tell me this just now; what in the hell am I going to do with him? What in the hell am I going to do with my life? I can´t stay here in this house; it´s a Navy house, and they´ll be sending some Navy councillor or social worker round soon to offer me a council house. Mother, I would rather cut my throat before that happens. Could you imagine what Felicity Ambrose-Smythe and that gang would say?"

"What I cannot understand, Alicia, is why you didn´t buy a bloody house like everyone else?"

"Mother, Alicia sighed, It´s all right in hindsight, but we were enjoying ourselves at the time; we were young and stupid ...and then the children arrived, and Simon wanted to wait until he knew if he would get a job in the Ministry of Defence."

The hours passed, another bottle opened, and a solution arrived at, whereupon Alicia would come up to Scotland to be near her mother and see how the land lay in relation to a permanent move away from Devonport, and the officer wives´ cliques. Francesca would stay at her school, and Jonathan boarded in a private school near to her mother. There was a little light moment when mother remembered that the school uniform was a kilt. How would Jonathan react to a kilt?

"Probably by throwing his sporran at the Principal" The two women laughed and embraced in a manner not known since Alicia´s childhood, and staggered upstairs to bed.

No one consulted Jonathan of course. The two women gave him a lecture on the family situation and realities, and he was finally assuaged on the idea by his grandmother, assuring him that she was nearby, and he could stay with her at weekends if he wished.

He was mortified with embarrassment when his uniform, including the kilt, arrived at his grandmother´s, and it took the two women some considerable effort of cajoling, threats and persuasion to have him dress. He bit back his tears of shame and self-consciousness, whilst Alicia and her mother strained themselves to hold in their amusement. Alicia had to go back down to Devonport to arrange her move north and to finalise the Will and other Legal procedures.

Chapter 19: Castle School, Dumbarton

Castle School was located in what was a millionaire Industrialist's mansion amidst extensive mature grounds beside the River Clyde. It followed an ethos common to many private schools with residential pupils, in that austerity, discipline and sports were on par with academic teaching.

About eighty percent of the students were from Scotland, the children of middle classes who aspired for a better education for their sons and daughters.

There were only about fifty boarders, and most of them went back to their homes in the Highlands and Islands at the weekend, leaving a few, including Jonathan to rattle about the dormitories. School uniform rules included compulsory wearing of the kilt at assemblies, church services and crucially, when any pupil left the grounds for any reason, including travelling home.

Unfortunately, a tough council house estate lay between Castle School, and the town centre of Dumbarton. The pupils therefore normally went about in groups, but even this did not protect them as they ran the gauntlet of the mob who would gather at various points to scream abuse and hurl all kinds of objects at the unfortunate pupils. The Principal insisted that the pupils wear the kilts, and that the experience formed an important character building for his alumni.

A few days before term began, Mrs Vickery, his grandmother accompanied Jonathan to Castle School.

The Principal, Dr Kennedy, as always, dressed in his academic gown, welcomed him and as he was going to board in the school, handed him over to the school Matron, Mrs MacDonald, who lived in the Gatekeepers lodge with her husband, the school Janitor.

Mrs MacDonald assured his grandmother that she would personally look after him; "Just as if he was my wee boy."

After he kissed his grandmother goodbye with trembling lips, Mrs MacDonald led him over the gravel path to one of the dormitories, all the while explaining some of the school regulations.

"This is Bute House," she said, "and over there is Argyll. The smaller building over to the right is Denny; that's where the girls are boarded, and it's strictly forbidden to go anywhere near that dormitory; do you understand Jonathan?"

"Yes Mrs MacDonald" replied a still nervous Jonathan.

Jonathan, although inwardly unhappy and melancholy, settled in school more easily than he had thought. The regulations, compared to St Martin's, were comparatively light, and all the boarders could mix freely in the common room after supper. The Scots were naturally superior in their attitude to the English pupils, but in general, in a jokey manner.

Jonathan, just as his father had been, was good looking and tall for his age, but took no interest whatsoever in the opposite sex, whether boarders or day pupils. Usually he kept himself to himself, and had a reputation as being something of a loner, not involving himself in the various sports, clubs and societies that flourished at the school. The others pupils recognised his strange aloofness, and except for the odd English bashing, left him alone to his own devices.

His first year passed reasonably quickly, and his mother had finally moved up to Scotland and found a job at the Clyde Royal Navy Submarine Base at Faslane.

She had taken an apartment, "just until I can find something more suitable," in an old converted mansion in Rhu, which however did not permit children to stay.

Jonathan, therefore, still went to his grandmother's cottage once a month or so. He spent most of a very boring summer holiday with her.

His mother took him out a few times, but it seemed to be a strained unhappy relationship on these days; she was unable to somehow relax and connect with her son.

Chapter 20: The Seduction

Jonathan was in his second year at Castle school, still keeping himself very much to himself and not achieving much in the way of academic excellence, but at least he had settled.

One afternoon, after a PT session running round the grounds, Jonathan was pleasuring himself in a shower cubicle. He was so intent, that he didn't notice the cubicle door was open, and two older boys were watching him. One of them, his House Prefect, George Watson, jolted him back to consciousness when he said, "That's a nice one you've got there Jono."

Jonathan almost died with fright, but the two older boys entered and George said, "Don't worry Jono; we all do it," and they dropped their shorts, pulled on their cocks until they were erect. "Come on Jono, we do it together," and they began pulling on one another.

Jonathan stared with disbelief, but felt his own penis erecting again, and began his own pleasuring until George transferred his hand to Jonathan, and clasped Jonathan's hand to his member. He was too flushed with pleasure and excitement to be embarrassed, and almost simultaneously came, as George's cum spread all over his hand. He had never experienced a thrill like that before, and as they all showered together, felt an almost euphoric rush in his head.

"Was that okay Jono?" William, the other Prefect said, "Better than wanking on your own...eh?"

George butted in, "Not a word to anybody wee man, understand? One stupid word to anyone and you will be in deep shit, *comprende?*"

"I won't say anything" replied Jonathan, recovering but still feeling the warmth of comradeship in a forbidden act.

It remained in Jonathan's mind over the next few days. He didn't feel ashamed in any way, on the contrary he felt a kind of release from pent up emotions. He felt a kind of comradeship with boys who had never really even spoken to him before.

After supper a few nights later, George came up to him and asked: "How´s things Jono, had a good time the other day?"

Jonathan blushed, but replied, "I´m fine George."

"Look Jono, some of the guys are having a bit of fun tonight, do you want to come?"

"What do you mean," asked Jonathan.

"I asked you if you want to cum you dope," George indicated with his hand signal.

"Okay count me in, and thanks George," a suddenly valiant, sure of himself Jonathan replied.

"Okay, I´ll meet you at the showers at midnight, and not a word to anyone, right? ... oh, and bring a towel."

Jonathan was positively shivering with nerves and excitement, as he lay between the sheets, waiting for midnight.

He felt, at last, to be part of a gang, comradeship, something he had denied himself for so long. He counted the minutes, and went down to the showers at exactly twelve o´clock, as the chapel bell was chiming.

George was waiting with two others Jonathan recognised, and they flashed him a grin. He felt positively exhilarated with sexual excitement, as they crept downstairs, through the kitchens and out the back door. They crossed the courtyard and filed silently across the playing fields and into the woods, until they came to a moonlit clearing where another five or six boys were waiting, drinking cans of beer.

They all greeted each other with hi-fives, and George pressed a beer into his hand. Someone passed around a half bottle of vodka. Jonathan, just like the others had a swig, and almost choked. He was feeling lightheaded, but drank another can of beer.

There was a nervous tension as they all swapped jokes, until someone said, "Well are we doing it or not?"

"Well that´s what we´re here for, said George."

"Let's do it." The boys stripped off their clothes, Jonathan following a little nervously. They were all in a circle, each one stroking their own cock, comparing the size of their erections. Someone came behind Jonathan, and began fondling him between his legs. This boy, he thought it was George, began stroking him, and another boy joined in. He was fully aroused with pleasure, and quickly spurted his semen.

He found himself on the ground, still pleasured, but realised that someone had his cock between his legs, trying to force it into him. He began to panic, and someone said in his ear, "Don't worry Jono, nobody is going to hurt you." He struggled to free himself, but others were too strong in holding him down. Finally, he began to cry in pain and fright, and vomited over someone's feet. Someone began punching him on the head until a voice said, "For fuck sake leave him alone, it's his fucking first time!"

Lifting the boy to his feet, George said, "Look Jono, this is our initiation ceremony, you're not damaged, we all went through it."

Jonathan was still crying and couldn't speak, as some boy cleaned him up a bit and told him, "Shut up you stupid little wanker, you're going to wake up the whole fucking school!"

His Prefect, George, took him back to the dormitory, and warned him that if he mentioned any of this to anyone, he would be dead.

Jonathan could only respond, "I just want to go the toilet." After throwing up again, Jonathan went into the shower, and scrubbed himself raw. He was in pain and disgusted with his body. He crept under the covers and slept fitfully, recurring nightmares of fire and monsters racking his sleep.

Next morning, he did not hear the breakfast bell, and only woke up to find Mrs MacDonald standing anxiously beside his bed, feeling his head. He was running a temperature, and he had a thumping headache.

"Looks like you have a bit of the ´flu, she said, but we´ll try some aspirins before we bother the Doctor. I´ll telephone your grandmother and let her know."

"I´ll be alright Matron, but can you tell the Housemaster I´m not going to classes today?"

"Don´t you worry young man, I´ll look after you. I´ll tell cook to send up some tea and biscuits later, when you´ve had another sleep."

Later on in the morning, George came by and anxiously asked him how he was.

"What do you care, your all just a bunch of filthy perverts!" Jonathan said furiously. "Just leave me alone."

George angrily responded, "Don´t be so fucking stupid, we´re not homos, we only like a bit of fun. Don´t worry, you´re out of it, but if you tell anyone, you´re dead; I fucking mean it!"

After this incident, Jonathan became almost a recluse and even more introverted, avoiding almost all contact with the other pupils, unless it was absolutely necessary.

The school Matron, Mrs MacDonald, called his grandmother on several occasions, but he shrugged off all adult concerns with, "I don´t like it here, and never will."

Chapter 21: The Captain

Captain Harry Wellesley was on an official inspection visit to Faslane, assessing first hand, the planning progress of the expansion of the Faslane and Coulport facilities to take the newly ordered Trident Ballistic Missile submarines.

As was the custom, the Commodore Clyde was hosting a dinner in honour of the visiting inspector from Northwood, the Joint Services HQ outside London.

In an unofficial extension to her job as Civilian Community Public Relations Officer, and given her attractive personality and single status, Alicia Amersbey often 'made up the numbers' to accompany visiting officials.

This time, she was partnered with Captain Harold Wellesley, and was enjoying the experience. *I could certainly fancy this one,* she thought.

Often she entertained the most God awful, egocentric bores; this captain was certainly not in that category!

Alicia had learned by her past mistakes, that the handsome young, ambitious Royal Navy officers she often encountered did not necessary make good partners, or even good lovers.

This captain was certainly different and she found herself immediately attracted to him. He was only just above average height, probably mid to late forties according to his speckling of grey hairs.

His demeanour suggested a pugnacious character, an intelligence and assurance, which seemed to pitch him above other taller, men. Nor could he be described as being strikingly good-looking, but with his solid chin line, rugby damaged nose, and piercing blue eyes, the overall effect was a man of intense masculinity.

Alicia had met him before, at the funeral of her late husband Simon. Commander Wellesley, as he was at the time, was officially representing the Royal Navy at the service. He had offered his personal, as well as the Royal Navy condolences, but little else rather than formal words had passed between them.

He was billeted, by chance, in the same apartment complex where she was renting. She had noticed a VIP being collected and brought back in an official Royal Navy car to and from the navy base without actually seeing the person in the back seat.

Alicia noted that although he was the guest of honour, and centre of attention for the table, he was attentive, inclusive and humorous to the rest of the guests. He seemed to possess an aura of power and authority, emanating from an otherwise reserved character; others were more intent in dominating the conversation, but when he contributed, the table listened.

During dinner, there wasn´t much time for anything other than pleasantries and small talk between them, but more than a few times their eyes met, resulting at times, to Alicia´s discomfort, finding herself unaccountably flushing and a little discomfit; something she had not done since she was a teenager.

Angry with herself, she manage to regain control, and asked of him a question she already knew the answer to, but wanted to hear his response anyway. "Is your wife staying in Devonport whilst you you´re working on the inspection tour Sir?"

"Oh please call me Harry, Mrs Amersbey. Actually, I live in London while I´m attached to the MOD for this exercise. As to the question of my wife, we should clear that up right away; there´s no Mrs Wellesley, I was divorced some years ago."

He said this with such candour, that Alicia was startled. She flushed again and stammered, "Oh I´m sorry I didn´t want to intrude, I just thought I could help her find her way around. Please call me Alicia, Captain. I believe we are neighbours, aren´t you staying at Kinsley House?"

"Yes I am; rather nice billet, isn´t it? Certainly beats the barracks in HM Neptune!"

"Feel free to pop around for a coffee, if you need company." As Alicia was saying this, her face unaccountably began reddening again. "I'm sorry, I'm being rather forward again."

"No need to be sorry, that would be great; I often get fed up talking to myself; it makes me realise what an insufferable bore I am! We'll make it tomorrow.... eleven, is that all right? I'll bring the biscuits!" He had this confident, easy, smile and a humorous twinkle in his eyes.

Shit! Alicia said to herself; she would have to cancel a hairdressing appointment, but instead replied, "That would lovely; I'll look forward to it, I'm number five, on the ground floor at the back."

Aware that others were listening into their conversation, they turned their attention back to the general table discussion, which had turned to the subject of the peace camp. The opinion was almost unanimous that they were a damn nuisance, having no effect other than causing annoyance and stress to their unfortunate neighbours, and the personnel going into Faslane.

Someone suggested stopping all the benefit handouts, whilst one wife, promoting a swell of laughter, suggested castration for all, so at least they would die out over time!

It was a pleasant evening, with little `shop talk´ going on, and it was midnight before they realised it. Two of the officers present had duty scheduled at six o´clock, and the party broke up. Captain Wellesley offered Alicia a lift home in his official car, but she declined gracefully, if a little reluctantly. She would need her car at home to go into town to buy some decent coffee in the morning.

Alicia was up early, fussing around, tidying up her women's magazines, her books, and as an afterthought, and with a wry smile on her face, her bedroom ...just in case! She decided on showering when she came back from the deli, threw on her favourite black tracksuit, and fled out of the door into a blustery showery day, and into her Mini. She was waiting at the door of Simonelli´s Delicatessen, as the staff opened the door. After buying her Arabic Italian Espresso mix and a packet of miniature amaretto biscuits, she glanced at her watch, she decided a quick espresso was in order; it would energise her!

Satisfied by the rush of caffeine, it was back into the Mini, and within five minutes she was back home thinking, *not bad timing, I think I´ll have a quick bath!*

She dressed carefully having decided on a pale blue Dior pashima wool jersey over pink slacks and midnight blue dance pumps. Hair and make-up meticulously applied she checked herself in her floor length mirror, turning this way and that, adjusting her hair this way and that. She was satisfied with the result and looked good, but...? *Christ let´s be daring Alicia,* took off her jumper, and decided on a midnight blue silk blouse. She decided, bra-less; she still had a very good breasts, *so why not show them off!* This time, adjusting the buttons and with a Kashmiri silk scarf, a spray of Chanel No.5, she felt she looked wonderfully sexy and feminine ... *and it´s only ten thirty in the morning!*

The telephone ringing brought her back down to earth giving a panic that he was calling it off; but no, it was her mother asking if she wanted to meet her for a coffee!

Alicia quickly related the story of last night´s dinner, and her invitation for coffee with the captain.

Her mother always aware of her daughter´s situation, told her she´d better hang up then ..."Phone me later!" and hung up.

The coffee was bubbling down into the Cona machine, when the doorbell went at precisely eleven o´clock.

Alicia allowed herself a quick check on her appearance, and shouted through, "just coming," as she undid yet another button, feeling a rush of sexual excitement as she did it; *Bloody hell, I´m just like a seventeen year old,* she smiled to herself.

Opening the door, she almost didn´t recognise him. Last night was semi-formal with the men in dark suits and ties, and today the captain was dressed casually in a blue denim button down shirt, jeans and sailing shoes.

He looked so much younger, and smiling in the rain announced, "'Morning, these are for you," handing her a bunch of old-fashioned red roses, and a presentation box of Italian Biscotti from Simonelli´s.

"They´re wonderful," she said, "I haven´t seen these old roses for ages!" taking them off him and smelling the fragrance. "Oh, you´d better come in, the coffee´s ready."

He followed her down the hall and into her lounge. Although it did not have sea views, the lounge looked onto a private wood. Sometimes she would spot a timid little roe deer here, as well as the blasted rabbits! The sitting area had a pleasing split-level design, and Alicia had decorated it in pastel and oatmeal creams with few pieces of furniture cluttering the space, making the room look bigger than it really was.

"This is very nice," he said, "You´ve made it look fabulous;" he continued talking as he walk around appreciating her decoration and little feminine touches. Turning to her he said, more softly, "and you look fabulous also; you do know you are very beautiful, don´t you?"

Alicia again felt the flush of embarrassment she had experienced the night before. Recovering she answered a little coyly, "thanks for that captain, it´s very much appreciated." They stood looking at each other for seemingly minutes, but actually a second or two, before he smiled and said, "It´s Harry, not captain, and I mean it, you are very beautiful."

Another awkward second of hesitation occurred as she took the word´s in before she kissed him on the side of his face, and said, "I really do appreciate it Harry, it´s a long time since I heard that from a man. Come on through to the kitchen, the coffee´s ready, and I´ll stick these into a vase."

It was obvious that they were very much at ease in each other´s company, as sat around the old bleached pine kitchen table, recounting their respective stories.

Before they knew it, it was almost one o´clock, and Harry suggested they go for a bar lunch somewhere. This promoted a little debate as both had decided anywhere but around Helensburgh or the base area; they were on their free time and didn´t want work to intrude on their day.

Harry went back round to his flat to pick up an anorak, whilst Alicia changed her sexy blouse for the Dior jersey she had on earlier; a quick touch up of her hair and make-up, and she was ready for her day out.

They took her Mini Cooper, having decided to head over to Drymen on the far side of Loch Lomond. Harry drove fast but confidently, not conversing too much as he concentrated on the road.

Arriving in the village square, they were surprised and disappointed to find that they were actually a quarter of a mile from Loch Lomond. The rain had stopped and the first rays of a weak sunshine were appearing, he stopped the car and asked a passing woman where he could have lunch beside the loch.

She replied that he would have to drive another seven miles or so to Balmaha, but advised they continue on to Rowardennan, to the hotel there, "The bar lunches there are historic" she affirmed.

They took her advice, treating themselves to one of the secrets of Scotland, and only about thirty miles from Glasgow.

They just had to stop and take in the peaceful ambiance tableau of the little boats bobbing on their moorings at Balmaha, Alicia linking her arm in his as they walked down the little jetty. The Moorings Tearoom wasn´t open, otherwise they were tempted to stay right there.

Back into the Mini, they climbed the narrow road to Rowardennan and within minutes being grateful for their decision to carry on, as lochside vistas opened up on the left hand side of the road.

The Rowardennan Hotel sat at the base of Ben Lomond, now shrouded in mist, and the bar was crowded with young people in a variety of walking and climbing gear.

Fortunately a group got up to leave, and Alicia promptly immediately sat down before anyone else had a chance to bag the table, smiling happily at the more reticent Harry.

"Well done," he acknowledged as he sat down beside her. Harry rose again as soon as they realised there was no table service, and after returning with a pint of Tennant's for him, half pint for her, advised her that the chef had run out of everything except the venison pie.

"Well I'm starving," she laughed, "If it had been pussy cat pie, I might, but just might have declined, so venison pie it is!"

In the event the pie was delicious, but they had to share their table with another younger couple, so intimate conversation was out of the question.

The young couple, who introduced themselves as Ron and Moyra from Glasgow, were obviously very much in love, holding hands and smiling into each others' eyes. They still had courtesy to keep up an animated conversation with their new English `friends´, extolling the virtues of climbing `the Ben´, which they assured was not that difficult. After a half an hour of this, and another drink, Harry made his excuses. After promising Moyra they would visit them in Glasgow, they escaped outside. They walked arm in arm down to the jetty, and spent some time looking over the loch to Inverbeg on the other side.

"Penny for your thoughts," he asked.

She didn't answer at first, causing him to look at her quizzically. "I'm having a wonderful day Harry; I haven't felt so relaxed and happy for years." She turned round, and they coincided with their lips, in a tender and warm kiss, embracing into a new loving experience.

A drenching squall suddenly whipped up, and Harry suggested they go back home, promising to come back and climb the Ben sometime soon.

"No Harry, let´s just go back up to the hotel, and take a room."

Alicia knelt, her hair brushing against his penis in her act of submission; he was her Lord, and she wanted him to know. She caressed his body, his wiry chest hair knotting in her fingers, hand running down to his thighs, his butt cheeks, and finally over his scrotum, caressing and testing lightly his hardness, all the while in her mouth, thrusting and sucking, massaging with her tongue.

He towered above her, silhouetted in the light; powerful, masculine, beginning to quiver, going in deep throat until his explosion, the release of his seed almost choking her, the warmth liquid in her mouth as he grunted in his spasms.

Never, in all his experiences had he realised such sexual satisfaction, complete release and fulfilment.

Now as they lay together on the bed, reflecting and resting, because he knew, he must return the gratification to this beautiful woman.

He realised that Alicia had loved him completely. She was special, feminine, a very complete woman who could satisfy a man´s desires so profoundly; she was elegant, intelligent and humorous.

Harry was flattered and thrilled she wanted him. She was the answer to his endless dissatisfaction, the lonely nights in oh, so many different postings. There was always a secretary or Wren to entertain and satisfy his immediate sexual needs. He was also honest enough to admit to himself that in a few short years, he would not be attracting beautiful women as he had in the past, on the strength of his power and authority in the Royal Navy.

Chapter 22: Commodore Harry

Jonathan was in the school dining hall, when one day, a year later, Mrs Morrison, the school secretary called him; his mother telephoned and invited him to lunch with her in a Helensburgh hotel, and to meet a special friend.

He wasn't particularly keen, but it had been almost a month since he had seen her, or his grandmother.

Jonathan left the school with another boy to go to the station, and almost immediately ran into the council house kids, who threw the usual trash and called them queers on account of their kilts. They ran for the station, the other boy going to Glasgow and Jonathan to Helensburgh. He still felt self-conscious in the kilt, and was aware of the amused expressions and comments of the other passengers. He sulked and fumed: *This is Scotland, and I'm English, but I'm the only one forced to wear this fucking skirt!* For the umpteenth time he thought of running away.

At the station in Helensburgh, for once Alicia was on time and waiting for him. She looked stunning in a tobacco coloured tweed jacket over a light cream dress, complemented by tobacco and cream handbag and shoes.

"Hello darling! How are you? Oh, Jonathan, that's a miserable expression for your mother, I haven't seen you in ages."

Jonathan greeted her without enthusiasm with a cursory "Hello mother."

They got into a taxi, and Alicia instructed, "The Commodore Hotel, please."

Jonathan asked, "Where's your car mummy?"

"My friend needed to borrow it this morning," she replied. "How is school Jonathan, are you playing any sport now?"

"Mother you know I don't like sport, and when I'm forced to play bloody football or rugby, the other boys kick and punch me because I'm English."

Alicia tried to laugh it off. "Don´t be silly Jonathan, we´ve been through all this before, sport is good for you, and I´m sure you´re exaggerating a bit." Taking his hand, she looked into his eyes, imploring, "Jonathan, I want you to be especially good today; I want you to meet a very special friend."

"What friend?" asked Jonathan, "and what´s so special about this one?"

"Just wait until we get to the hotel."

Intrigued, Jonathan persevered: "Is it a man, mother? Are you going to marry him?"

"Yes it´s a man, Jonathan, and he´s become very important to me. I want you to be on your very best behaviour when you meet him; please, for my sake Jonathan."

At the hotel, Anne paid off the driver and, as she fussed over his tie and straightened his sporran, again reminded him to make a good impression. They entered the Carvery Restaurant, and crossed over to where a solitary man was reading his newspaper.

He looked up and exclaimed, "Hello darling, and kissed and embraced Alicia tenderly; and this must be young Jonathan? How do you do young man?" He shook Jonathan´s hand firmly, "I´ve been waiting to meet you Jonathan, I´m Harry Wellesley."

Jonathan, with his eyes cast to the floor replied, "I´m pleased to meet you, Sir."

"That´s a fine kilt your wearing Jonathan, is it your school uniform?"

Blushing with embarrassment the boy replied, "Yes Sir, but I bloody well hate it!"

The Commodore responded, "Ah, sometimes we have to endure things we don´t understand son, but it probably helps to build your character as an adult."

Alicia intervened, shooting a pleading look in her son´s direction. "Let´s sit down and have a drink before lunch. What are you drinking darling?"

"Just a martini cocktail, would you like one?"

Responding with a smile, she said, "As long as it's desert dry."

"Jonathan?"

"A Coca Cola," was the almost inaudible reply.

Harry looked at Alicia, and received a resignation shrug from her shoulders in reply, and signalled to the waitress, a young girl of around eighteen years old.

Harry ordered, "Two Martini cocktails, and a Coca Cola for this young man."

"I'm sorry Sir, we don't have Coca Cola, only Pepsi."

Jonathan interjected, "Pepsi is not Coke, it's not the same. I'll just have a Fanta Orange."

The girl was getting embarrassed, and said, "I'm sorry again Sir, but it's Pepsi's brand of orange we have, but it's much the same taste."

Jonathan scowled, "Look, just bring me anything; what's the point in asking me when you obviously don't have what I want?"

The commodore intervened, saying: "I'm sure it will be fine," to the waitress, and then to the boy, "Jonathan, there's no need to be rude to the waitress, she is only doing her job."

Jonathan shot a venomous look at his mother, and slunk further down in the banquet until his head was barely level with the table.

The adults decided to more-or-less ignore him for the rest of the meal, only now and again bringing him into the conversation about how is his food and so on.

Jonathan was feeling more and more isolated, but finally asked, "Mother, can we go and buy some ice cream and visit grandmother?"

Alicia looked directly at Harry, and lied, "Not this time Jonathan; Harry has to go back to London today, and I must drive him to the airport; perhaps the next time."

They left shortly after, the commodore shaking Jonathan's hand again, and saying, "It was good to meet you young man, and I do hope we will become firm friends."

In the taxi, Alicia scolded her son for his rudeness. "Jonathan, you don´t know how hard it is for me, I am alone, whilst you and Francesca have your friends at school. I´ve grown very fond of Harry, and I don´t want you ruining it by your bad manners."

"Mother, he is much older than you; he looks like your father!"

"Jonathan, it´s none of your business how old Commodore Wellesley is, he is very important to me, and that´s that!"

At the station, Alicia asked the Taxi to wait, bought his ticket, glanced at the timetable, and pressed ten pounds into Jonathan´s hand. "The train leaves in fifteen minutes Jonathan, I must rush or Harry will miss his plane. Please be good!" She gave him a brief hug before running outside without looking back.

Chapter 23: Megan

Jonathan bought a comic, and an ice cream at the Kiosk, and settled down on a bench near to the platform for the Dumbarton train.

Shortly after, a train pulled into the station and disgorged a load of drunken, rowdy, football supporters returning from a local derby match. When they saw the young lad in a kilt, a group quickly surrounded him, shouting insults and spraying him with beer. He tried to get away, but two of them tore the kilt from his body, and pissed all over it; apparently, it was the wrong colour or something.

The arrival of a solitary policeman saved Jonathan from further indignity, but enough damage had been inflicted upon him to leave him shaken and distressed. No one had come to his assistance, and as his train arrived, he put on his urine sodden kilt and collapsed in the last seat of the train, shame and humiliation all but overcoming him.

Just as the doors were closing, a girl jumped aboard, but he only looked up when she said, "What in the fuck has happened to you?"

"Nothing" he said, dropping his eyes to the floor.

"Nothing? You pissed yourself then?"

He recognised her now, a rebellious nonconformist; different from the others, she was in the year above at school, but she wasn't wearing the uniform. She was dressed in a red stripe tank top, black jeans and short black bomber jacket. She had red Doc Martin's boots on her feet, black make-up on her eyes and black lipstick. Her hair was all over her face, and she sported a safety pin through one of her ears.

"Some bastards thought that my kilt deserved to be pissed on." He conceded morosely.

"Why are you wearing that stupid fucking kilt anyway?" she demanded.

"It's the stupid fucking school rules; where's your uniform?" he retorted.

"It's in my rucksack you stupid bastard! Don't you have the sense to take a change of clothes?" She sneered at him, "You're just asking to get a kicking in that outfit. Look around you moron, how many fucking kilts have you seen today? Jesus, you are really thick!" Softening her tone a little, she asked, "What are you doing in Helensburgh anyway?"

"I was having lunch with my mother and her boyfriend."

"And where is mummy now?" she asked.

Crestfallen but defiant he replied, "Probably at home having sex with her boyfriend before he goes back to London."

"You mean your mother lives in Helensburgh? Why are you fucking boarding at the school?"

"She lives in a flat in Rhu, but children are not allowed. Anyway, it´s no big deal, I´ve always been at a boarding school."

Shaking her head, the girl said, disbelievingly, "Fucking hell, these adults are really something."

"What are you doing here?" queried Jonathan. "Why are you dressed like a skinhead?

"I´m not a skinhead, I´m an anarchist you fool. I´ve been demonstrating at the peace camp. It was really cool! Boy did we have a laugh today! I threw a flour bomb over a pig´s head, just as he was plastered with an egg! It was so fucking funny, he was fucking raging, and ran after me, but some guy tripped him up!" She shrieked with laughter at the memory, whilst Jonathan watched on with amazement.

"What´s an anarchist, anyway?" Jonathan asked.

"Jesus, you really are a dickhead, aren´t you? She retorted. We are against the establishment, the capitalists, the banks, the government and the fucking nuclear weapons that are going to blow us all to hell even if the banks don´t fuck us first! What´s your name anyway, handsome?" the girl asked.

"Jonathan Amersbey," he replied flushing a little, then asking, "What´s your name?"

"I´m Megan, and before you say anything about my accent, I´m from Wales"

Jonathan, felt somehow at ease with this strange girl, and as the train pulled into Dumbarton station, he asked, "Aren´t you going to get changed?"

"Of course, sonny boy; I´ll get changed in MacDonald´s. Come on, I´ll treat you to a ´burger and you can change out that piss ridden skirt you´ve got on. You can wear these jeans, and if anyone at school says anything, I´ll kick them in the nuts!"

With that remark, Jonathan felt his face flush again, but nodded gratefully.

They changed in the MacDonald´s toilets, and Megan emerged more or less like any other private school girl in her uniform, and with pearl earrings replacing the safety pin. Jonathan felt much more comfortable, but aware it was a pair of girl´s jeans´ he was wearing.

They exchanged histories as they ate, Megan sympathised with the boy for the death of his father, but affirming her opinion his mother, Alicia was a cold-hearted bitch in not having him at home.

She explained her own parent free situation, as being the result of divorce. Her father, a Senior Civil Servant in the Welsh Office, had married his secretary, a younger woman, who wanted nothing to do with Megan. Her mother had also remarried, but to an older divorcee with two teenage boys, who had taken an unhealthy sexual interest in their new twelve years old step-sister. The resulting accusation, denials and arguments resulted in a boarding school education for Megan. Castle School was her second school; she had been expelled from the first boarding school for fighting, and badly injuring another girl.

It was the beginning of a new relationship for both of them. Both of them were misfits and without friends at Castle School. She being older, and of a more capable nature, acted as a kind of friend, protector and mentor to the boy. He in turn, gave her companionship and a chance for her to expound her political and social idealism.

Time passed by much more quickly for Jonathan now that he had a friend and confidant. Some Saturday´s Megan would suggest a trip up to Glasgow, where they would have a laugh shoplifting in the big emporiums.

Once the security staff almost caught them, and after running halfway along Argyle Street, Megan erupted in a fit of uncontrolled laughter whilst Jonathan almost wet his trousers.

They would take in an early session at the cinema, before catching the train down to Dumbarton, and their customary 'burger and change of clothes at MacDonald's. At school, they met most evenings after supper in the common room, playing scrabble, chess or other board games. The others ignored them, or at least didn't bother them, after Megan had bared her teeth at their first comments.

Chapter 24: Jonathan the Activist

Megan began taking him to the peace camp, where he found, a kind of empathy among the dropouts, anarchists, CND militants and assorted socialist extremists. As a friend of Megan's, they regarded him as one of their own, although at times he took some teasing about his English middle class accent.

The peace camp leader, an American-Japanese woman took a liking to him, explaining with much patience, theories of Unilateral Nuclear Disarmament in a profligate nuclear arms world. She was aware of his family background, and that his mother held an important PR job at the base. He was closely, but carefully questioned on his `inside knowledge´, but it soon became clear he had little information they did not already have in their intelligence files.

Jonathan was welcomed and permitted to stay, and help around the peace camp, doing general duties, preparing banners, flour bombs, and the like; however in order to protect him, he was never permitted to take part in any of the demonstrations for fear of his arrest.

One night, after supper, they were in the common room, Megan suddenly asked, "What are you going to do when you finish with this place Jono?"

Jonathan thought a bit and confessed, "I honestly have no idea. I always thought that I go down to Dartmouth and become a naval officer. The navy is in my genes, or so my mother and grandmother keep telling me. Now I´m not so sure that I want to, but I haven´t a clue what else I can do; if I don´t join up, my mother will go mad!" He continued reflectively: "I´m sure she and the commodore are going to get married; my grandmother has been hinting this to me for ages. I certainly don´t want to go and live with them either. I´d get my accommodation with the navy, so it looks like the best option for me."

"You could always stay with your grandmother Jono." Megan suggested.

"Megan, be serious, have you seen my grandmother´s cottage? It´s tiny, we trip over each other when I visit her at weekends. Holidays are a nightmare; she wouldn´t want me there permanently, and besides, I still need to find a career."

"Poor Jono, that´s what I mean when I say we´re trapped in a bourgeois capitalist establishment system. We don´t have no fucking choice or freedom! We´ve just got to comply and obey the Mr Big´s of this world; well, I´m fucked if I´m going to join the brolly brigade."

Megan admitted to Jonathan, that she was only passing out the time at Castle School, as she intended to `escape the rat trap´ as she put it, just as soon as she was sixteen years old, at the end of June.

Jonathan´s stomach gave a jolt, and he had to fight emotions as he realised she was serious, but managed to ask, "What are you going to do Meg?"

"I´ll join the peace camp or maybe go down to Newtownbury and join the eco-commune there." She had enthused about the ecological warriors' movement that was protesting against the building of a controversial by-pass road around Newtownbury in Buckinghamshire.

"Meg, what are you going to do about money? I can't see your father forking out for an eco warrior career!"

"Jono, sometimes I really do think you are retarded! What do the peace campers do every fortnight? They go down to the social security and there a nice man behind the counter hands out dole and social benefit money. When there's a demo going down at Aldermaston Nuke site, or anywhere else, they just go along to the dole, say they need money to go to London for an interview, and another nice man gives them more money…no questions asked." Laughing she punched him on the arm, "So, Jono boy, I'm joining the professional protest industry."

Concerned, but smiling at her carefree happiness, he asked, "Won't you need a career after all this protesting is finished?"

"The protest industry will never finish Jono, until the people regain power, and that's not going to happen any time soon! Besides, can you see me working in a bank, or as a nurse wiping old peoples arses, or do you think I'd make a good police officer? When tomorrow comes, I'll think about tomorrow, meanwhile I want to throw flour bombs as a profession!" She said this with her customary shriek of laughter, which made some of the others in the common room hiss, "Shut up, we're trying to study."

"Fuck off you miserable bastards," was Megan's riposte.

With a lump in his throat, Jonathan asked, "Meg, if you're going down to the commune, can I come with you for a few weeks at the holidays? Mother's going off to Gibraltar with her commodore, and I'm stuck here, or with my grandmother."

"Don't be daft Jono, you're only fifteen, and they'll just drag you back. Besides, I'm an anarchist, you're going to be the fucking captain of the ship."

"Just let me come for a week or so Meg; I know how to rough it. I promise I won't get in the way. I'd really like to see the action. Please Meg."

"Jono, how the hell would you explain it to your mother?" She put on his accent, "Mother, I'm just off for a week or two throwing rocks at the fuzz!" The raucous laughter drew the hisses again, this time disdainfully ignored.

Jonathan had an idea: "Look, suppose I say we're joining an archaeological dig in Cornwall or something? We could ask Meryl at the peace camp to make up an official document, and ask for a fee of say, a hundred pounds."

"Hah! Now, *that's* a brilliant idea!" She laughed, "Mummy will give you a hundred pounds to throw stones at the police? Hah! That is a good one!" Reflecting a little, she agreed, "Okay, if you really want to come, why not?" Megan in fact was secretly pleased she would have his company in the summer.

In the event Meryl would not cooperate in the subterfuge, but another, well-spoken CND activist agreed to telephone his grandmother on his behalf, pretending to be Mr Jackson the Geography Master, and supporting his wish to go on the expedition. The cover would be that one of the original pupils had dropped out, and Jonathan had expressed an interest in replacing him.

The friend even produced an authentic looking copy of an official Archaeological Site to add to the deception. On the `phone he assured the old lady that it was combined schools and university organised archaeological dig in Bristol. He provided her with an emergency telephone number if she needed to contact Jonathan over the summer.

The deceit worked, with a the old lady expressing mild, but pleasant, surprise that her grandson was, at last, taking an interest in something tangible.

Chapter 25: Newtownbury

Newtownbury, a small market town in Southern England sat on the route from the Midlands Industrial belt to the ports of Southampton and Portsmouth. It had suffered decades of heavy lorry traffic choking the narrow town centre through route.

A by-pass had been proposed and planned for years. Much to the fury of the local townsfolk and businesses, the construction had been delayed for many years. One planning enquiry followed another, following the objections and procrastinations of various ecological groups and local landowners. When the project had finally cleared all the planning and judicial processes, the ecological militants swung into action, to physically block the by-pass construction.

The eco-warriors, and their more conventional allies Greenpeace, and Friends of the Earth, focused on a particular contentious stretch of the proposed road, which was to be routed through an ancient oak wood.

By a campaign of court injunctions, whenever a possible endangered species of plant or animal life was uncovered, an application for an injunction to stop work would be lodged in the Court, further delaying the project. Allegations of dirty tricks abounded, with the pro-by-pass lobby alleging that some of these endangered species had been imported from other areas.

The eco-warriors excavated Viet Cong style tunnels under the proposed route, and chained themselves to the topmost branches of the trees overhead, physically preventing construction for many months, and in the process, tying up a huge amount of police resources.

People come and go in these camps, and no one questioned them, or asked for identity. Megan had forewarned Jonathan that if asked he was to say he was seventeen.

Arriving at the camp, after hitching lifts all the way from Scotland, they met the commune leader. Archie McGlyn was a Glaswegian with an almost cadaver look; pale grey faced, despite having spent several years living out of doors, and permanent dirty stubble; He was tall, rake thin with piercing blue eyes behind National Health round glasses, and sported pony tail which emphasised a shaved bald head.

In an aggressive broad Glasgow accent, he stressed that this was no holiday camp; timewasters would be booted out, and then basically explained the purpose of the protest and communal rules. The eco- warriors were, in the main, the same mixture of drop-outs, anarchists and hippy types they were used to at the peace camp

The commune had, at this time almost sixty full time eco-warriors, as they styled themselves. It had been built in a large clearing in the wood, surrounded by a makeshift barrier of barbed wire and branch fence. In the centre stood a large makeshift canvas and wood communal tent, used for meals and meetings, with a basic cooking area just off to one side. There were rudimentary washing and toilet facilities nearby, and trench latrines had been dug around the perimeter of the camp. Sleeping quarters were an assortment of tents or basic shelters grouped around the commune's centre. They were, in the main, constructed from plastic sheeting, branches from the trees or whatever material could be scavenged by the eco-militants.

Jonathan and Megan opted to build their own shelter away from the centre, mostly because they did not know the others, and so far had little confidence in them.

The day after they arrived at the commune, they went into Newtownbury. Megan registered at the local unemployment office, where she was issued with a cheque worth one hundred and fifty pounds to cover her immediate accommodation and living expense, and a list of job vacancies in the town.

She immediately went round the corner to Barclays Bank to cash her cheque, and on the way, tossed the job vacancies list in a bin.

Jonathan had received two hundred pounds from his mother, and a further one hundred to cover the expedition fee from his grandmother, therefore money would not be a problem.

Next stop was the local swimming pool for a shower, and then to a MacDonald´s for a 'burger. Suitably replete, they wandered through Newtownbury, not even noticing the traffic noise and fumes in the town centre. They did some shopping for food other essentials, and finally made their way back to the camp by bus.

Jonathan and Megan thrived in the hippy style environment. The deprivations of their makeshift shelter and camp conditions escaped them. They were accustomed to this in the peace camp.

A roster of duties had been established, with the shifts of tree chaining, or manning the tunnels not too onerous, as yet another Court Order had stopped construction work at this time.

The weather that summer was balmy. The police were powerless to disturb the almost holiday camp atmosphere of the commune. Most evenings there would be a guitar led, sing song around a campfire, or some frivolous games and jokes being played, all fuelled by a plentiful supplies of cider or beer, and the odd joint being passed around.

The freedom from the stifling restrictions and control of school; the ambiance of being among rebellious young people was playing tricks in the minds of the Jonathan and Meg.

Chapter 26: Gibraltar

Harry was now Vice Admiral Wellesley, having been fast-tracked to a special coordination position within NATO Naval Command. A huge NATO War Games exercise was in the long and complicated planning process, and he was responsible for coordinating Royal Navy manoeuvres with the other members of the NATO Alliance.

Harry was by now besotted. Alicia was the woman he had dreamed about, beautiful, vivacious, intelligent and interesting, and above all, he thought she would be loyal, unlike his first wife.

She had left him for another Royal Navy officer; a real prick; a desk jockey who fought the finest sea-battles across his Whitehall desk. It had been a shock to begin with, but the humiliation and pain had subsided over time, and he had finally realised, he had been a rotten husband. He had a full time commitment to the Navy; Singapore to Malta, Hong Kong to Canada; everywhere but home in the interest of his career.

Now he had changed, but still Her Majesty´s Royal Navy man to the core. He had never lacked the seductive company of women in the twenty years he had been divorced. Sea-going duties were over at his rank, and politically, if he was honest with himself, he needed a wife beside him.

Harry and Alicia had been seeing each other for two years now, spending the weekends together either in London or at her apartment in Rhu. His old friends had noticed the difference in him; he was much more outgoing than before, a new spring in his step. He laughed easier and longer; they made a nice couple. They were happy for him, and very much liked his beautiful vivacious companion.

Privately they worried about him marrying Alicia....not Alicia, but the baggage of a dysfunctional son she would bring with her. It was this issue about Jonathan that had in fact delayed Harry from asking Alicia to marry before now.

He couldn´t expect her to wait forever, and perhaps sometime soon, she would be looking for a more permanent commitment, if not with him, then someone else.

Finally, he made up his mind to propose to her in Gibraltar, where he was now spending the bulk of his time. He asked her to join him for an extended holiday.

Alicia took a month´s leave from her job at the Clyde Navy Base, and they had the use of a luxury apartment belonging to a friend of Harry.

His favourite restaurant had agreed to provide the service, for a surprise romantic candle lit dinner on the apartment terrace, overlooking the Gibraltar Bay, with the lights of Tangiers in the distance.

After dinner, as they were relaxed, talking quietly and enjoying the ambience of a warm summer evening, he produced a beautiful sapphire and diamond ring and asked her to marry him.

Alicia was overwhelmed with emotion, and taking his face in her hands kissed him tenderly, accepting his proposal. "I love you Harry, and I promise you I´ll be a good wife to you." She was like a school-girl in her euphoria.

They discussed the marriage. Harry wanted an immediate quiet, discrete wedding for family members only. Alicia agreed, being careful not to show her disappointment. She would have preferred a grand affair in order to poke the noses of the so-called friends who had been back-stabbing her for years, but a quiet wedding was a small price to pay for her future as an Admiral´s wife.

She telephoned her mother with the good news, adding that she wanted her, Francesca and Jonathan to fly out immediately. Harry would arrange a special license for the wedding.

Mrs Vickery was delighted for her daughter. She had genuinely been concerned at the lack of a good husband by her side, and had been silently praying for this to happen. She went on to explain that Jonathan was on some kind of field trip with the school, but she would contact him, and bring him back.

It was with a tremendous shock, when next morning Mrs Vickery phoned the emergency contact number given by the nice Mr Jackson, the Geography Master she was answered by a rude young woman in Bristol, who asked: "What in the fuck you are talking about!"

The old lady pressed her, and demanded to know where her grandson was.

She was told in brutal fashion, "Get off the ´phone you demented old bitch!" and the receiver slammed down on her.

Mrs Vickery then telephoned the school, which was under the care of the Science Master over the holidays.

He was mystified. There was no Mr Jackson at the school, and he had no knowledge of any archaeological dig. However, he would telephone the headmaster at his holiday home in Brittany, and ask him if he knew of the expedition.

Mrs Vickery immediately telephoned Alicia in Gibraltar, and informed her of the mysterious circumstances surrounding Jonathan.

"Oh my God mother!" she exclaimed. "If Harry hears of this, he´ll be absolutely furious! He likes to be discrete, if this comes out in public, he´ll call off the wedding, I´m sure he will."

"Alicia! Your only son is missing!" "Forget the bloody wedding and get back here now!"

"Mother, I can´t, I´ve got to keep this from Harry. I´m sure nothing´s happened to him, he´s off on some rebellion to spite me, I´m sure of it."

Alicia was forced to explain the situation to Harry after being informed that the Headmaster had insisted that the police had been informed of the boy´s disappearance. Jonathan was after all, a boarding pupil, in the care of the school, and in the absence of a signed holiday release certificate, which apparently had not been issued to the boy´s guardian.

Alicia was indeed correct in her assessment of the Vice Admiral´s reaction to the news.

He blew his top! "My God, Alicia, I told you that the boy needed a stronger hand on him. That bloody school he´s at is no more than a damn kindergarten!" He looked worried as well as furious, "Christ if the Admiral hears about this! I´ve just informed him of our decision to get married! Jesus, he´s absolutely firm on things like this damaging the Navy´s discipline reputation."

Although she had heard of his famous rages against inefficient or incompetent junior officers, Alicia had never seen him so angry, and in consequence began to sob quietly.

After a while, noticing how upset Alicia was, he calmed down. "Alicia, my darling, I love you, and this will not change anything between you and I, but this lad needs a strong dose of discipline, mark my words! As his future stepfather, I intend to take an active role in his upbringing from now on. He´s been allowed to drift along far too long." Taking her in his arms, he said, "You´d better go back and sort things out. I´ll phone a friend of mine in the Strathclyde Police at Dumbarton, and see if he can help." Reassuringly he added, "I´m as sure as you are that he´s up to some bloody stupid schoolboy escapade."

They were up at six o´clock next morning. Alicia hadn´t slept all night and Harry wasn´t his normal easy going self at home. Breakfast was a coffee and a cigarette, with few words passing between them. The situation was obviously worrying him, and although he didn´t say it, she was sure that it was his close relationship with the Admiral he was concerned about, and not Jonathan.

She was more than a little hurt, when Harry got his navy driver to run her over to the airport, less than ten minutes from their front door, giving her a desultory peck on the cheek, and a "Take care, darling."

At least he had been able to swing a Business Class ticket on the seven thirty flight into London Heathrow, and then a connection to Glasgow, landing at one o´clock. An expensive

Taxi ride took her the thirty odd miles to her mother's cottage in Helensburgh by two.

Almost before her mother had a chance to close the door, Alicia immediately began berating her over the apparent disappearance of her son. "Mother, you've been such a fool, didn't you think to ask for proper documentation from the school?"

An embarrassed but furious grandmother threw back, "Now, after all these years when I've had to look after your son, while you have been swanning around looking pretty, you have the nerve to castigate me when something goes wrong?"

"God almighty!" Alicia swore, "Don't you know what trouble I'm in mother? Harry is beside himself with fury. The Social Services are blaming me for Jonathan's disappearance! Harry spoke last night to the Chief Constable at Dumbarton, and they are taking it very serious; they've put out a nationwide alert for a missing person!"

"He's almost certainly with that girl from school, Alicia," her mother interjected. "These young people have absolutely no morals nowadays, I just hope she doesn't get pregnant!"

Oh my God! ...mother, don't even think something like that! What a bloody mess! The little shit! How could he do this to me? I'll kill him!"

Chapter 27: The eco-warrior camp

Jonathan had matured significantly in the seven weeks he was in the commune. He had grown up physically and mentally. He had a new confidence to add to his already good looks. Like most of the others, he had allowed his normally short, tidy hair to grow into a hippy, unkempt look. He was careful to keep himself clean, and had taken on a deep weathered tan, which made look older than his years. He loved a woman for the first time.

Meg and he had indulged in some adolescent petting and kissing before, which she always controlled firmly when it was in danger of getting out of hand. He was young and in love, irresponsible, free; but she being older, and more in control of herself and her emotions, denied his love. She had reminded him that he was still only fifteen, and she sixteen, and she was buggered if she was going to be trapped into any long-term relationships. However, she admitted to him and to herself, she was very fond of him.

It happened quite naturally and almost accidently, after a really raucous party that must have had the police on duty fuming.

They stumbled back to their shelter, and fell onto the bed, Meg landing on top of Jonathan, hungrily kissing and biting his neck.

Jonathan detected immediately a change in atmosphere; it was not the usual French kissing and groping, there was an urgency in her; a primal sexual lust in need of satisfaction.

She simply said, through cider full breath, "Jonathan, fuck me, fuck me now."

Jonathan, lying on top of their sleeping bags, stunned, afraid, but already with an erection, could only breathe, "Are you sure Meg?"

She was already pulling his trousers down, which released his erection. "Whaee! What have we got here?" She said, smiling happily and lustfully, as she took him in hand.

Jonathan was almost coming, and said, "Wait a minute, Meg, *please!*"
She released him and they almost tore each other´s clothes from their bodies.

It was inevitable that the inexperience of Jonathan made him ejaculate almost immediately he entered her, but she gripped him inside of her, until she shuddered in her pleasure, escaping her lips in the form of a low moan.

He began to say sorry, but she placed a hand over his mouth, "Shush, you were just fine."

After falling back, and resting, held tight in each other's arms, they began their lovemaking again, this time Jonathan had more control over his sexual urges. Although still inexperienced, he was more in control, achieving the pleasure and satisfaction of almost simultaneous climax. Exhausted, happy and replete, they both climbed into one of the sleeping bags and fell into a dreamless sleep.

The commune and the police had a kind of unofficial accord. In times of a judicial stalemate, the eco warriors would not cause problems in Newtownbury. The Police in their part of the agreement left the commune in peace. Therefore, it was quite unusual when four policemen, one of which was an inspector, appeared early next morning at the guarded entrance to the protest camp.

The two eco-warriors on guard sounded an alarm, which brought a couple of dozen militants running to the gate fearing a police or security company attack.

Archie McGlyn quickly calmed everyone by making the comment, "It's okay folks, this is not an eviction, there's only four of the pigs."

The inspector overheard this, and face reddening with anger said, "There's no need for insulting language Sir, show a bit of respect please."

"We'll give you respect, when you take your troops and machines and get to hell out of this wood!" Archie was playing to his audience, which responded with a collection of "fuck off's," and "arrogant bastards."

Ignoring this, the inspector continued, "I am Inspector John McKinnon," holding up his warrant card for inspection. Can I talk to the person in charge?"

Archie responded, "No one, and everyone's in charge here Inspector, but you can talk to me, and I'll pass it on to the rest of our commune."

"I take it you have the confidence of the commune then, Mister…?"

"Just call me Archie."

"Can we talk in private Archie? It´s serious, it involves a search for a missing person."

"Okay Inspector Mac, but don´t expect me to be `shopping´ on anyone here, if they don´t want to be found."

They walked up to the communal tent, and still standing, the Inspector explained his `problem´. "A young boy, Jonathan Amersbey, aged fifteen, has been reported missing from his school in Dumbarton, Scotland. He was last seen on June twenty eighth, but was not reported as missing until the Wednesday last."

He went on: His mother and grandmother are desperately worried that he has come to some harm. He is still under the age of consent, and that is why the police, as well as the social services, have become involved."

The inspector explained, "Archie, we know he left the school in the company of a young lady, and has done so willingly; she´s been identified as Megan Smith-Jones, aged sixteen years, and there is no complaint or enquiry about her status. We are, at this time treating this case as a `running away from home´ more than a criminal intent case. As I´m sure you are aware," this was said as the Inspector was looking distastefully around, "fifteen year olds run away from home all of the time, most make some contact with their families after a few days, whether they return home or not. It pricks their conscious, or so it seems, they don´t want their mummy´s to be worried." Continuing he stressed, "In this case however, the school was still technically in charge of this boy, and there has been some kind of fraudulent misrepresentation by someone, so far unidentified, to delay enquiries as to the whereabouts of Jonathan Amersbey. We have a situation here where the school, as well as his mother, is insisting upon a full investigation into this boy´s disappearance."

"What exactly is your point in coming here then Inspector?" interrupted Archie.

"Inquiries in Scotland have revealed that Miss Smith-Jones has been an active participant at the Faslane Peace Camp Archie, and we have ascertained that she has signed on, and received unemployment benefits here, in Newtownbury, and that she is usually accompanied by a young boy, fitting Jonathan Amersbey's description."

Again, he stressed, "I am asking for your cooperation Sir. I am not here to arrest anyone, but I need to see, and ascertain that this young man is in good health, and is here on his own accord, and not a captive. I am duty bound to interview him, as you can understand, and I'll say it again, not to arrest him and take him back in chains, but to clear up matters with his mother, and the authorities in Scotland."

"Mister Policeman, I'm not going to confirm or deny the presence of anyone in this commune, people come and go as they please, and fifteen years old is hardly a child."

"Archie", the Inspector interposed, "In the eyes of the Law, fifteen *is* a child, and I'm sure you are aware, that in today's climate, knowingly harbouring a child runaway is a serious criminal offence." He hardened his tone, and looked Archie in the eye, "Let's cut the crap Archie; I will come back at two o'clock, with enough substantial reinforcements to carry out a thorough search of your camp. Alternatively, and much preferably to me, and I suspect to you and your members, is that he turns up in my office in Newtownbury Police Station before that time."

With a curt nod of his head, he turned about sharply, strode back down to the gate, ignoring the sullen and slightly infantile menacing of the eco-warriors. "Let's go sergeant", and the four policemen turned away down the track to a cacophony of catcalls and insults.

"Ginger! Go and find Meg and Jono. I want them here NOW!" When Archie was angry, everyone knew it, and kept out of his way. Although thin as a beanpole, he had learned his fighting skills in the streets of Springburn, a notoriously hard area of Glasgow. He never showed fear, and had beaten men twice his weight into tearful submission over relatively minor arguments. Ginger his runner, did not argue, question, or do anything more than run to Meg and Jonathan´s shelter.

They were still blissfully sleeping, but one or the other had kicked off the sleeping bag, and they were lying completely naked, exposed to the avaricious eyes of Ginger, as he took his time over his good fortune. Megan was lying with one arm over Jonathan, but her young pert breasts were within a foot of Ginger´s nose, and by the angle of her legs, he had a full view of her sex.

After a few minutes ogling, Ginger almost shouted, "Well, well now, I hope you had a real good shag Jono boy, because I think it´s going to be your last one in this camp!"

Megan was instantly awake and screamed, "Get the fuck out of here you fucking arsehole."

Jonathan, still groggy, could only say, "What in the fuck are you doing here Ginger," as he was trying to cover them up with the sleeping bag.

"Just get fucking out, NOW!" Megan screamed again.

"It´s okay, I´ve seen enough to have a toss in the toilets, thanks Megan", Ginger shot back. "Oh by the way, Archie wants to see Jono…hmm, right NOW!" With that, he backed out of their shelter a smirk almost splitting his face in half.

"Jesus Christ! What have I fucking done?" asked Megan almost to herself …oh fucking hell, what a fucking idiot."

"Misunderstanding, Jonathan said, "It can´t be serious Meg, we´re not on duty ´till four today."

"Not that, you stupid fuck; were you wearing a fucking condom? No? I don´t think so, so what fucking happens now?"

"Shit Meg, don´t worry, we´ll always be together anyway. You won´t be pregnant we only did it once…twice."

"Jonathan, what happened last night was a one off, got it? We are not lovers, or even boy and girlfriend. It was a fucking mistake. I told you I don't want a long term fucking relationship with you, or anyone else right now." She threw him a withering look, "I'm off to the latrine; you'd better get down and see the Mr fucking Big Boss man. Jesus! Even a camp of anarchists' has got to have a fucking boss man!"

Archie was pacing up and down outside the communal tent, when Jonathan arrived, breathless and more than a little apprehensive.

"Where's Megan," demanded Archie.

"She's in the toilet, Archie," Jonathan answered fearfully.

"Well, get your arse over there and get her!" Archie spat. "No, you wait here! Ginger! Go over to the latrine and bring Megan down here."

Ginger ran off again, and Archie asked Jonathan, "What age are you Jono?"

"Seventeen Archie, why?"

"You're a lying little cunt, and if you tell me one more fucking lie, I'll floor you!" He raised his fist as he said this and Jonathan almost peed into his pants. "Now once again, what age are you, Jono?"

"Fifteen, Archie, I'm sorry."

"Not half as sorry as you will be, if we get more fucking trouble over you."

Ginger and Megan arrived on the scene.

Megan shouted, "Archie, keep this fucking peeping-tom pervert away from me."

Archie looked quizzically at Ginger, who shrugged his shoulders, as if to say, "Who me?"

"Megan, what fucking age is your boyfriend? ...and before you give me a piece of shite, I know!"

Defiant, Megan answered, "Well then Archie, if you know, why are you asking me?"

"You'll get a smack in the mouth if you carry on like this!" He snarled, "Well, you two have given me a fucking headache; dae ye know why? Mummy has been looking for her little Jonathan, who seems to have run away from home."

Eyes blazing he continued, "She´s sent the pigs around here looking for him, and no doubt the fucking child support brigade will be here this afternoon!" He shouted, "You fucking know we don´t allow kids here! If the Press happen to get hold of it, we get tagged up as a Satanist cult molesting kids!"

Archie raised his finger and pointing directly at Jonathan, "So I´ll tell *you* what you are going to do. You can pack whatever two-pence worth of gear, except any food or booze you have, which we will accept as a donation. Then you will catch the eleven-o´clock bus into town, walk to the police station, and you ask for Inspector Mackinnon. He will then do what´s necessary to get you back home to mummy before it´s dark. GOT IT?"

Jonathan could only say a meek "Yes Archie, I´m really sorry!"

"I´ve got a feeling son, you are going to be a hell of a lot more sorry before too long!"

"Archie, Megan interposed, I´m not going back, can´t I stay on?"

"No fucking chance sunshine! You´re both out! Ginger! Get Gordo to go with them and make sure they go to the pigs." With that, he took one last withering look at them, and strode off.

They packed in silence, Megan refusing to look in Jonathan´s direction. On the bus, accompanied by the camp gorilla Gordo, they didn´t speak. Only when they were about to enter the Police Station, Megan turned to Gordo and told him, "Run back to your master Gordo, we can make it through the door."

"That´s funny Megan, but I´ll just wait to make sure you go in."

Megan furiously crashed the door open, causing the desk sergeant to frown and say, "What´s the hurry Miss? Desperate to get into a cell are we?"

They asked for the Inspector, and while waiting, Megan warned Jonathan not to shop the CND activist who had helped him with his subterfuge. "Remember, no comment without a lawyer!"

The interview with the Inspector went better than they had feared. He simply wanted to clear up some administration, on what was a Dumbarton police matter. He asked Jonathan, if he willingly left the school, and was not coerced in any way into joining the eco- warriors at the commune. Satisfied, with his answers, he insisted that Jonathan phoned his mother.

His grandmother answered, and the old woman tearfully thanked God he was fine, and would be returning home. His mother apparently was at Castle school, in conference with the principal who had cut short his holiday in France, given the seriousness of the situation.

Megan and Jonathan were not allowed to be alone in the police station, and, when the inspector handed him a Rail Warrant to take him back to Dumbarton, Jonathan asked for one for Megan.

The Inspector explained that Megan was an adult, and no one had reported her missing, therefore he had no jurisdiction over her movements.

Jonathan looked at Megan, pleading with his eyes, but she looked away, and said nothing.

He went to say something, but she pre-empted him by stating in a dull, lifeless voice, "I'm not going back Jonathan. I'm sorry, but I can't, I've got to sort myself out."

He felt his eyes fill up, but held the tears back, and simply nodded. "Meg, you've got my grandmother's address, let me know where you are, please."

"Right my lad, let's get you on your way then." The inspector handed him over to a uniformed constable who would take him to train station and hand him over to the Transport Police, who were to accompany him north.

They parted at the entrance to the train station, she hugged him tightly for a few moments, and he detected wetness in her eyes, but she simply said, "Jonathan, we´ve had a great time, but it´s over now, I´m sorry."

He was about to plead again, but realised it was useless, and merely muttered, "I love you Megan."

The constable interrupted, "Come on son, you´ve got a train to catch," and gently led him away.

Chapter 28: Resolution of a rebel

The journey back to Scotland seemed to last forever for Jonathan. A series of older Transport Police officers accompanied him; they obviously resented having to escort a young thug home. There was no attempt made to communicate with the boy, other than at the times he was taken to the buffet car, and then only to ask him what he wanted to eat or drink, and to stand outside the toilet door when he wanted to pee.

It was not as if the boy wanted company. Sunk in despair, he was trying to come to terms Megan´s brutal rejection of his love, and still dazed by the events that had occurred in less than twenty-four hours. He reasoned, she must love him, otherwise she wouldn´t have made love to him. *We could have stayed together once the school business had been sorted out,* he thought. He resolved that he would try find her through her friends at the peace camp; someone would know where she was, maybe in fact, she would go back there. She had loved the weekends and the demos there. *Yes, she would probably go back and he would get her to see reason.*

Jonathan had long inculcated her arguments on capitalism and the establishment enslaving the rest of us in their systems. There was no way that he was going back as the meek little schoolboy he was last month. No, Jonathan Amersbey could think, act and make decisions for himself. There was absolutely no chance he was going to wear that fucking kilt again. Principal Kennedy could shove it up his arse.

His mother was waiting along with several other police officers when the train arrived in Glasgow Central Station. Immediately the train arrived in the station, he was taken to the Police Office, through the crowds of curious on-lookers.

Alicia, appalled at her son´s appearance, exclaimed, "My God, Jonathan, look at yourself ...you look like a bloody tramp! What´s happened? ...Jonathan," she admonished, "you´ve really got your-self into trouble this time."

Jonathan, scowled at her, but didn´t say anything. *Jesus has she always got to be like this?*

He looked on as the Transport Police officer produced some documents, which one of the local policemen, a sergeant checked over.

"You are Jonathan, Amersbey, aged fifteen years old, and a pupil at Castle School, Dumbarton?" he asked.

"Who else would I be?" Jonathan shot back, "Prince Charles?"

"Just answer the question!" demanded the sergeant, visibly angry and colouring red. "Have you any idea of what trouble and expense you have caused us?"

"That´s your problem, I didn´t ask to get hauled back here by you people."

"Jonathan! Show some respect! What in the hell´s got into you?" Alicia shouted. "The police are only doing their job! You gave us all a terrible scare going off like that, and just look at you," she repeated, still unable to believe her eyes.

The sergeant intervened, "Listen to me, if you do not cooperate with these identification procedures, I´ll have you arrested; is that clear?"

Defeated for the moment, but still defiant, Jonathan said, "Okay, I admit it, I´m Jonathan Amersbey, aged fifteen and two months, and this is my mother! Oh, I forgot, I used to go to Castle School."

"Now that´s been cleared up ... Mrs Amersbey, I have to ask you to affirm that this is your son Jonathan, and he is, in your opinion, sound in health. This may seem a little stupid to you, but I must sign this document as having received your son in good health from the Transport Police."

Wearily, Alicia affirmed, "Yes sergeant, this is my son Jonathan, and he appears to be in good health," *If a not a bit filthy and smelly!*

The police officers signed and stamped the receiving documents, and the party moved outside to where a police patrol car was awaiting them.

The sergeant advised them, that they were going back to Strathclyde Police HQ at Dumbarton, and Jonathan would be interviewed by his Chief Superintendent, and a member of the Council Children´s Support staff.

Alicia protested, "Sergeant, I´m tired, the boy is tired, he needs a bath and a meal; can it not wait until tomorrow?"

"I´m sorry, Mrs Amersbey, but these are my instructions. The headmaster of Castle School has made an official complaint concerning falsification of documents, and misrepresentation of a teacher at the school, and this will have to be investigated properly. I understand that the social services may be pressing some kind of charges of child neglect also, so it´s probably in your best interest to cooperate and attend these interviews voluntarily, and, as soon as possible."

Malevolent Karma

"Jesus Christ, what a bloody mess." Alicia shot a venomous look at her son, who simply shrugged his shoulders in return.

The police driver, rather unnecessarily, used his flashing blue emergency lights, to exit the station, and weave through the six-o´clock rush hour. He sped down Dumbarton Road, and through the Clyde Tunnel to access the M8 Motorway. No one spoke and as they were passing Glasgow Airport at seventy miles per hour.

Alicia was gazing at her own reflection in the rain-streaked glass, depressingly thinking, that just a couple of days ago, she was in a balmy Gibraltar with Harry, planning their wedding. *Shit! It would have been taking place in a day or so from now, but for this idiot son of hers.* God knows, she thought with a horrible lurch of her stomach, when, or even if it will take place. Jesus, she could kill him!

As the car shot across the Erskine Bridge, she looked down on the river and watched a ship moving slowly downstream. She would not have known the ship, but it was MV Dalmarnock, which takes the human waste residue from the Shieldhall Sewage Processing Plant out into the Firth of Clyde, where it´s dumped onto the seabed. The irony would not have been lost on her, that much of this filth gets washed back ashore later, to coat the skins of Glasgow day trippers on the beaches of Ayrshire.

At Dunbartonshire Police HQ, they were shown into an interview room. A cup of tea was offered to Alicia and Jonathan a can of Coca Cola from a vending machine. They were left waiting for what seemed like ages, but it was more or less twenty minutes.

Alicia tried to solicit information from her son, about what had happened, and what he had been doing the past month. Jonathan, in his new role of anarchist, simply refused to answer. Finally, Alicia gave up in exasperation.

A tall, grey haired distinguished looking man, in civilian clothes, entered accompanied by a young uniformed woman police officer.

"I'm Chief Superintendent Nisbett, he said as he shook hands with Alicia, and you are Mrs Amersbey? ... and this will be the young man who has created all this nonsense," as he appraised Jonathan with a critical eye, noting the sullen expression, and his general tramp-like appearance.

"Constable Maguire, can you take this young man into the showers and get him cleaned up a bit whilst I have a talk with his mother?"

"Of course Sir", she replied, and took Jonathan's arm, saying, "don't worry Jonathan, but you really could do with freshen up."

When the door closed behind them, the Superintendent began, "Mrs Amersbey, I have spoken to Harry Wellesley about the situation. I've known Harry since he was at Faslane when he was on the submarines; we played golf together, he's a very good friend."

Alicia relaxed, and thought, *Harry has sorted things out.*

The Superintendent went on: "We still have a problem Mrs Amersbey; not from my police point of view, we get kids running away every day of the week, but the school has made a formal complaint, and Social Services are also poking their noses into the case."

Alicia was about to say something, but Nisbett held up his hand; "Before you say anything, I want to help, and I have several suggestions on how we should proceed. Firstly, I have had a lengthy conversation with Jim Kennedy, Jonathan's headmaster, and he is reluctantly willing to drop the complaint, if Jonathan gives him a full apology, and leaves the school voluntarily. He doesn't want the publicity anymore than we do. Do you think Jonathan will comply?"

"Yes, I'll make sure he does!" replied a grim faced Alicia.

"Fine, next, we have to satisfy the Child Support unit that Jonathan has not been neglected."

Aghast, Alicia almost shouted, "Neglected? How dare they suggest this, he has been sent to private school; always well cared for, healthy ... he's never even had a hand laid on him, although at times I've been sorely tempted! It's all been a mistake, and remember some adult has helped him deceived us all!"

"Yes I know about the false document and phone calls," Nisbett interrupted, "but please listen to me. The Social Services weald a lot of power in Dumbarton District Council, and we have to make sure that they have satisfactory explanations, and apologies if necessary, or you may find yourself in court on a child neglect charge."

"This is a bloody nightmare!" Alicia interjected, "What are you suggesting Superintendent?"

"I know the head of Children's Support quite well, we're on several committees together. She's a typical career zealot, but I'll have a word in her ear, and try work out some agreement. I think it will involve some kind of statement a `misunderstanding´ between your mother and yourself, and a promise to be more careful in the future; but, Mrs Amersbey, if she wants you to grovel, my advice is, grovel!"

"When am I to do this grovelling, Mr Nesbitt? Alicia asked, through a rigid jaw.

"As soon as we can arrange a meeting, don't you think? The sooner this is all put to bed, the best for all, and you can get back to marrying Harry Wellesley!" He said this with a smile, which lifted her spirits a little. "Yes, Harry has explained everything; if I were in your shoes I would want to strangle our young delinquent also!"

The meeting, next day, with the Social Service woman went as bad as Alicia had feared. Alicia was ten minutes early for the meeting, wearing a smart business suit, and pearl earrings to make a good impression, but realised too late, it was a bad idea...too smart!

A small, mousy haired woman, in a shapeless dress, wearing no make-up, eventually came out meet her.

"I'm Anne Robertson, the Head of Children's Support" she announced to Alicia, as she showed her into her rather austere, functional and soul-less office.

She had been in a meeting, which had over run by twenty-five minutes, but she made no attempt to apologise to Alicia. Instead went straight into a tirade about the difficult job her department was experiencing with a positive epidemic of neglected children. "And it's not only to be found in the underclass either!" she lectured pointedly at Alicia.

Alicia kept her cool though, and allowed the woman to vent her spleen. The meeting ended with a chastened, humiliated Alicia, but with a satisfactory `No Action Required´, stamped upon the case file.

At his grandmother's, the two women tried to get some kind of explanation out of the boy, but he kept a surly, morose silence, refusing to discuss the events of the summer.

They pleaded and cajoled the still sullen, uncooperative Jonathan to tell them who had telephoned his grandmother, and forged the Archaeological Dig document to no avail; but in the knowledge that he was not going back to the Castle School, and the detested kilt uniform; he acquiesced in making a personal apology to the principal.

The interview only spoiled a little, when Doctor Kennedy told him that he had no future.

Jonathan riposted "The majority of your pupils don't have a future; they're in a "fucking shit school!"
Alicia practically threw him out the door, before the Head could get to him.

Alicia had kept the Harry abreast of developments, and told him she loved him more than ever, and thanked him for all he had done to resolve the problem. His friend Superintendent Nesbitt had been very kind and helpful.

Harry in turn, assured her that he still adored her, and they would get married as soon as possible. He had an idea about Jonathan's education and future, but didn't want to elaborate at this moment in time as he still had enquiries to complete. He added, "Darling, I'll be in London at the weekend for a conference at the MOD, can you make it down for an overnight, at least?"

"Harry, my love, I would fly to Singapore for a chance to be with you!" she almost choked out.

"Great, I'll call you in the morning; leave your flights to me, I'll reserve through my Public Relations account! I love you, 'Bye for now."

Chapter 29: Vice Admiral Harry and Mrs Wellesley

Harry and Alicia had a quiet wedding in Gibraltar a few weeks later, attended only by the Best Man and Bridesmaid as witnesses; both were friends of the happy couple. There were no family members present; it was for the best in the circumstances. They allocated a Royal Navy Senior Officer's residence as befitting the rank, but would be commuting often to Harry's flat in London as his duty required.

Jonathan remained a problem, he couldn't live with his grandmother on a long-term basis. Moving in with Harry and Alicia was also out of the question, therefore, on Harry's suggestion, he was packed off to an outward-bound school near Forres in the North of Scotland. They specialised on the problem children of the rich and famous.

Jonathan´s response to this move could have been predicted by anyone who knew him, as he was now a radicalised and dysfunctional individual with no desire to please anyone. However, he stuck out the regime of early morning runs over freezing rain-soaked moorland, porridge for breakfast and rigorous exercise routines until he could figure out what to do next.

A chance meeting in Forres, with some sympathetic hippies from the commune in Findhorn gave him the opportunity.

He telephoned his grandmother and told her of his intention to leave the school, pointing out that he was now over sixteen, and could now do what he wanted with his own life.

The old woman tried desperately to get him to change his mind; "at least speak to your mother and the Commodore," she pleaded, "Honestly Jonathan, they have your best interest at heart."

"No grandmother, they´re not interested in me and never have been!" He gave her his address at the Commune to save the police wasting their time looking for him, and promised to keep in touch with her.

Alicia´s response to this latest crisis was frustration and resignation. They were in London this week, and Harry had so much on his plate with his NATO coordination role, he could not spare the time trying to resolve Jonathan´s problems, but she had to tell him in any case.

This time he wasn´t angry, but advised her to go up North to Findhorn and try to persuade her son to go back to the school.

She flew into Inverness the next day, and hired a car to drive the the thirty miles or so along the Moray Firth coast. It was a beautiful, bright winter´s day, very little traffic on the road and a blessing to the soul after the traffic and chaos of Central London. She drove through the pretty town of Nairn and on to Forres and Findhorn Bay, where the commune was located.

Alicia drove down the road through the sand dunes to the little village of Findhorn, and asked at the local pub where the commune was. She took the opportunity to refresh herself with a welcome half pint of beer, as the barman filled her in on the hippies at the community.

They seemed to be decent people he assured her, a strange lifestyle though; frequent customers at the pub, although they made their own brew. The locals had no problem with them, after all they had been here since the sixties; mind you, he didn´t want to speculate on their attitude to marriage, as he gave her a wink.

As soon as she saw the commune, her heart sank, but at the same time, a sensation of relief also overtook her. This was not at all like Newtownbury, or the peace camp at Faslane. It was set on the beautiful Findhorn Bay and true it was run by hippies as a cooperative, but it appeared to be tidy, organised, and the caravans painted neatly, if not aesthetically in pastel colours. She was politely received by a slim, dark haired, woman of about her own age at the Reception/Office. Alicia began on the wrong foot, by commenting on how nice the commune was.

The receptionist quickly informed her that this was an eco-village, not a hippie colony.

Alicia asked to speak to her son, Jonathan Amersbey.

The receptionist instantly knew whom she was talking about. He just arrived the other day, she asked; "Are you his mother?" At the same time checking a roster, and surreptitiously appraising Alicia´s expensive, London bought clothes.

"Jonathan´s out working on the sands;" she announced, "we harvest our own cockles and mussels, but I´ll send for him; would you like some tea?"

Alicia declined, and asked if she could have a look around.

"Of course you can, we welcome visitors; we have a craft shop and donations to our Eco-Fund are welcome," said with that supercilious smile only the righteous can invoke.

Half an hour passed, and Alicia feeling abandoned, felt the anger arising in her throat.

An older man, this time recognizable as a hippie, long hair and beard going past grey into white, and wearing a woollen fisherman's jumper, jeans and moccasins; homemade, by the look of them, approached. "Mrs Amersbey?" he enquired.

"Yes, well no, I'm now Mrs Wellesley, I've remarried," Alicia awkwardly replied with a tight smile.

"I'm Saul Arkwright," he said extending his hand, I'm the current leader here," he added.

Alicia took his hand, it was calloused from manual work and the handshake was honest and firm.

"Mrs Am.... Wellesley, I'm sorry, but Jonathan doesn't want to see you; he's refusing to come and talk to you."

"What do you mean, he's not going to see me," she demanded, "I've come all the way up from London to see him!" Her heart was beating like a drum, and her voice quivered as she uttered the last sentence. "I'm not going back without talking to him ...for all I know you are holding him against his will ...I'll get the police!"

Patiently Saul answered her, "You are welcome to telephone the police, Mrs Am...Wellesley, but the first thing they will ask is, what age is the young man? ...and if he is over sixteen years old, they will tell you that they cannot interfere. Look, there's a tearoom beside the craft-shop, if you wait there, I'll try and convince the lad to come and see you, as you've travelled so far."

A spasm of nervous hunger crossed her stomach, so his time she bought a pot of tea, and a finger of shortbread. Sitting in the tearoom, Alicia felt foolish and impotent; people were passing to-and-fro, some tourists but most obviously members of the commune. She was imagining them talking about her.

Finally, she was startled out of her thoughts by the familiar "Hello mother" of Jonathan.

It had been six months since Alicia had last seen her son, she almost didn´t recognise him; her imagination still focused on a small boy in his kilt at Castle School. He had grown taller and looked very fit; he had changed; there was no warmth in his face or his greeting.

"Jonathan, you´ve grown up so much..."

"Why are you here," he interrupted, "you never came to see me in that fucking Gulag you and your commodore sent me to; so why come here to see me?"

Taken aback, by the force of his anger, she was momentarily stunned into silence. "Jonathan, we are doing the best for you, can´t you see? Harry and I only want to see you happy and finish your education; after that, it´s your decision as to what career you want to have. Harry would get you into Devonport, for God´s sake!"

He snarled back, "I´ve made my decision; my so-called fucking porridge-in-the-morning-education days are over, and you can tell your admiral to stuff his Devonport up his arse!"

"Good God Jonathan ...." but Jonathan had already turned on his heel and walked away.

Alicia was left standing, looking and feeling forlorn and useless. She was aware that the receptionist was staring at her. Squaring her shoulders, she shook her head sadly and left.

BOOK TWO

Alistair MacLeod's Story

"There is no love sincerer than the love of food."
~George Bernard Shaw

Chapter 30: 1964 Glasgow, Scotland.

"Beautiful, isn´t it? Look at the details on these figurines. I love the theme as well." The fresh-faced young woman was addressing a stranger. Both were admiring Checkmate, the Medal d´Honneur prize-winning exhibit in the Salon Culinaire d´Ecosse at the Kelvin Hall in Glasgow.

The object of their attention was a chess set, modelled on the classic Reynard the Fox figures, the sculpture had been hand carved in white and black butter. The marble-effect chessboard was a composition in the shape of Africa, and represented the political changes taking place on that continent. Black Africa chessmen had Colonial White Africa in a checkmate situation.

"It´s quite good," the young man replied, "a few months' work, I think."

In her soft lilting accent she added; "It´s fabulous; look at the detail on the pawns, he´s even got detail on the buttons of their waist coats!" She looked closer at the card giving the winner´s name; "Hamish MacLeod, I wonder if he´s from the Islands?"

The young man replied, "I think his parents came from the Islands, from Lewis, in fact."

"Do you know him?" she was now studying the man a little more closely. *He's not bad looking;* she thought, *a bit French looking, with that beard and soft leather jacket. I bet he's a Mod!*

"Want to meet him?" he asked.

"Yes, that would be great; I'd like to find out how he coloured these black pieces; food colouring is water based, so how did he get them to emulsify?"

"I'll tell you how in time for the next Salon. That's probably the best thing I've ever done," Hamish said.

At last, she cottoned on. "You're Hamish MacLeod!" she exclaimed.

He laughed, "I was waiting until you said something nasty! Pleased to meet you; I'm Hamish, and you are Miss?"

"That's not nice, I might have said something embarrassing!"

"You should have been here a few minutes ago; some idiots were demanding that Check Mate! should be disqualified. `It's a political statement!´ or some rubbish like that. The fools were typical opinionated ruling-class loudmouths. They couldn't stomach the idea that the sun was setting over the Empire, and that Blacks could be winning!" Calming down and smiling at her he continued, "You still haven't told me your name... definitely from the Islands, with that accent; ochone, ochone Flora!"

"I'm not Flora, I'm Lorna, and don't make fun of my nice accent; I'm proud to come from Barra, you know."
He noticed her clear blue eyes, beneath long dark eyelashes, and an almost prim, but a humorous, warm smile.

"I think we'd better move on, Lorna de Barra, we're kind of blocking the view, and spoiling my fifteen minutes of fame! Fancy a coffee?"

"Only if we can pass by the Junior Chaudfroid Hams, I've got something to show you, Mister Big Cheese."

They forced their way through the crowds, Hamish responding to various friends' greetings and congratulations; secretly pleased that she was with him. She really was a good-looking lassie; pert, confident, with her pony tail hair bobbing as she kept up with him. They reached the Junior (under 21) section, and the Cold Buffet Exhibition.

"What do you think," she asked excitedly, awaiting his reaction. She was pointing to the Gold Medal Award for `Works in Chaudfroid´. There was a whole ham, covered in a creamy white velouté, and exquisitely decorated with a brilliant, fine bouquet of vegetable orchids, and finished in a crystal clear aspic glaze.

The Gold Medal ticket, announced Winner: `Lorna McIntosh, Queen´s College´.

"Lorna! This is fabulous!" He pressed through the crowd to get a closer inspection; "Seriously, this would probably beat the senior category; I´m not joking, this is good stuff, congratulations!"

Just then, several of her college friends came by, and shrieked their congratulations, surrounding her.

Hamish was forced away from her, thinking to himself; "Shit she´s only a student, too young; and tapped her shoulder. "I´m off for a coffee," he shouted over the noise.

She looked startled, and shouted in reply, "Wait a minute, I´m coming too."

She said goodbye to her friends, who looked on a little mystified, as she followed Hamish through the throngs to a Gaggia coffee machines stand. He flashed a VIP card at the receptionist, and they were ushered into the VIP lounge area.

"Mama Mia, if it´s not the champion himself!" cried an enormously fat Italian. "How´s the craic Hamish? ...and who´s this *bellissima* with you!"

"Hi, Mario, this here is the Junior Champion Chaudfroid Chef! Can we get two cappuccinos?" Aside to Lorna, he said, "Don´t mind him, he´s from Govan, but he sells these fantastic coffee machines."

After a few more minutes of back and forth ribbing, Mariano got back to selling his five thousand pound coffee machines, and they had peace to talk about themselves.

Inspecting him closely, the girl asked; "So, Hamish MacLeod, in between chopping up butter, do you work?"

"I´m a senior Sous Chef at the Central Hotel; I look after the Malmaison Restaurant." He answered, with just a little pride in his voice.

"Oh my; I´m definitely in exalted company today!" she exclaimed, "aren´t you not a bit young for that?"

"I´m twenty three, and served my time in the Central and Gleneagles, so, not so young."

"Is that what your ambition, to become Chef de Cuisine at Gleneagles?" she enquired.

"That´s not a bad ambition, but I´m not sure; I think I would like my own restaurant; a small French Bistro type place, but money is the problem. I´ve been offered a lecturer´s job in the new College at Clydebank, I quite fancy that also; the only problem is the salary is not so good, but the hours are better, no more split shifts, and weekends off."

He asked her, "What about you? What do you want to be? Not school meals I hope, with your talent! I can´t imagine you dolloping sago pudding onto snotty nosed kids plates in an Easterhouse school."

Indignantly she answered, "What do you take me for? Do you think I´ll have done three years at Queen´s for that? I´ve been working Saturday´s up in the restaurant in Fraser´s in Buchanan Street. They´ve offered me a Trainee Manager´s post, starting in June when I finish at Queen´s. Eventually, I´m going to have my own place though, maybe a coffee shop. Have you any idea how much money can be made in a coffee shop?"

"Not as much as in a restaurant," responded Hamish. "Good luck with your new job though." He liked this girl, she was so positive and sure of herself but not pushy with it. They chatted a bit about their families, over another free cappuccino.

Lorna´s father had a croft on Barra, in the Hebrides, whilst her mother was a primary school teacher in Castlebay, the island capital. She had an older, married sister, with whom she stayed in Glasgow.

Hamish´s mother and father had migrated from Lewis, to Clydebank in the Thirties. He was an engineer, and he, and Hamish´s two brothers worked in Yarrows shipyard at Scotstoun. Hamish rebelled, and quit his engineering apprenticeship scheme, much to his father´s fury to enter into an Apprenticeship for Chefs programme, with BT Hotels, a leading hotel group.

They talked a bit more, but Hamish said he had to get back to the restaurant for the lunch service. Before he left, he asked "Lorna, if you don´t mind me asking, how old are you? It´s only because of the standard of your exhibit," he hastened to lie.

"Have you no finesse? Bloody hell, I´d thought I´d left the clod-hoppers behind in Barra," she replied, just a little angrily.

"Sorry, but I would like to know, if..."

"If what teuchter? If I´m out of nappies yet? Listen mister, I´m just asking myself if I want to go out with you, when you might be old enough to be my dad! I don´t think so."

Christ, she´s feisty for all her innocent wee lassie looks, "Right, I´ll start again; I´m twenty three, and if you were only sixteen, and if I wanted to ask you if you fancied going to the Highlanders Institute with me, you wouldn´t get in, and I would miss my Gay Gordon´s dance. So Miss Lorna McBarra, I´m off this Saturday night, would you like to come with me to the Highlanders, and more importantly, will they let you in?"

She lost her anger, "Well now, if I go to the Highlanders Institute, can you do a Strathspey Reel?... by the way, I´m twenty; you don´t get into the Dough School, until you are seventeen and I´m finishing this year; is that alright for you exacting requirements?"

"Perfectly, and now that I´m not going to be up for baby snatching, if we´re going to the Highlanders! I finish work at six, so can we meet under the Heilan´ Man´s Umbrella at seven? We´ll go for something to eat first, okay?"

"No, it´s not okay," she replied annoyed, "I´m not standing there waiting for you to turn up; people will think I´m on the game! No, Mr MacLeod, you can come to my sister´s to pick me up. Number 245 Woodlands Road, first floor right. It´s right behind the Grand Hotel, at Charing Cross. My sister will want to see what teuchter is taking me to the Institute!"

"That´s amazing! ...that´s just round the corner from me! I´ve rented a flat in St Georges Road! Fine, I´ll wear my best Sunday suit for your sister! He escorted her as far as the Petit Fours´ exhibition, and said, "See you Saturday!"

Her answering smile, stayed in his memory for the rest of the week.

Saturday came, and he was unaccountably nervous, throughout the lunch service, making several mistakes in the orders, much to the fury of the Luigi the Head Waiter, who had to pacify some very angry customers.

At four o´clock, when he clocked off, the streets were still busy with the Saturday shoppers in from the big housing estates scattered around Glasgow. He was lucky to find a place to stand on the bus from Renfield Street, to Charing Cross, not a great distance, but he was in a hurry.

Ian, his flatmate was still at work, so he put two shillings in the gas meter, and treated himself to a bath, taking care to wash away the accumulated kitchen smells from his body.

Dressed in his new tight black jeans, his black Beatles style shirt and narrow white tie; longish hair carefully styled *aux française,* he splashed on some of Ian´s Old Spice. He put on his still to be paid for, soft French leather jacket. Checking him-self in the old dresser mirror, he felt satisfied that he looked good enough for a lassie down from Barra.

Lorna´s sister lived less than a quarter of a mile away. Half of the migrants from the Highlands, who came down to

Glasgow for work, seemed to live in the red sandstone tenements around Woodlands Road. The area was considered not bad, and certainly one up from Maryhill.

He quickly found number 245, but had forgotten which door it was in the tenement, and what Lorna´s sister´s married name was.

Sheepishly, he had to knock on the first door and asked the old man who answered, if he knew of a lassie called Lorna in the close.

"Aye, ah do, but what business is it of you?" was the response.

"I´m taking her out and I´ve forgotten which flat she lives in."

Looking Hamish up and down, the old fellow said, "Ah thought she had better taste, but it´s her choice I suppose; upstairs, right door, the names McDonald."

"Thanks a lot Mr McDonald," said Hamish, and made as if to go.

"Laddie, my name´s Anderson; Lorna´s sister is married to Archie McDonald, from Tobermory, right?"

"Thanks anyway Mr Anderson, I´ll be away upstairs then." Taking the steps two at a time, he quickly found the correct flat. Checking the name plate, `Norman McDonald´, he couldn´t help but take in the highly polished brass letter box, knocker and door handle, set in a gleaming black painted door.

Here goes, he thought, checking his appearance in the mirror of the letterbox brass, and adjusting a stray hair lock, he pressed the bell.

After a long few minutes, the door opened to an older version of Lorna, carrying a baby in her arms.

"You must be the Hamish, the teuchter from Clydebank then; I´m Shona, and this here is wee Davie," indicating the baby in her arms, "and this one hanging on to my legs is wee Norman. Opening the door wider, she smiled, "Come on in, Lorna´s still getting ready, she was late coming back from Frasers."

Malevolent Karma

"Lorna, you´re teuchter´s here," she shouted, answered by a muffled "just coming" from one of the bedrooms.

The flat was a typical two room, kitchen and bathroom arrangement, which meant that the kitchen also served as a sitting room; the furniture appeared basic, but everything, including the old `granny style´ cooker was immaculate, only spoiled by the line of babies nappies, strung across the top of the cooker drying.

"Lorna´s been telling me you´re a top chef, then, at the Malmaison, and you´ve won a few medals, eh?"

"I try my best, Mrs McDonald," he replied, more than a little self consciously, "but Lorna is really good as well. Her chaudfroid ham at the Salon Culinaire was brilliant."

"Yes, we´re all quite proud of her, she´ll go places that lassie, if only some stupid teuchter laddie doesn´t turn her head first!" She said this with an obvious sense of humour that had Hamish smiling also.

He objected, "But, Mrs McDonald, I´m no´ a Highland teuchter, I´m from Clydebank!"

"That´s worse still, a Bankie is no use for my wee sister!" Thankfully, Lorna appeared in the door, and said, "Don´t take any notice of her, *she* married a *real* teuchter, from Mull! ...would you believe it?"

"What do you think?" She paraded in front of them, twirling around, in her just purchased figure hugging dark blue and white lace dress, pouting provocatively.

"I think you look great," said Hamish, "blue really suits you."

"How in the hell are you going to do an Eight-some Reel in that?" asked her sister.

"I´ll manage; where´s Norman?" Lorna asked, "He´s not back yet?"

"No, it´ll be a while yet. Celtic were playing Hearts in Edinburgh, and I heard they´d won, so he´ll be pissed as a fart when he eventually get´s home. He´ll be away again next week, so he needs a bit of time with his mates."

"Norman's a chief engineer in the Merchant Navy," Lorna explained; "Sometimes he's away for months on the cruise ships;" She proudly added, "he works for Cunard you know."

Shona intervened, "Right you two, bugger off, I've got a wean to feed and bath for his bed."

On the way downstairs, Hamish asked, "Where do you fancy eating?"

"You decide, was the answer, that way I can tell if you're for real, or just another cheapskate Bankie."

"OK, I'll demonstrate just how sophisticated I am. We're going to the Courtyard. It's Italian; I know the Chef, Sylvester, and he makes the best *Cervella Fritta* I've ever tasted, quite brilliant."

".... and what is *Cervella Fritta?* Mr Know All."

"Fried calves brains" he laughed, "it's good for developing intelligence."

"Yuk!" she responded, "I'll stick to spaghetti bolognaise, if he can rise to that."

Chapter 31: The Courtyard Restaurant

The Courtyard was probably the best Italian restaurant in Glasgow. It was in an old Townhouse in Landsdowne Crescent, in the City's west end. Part owned by a famous Scottish international football star, the Courtyard was patronised by the TV celebrity crowd as well as the Celtic and Rangers footballers.

Hamish had taken the precaution of phoning his friend, Sylvester, and reserving a table. They would be well looked after, as befitting fellow professionals.

Agnelli, the Head Waiter, greeted them like old friends, as was his wont, making a fuss of Lorna, kissing her hand and looking at her appreciatively. Showing them to a table in an alcove, and whilst lighting the candle, he said that Chef Sylvester, had prepared something special for them; "would they like this, or prefer the Menu?"

Hamish, first checking with Lorna, who nodded affirmation, said "That would be great, but remind the Chef, that we´re going dancing later, so not too heavy please."

A couple of very dry martini´s, appeared with a plate of Tuscan olives in a basil flavoured virgin olive oil.

"My God, Hamish," Lorna exclaimed, "I thought I was coming out for spaghetti bolognaise, this will cost a fortune; can you afford it?"

He put on a broad Glasgow accent "Don´t you worry hen, when these guys come to the Malmaison, we make some, ahem ... adjustments to the Bill. It´s called `perks of the trade´."

They had a truly excellent meal, starting with *Gamberetti all´olio e limone*, Shrimps in oil and lemon, served with a light Pinot Grigio, and then a simple *Arrosti di vitello*, Roast loin of veal, with dainty roast potatoes and a green leaf salad.

Agnelli ordered the wine waiter to serve a bottle of Chianti Classico, vintage 1951 with the main course. Lorna asked about the missing wicker basket, Agnelli just smiled and murmured, "The best wine is inside the bottle, *bella*." They finished with an exquisite but potent desert of *Baba e Ron con Gelato*, Rum Baba with homemade vanilla ice cream.

The restaurant now had filled up, and Hamish explained who was who among the celebrities. At about half past nine, several of the Celtic players arrived with their partners, to a loud applause from the diners, which included a couple of Rangers players!

Over coffee, accompanied by tiny marzipan biscuits, and old Marsala, Lorna asked, "Hamish, do we really have to go to the Highlanders Institute this time? I´ve eaten and drank so much, I can´t see me flinging myself into a Reel tonight."

"Thank God you said that," he replied, "I was scared to ask you! We´ll go to the Student Union, they´ve got a Trad Jazz Band on Saturday´s."

Smiling she agreed, "Sounds good to me, but we´d better say thanks to Chef Sylvester on the way out."

Agnelli brought the severely reduced Bill. Hamish paid, and left a generous tip for the staff.

.

They went through to the inferno that was the kitchen, dodging chefs, flaming steaks, and waiters running madly around. The noise and heat, after the calm of the restaurant, assailed the senses.

The Chef, standing by the serving counter, paused for a moment in his direction, to greet them; "Ciao Hamish, an´ this a´ here is la Donna Bella… si?"

"Ciao Chef, great food as usual, look, your too busy, see you tomorrow at Pino´s… okay?"

"Okay, Ciao!" as he threw a friendly wave, he began berating a young commis chef in Italian.

The night was dry and cold enough for frost to be on the railings of the gardens in Lansdowne Crescent. Lorna professed to feeling a little tipsy from all the wine she had drunk, and held on tight to Hamish, as they walked the half mile to Glasgow University Student Union.

As they crossed the bridge over the River Kelvin, she suddenly stopped, and kissed him, leaving him a little surprised, but extremely pleased with him-self.

He thought to himself, *She´s a lovely girl, her honest nature, her personality, her looks … just a nice, smart Highland lassie!*

The Union enjoyed a certain reputation for booking great bands at the weekends, and tonight was no different. They enjoyed the trad jazz band, the Clyde Valley Stompers, and stayed on the floor until last.

Walking home, they snuggled close, and took a small detour around Park Gardens for a spot of `winching´, courting on a bench in the park, until the cold forced them to get up and walk home.

The Malmaison closed on Sunday´s, therefore they both had a day off, and they arranged to meet at Pino´s Park Cafe, further up Woodlands Road after Lorna had been to Mass at St Mary´s Church.

When they arrived at Lorna´s close, her sister was anxiously looking out of the window for her.

"For God´s sake, Shona!" whispered Lorna, "I´m twenty years old, it´s only one o´clock!"

"I´m responsible for you!" her sister hissed back down on her.

They only had time for one passionate kiss, when they heard the flat door opening on the first floor.

"See you tomorrow!" and she ran upstairs.

Hamish leaned against the tiled wall of the close, and smiling, *Christ, she´s a darling.*

Chapter 32: The Vespa Trip

Early next morning, Sunday, Hamish went round to his lock-up garage, and hauled out his pride and joy, a midnight blue, Vespa 150 GS scooter. He washed and polished, until all the chrome on his protector bars, mirrors and lights were gleaming, filling it up with petrol. The weather was still freezing, but an almost cloudless sky encouraged his surprise for the day.

Back in the flat, he woke up Ian, and asked him if he borrow his fleece flying jacket. "Borrow what you like, came the sleepy reply, just bugger off, and let me sleep!"

Sticking the jacket and a spare crash helmet on the pannier rack, Hamish headed up to Pino´s Cafe. The usual crowd already there, included Sylvester, and a few others from the restaurant world who had Sunday as their free day. Even though it was just going on twelve, the jukebox was already belting out the Rolling Stones, "Nineteenth Nervous Breakdown," as the catering trade wound down the stress of their jobs.

Smoke and animated conversation filled the air, and strong Italian espressos´ consumed as fast as Pino could extract them from his Gaggia.

The door opened, and Lorna peered in through the smog, but Hamish had seen her first; he was on his feet, almost turning over the table, to a chorus of "Jesus Christ Hamish, what´s the panic!"

His heart missed a beat. She looked great, in blue jeans, tucked into black fur topped boots, and a short sheepskin jacket counteracting the cold. He was at her side, and a wide-eyed smile welcomed him, as she gave him a quick confident hug and kiss, before he began introducing his mates. My, did he feel good!

Over a coffee, eaten with some of Signora Bertocelli´s amaretto biscuits, he outlined his plans for the day.

"Sounds good," she said, "but how do we get up to Loch Lomond?"

"Come on and I'll show you," as he dragged her outside.

"Is this yours?" she asked, "it's beautiful! I knew you were a Mod!"

"Well I used to be, before I grew up! I've kept the wheels though, but hardly ever use it now. Today's perfect though, it'll be nice on the lochside today." He added, "I brought crash helmet and a fleece for you, but you look okay in that jacket."

"Well are we going then?" she asked, obviously keen to get on the Vespa.

"We'd better pay, and say cheerio to the crowd!"

They left to a chorus of whistles and cheers from the crowd.

There was almost no traffic, but he took it easy, until they were on the Great Western Boulevard, after Anniesland Cross. He began to open it up a little, the distinctive, throaty 150cc Vespa engine sound belaying the power of the scooter.

He felt her close, her arms around his body, her mouth breathing her femininity on the side of his neck, her legs tight on his thighs. Oh, it felt good, he was on a high, they weren't talking, but they were communicating.

At the Parkhall roundabout at Clydebank, he slowed a little, and asked if she was okay. The excited sparkle in her eyes, and flush on the cheeks, did not need the "Loving it!" she gave. After the roundabout, he took the Vespa up to eighty, and enjoyed the rush of speed, and the tightening of her grip around his body and thighs until they were entering Dumbarton. Slowing down to the limit of thirty miles per hour, they were passing the great warehouses filled with the Ballantyne's and Hiram Walker whisky. He stopped to show her the security patrol; a flock of geese at each warehouse, who squawked a warning, or would even attack unauthorised intruders.

By-passing the villages of Jamestown and Alexandria, they paused again for a moment, in Balloch, where he showed her the `Maid of the Loch´, a beautiful old paddle steamer, that took tourists a voyage up and around the islands on Loch Lomond. Five minutes further on, they once again admired the view from Duck Bay Marina, over the loch vistas, to the magnificent snow covered Ben Lomond.

Being from Barra, she was used to lovely surroundings, but she felt a lump in her throat, at the sheer beauty of the scene before them. Again, she gave him the special warmth of her embrace, and this time, not so warm kiss from her frozen face.

Twenty minutes further on, following the Loch shore, they were in the warmth of the public bar of the Inverbeg Inn. The bar was packed, but they managed to squeeze into a table beside the roaring log fire, where they quickly thawed out. A fiddler and accordionist were leading some of the crowd in traditional Scottish songs; The Bonnie Banks of Loch Lomond receiving a special rendition with various choruses being belted out by the crowd.

They thoroughly enjoyed the scotch broth, and the haggis and neeps lunch, washed down by a couple of pints of Tennant´s lager; soaking up the high spirited ambience, and each other, as they happily joined in the spirit of the bar.

Darkness falls early at this latitude, and by half past four, they were making their way back to Glasgow, Lorna locked around him in an embrace, which warmed them both to the core. They went back to Pino´s for a warming coffee and sat a bit holding hands, and just being close. The catering crowd weren´t in, only a few other young couples and they had a chance to talk, and plan their next date.

Hamish´s hours of split shifts and few nights free, made things complicated. Lorna was at Queens College until five o´clock, therefore there were complications to be resolved. They agreed he would meet her outside the college at five, and she could accompany him down to his work. Other than that, they could only squeeze the odd phone call, the odd coffee break, and Sundays, which became sacrosanct for them, usually going out on the Vespa, unless the weather was particularly foul.

Chapter 33: The Gala Dinner

They were `steady´ after that first weekend and obviously very much in love by the time the Salon Culinaire Gala Dinner came about six weeks later.

It was a formal affair, and Hamish decided that he should hire a formal dinner suit for the occasion, as he only had an informal kilt outfit.

Lorna´s mother had come down from Barra, to see her daughter receiving her gold medal.

Hamish came round to the apartment to escort Lorna and her mother to the ceremony. Her mother was cool and unfriendly to him, and when he attempted conversation in the taxi, she cut him off, talking to her daughter about life on Barra. By the time they took their place at the table, he was more than just a little apprehensive. Some of Lorna´s Queen´s College lecturers´ and friends helped to keep the table lively, and he soon forgot his nervousness. Throughout dinner, he had a good discussion with one of the lecturer´s about his plans to take the Clydebank College job.

Dinner over, the hush of expectancy fell across the room, as the chairman of the Scottish Cookery and Food Association rose, to give his speech, praising the standard and quality of the exhibits, particularly of the young, up and coming chefs.

He raised a laugh, when he described his own first 'live' competition. He was overzealous with the brandy as he flambéed a shrimp dish, resulting in the shrimps exploding out of the frying pan, and setting fire to the sponsors advertising over the Stand. Amidst the laughter he finished with, "No medal for the food, but I definitely deserved one for the entertainment value!"

Lorna was positively aglow with excitement; she looked lovely, beaming in the pride and pleasure of her success, when her name was announced to go up onto the podium to receive her gold medal.

Hamish was, by now, an old hand as these awards ceremonies, but still had a thrill, when his fellow professionals gave him a standing ovation for his medal d´honneur, the Salon´s top award.

The band struck up for the first waltz; Hamish asked Lorna to dance. She looked at her mother, as if for permission. Mrs McIntosh gave her a tight nod, and turned away to talk to her neighbour. Quizzically, Hamish looked at Lorna, and she gave a nervous shrug as they made their way onto the floor. Once in his arms, Hamish detected Lorna wasn´t her normal self. She was wearing an unaccustomed frown, a little tense. Mrs McIntosh was watching every move as they danced around the floor.

Lorna admitted that her mother was giving her a hard time, and was rather overbearing, and she wished to hell, she hadn´t come down to Glasgow. "The sooner she goes home the better," she said, just a little upset. She went on, "Hamish, it´s better that we don´t see each other until she goes home, it´s only until next weekend."

"I take it she doesn´t approve of me," he replied, dismayed at this turn of events.

"Don´t worry, I can´t talk now, but we´re okay, aren´t we?" she looked into his eyes with a kind of pleading expression.

Malevolent Karma

Anxiously he replied, "Lorna, you know I love you; I know you feel the same; maybe it will take time before your mother get's used to the idea, but she will, I promise."

Frowning she whispered, "We can't talk now, darling, let's enjoy the evening, just be patient this week, I'll 'phone you, okay?"

Unhappily, he had to agree, "'Phone me at work, before seven, if you can; remember I love you, and we'll have that Bistro some day!"

The restaurant was very busy all of that week, due to an international Pharmaceutical conference in the Hotel. A Royal Princess attended as guest of honour, and her demands for room service kept the chefs running day and night until she had left.

Much of the real business was conducted over the expense account lunches and dinners in the Malmaison, and Hamish had to be on his toes day and night for the week of the conference.

Lorna phoned several times but he had no time to speak to her, only promising to see her on Sunday. Thankfully, her mother was leaving for home on the Saturday. She asked him if they could meet somewhere else, as she had to talk to him, without his crowd being around, and no, he couldn't pick her up at her Shona's.

They agreed to meet in the Cafe Rossini on Great Western Road after Sunday Mass at St. Mary's.

Sunday came by; he was still tired and tense from his frenetic week at the Malmaison, and he was worried about Lorna; he was sure there was something wrong.

He was there before her, and when she entered the cafe, she looked strained and upset. Her normal young, fresh look had been replaced by lack-lustre greyness; dark shadows showed tiredness under her eyes. Looking around at the others in the cafe, she declined a coffee, and asked if he would mind they went for a walk in the Botanical Gardens.

His mind was racing, but he readily agreed, paying for his own coffee, and walking out behind her. "What's the matter, Lorna, tell me what's up?"

"Let's wait 'till we get to the park," she said, giving him a bleak smile.

It was a beautiful day, the sun was out, and the birds singing up in the branches of the Botanical Gardens trees. Families with excited children, and older couples were strolling and enjoying the park. They walked in silence, and found a free bench in a secluded, quiet corner. Still, she hadn't kissed him, and he felt a cold dread entering his stomach.

"Hamish, you know how much I love you," she began, "but we've got to stop seeing each other."

Incredulous, he looked at her, "Jesus Christ, Lorna, what are you talking about? I know your mother isn't keen on me, but she doesn't know me yet!"

"Please listen to me, Hamish; it's not you, it's your religion; you are Protestant, and from Lewis, which is staunch Protestant. I am Roman Catholic from Catholic Barra. My mother and father think you lot are pagans!"

Panicking, an angry edge entered his voice, "What are you talking about? I want to marry you, not your mother! I've had this shit from my lot about marrying Catholics, and funny enough, those who shout loudest never go near a bloody church!"

"Hamish, you don't really understand. My family are strong practicing Catholics, and my religion is important to me."

He was about to interrupt and say he understood, and that wasn't a problem, but she went on, "No, listen a minute; my mother and father have supported me, and paid for me to come to Queens College. I don't want to repay them in this way. If I marry a Protestant, I will be ex-communicated from the church. My father would disown me, that's certain, and probably my mother also." She looked at him pleading with her eyes, "Hamish, we've only known each other seven weeks, and it's been wonderful, truly wonderful. But I don't want to lose my family and my religion, can't you understand?"

Hamish was doing his best to restrain his emotions, and his anger, "Lorna, for fuck sake, this mixed marriage stuff belongs in the seventeenth century; don't let these people rule you in this manner! I love you and you love me! We're a great couple; one day we'll have babies, and our own restaurant; we've got a great future ahead of us! Please think for yourself, think of us, not your mother and father!"

At this point, she got up and began crying softly; "Please Hamish, try and understand, I can't do this to my family." She walked away, leaving him stunned, shaken to the core, and eyes beginning to water.

Sick to the stomach, he knew he had lost her. He was about to run after her, but knew that would only prolong the agony of their lost love. He sat for an eternity, shaking his head in disbelief. "Fucking bigots!" he exclaimed, causing a passerby to stare at him.

Into himself, he tried to find an adequate rationale, but kept coming back to the injustice of the so-called Christians, from both camps, determined to maintain their tribal numbers.

The bright sunny day only seemed to add torment to his misery as he sat and pondered, until finally, he got up from the bench, and began the long cheerless, lonely walk back along Great Western road, to his now depressingly lifeless flat. At the last minute, he made a detour around Woodlands Road, and looked up at her flat, but there was no sign of life and he continued on his way home

Norman MacRitchie Reeley

Chapter 34: The Escape

Hamish suffered a sleepless night, bitter thoughts racing around in his head. He made a decision to get on with his life. His first task was to telephone the principal at Clydebank College to confirm his acceptance of the Chef Lecturer post he had formally received. Instructed to respond in writing, he wrote it out and posted it on his way to work.

As soon as he arrived at the Central Hotel, he spoke to his Chef de Cuisine, and explained he had a personal problem. He asked for an immediate transfer up to the Gleneagles Hotel, the flagship of the group.

The Chef was sorry to lose him, but knew and respected Hamish well enough not to object, or block his transfer. He had another very promising young Chef de Partie whom he would promote to Sous Chef. The hotel would be quiet, after the mayhem of the conference last week, so he had his permission to leave if there was a vacancy at Gleneagles.

Hamish then telephoned the Chef de Cuisine at Gleneagles, with whom he´d worked for in the past summer season, and asked if he needed a Sous Chef. The answer was a definite yes; good Sous Chefs were in very short supply. There was an oversupply of `cowboys´ who´s limitations became apparent very quickly at Gleneagles.

A visit to the Personnel Department to obtain the transfer documentation, and he was officially free. He returned to the subterranean kitchens, and made his farewells to his companions. He made his escape, just as the first orders for lunch were called out in the kitchen.

Chapter 35: Island of Barra

The overnight crossing was reasonably smooth, unlike her previous experience, when the weather had turned bad and the ferry had tossed and heaved all the way down the Inner Minch. Lorna slept, and it was the announcement of entering Castlebay harbour that woke her. She had not advised her parent´s she was coming, and now began to experience the sinking feeling of apprehension in her stomach. She was surprised and dismayed to see her mother and father waiting on the dock, realizing that Shona must have phoned them!

It was a lovely clear, but fresh morning, but the welcome was frosty to say the least. Her father had a face of thunder, as did her mother whose first words were; "Lorna, what are you doing here? I´ve got to be at the school in five minutes, so you´d better explain yourself."

"Mother, let me get my feet on the ground first."

"No, you´re going straight back on that ferry," she shouted.

Lorna´s father came to the temporary rescue, "Shona, that´s not practical, people are watching, let´s get out of here."

Lorna´s three days on Barra turned out to be a prolonged nightmare of blazing family rows. She had naively thought that her pleadings and reasoning would soften her parent´s opposition to her going out with, and eventually marrying a Protestant. Her two brothers on Barra were also brought in, to persuade her to give Hamish up, one of them, Angus, even threatening to go down to Glasgow to `sort him out´!

Her mother took her to see the parish priest, a family friend. Father O´Brien had known her all of her life.

He reminded her, that he had baptised her, had given her first communion, and she was a daughter of the Church. After her confession, he berated her for her selfishness; she had scant regard for her parents´ beliefs and wishes; the Church was under constant attack from these heathen´s on the other islands. He further threatened her with excommunication from the Catholic faith; she would not be able to receive communion from that day; furthermore, any child of this union would not be received into the Roman Catholic faith.

It was a defeated; tear stained and depressed Lorna that boarded the Caledonian MacBrayne ferry, to take her back down the Minch to Oban.

Chapter 36: Aunt Theresa

This time the weather was foul; the ferry was being heaved around in the westerly gale, and rain was sweeping the decks and windows of the public areas. Lorna took to her bunk; the violent movement of the ship made her sea sick, and she had to take frequent trips to the toilet to throw up. As she passed away these miserable hours, she once again felt a rebelliousness rising from within. Then, she would suppress it; she owed her father and mother, everything, and the thought of ex-communication, terrified her.

As the ferry blew it´s horn in the Sound of Lorne, approaching Oban, her thoughts had returned once again to rebel mode; she thought of Aunt Theresa, and decided that she would speak to her.

Aunt Theresa ran a small bed and breakfast guesthouse, just below McCaig´s Folly. When she answered the door to Lorna´s knock, she couldn´t help but cry out, "Why hello Lorna! What a lovely surprise! Come in, come in; you´re soaked to the skin, did you walk all the way up the hill? Come away through to the kitchen lassie, and we´ll get you warmed up! Have you just come off the ferry? Or, are you going back to the Island now?" A flood of questions spilled out from Aunt Theresa, mostly going unanswered, except for a brief yes, or no, when Lorna was able to interrupt.

They settled down around the big bleached pine table laid out with tea and fresh scones, with homemade raspberry jam and butter. Lorna had not eaten anything on the ferry, and very little during the traumatic few days on Barra, but suddenly found her appetite in the warmth of the welcome in Aunt Theresa´s kitchen.

Theresa was born a year after Lorna´s mother, but appeared ten years younger. She was very good looking forty-seven year old, and, although she was in working mode, was fashionably dressed; she had an air of friendly confidence around her.

Lorna found herself pouring out her troubles to her aunt, breaking into sobbing heaves of tears, as she related her story.

Theresa listened, and, when she broke down, gently took her to her breast; "There Lassie, dinnae fret yourself; we´ll work something out. You stay the night with us; I´m going down to the cash and carry in Glasgow tomorrow, so I´ll take you down in the car. Donald is on the back shift, he won´t be in until half past ten so we´ll have time to talk after I serve dinner …come to think of it you can give me a hand! It´s not every day we have a gold medallist staying here! Your photograph was in the Stornaway Gazette!"

Theresa showed her niece up to a room with a lovely view overlooking Oban Bay, and the islands beyond. As she was closing the door, Theresa said, "Have a bath and a rest dear, and we´ll have that talk later."

Lorna felt much better, and after a long bath, she lay down on the bed, and fell fast asleep. It was after nine o´clock, and dark, when she awoke, feeling a wave of guilt sweeping over her as she rushed downstairs to help her aunt. Theresa shushed away her embarrassment. "The Residents have been served, Lassie, and the dishes are in the dishwasher, so do you fancy a glass of wine before Donald get´s home?" she asked.

Just the telephone rang and Theresa went out to the hall to answer it. She was back in a few minutes, "That was Donald, he won´t be home for hours; there´s been a bad accident down at Melfort, and he´s down there just now. We´ll have our dinner then, but first things first, a nice glass of Rioja, Cheers!"

The two women sat down and talked.
Theresa related her traumatic story when she and Donald first began courting, more than twenty years before, and when conflicting religious attitudes were even more deeply entrenched.

She was thrown out of the house by her father; she drily remarked, "It didn´t matter anyway, I was away from home, working in Oban as a chambermaid when we met, but it hurt me a lot at the time. The hatred was ridiculous; my thick, stupid brothers actually came down to Oban to give Donald a thrashing. Donald had just started in the police at the time, and as you know, the police were almost one hundred percent Masonic Protestants. The local sergeant simply arrested them, and put them back on the ferry." She laughed, "My brothers were in Oban for about three minutes!"

Frowning now she continued, "It caused so much trouble, they haven´t spoken to me since, not even at my father´s funeral. Imagine, twenty-seven years of hatred over Religion, of all things! The irony was, that I wasn´t all that religious after I had left home, but that experience finished it for me; I have never entered a church since then."

Bitterly, she continued, "It´s just so hypocritical; they have all forgotten the Christian ideal of love thy neighbour. Each side is so afraid of losing members, that they preach hate, instead of love! You mentioned Hamish´s family are from Lewis, I´ll bet they behave in the same way; one lot´s as bad as the other!" Perking up, she smiled, "Here, another glass, and let´s cheer up! How is your sister Shona doing in Glasgow? She married a McDonald from Mull did she not?"

Lorna explained she was staying with Shona, her circumstances, and her third pregnancy in four years.

Theresa exploded; "How in the hell can any woman be happy in these conditions! She´s alone down in Glasgow, her man away most of the time and nothing more than weans, nappies and four walls to keep her company. I´ll bet your mother´s happy though! She got up from the table; "Come on, let´s eat; I´m starving, and I´ll bet you are too!"

They had their dinner of a homemade steak pie, with lovely steaming mashed potato, talking all the while. Finally, it was after midnight, and just as the key was turning in the lock, and Donald shouted, "Home at last!"

Theresa said, "Look Lorna, I can´t tell you what to do, that´s your decision to make, and yours alone. Just remember it´s your life; it´s not anybody else´s, and certainly not that snivelling little hypocrite Father O´Brien!"

Next morning, after a hearty traditional Scottish breakfast, and leaving Mrs Mulgrew, Theresa´s daily help in charge, they set off in the black Mini Cooper estate, back out north, to swing around east at the Connal Bridge to take the A85 to Tyndrum, and then the A82, almost retracing the railway line, back to Glasgow. Theresa drove fast and expertly, the Mini sticking to the road on the many bends through the mountains and loch-sides, entertained by Jimmy Young on the radio, and taking in the scenery as it flashed past. The two women didn´t return to the topic of conversation the night before, now talking fashions and life in general. They were parked in front of the flat in Woodlands Road by twelve o´clock.

Theresa wasn't keen to come upstairs, citing her need to get on with her business, but Lorna pleaded with her, just to say hello to her sister. Upon entering, she instantly regretted her insistence. Shona was still in an old dressing gown, and looked ill. Perhaps out of embarrassment, her welcome was lacklustre, at best, throwing a vicious look at her sister. The flat was untidy, and the smell of stale nappies hung around the kitchen. The little two year old, Norman, had a runny nose, and was running around in a dirty vest, banging on his old saucepan.

Theresa was shocked at Shona's appearance, and the general state of the apartment. In her eyes, Shona had aged from being a carefree, if a little wild teenager, into a housewife with kids, with a grey defeatist aura around her, compounded by the conditions around. She didn't stay long, declining a cup of tea, as she had to do some shopping, and collect supplies at the cash and carry, before meeting a friend for a late lunch. Lorna accompanied her downstairs, apologising on the way, and excusing Shona's appearance was a result of her pregnancy.

Giving her an intense look, and hug, Theresa said, "Think hard Lorna, that's a prime example of marrying a good Catholic boy! No contraception, breed for the Church, and the man is off to the football, to leave you to bring up the bairns! Just remember though, whatever you decide, you'll always be welcome at Aunt Theresa's." A brief smile, another hug, and she was off, down Woodlands Road and heading for the Sauchiehall Street shops.

Lorna wearily climbed the stairs again, dreading the confrontation she knew she was going to have with her sister.

Entering the kitchen, she was greeted with; "What in the fuck do you think you're doing? You couldn't think of giving me a phone to warn me she was coming for a visit? Is this your way of humiliating me further?" Shona's face contorted with fury, as she spat out her venom.

"I'm sorry Shona, I thought you would be up and about", was all Lorna could respond. "I thought it would be a nice surprise for you."

"Some fucking surprise; if mammy finds out she's been here, you'll be in even more trouble."

"Shona, what's wrong with you anyway? Lorna asked. You've never acted like this before."

Abruptly, Shona burst into great sobbing tears; "I'm fucking pregnant again! Is that enough wrong for you? You have no idea of real life yet Lorna." She sobbed, "How am I to cope with another bairn? These two are a handful as it is, how am I going to look after another?"

Lorna took her sister in her arms, and comforted her as best as she could. When she had settled down, Lorna made a pot of tea, and the sisters began a long, overdue conversation, thankfully uninterrupted by the children.

Shona was deeply unhappy with her life, but there didn't seem to be a way out. Her husband, Norman, was away most of the time, and when he got back, he wanted to be with his mates. She felt neglected and trapped.

She had wanted to be a good Catholic, but realised she had been a fool not to take the Pill. Finally, she advised; "Lorna, don't follow my example, you're much more intelligent than me; I'm not going to say marry your Proddy, but you make up your own mind about it. Listen to mammy, but don't just obey her for obedience sake."

Lorna replied, "Listen to me Shona, your obviously tired, and feeling really low. You've always been the lively one of the family; I'll give you a hand to get things cleared up, and when the baby wakes up, we'll go for a walk up the park. I've got to register I'm back at the college anyway, but that won't take a minute." In an effort to cheer her sister up, she continued; "It's a lovely day out, wee Norman will love the swings, and we'll buy an ice cream from Pino's."

In reality, Lorna had made up her mind before going up to Barra, but had wanted the approval of her parent's and the Church. She had needed to talk to her Aunt Theresa as a kind of support system for her plans, and had been grateful to learn firsthand, that defying the Church and family wasn't the end of the world. Without any doubt, there was going to be anger, tears and confrontations, but she loved Hamish, and she was going to get him back somehow

That same evening, at six o'clock, she was at the staff entrance of the Central Hotel, and asked to see Hamish. Old Eric, the timekeeper, shocked her, when he said, "I'm sorry hen, Hamish disnae work here now, he's transferred up to Gleneagles Hotel."

She stared at him in disbelief, before he suggested that she could talk to someone in kitchen, who could maybe help her. She was spared the trip down to the kitchens, when one of Hamish's friends, Henri, just came off his shift.

Spotting her, he asked what she was doing there.

She briefly explained what had happened, and she was desperate to talk to Hamish again.

Henri suggested they go round to the bar for a drink. In the bar, he explained the situation. Hamish had been so upset he needed to get away. He had talked to him on the phone last night, and he still sounded unhappy and depressed. Henri added that he was going up to see Hamish on Saturday, his day off, and suggested that he would talk to him about her.

"Oh please, Henri, can I not just come with you? Doubtfully she asked, "Would he want to see me Henri? I was stupid; I listened too much to my mother. I love him.

"I would bet on it, Lorna, but don't confuse him; only come up if you want to get back with him, please. He was very badly hurt when you stopped seeing him last week." Looking at her sympathetically, he agreed, "Okay, I hope I'm doing the right thing here; if you sure you're serious, I'll pick you up at Charing Cross at eight; I'll be in a yellow Triumph Herald."

Chapter 37: Gleneagles Hotel, Perthshire.

Hamish was free in his room, about to go for a shower, having just finished supervising the Breakfast and Room Service shift, when Henri called in. They greeted each other effusively, and Henri invited him down to see his new car, parked outside the staff quarters.

Lorna was sitting in the passenger seat, and when Hamish saw her, his heart missed a beat; ... instantly he knew she was back!

Lorna got out of the car, and could only get out "I´m sorry, Hamish ..." They flung themselves into each other´s arms, clutching and kissing, enfolded in emotion.

For a few minutes, Henri was content to look on in amusement, until he said; "Any chance of a cup of tea for the chauffeur?

They finally split apart, Lorna eyes wet with happiness and relief, and Hamish feeling a foot taller, and with a wide smile on his face, the first for in a week.

They all piled into the Triumph, and went down to Auchterarder Tea Room. In the back seat, Lorna related her journey up to Barra, and its consequences. She had been a fool to think her parent´s would change their attitude. She told him of Aunt Theresa and Donald her Protestant husband, and the treatment she had received when she married him. Finally, she told him how much she loved him. No one was going to come between them, ever again.

After their delicious tea, accompanied by freshly baked scones and cakes, they were all in a happy carefree mood.

Hamish exchanged shifts with another Sous Chef, and was not on duty until six o´clock. They decided to go for a run around, but first, at Henri´s insistence they went back to the hotel to find another girl to make up a foursome.

Luck was with them, and a pretty young Italian student, working in the Housekeeping Department, was only too delighted to see some of the countryside, as well as partnering the handsome Frenchman!

It was a wonderful day out, and with regret, they headed back to Gleneagles in time for Hamish to begin his work. After some discussion and a phone call to the Central Hotel to readjust Henri´s next day off. It was proposed and quickly agreed, the visitors from Glasgow would stay overnight, to take in the local barn dance. Lorna would stay in Ana´s room, and Henri with Hamish. Fortunately, the hotel still wasn´t fully staffed, and both Hamish and Ana had rooms to themselves in the staff annexe.

Lorna and Ana had hit off. They were the same age, and both were students; Ana had finished her examinations at the University of Perugia. She was working at Gleneagles to improve her already excellent English, before taking a job in her father´s business.

They whiled away the hours waiting on Hamish to finish work, resting and chatting. They took turns in putting their hair in heated rollers, putting on their makeup. At last, it was time to get ready for the dance. Ana lent Lorna, a pretty, shocking pink blouse, and dark blue skirt to wear, with matching blue pumps. Ana looked gorgeous in a sensual red dress, which accented her full figure. Her dark Italian looks was going to turn a few heads.

The boys were suitably impressed; they also had done their best to dress up for the occasion.

On the way to the barn dance, they passed around a half flask of vodka, which had the girls gasping, but happily warmed up. It was a typical Scottish country dance band, and they had a wonderful time, made all the funnier at Henri and Ana´s attempts at the more intricate dances. They visited the bar more than a few times, and it was a very merry quartet that drove slowly back to the hotel at two in the morning.

Approaching the hotel, they could make out the night staff moving around, but not paying attention to the outside. They stopped talking as they crept around to the staff annexe.
Henri looked at Ana, and a nod given. Hamish looked at Lorna, and received a smile in return; the couples split, and crept into the respective Women Only, and Men Only quarters.

He had some experience, she was a virgin but willing in his lovemaking. She gasped and endured the pain of penetration, but he was considerate and gentle; soon the passion and pleasure overtook the discomfort, and she loved him at this moment, more than anything else in her life. He was careful to withdraw as they reached their climax, but still a little shocked by the warm spurt on her thigh but clung to him in his spasms.

They fell asleep in a crushing embrace. At five thirty in the morning, the lovers were wakened-up by a gentle knocking on the door.
 Henri poked his head around the door; "Time to change places, before the dragon does her rounds in the female quarters."
He waited outside, and escorted Lorna to the women´s annexe, and with a wink, went back to Hamish´s room.
 Ana was awake and getting ready to start work at six o´clock. "I´m dead," Lorna admitted, "you must be shattered also."
 Ana replied, "I am, but sometimes it´s worth it! I´ll get some breakfast for you at ten o´clock, so don´t wake up."

Sunday was the busiest day of the week in the Gleneagles kitchen´s. As well as the residents, the hotel was famous for its Sunday lunch, and the well-to-do would travel from Edinburgh and Glasgow to be seen dining there, and enjoy the excellent food at the same time.

Hamish was at his post at nine, and did not finish the service until four o´clock. He was due back on duty at six-o´clock therefore they only had a brief two hours together. He had prepared a picnic, and they spent talking about their future together in a quiet corner of the hotel grounds.

They concluded that the best way forward, was for Lorna to take her finals, and then take a job at Gleneagles. He could fix that, except it would not be in the kitchen. Chef de Cuisine Rouget did not tolerate women in the kitchen! When the season was finished, he was going to work as a lecturer at Clydebank College, and she could take up her position in Fraser´s as Trainee Manager.

Hamish´s father was a member of the Orange Order and a Freemason, and his family would be as opposed to a mixed marriage as Lorna´s, but with a bit of luck, both sets of parents would come round in time. If not, it would be too bad; they were going to get married!

They held each tight, and the parting was warm and comfortable; both were confident in their love for each other, and now was the time to begin the practicalities of living their lives as a couple.

Chapter 38: Annie Grigor

After their summer at Gleneagles Hotel, where inhibitions had disappeared like the mists in the glen, they rented a flat above a small bakery and tearoom in Ruthven Lane, in the West End of Glasgow.

Hamish and Lorna had been lucky in finding such a good flat in the area. Aunt Theresa, had a friend who lived in the top floor, and she had given Mrs Grigor the references required of the young couple.

Mrs Grigor was by no means a prude, but she knew Hamish and Lorna were not married, but she had also been impressed, by the fact that they had been working at Gleneagles Hotel. She´d had an afternoon tea there once.

Annie Grigor had been widowed during the Korean War. She was a small, thin, ferrety looking woman; her hair and skin almost the same colour of grey, due to the lack of sunlight in her life. However, her eyes shone with the energy and enthusiasm of a liberated woman, proud of her `wee business´, as she put it.

Annie was in her shop from six in the morning, until about seven at night with only Sunday as a day off. She said it was her life, and both Hamish and Lorna believed it! She had no children of her own so she took to the young couple, and fussed over Lorna as if she was her own daughter.

Mrs Grigor employed a Polish ex-prisoner of war as baker. Vilius had been conscripted into the German Army when the German´s over-ran Poland at the start of World War 2. Interned in a POW Camp in Ayrshire, he had stayed on after the war.

Tall, with a shock of white hair, and, despite his profession, thin as a rake, Vilius retained a thick Polish accent and rarely talked to anyone. He was always courteous, but appeared to be timid, and no one had heard him talking about his past, or wartime experiences. He lived in the converted flour loft above the bake-house.

Vilius, (Annie called him Willie), and his apprentice, produced the breads and baked goods, while she made the finer cakes and gateaux which proudly filled her display cabinets. She employed students from the nearby Glasgow University, to serve in the tearoom, and work the busy shifts at the weekends.

Malevolent Karma

Hamish and Lorna quickly redecorated the two bedrooms, kitchen and bathroom flat all in white, and using brightly painted old furniture, bought from Paddy's Market and Barrowland, to contrast. They were deliriously happy, in their own home, and the excommunication from their families had ceased to be a source of despondency.

The advantage of living above a bakery, is, that you can have fresh bread or rolls, first thing in the morning. The disadvantage is, of course, the delicious smell of baking is always there to torment the wicked.

Hamish was enjoying his job at the college; it was far less pressure than his Sous Chef roles at Gleneagles and the Malmaison, and he was revelling in imparting his knowledge on his students.

Money was tight however; his salary had been much reduced, and he had to supplement his income by 'jobbing' for a catering company that specialised in weddings. After a while, he was working many more hours than when he worked in the hotels, but in recompense was able to save money towards their own ambition, a restaurant of their own.

Lorna's job as a Trainee Assistant Manager in Fraser's Department Store had proved to be huge disappointment to her. At Gleneagles, she had worked as a junior in the reception, and had gained confidence and experience in meeting important VIP's and celebrities, and resolving many of their petty complaints and problems. As Trainee Assistant Manager at House of Fraser's, she found herself working as a glorified office girl, fetching the tea, filing documents, and taking messages around the shop. She was bored and unhappy, but was sticking it out as they needed the money, now that she was expecting a baby!

They had a quiet, Register Office wedding, witnessed only by his Best Man Henri, and Ana, his Italian girlfriend, who was acting as her Best Maid. Ana had become Lorna's closest friend over the past year. The only family members present from both sides were Lorna's Aunt Theresa, her husband Donald, and Lorna's sister Shona. The rest, including both sets of parents, had refused to attend on opposing religious grounds, which, despite the efforts of the happy newlyweds and their friends, still managed to put a small shadow over the proceedings.

Lorna and Hamish both had accepted long ago that this would be the case. Their respective families were too deeply entrenched in their bigotry, to accept a `mixed´ marriage.

The Reception was in the Ruthven Court Tearoom. It was a wild, lovely, happy night, almost all their friends being able to attend. They spent their wedding night upstairs, in their own bed, but only after they had expelled thirty or so drunken happy friends from the flat, and then spending twenty minutes trying to clear the confetti out of their bed.

Next day, they were off in Henri´s Triumph Herald to the Lake District for three days of honeymoon bliss.

Lorna´s baby-bump soon became too pronounced to hide, and she felt she had to leave her job at Fraser´s. This was going to be a further blow to their finances, but Annie Grigor stepped in, and insisted that she came and worked for her.

It was a wise move; Lorna took much of the pressure from her, and her professionalism paid off. She suggested increasing the range of products, to include soups and hot snacks, resulting in a considerable increased lunchtime trade from Byres Road shoppers.

Baby Alistair MacLeod came into the world three weeks earlier than expected.

Lorna had been cleaning down the shelves of the big display cabinet in the shop, her belly perched over the rim, as she reached into a corner, when she had a spasm, which forced her to sit down on a stool.

"Are you alright Lorna?" Mrs Grigor asked.

"Just a spasm, I think," she replied weakly, just as her waters broke.

Alistair entered the world of catering when he was one week old. His pram was placed in a recess, between the bake-house and the tearoom. By the time his fourth birthday came around, he would be pressing out scones and empire biscuits, and spreading the icing on them after they were baked.

Annie Grigor had come to rely on Lorna, to more or less run the business. She had not been feeling too well for some time. Her normal gray pallor had not changed, but her eyes had lost the vitality, and she tired easily; she was frequently struggling for breath after busy sessions in the shop.

Lorna was insisting she saw a doctor, but she replied, "I haven´t seen a quack for thirty odd years, and I´m not bothering one now…it´s only old age creeping up on me."

A few weeks later, however, she caused a scare in the tea room, when she had a faint, falling right across a table of matrons enjoying their afternoon tea. Amidst the chaos of hysterical pensioners, Lorna called an ambulance from the nearby Western Infirmary. Willie had come running through from the bake-house, summoned by the clamour, and immediately cleared everyone from the tearoom.

Annie had a gash on her eye from her fall, but was beginning to come round, as Willie was loosening her blouse and overall, to give her air.

"What are you doing… you dope," she said, "Stop that! I´m alright!"

The big man replied tenderly, "You no´ alright Annie, you fall down. You go to hospital now."

Before she could object further, the ambulance crew arrived, and after checking her vital signs, and administering first aid on her cut eye, put her on the stretcher and into the ambulance. Willie insisted in accompanying her, whilst Lorna remained behind to close up the tearoom for the day.

Chapter 39: Annie's proposition

Annie was diagnosed with a faulty heart valve, which could be life threatening, meaning that she would have to take it easier in her lifestyle from now on. She relented to having a week off, and then returned to work much to Lorna's objections. Later that same night, after Alistair had been put to bed, she came up to their flat, and asked to speak to them.

Hamish and Lorna had talked about the situation and were expecting the worst; they just knew that Annie was going to sell up! They were hoping she would consider selling them the flat. They liked the West End, and the apartment was perfect for them. Both of them felt sure that the Byres Road area was becoming a fashionable area; perfect for their plans for a small bistro someday.

Nervously, Hamish poured out a small Bristol Cream Sherry that he knew Annie enjoyed and a glass of wine for Lorna and himself, whilst maintaining small talk about his students' disasters of the day.

Annie brusquely interrupted him, "I have something to say to you Hamish, so stop prattling on, and listen to me." She went on; "I'm sure that you are aware, that Willie and I have more than a boss and worker relationship."

Lorna looked at Hamish, and he returned the surprise, and said, "To be honest Annie, we know you two are very close; you've been working together for more than twenty years, but anything else, no."

"Well, yes, we have been very discreet; we had our reasons; but to get to the point, Willie and I want to retire down to Troon."

Lorna interrupted, a little anxiously, "What about the business then Annie?"

"That's why I'm up her talking to you, Lorna, I want to sell the business. What I want to know is, are you two interested in taking it on?"

Hamish replied, "We'd love to Annie, but we don't have that kind of money just now; we were hoping that we might buy the flat, but we can't afford the business as well."

"Jesus Hamish, don't you think I know that? You give me what you can now, and pay the rest to me over time, how about that?"

Lorna interposed between them; "Annie, that's really very generous of you, and we'd love to buy it all, but don't you need the money up-front to buy your house in Troon?"

"I've already got my bungalow bought and paid for Lorna; why in the hell do you think I've worked so hard all my life?" She finished her sherry, handing the glass to Hamish to refill and continued, "Willie and I have been planning this for years, and now is the time to do it. I'm tired, he's nearly sixty five, and we have enough to live on, so finally, are you interested?"

They looked at each other, smiled and yelled, "Yes, we would love it!" Lorna leapt up, and hugged Annie, laughing, "Annie, you're just the loveliest person I've ever met!"

Hamish, looked on, his eyes glazing as he was working on his plans for the bistro.

Chapter 40: 1975 The MacLeods

The Ruthven Court Tearoom and Bistro was booming. Hamish and Lorna had worked their socks off, putting in the long hours and hard graft to make it one of the most profitable and successful businesses in the West End.

The family practically lived in the teashop.
Alistair, when he came home from school, had his milk and his shortbread biscuit in a corner table, and do whatever

homework he had to do. More often than not, some of his pals would call round for him to go out and play. They were always hungry, looking at the cake displays and would be rewarded with a biscuit or cake before they ran out the door, with a "Be careful, cross at the Green Man and keep away from the river, and be back by six!" ringing in their ears.

The gang would tear about Kelvingrove Park on their chopper bikes, frightening the old ladies walking their little Poodles and Scotch Terriers, and of course at times returning home in tears with bleeding elbows and knees when the fun turned into drama. Often, when it was raining, the boys would be found in the Kelvingrove Art Gallery, peering at the scale models of the great ships that had been built in the Clyde shipyards, boasting that their dad´s had built this one, or that one.

Kirsty, their little princess of a daughter, had been born five years earlier, had made her first scones, and was about to begin school. She would be entering the first year of school just as her big brother Alistair would be in changing to a senior school.

Lorna had rejected the idea of a Roman Catholic education for the children although Hamish had said he wasn´t bothered as long as the school was a good one. She was however determined they would go to a private school when they changed into the senior school, and had been saving hard to send Alistair to Glasgow Academy.

The only black cloud in their life came when their friend and benefactor, Annie Grigor succumbed to her heart condition. Hamish and Lorna had kept up close contact with Annie and Willie in Troon, often on Sundays driving down for the day with the children to her house on the beach.

Sadly, they were witnessing a steady deterioration in her health, but she completely rejected the idea of a heart by-pass operation.

"When it´s my time to go, I´ll go," she would breathlessly rasp at them when it was suggested. Just promise me one thing, when I'm gone, keep an eye on Willie for me, his eyesight is beginning to fail, and he hasn't anyone to look after him."

When she eventually yielded to her condition, they discovered that even this black cloud had a silver lining. They found out that she had cancelled their remaining debt in her will; effectively, they were inheriting the Ruthven Tearoom and Bistro. They were left reflecting upon the memory of a remarkable and generous woman who had continued to be their benefactor, even in death.

Hamish had kept on working at the college, and was now a Senior Lecturer, but he now knew there would be no more promotion for him in the Socialist world that reigned in the education system. In socialist eyes, he was a businessman; a capitalist feeding on the blood of the oppressed workers. Unemployment was rising. Inflation had hit twenty-four percent, and the greedy capitalists were getting the blame.

Hamish had begun to despise his job; the students were great but he was having frequent quarrels with his superiors in the college. Budget cuts meant there wasn't enough money to buy food for student practice. Hamish argued vehemently that the students were being let down at a critical point in their careers. The college hierarchy thought Hamish was just a troublemaker, and should stick to following orders. The Head of Department began a campaign to discredit him. His students work was put under the microscope, but this was abandoned after seven of them gained gold medals in the Junior Salon Culinaire that year.

Then it was discovered that Hamish was employing some of his students to work at night in the bistro! He was hauled in front of a disciplinary committee alleging child labour abuse among other things.

Hamish pointed out they were all over seventeen years of age, all had permission from their parent's to work; it gave them valuable experience and they were paid the same rate as the other employees.

He still received a Censure as some other lecturers complained that some students were coming to class tired in the morning. The stress of the constant bickering was getting him down and even in the staffroom, others were eyeing up his desk.

It was customary that on the busy Saturday nights, Lorna brought in a babysitter and came down stairs to help-out in the bistro. It wasn´t hard physical work, but after they had served several hundred lunches and teas during the day, even greeting the customers and preparing the Bills was tiring enough!
It was one in the morning, the staff had left for the night, and it was just the two of them having a drink at a corner table. She had her shoes off, feet stretched out over another chair, and nursing her favourite Benedict cocktail, whilst Hamish was on his second Highland Park Malt. They had discussed the week´s business, when suddenly Lorna brought up the subject of the future.

"What future," he said, just a little tiredly.

"Well, we can´t go on like this forever," she said, "I´m not stupid, I know you´re absolutely sick of the college, and we´re working too hard. We hardly ever have time to ourselves; sex is a chore for Sunday mornings only, so I think it´s time to think of a change."

Brightening up he responded, "That´s true enough, but you love your tearoom, Lorna, and it brings in good money; we´ve done really well here. Anyhow, what would your little old ladies do if you were not here to pour their tea for them? What are you thinking about?"

She sat up, concentrating now; "Well, I´ve been thinking a lot about this; I think we should move back out to the country, or the coast, not too far from Glasgow. I would love to wake up and see some sheep, or the sea; something other than buses going up and down Byre´s Road."

He lit up a broad smile, "I´ve been thinking the same for ages!"

"Why didn´t you say something then," she asked.

"Like I said, I thought that you loved the tearoom, and the time was never right to talk about it."

"God Almighty!" she exclaimed, "do you think the limit to my ambitions and ability is serving refined Kelvinside ladies tea and cakes? Has it never crossed your mind that I might want a change, or is these important thoughts only for the men-folk?"

Meekly he replied, "Of course not, I just didn´t think about it in that way."

"Get me another drink you plonker," she smiled, holding out her empty glass, and letting him off the hook.

As he was preparing the Benedict, he ruminated aloud. "Listen, that BBC crowd; a lot of them live in the Helensburgh, Loch Lomond vicinity, if we found a place around that area, we would have a following right away, and it´s not too far away from the city." Passing her drink, and topping up his Highland Park, he continued, "and I could keep on at the college for a while longer until we got established. God it would be worth it to give these bastards the finger when I leave for good!"

Lorna, flushed with her third Benedict cocktail exclaimed, "And my old ladies could drive out on a Sunday for lunch! It would be better for the kids also."

"Right that settles tomorrow then," he exclaimed, "we´ll have a look around the area; it will give us some ideas."

She fixed him with a slightly inebriated coquettish smile; "Come on you big teuchter, we haven´t done it on the carpet for years!"

Chapter 41: Chasing a Dream

They had checked out a dozen small hotels for sale in the area; from Cardross, on the Clyde Estuary, all the way to Lochgilphead on Loch Fyne, which was much further north than they really wanted.

Hamish was a stickler for Conrad Hilton´s advice of location, location, location, being the dominant factor in buying a hotel. The hotel´s that were on the market that measured up to their specifications were either in very poor condition, requiring extensive renovations, or the one or two good properties priced way beyond their modest budget.

A month later, the first signs of discouragement were appearing. They had just inspected and discounted an old church conversion near to Arrochar, they had one more to check out, a `just on the market´ hotel in Cove, which look lovely on the brochure and worth looking at, but Hamish thought that it was too far out of the way from civilization.

They drove down the A814 road towards Garelochhead. The narrow road followed the side of Loch Long and brought back pleasant memories of their courtship, on the back of Hamish´s Vespa GS.

Passing the Finnart Oil Terminal, they decided to stop at the old Green Kettle Tearoom and indulge in Mary MacGregor´s delicious home baking. This used to be a favourite stop on their three lochs tours over ten years ago, but never had the time to return since then.

Within a couple of minutes they were passing under the West Highland Line railway bridge, and the unique and distinct old Green Kettle sign was there, on the left, where it had hung for forty years or more, swaying in the wind.

There was a near gale blowing as they stepped out of their old Volvo. Entering the little shop, they laughed as the heavy door almost flew away when they opened it, the little shop bell tinkling merrily.

"This place is not called Whistlefield for nothing," Hamish commented.

They stood in the shop reminiscing a little at the pink painted walls and shelving, stacked with tins of beans, sausages, corned beef, coffee, tea and the multitude of requisites that fishermen camping at the weekends down in Portincaple would need to buy.

A little kitten suddenly popped his head out of a box of crisps, just as Mary MacGregor pushed through the curtain from her kitchen; another cat, probably the mother, following behind her. A waft of fresh baking escaped through the curtain, whetting the appetite of the young couple.

"Hello, can I help you?" smiling and standing in her white overall. She had changed little in ten years; grey hair tied up in a bun, her eyes still sparkled with humour, but now hidden a behind enormous pink glasses.

"Can we have tea?" asked Lorna, as Hamish continued with his inspection of the little pink shop.

"Of course you can….and you´ll have some scones also?"

Lorna asked, "Do you still do the treacle ones; we used to come here years ago"

"I remember you," Mary replied, smiling warmly, "you come from Barra, or was it Uist? You used to come here on your young man´s scooter I think, because you were always wet or frozen stiff. Didn´t you open a tearoom in Glasgow?" she asked.

"Yes, we did, but how did you know that?"

Mary explained, "It´s a small world dear, Glasgow is not that far away and we old bizzy-bodies from the Islands love to gossip. Your aunt sometimes comes in on her way back to Oban….she´s very proud of both of you."

Hamish had stopped his inventory of the shop, and intervened, "When you two Highland ladies have finished, can I get my tea?"

Mary put her hand on Lorna´s arm and remarked, "We´d better feed the young man, and then we can have a chin wag. Go on through, and I´ll bring the tea."

They pushed open the door into the tea room, to be met by the ubiquitous pink decoration, which extended from a brown wainscoting to include the ceiling, only broken up in parts by a selection of flower prints and an oval mirror over the fireplace.

Nothing had changed here in the thirty years that Mary, and her rotund and jovial husband Jimmy had owned the place; but such was the fame of her delicious home baking, people forgave the worn oilcloth table covers, the cracked cups and saucers, and the rickety unmatched chairs that they had to balance on. On each table sat a tarnished silver cake-stand, with its matching milk jug and sugar bowl. Pink tri-angled serviettes, a re-cycled sauce bottle housing a tired looking plastic pink carnation provided the table decoration.

"It´s quaint, isn´t it," would be the comments of the refined ladies from Bearsden or Helensburgh, who normally would have had a fainting turn if similar conditions reigned in the tearooms of their own town.

The only other customers were two such ladies, who were sitting directly in front of the coal fire burning in the grate.

As Lorna and Hamish sat down by the window, the women prepared to leave. One of them laughed and looked over, "Don´t think we´re leaving because you´ve just come in, we´ve sat here an hour already!" As they smiled a reply, she added, "Do have a meringue, they are absolutely scrumptious!"

Hamish noticed one had a walking stick, and he got up to open the door.

"Oh don´t fuss, young man, I can manage quite well yet; enjoy your meringues!"

Lorna dug into her bag and fished out the details of their next inspection stop, the Knockderry Hotel in Cove, out and along the Rosneath peninsula.

It was a fine looking red sandstone baronial manor building, within its own grounds, and with extensive sea views looking over the Clyde estuary. As they were checking the details, Hamish remarked again about the location being too far out from Helensburgh and Rhu, which in his mind, provide the bread and butter of the business. The asking price was also beyond their budget, so they would be depending on a substantial reduction, but they agreed it might be worth having a look as they were in the area in any case.

The door to the kitchen swung open, and Mary MacGregor appeared with the pots of tea and hot water, setting them down on the table. She lifted the empty cake-stand away, and went back into the kitchen, returning with another one, piled high with homemade scones, pastries and the fresh cream filled meringues that did indeed look scrumptious.

Noticing the Estate Agent's folder on the table, she enquired nosily, "Are you thinking of buying the Knockderry then?"

Hamish glancing up replied, "Oh we're only looking around to see what's on the market."

"Just be careful with that place," she advised, no one's ever made a go of it, and I'm told it's full of dry rot." She added, "Have your tea, and if half of that stand is not eaten, I'll be very angry!"

Lorna protested, "Mary, it's all delicious, but it's impossible to eat all of that."

"Well, do your best then," she sniffed and went back to her kitchen.

Hamish, still glancing through the folder observed, "You know, something in this area would be ideal, it's in the country, the sea is just down there, and it's not too far from the crowd. Maybe we should ask old Mary, if she knows of something nearby?"

Just then, Mary came back through, with a Helensburgh Advertiser in her hand. "Look at this," she pointed to an advert, "if I was you, I'd have a look at this place; you could easily convert it to a restaurant and bed and breakfast."

It was an advertisement from the Ministry of Defence for the sale of ex-officer's accommodation located at Whistlefield, Garelochhead. The accompanying photograph, showed a grey painted, Swiss Lodge type of building, in what seemed to be a considerably run down condition.

Hamish pulled a face at Lorna, which didn't go unnoticed from Mary.

"Listen, you two, this place isn't as bad as it looks, and they've been trying to sell it off for years; you could get it really cheap, and do it up."

Hamish laughed just a little sarcastically, "It would have to be cheap, because it looks as if it's going to fall down!"

Lorna interrupted, "Go on Mary, tell us about it, where is it, this is Whistlefield, is it not."

Mary explained the history: "It used to be a millionaires holiday home before the First World War, but somehow the Ministry of Defence took it over during the War, and converted it into an officers billet. It lay empty for years. Then it got used as offices when they started building the extension to Faslane for the Polaris submarines, but it's been empty again for at least seven or eight years."

"But where is it?" Lorna asked again.

Pointing out of the window, and up the hill in the direction of Garelochhead, she explained, "It's just up the top of the road; before you come to the corrugated iron house, you will see a barred gate with a gravel road on the right. You go down that road, over the railway and it's just over the hill. The views are lovely, but I expect that it's become very overgrown by now." She insisted, "Listen to me, this is just right for you two; finish your tea, and go and have a look. I know the caretaker, he works for the MOD, and he'll come up and show you inside if you want."

Hamish interrupted, "I think we'd better have a look at it first before bothering anyone."

Lorna with a sparkle of interest in her eyes, asked; "Can we get over the gate, or will the caretaker have to let us in?"

"You can climb the gate easily; just ignore the KEEP OUT sign; there's no dogs or anything, and walk the rest of the way; it's only about two hundred yards."

Noticing they had stopped eating, and their cups were empty, Mary shooed them out of the door, both struggling to put on their jackets.

Trudging up the hill against the wind they debated the wisdom of bothering to look, but Lorna insisted that Mary would know if they hadn't looked at it; she would be sure to question them when they returned, "So just let's get on with it."

They found the road and gate within minutes, and climbed over, a little fearful of the sign to KEEP OUT! After all, this was a military training area, with a live firing range on the hills across from where they were standing! Following the track, now overgrown with grass, they breasted the hill, and just below them were the buildings.

They main building was indeed Swiss style, and much larger than they had thought. There were two smaller Nissen type huts behind a hedge to one side; all painted in the same camouflage grey.

Hamish now had a surge of excitement; the view over the two sea lochs was magnificent. Sure enough, the trees, ferns and brambles were obliterating the outlook now, but without doubt, *this had possibilities.*

They walked down and picked their way around, not saying anything, until Lorna said in a hushed tone, "Hamish, I think this might be it!"

Hamish replied cautiously, but with a hint of excitement in his voice, "Well the situation is fabulous, I'm sure we could do a good conversion here, but it very much depends on the price; this will take serious money to upgrade."

Just then, they were startled by a shout, "What are you doing here!" An older man, carrying a stout walking stick, came down the hill towards them. As he came nearer, he was smiling broadly, "That gave you a start, didn´t it!" he laughed.

Hamish began to explain, but the man interrupted, holding out his hand, "I´m Douglas Mackenzie, I know who you are, Mary phoned me to come over. I look after this place…just to keep it watertight you know, not to do the garden," sweeping his hand around the area. "I´ve brought the keys, but it´ll have to be a quick look, I´m due in Helensburgh at five."

Aside from the paint, grey on the outside, and a pale green inside, the building was in very good condition. Douglas explained the history as they walked through, peering in all the rooms. It had been built in the late eighteen nineties for a Glasgow shipping magnate, who had married a Swiss countess.

The hardwoods used were of the finest marine quality, and he assured them, there was not a trace of rot in the entire building. This was the third time that the MOD had advertised to sell, but it seemed to be too big for a home, and the fact that it was a wooden construction also put people off.

Hamish and Lorna could hardly suppress their excitement, as they went back up the hill with Douglas.

As he was locking the gate behind them, Hamish asked him "Mr Mackenzie, how much are they looking for this place?"

"Well, to be honest son, I don´t really know, but they are keen to get rid of it. I know that it´s costing them more in maintenance than what it´s worth. Listen, I´m in the office tomorrow, I´ll ask the Quantity Surveyor what he thinks it´s worth, but it has to go through the Official Solicitors Office, you know that, don´t you?"

"Of course, I didn't think I could slip you a pound or two," Hamish joked, nervous now at the idea.

"No chance of that son," he smiled, "right then, I'm away; tell Mary I'll see her tonight. Leave a phone number with her where I can contact you." He shook both of their hands, and drove away towards Garelochhead.

They talked animatedly going back down to the Green Kettle. Lorna was beside herself with excitement, and Hamish had a brainwave.

The college had a building department, and Hamish had very good relationships with the Head of Department, and most of the lecturers. For four years, he had hosted their end of term dinners at the bistro at knock down prices. They were a great bunch of guys' and provided the Union back up for Hamish's many disputes with the authorities!

Excitedly he explained, "Lorna, I can get the builders in the college to prepare the plans, and give us a quote for the building work; they are always building houses and extensions at the weekends and holidays."

Entering the Green Kettle tearoom, Mary saw by their faces that they were more than interested. "Well what did I tell you," she smiled at their enthusiasm. "Mind you, there's a lot of work to be done, but you'll find that Douglas will help as much as he can. It's a shame the place has been lying empty all those years."

In the event, their offer to buy was the only one presented. They had the cash in the bank and therefore there was no obstacle in waiting for a mortgage.

It took them a full year to get their project to fruition. The guys' in the Building Department in the college were their greatest allies.

They were experts at their craft, negotiating directly with the Local Authority, producing plans and after they had agreed a price for the work with Hamish, they also acted contract supervisors. Each weekend, and sometimes during the week, a group would come up to Whistlefield, staying overnight in one of the Nissen Huts to crack on with the work. Hamish and Lorna scoured the auction rooms, second hand markets and scrap yards, buying up almost all of the furniture and kitchen equipment at knockdown prices.

They had another stroke of luck, when one of Hamish´s former star gold medal students decided to marry, and asked him if they would provide the catering for her wedding reception. Her father was a successful stockbroker and they lived in a mansion in the wealthy part of Upper Helensburgh. They wanted a society wedding and reception for their only daughter; two hundred guests in a marquee in the garden, no expense spared.

It was an astounding success, and they soon had requests for more events than they could handle, given that they were still running the teashop and bistro, and Hamish was still working in the college.

Their fame for top-level cuisine hit new heights when a well-known film and television producer relocated from London to the Helensburgh area.

George Samson commissioned them to produce something extra special for his housewarming. Over two hundred of `La crème de la crème´ of television and local society were invited to the event.

Hamish used this opportunity to begin his marketing campaign by discretely handing out his new business cards, an artist´s sketch of the hotel, with the mountains and lochs in the background and with the legend;

Lochview Lodge Hotel and Restaurant.
Whistlefield; by Garelochhead. Tel: 042608******
Proprietors; Hamish, and Lorna MacLeod.

The cumulative effect of all this hard work, effort and a little luck resulted in an important word by mouth reputation, gossip, and eager anticipation amongst their prime clientele base.

Hamish and Lorna did not even have to advertise the sale of the Ruthven Court Tearoom and Bistro. Their best friends, Henri and Ana, now with three children of their own, made them a very fair offer to take over the business. Henri was now the Chef de Cuisine at the Central Hotel, but the business was changing; good staff was becoming impossible to find, and the kitchens were almost medieval. He needed a stimulus, and the Ruthven Court Tearoom and Bistro was perfect for them.

Chapter 42: The Lochview Lodge Hotel

The Lodge had turned out better than they had hoped; after all, they had been working to a very tight budget in the end.

The attic now housed six bedrooms all en-suite. All had magnificent views over the lochs and mountains and were nicely finished in bleached pine and pastel shades.

They had considered using the attic as family accommodation, but Lorna had a nagging fear of sleeping in a wooden building, above the kitchen and restaurant. "Besides," she argued, "the income from the bedrooms would help fund a proper house for the family in the grounds."

They converted one of the Nissen huts into a temporary home; the kids loved it, they had plenty of space and it was just like being camping with the Boy's Brigade, according to Alistair.

Owing to the sloping site, the best place for the restaurant, they felt, was in the old billiard room. This was restored, back to the original teak walls, with nineteen twenties Rennie MacIntosh Art Deco prints and lighting. A recycled, MacIntosh cast iron fireplace, gave the restaurant a pleasing theme, as well as a name; `Rennie´s at the Lodge´.

The boiler house was down at this level, excavated into the slope, with its feeder high pressure propane gas tank hidden by the side behind a wooden ranch style fence.

The ground floor was the centre of the business, with its small reception, The Lobster Pot Bar with a cast iron stove, and decorated with old ships lamps, tables, spars, ropes and lobster pots in a marine theme.

The windows again offered spectacular views, and curiously, they had a view of the main road from the side windows beside the fire. Also on this level, an enormous chunk of their budget had gone into a modern kitchen with its ancillary rooms.

They painstakingly sanded the whole of the outside, back down to its former red cedar colour, and the red painted eve´s, contrasting pleasingly with the green and red of the hanging baskets and planters on the building.

They hadn´t had to do too much to the grounds, except cut back the undergrowth and rhododendrons and restore some overgrown pathways leading down to the loch shore.

Lorna had insisted that Hamish adopts the front of house role, and she would run the kitchen. She argued that the most important social decision maker was the woman of the house. She said that women preferred to be fussed over by a good male host.

Hamish acquiesced with reservations; he was certainly the better chef, and Lorna could charm the pants of anybody, but she had a point, and anyway she would not back down on the subject.

Chapter 43: The Inauguration

It was a fine, warm late summer evening, the sun still hanging in the sky over the mountains above Carrick Castle on the other side of the loch, and a light wind was keeping the local midge population under control.

The staff, supplemented by a few of the brightest of students from the college went about last minute preparation for the Gala opening. Hamish and Lorna took time to stand in front of the Lodge, arms round each other, gazing at their creation with a slight sensation of awe, but with much pride in their hearts.

Hamish had asked one of his regular bistro clients, a very attractive, celebrity BBC News presenter if she would officially open the hotel. She immediately agreed to do it for a free meal, but her manager was a tougher nut to crack, negotiating a modest fee; "Business is business….nothing personal," he said.

They invited over two hundred guests, drawn from a wide selection of the area's movers and shakers who could spread the word; the feature editors from the National and Local newspapers and their established friends and clients from the bistro. The ambiance was relaxed and fun, and the liberal sprinkling of famous faces mingling added the glamour to the occasion.

The TV presenter, made a very amusing speech at Hamish's expense, but assuaged his feelings by reflecting on the many lovely evenings she had spent with her family and friends in the Ruthven Court Bistro. A jeroboam of Veuve Cliquot Vintage Champagne was popped open, and the Lochview Lodge Hotel declared officially open for business.

Later, after the last of the guests had left, Hamish gave a speech of thanks to the staff for their hard work on and professionalism on the night. It had been a stunning success, and he and Lorna were proud of the professional way they had all set about their jobs.

Chapter 44: Alistair's School

When the question of schooling arose, Kirsty didn´t pose any undue problem as the local Garelochhead Primary School had a very good reputation.

Alistair was different; his reports from Hillhead Primary were not good. His teachers assessed he had problems of concentration; he was always getting into mischief and distracting other pupils by playing the funny man. "Must try harder" was the verdict.

Lorna was determined to send him to a private school, and had her sights set on Glasgow Academy, but distance and transport dictated that this was not an option now.

When they were registering the family at the Medical Centre, they consulted the local doctor, whom they had been informed, was sending his two children to Castle School in Dumbarton.

Dr Jeremy St Clair was a few years older than they were, but had an easy, confident relaxed way about him.

After dispensing with the formalities of registration, and making appointments for a medical check-up for the adults, he explained that he and his wife were very satisfied with the academic and discipline standards they set at the Castle School.

"It starts with the uniform," he laughed, "the pupils must wear kilts, and if that is not character building, nothing is!" He added, "There are quite a few kids from around here enrolled, and a minibus collects them from Garelochhead at eight in the morning, bringing them back at six; mind you, that´s an extra cost, but it saves a hell of a lot of bother for us."

Hamish telephoned and made an appointment at the school the following day. Both of them then spent half of the night trying to convince a very sceptical and frightened eleven year old that wearing the kilt to school was a very grown up, responsible thing to do…..and he was very lucky to get the opportunity to attend Castle School….they are very selective!

Next morning the weather had changed, but even in a downpour, Castle School appeared quite impressive. It was situated on the outskirts of Dumbarton in an old red sandstone mansion, set in extensive wooded grounds, sloping down to the Clyde estuary.

The Term had not begun yet, but their appeared to be a few students about the place, which they assumed correctly, might be living-in boarders.

Entering the vestibule, they detected the normal sights and smells of a school. There was an order about the place, a smell of floor polish and distant stifled conversations taking place in unseen rooms.

A kindly middle-aged secretary greeted them, who introduced herself as Mrs Morrison. She then asked them if they had brought Alistair´s school report. She then indicated they should take a seat on a hard wooden bench against the wall. Next to the Principal´s Study, the school coat of arms with its Latin Motto took pride of place. Looking around, there was the usual timetable and school notice boards pinned to the old oak wall panels.

Hamish and Lorna had never been in a Private school before, and shared the nervousness been felt by their son Alistair. Alistair was white faced and when Hamish asked him if he was alright, he croaked a nervous, "Yes Dad."

Lorna put a comforting arm around his shoulder smiling an assurance that she still didn´t feel, before straightening her back and thinking, "Bloody Hell, we´re the clients here!" Presently, the door opened and a tall man, looking distinguished in an academic gown came out and introduced himself as Dr Kennedy.

They all stood, and Hamish introduced himself and Lorna, "…..and this must be Alistair," Dr Kennedy interrupted, shaking hands all round. Taking charge, he ushered into his study, seating them on three chairs already placed in front of his imposing desk.

Mrs Morrison asked, "is there was anything else Dr Kennedy?"

"Yes, Mrs Morrison, can you get me one of the boys to show Alistair around the school while I talk to his parents?"

"Yes, of course, I think Cameron Rawstron is still in the Library, I´ll get him." She closed the door quietly behind her. The Principal tried to make them feel more at ease by telling them he had heard about their new business venture, and had read about the opening in the Glasgow Herald. He wished them well in the new venture before handing them three copies of the School Prospectus, adding hastily that they could read it at home.

A knock came to the door, and Mrs Morrison entered with a very tall, lanky boy of about seventeen, looking a little incongruous dressed in a navy polo shirt and a Royal Stewart tartan kilt; a lock of dank black hair falling across his glasses temporarily blinding him.

He strode confidently into the room, and almost saluting the Principal asked, "You sent for me, Sir?"

"Yes Cameron," turning to the MacLeod´s, he said, "this is Cameron, he´s one of the Senior Prefects in the school, he´ll take young Alistair a tour of the school now."

Cameron bounded over, and awkwardly shook Lorna and Hamish's hand, before they could get to their feet. Alistair was almost yanked to his feet as he gripped his hand, saying, "Come on, I'll show you around; are you boarding?"

Lorna quickly intervened, "No, he's going to travel every day!"

Looking a little put out, Cameron hesitantly said, "Oh....that's alright then" as he hustled a startled looking Alistair out of the room.

A bemused Hamish wondered if they would be getting a tour, when Dr Kennedy began his talk.

An hour later, they had joined up again with their son Alistair, who in fact looked a lot more happier and settled than they did, having endured a prolonged lecture about Castle School standards, and parental responsibilities. They had been issued with a list of required uniform and sports equipment and instruction that "Fraser's in Glasgow are our appointed suppliers." Hamish had also written a substantial cheque covering the first year's schooling.

Hamish kept thinking that he had been mugged by Doctor Kennedy. They hadn't got their tour, and they had listened what amounted to a very successful Sales pitch. Kennedy had subjected them to an avalanche of educational statistics, and told the names of every graduate that had made good in the world, a substantial proportion of which seemed to be Generals or Admirals!

They quizzed Alistair on his tour with Cameron; but all he would say that it was good and he had met a few boys and girls of his own age, who were boarding at the school. Alistair likened the playing fields and grounds to being about the size of Kelvingrove Park, which they accepted as being an exaggeration, but they were happy, if not surprised at his enthusiasm. The only fly in the ointment was the kilt. Alistair wasn't happy, but recognised that it wasn't an option. Lorna was thinking that he might have to wear braces to hold the kilt up, as her son had no hips to talk about!

However, an important hurdle had been surmounted, and they drove through the rain to Glasgow, firstly to buy the uniform and sports gear, and secondly, and more happily, to have lunch with their friends at the new Chez Ana restaurant, which was until recently Ruthven Court Tearoom and Bistro.

Next day, Jeremy St Clair, the local GP called in at the Lochview. He explained he had been visiting old Mrs Manningly down in Portincaple, and was interested in how Hamish and Lorna had fared at the school.
Lorna came out of the kitchen and exchanged pleasantries, but apologised she had things on the go in the kitchen.
Over a coffee, Hamish recounted the details including the feeling he had been mugged. "We didn´t even get a tour!" he laughed.
"Kennedy is like that," Dr Jeremy assured him, "no time for the parent´s; as far as he is concerned, we should stay out of the way and just send him the cheques; but he runs a good school." He talked a bit about the social scene in the area, who was who, and who to avoid, but Hamish reminded him that they were just in the first stage of building the business and really didn´t have any real free time. Any socializing would have to be done at the Lochview Lodge! Finally, as he was leaving to see another patient, he suggested that he would bring his brood, as he called them up for dinner this week sometime, and introduce them to Alistair, in order he had someone he could talk to at school.

After he had gone, Hamish went into the kitchen and told Lorna the details of the conversation. They both agreed he was being very kind and helpful in helping them settle in; "maybe I should have invited them up for a freebie," Hamish added.
Lorna retorted, "Enough of the freebies for now Hamish MacLeod; remember, they were at the opening night."

Malevolent Karma

Doctor Jeremy surprised them again by bringing his family up for a bar snack that very evening.

The Lodge was very quiet, weeknight business had not really taken off yet, and they closed Rennie's restaurant.

This time Lorna had some time to spare, and sit and chat a bit with Sonia, Jeremy's very attractive Swedish wife. Their children Robbie who was thirteen, and Julia at fourteen were so well behaved, that Lorna remarked later she thought they were being tortured at home!

The St Clair's invited Alistair and Kirsty to join them. They needed a little bit of gentle persuasion from Lorna to help overcome their shyness. Within a few minutes, the timidity had vanished, and the kids were out exploring and running around the grounds as the adults cemented a friendship.

Much to his parent's delight, Alistair quickly adapted to private school life. He was nicknamed Sandy by the other pupils, Alistair being too sissy!

The academic rigor and discipline at the Castle School brought out the best in him. He became much more confident without losing his impish sense of humour. He applied himself and studied harder, but struggled in various academic subjects much to Lorna's chagrin. She was determined that Alistair would become a Lawyer or Accountant.

Alistair became friends with Robbie St Clair. They went everywhere together, even when Alistair had his work to do at the weekends, Robbie would be there also, Hamish grumbling good-naturedly about the extra wages to be paid!

The boys joined the school Army Cadet Force, the junior football team and the local Sailing Club ...they were never bored.

A year later, the MacLeods' were working harder than ever, but they were enjoying the buzz of excitement that each day brought to them. They were singularly proud of their creation; after all, it was built from scratch out of a disused MOD building. Business had steadily increased at the Lochview Lodge Hotel. Their reputation had extended over a wide area, and they had several very good write ups in the quality press and magazines. Rumours began to circulate about a possible extension to Faslane Submarine Base, which could only provide further benefit to the business.

The children were happy and thriving; Kirsty with her own circle of friends down in the village, her Brownie's group on a Thursday night, and Saturday morning cinema club. Alistair and Robbie had become fervent Rangers football club fans, after Maurice Gibson, a football player at Glasgow Rangers had given them a couple of VIP tickets for a Rangers cup-tie at Ibrox Park. It was a bright winter Sunday, and the boys were tidying up outside, he had swept into the car park in his racing green E Type Jaguar. They had drifted over casually to stare at the car, and the leggy blonde showing more inches of leg than she thought. The boys had instantly recognised him, and later in the bar, had shyly asked for his autograph. Maurice obliged, chatted with them a bit, and gave them the tickets for the following Saturday cup-tie against Dundee United.

One Saturday morning, Lorna had driven into Helensburgh with Alistair for some supplies. As they parked across from the station, Alistair recognised Jonathan Amersbey, dressed in his school uniform kilt, standing outside at the edge of the pavement anxiously looking up and down for someone. Although in the same year as Alistair, they were in different Houses, and therefore did not mix in class, or for that matter, socially.

Lorna asked, "Who is that Alistair, why is he wearing his kilt on a Saturday?"

"Jonathan Amersbey mum; he's a boarder, and they have to wear the kilt when they leave the school."

"We'd better say hello then," she said, is he one of your friends?"

"No mum, the boarders' don't really mix with the day pupils; and besides he's a bit strange."

"Well let's go over and talk to him anyway; he looks a bit lost, poor boy."

They crossed the street and Alistair said hello, introduced his mother, and asked what he was doing in Helensburgh.

Sullenly Jonathan answered, "I'm waiting for my mother, and then we're going up to my grandmother's; it's her birthday today." He added furiously, "she's always bloody late!"

Just then, a black Mini Cooper drew up, beeping the horn. "That's her now, Jonathan said, as he opened the passenger door. "See you!"

Lorna had a brief look at the smartly dressed woman inside, recognizing her as one of the Base crowd who often came up for lunch in the bar, but before she could say anything, the Mini roared away.

That was a bit rude! she thought, but a little perplexed asked Alistair, "I recognise that woman, I'm sure she works at the Base, why is that boy boarding at school?"

"I don't really know mum, his grandmother lives in Helensburgh also; the others say he doesn't get on with his mother."

"Well I find that very strange; he's only your age! Just you watch your step my lad, or you'll be boarding as well!" she joked.

"Then you'd have to pay someone to wash the dishes and do all my work, mum; no it's cheaper for you if I live at home!"

Lorna gave him a playful smack on the side of his head, and suggested a coffee at the Oxfam Café.

Chapter 45: Alistair´s Summer in France

At the precise point in time that his schoolmate Jonathan Amersbey was putting into effect his subterfuge to go down to Newtownbury for a summer of protesting with Megan, Alistair MacLeod was on his way to Saumur, in France, to work in a Michelin Starred French restaurant for the summer.

An uncle of Hamish´s best friend Henri owned Le Coq d´Or in Saumur. Claude Langlasse drove his Chef´s mercilessly; the attention to detail was as impressive as the enthusiasm he instilled upon his staff. He was a pioneer of the newly fashionable Cuisine Nouvelle style of cooking.

Madame Langlasse ruled the restaurant equally with a rod of iron; no one went home at night after a long tiring day without an analysis of how the service went, and appropriate critiques or praise handed out; then the restaurant had to be cleaned, ready for next day!

Hamish, (shared by Lorna) held the opinion that hard work didn´t harm anyone, indeed it should be a source of personal pride and satisfaction to stand back after a hard days graft, and congratulate oneself on a job well done. He also held aspirations, (not shared by Lorna), that his son would follow in his footsteps, therefore a summer or two in a top class French restaurant would not be a bad idea.

Lorna was less sure, but for purely maternal reasons. The idea of the hard work didn´t bother her; nor was the fact that he would be in a foreign country. When she had first left Barra, Glasgow felt like a foreign country at first!

She also had every confidence in the Langlasse family to look after her baby, having met them before.

Alistair had been consulted of course, and was looking forward, if a little nervously, to the prospect of a summer away from home. He would improve on his French language, and the fact that he would be seeing Claude Langlasse´s very pretty daughter Sophie again, helped soothe the prospect of the actual kitchen work.

Sophie had spent last summer working at the Lochview Lodge, and although she was a year older than he was, they'd had a great time together in their free time, usually sailing in Alistair's dinghy over to Carrick Castle and up to Lochgoilhead. Being fourteen at the time, with his hormones causing strife in his body, Alistair naturally had taken a serious crush for her.

Sophie had more or less kept him at arm's length, allowing only the occasional relatively innocent kissing and petting.

Lorna had for a time been slightly concerned for her son, as he followed Sophie around like a love-sick poodle, and had insisted that Hamish took him aside for a fatherly chat about the `facts of life´, much to Hamish's embarrassment. This torturous `education´ was carried out at home, with Lorna's ear to the kitchen door, trying hard not to giggle too loud. Alistair clearly knew as much, if not more than his dad, but was milking the opportunity of witnessing his father dry up and squirm in his discomfiture.

A year on, Alistair had shot up in height, he looked older, had the first signs of a blonde fluff on his top lip, and confidence now replaced the timidity he once suffered. Crucially, he had learned to keep his glasses pushed back up on his nose, which meant he didn't have to bend his head to peer over at whoever was talking to him. He and Sophie had been exchanging letters since last summer; he in his convoluted French, she in a very Gallic version of English, but the message he thought he was detecting was one of romantic interest. This year he felt he was definitely in with a chance!

In the event, when Alistair got to Saumur, it was to find that Sophie already had a steady boyfriend, a young wine grower called Marc, who also raced rally cars!

In his first days of misery, he wanted to come home. He was angry and hurt to the stomach; he felt foolish ...betrayed almost. She hadn't mentioned anything of her new boyfriend in her letters; maybe if she had, he would not have built up his hopes and feelings so much. Maybe he would not have come to this bloody place at all!

Everyone was friendly and helpful, but he was struggling with his French, and the work was much harder than the Lodge ...and he was working ten hours a day!

Sophie was aware of his feelings, but just shrugged her pretty Gallic shoulders, saying to her friends, "I´m not his bloody mother!"

One afternoon, Paul, the commis chef who was mentoring Alistair, asked him if he wanted to make up a foursome on a picnic down on the banks of the River Loire.

Alistair declined, citing he was tired, but Paul persevered, and at three-o´clock he was installed in the back of a battered old corrugated sided Citroen CV van. As they bounced along, he was squeezed up against Marie, the dark haired, demure waitress from Paris working the summer at Le Coq D´Or.

They were speeding along a farm road alongside the river Loire, Paul was swerving from one side of the road to the other causing the rear occupants to collide with the sides of the van and then each other. Alistair found himself almost astraddle Marie at one point, but no one was complaining. Everyone was shouting and laughing hysterically at Paul to stop it, when suddenly a tractor came out of a gate ahead of them. There was nowhere to go and he swerved off the road and down the sloping bank, managing to turn the van away in time before coming to a halt about three meters from the river! The old van was teetering at a crazy angle, and almost as in slow motion, it fell onto its side piling everyone on top of one another.

"Merde! That was close," was Paul´s laughing comment as they all climbed out of the back doors of the van, "I hope it´s not broken the wine bottles!"

The Farmer had stopped and came running down the slope to help. *"Putain! Êtes-vous baiser fou ou quoi?* Are you fucking crazy or what?" Calming down a bit, he asked, "Is anyone hurt?"

Surprisingly no one was hurt, only a couple of bruises, which could have been caused by Paul´s antics before the crash. Paul apologised profusely and assured the farmer, that everyone was okay. He added that Alistair was from Scotland and he had wanted to find out if he possessed *les boules* enough to be his friend!

The farmer grumbled, but was satisfied no one had been injured, and muttering under his breath, "*Jeunes fous vont se faire tuer*, Crazy youngsters will get them-selves killed. I´ll bring the tractor down and right the car."

The tough old Citroen was up-righted; it started first time, and drove on to their picnic spot, beside a sandy beach on the river.

The incident proved to be a subject of hilarity all of that summer. Outside of the work, which got easier as Alistair gained more experience, the four went everywhere together, always laughing at Paul´s extrovert, gregarious behaviour. The added bonus for Alistair was that the demure Maria turned out to be less coy than people generally thought. He spent the last three days of his holidays with Marie at her mother´s house in Paris.

Her mother was a tall, severe, puritanical in looks as well as actions; a teacher of the piano, and treated Alistair with a cool reserve. It was very apparent that he was not good enough for her daughter ...but it was only for a few days. When Madame du Pont left each morning to teach at the private music conservatory, they would leave with her to do some sightseeing, only to be back in Maria´s bed within half an hour!

After a memorable summer, he returned to Lochview Lodge just in time to start his fourth year at Castle school, matured beyond his years in all senses of the word.

Lorna gasped as she hugged him at Glasgow Airport, "My son left here only ten weeks ago a boy, and has returned a man."
Hamish only looked on and smiled knowingly, before shaking his son´s hand in welcome back.

Book Three

In Mitigation of Iñaki Anton.

"...if you travel in isolation in your dreams, you will lose your soul"
~*Virginia Murillo*

Chapter 46: 1983, Bilbao, Spain

Eighteen-year old Iñaki Anton left the library building of the Universidad de Deusto, and ran, rucksack full of textbooks, to catch a bus along to Casco Viejo, the Old Town. He was late for his date with his current *novia*, girl friend Mercedes, and in his haste and blindness crashed into a stout old matron taking her Poodle dog for its evening walk.

"Imbecile!" she shouted, as she struggled to get back on her feet.

He breathlessly apologised with a *"Lo siento*, I'm sorry Señora", as he helped her up, the Poodle meanwhile yelping and yapping at his ankles.

He was very late as was usual lately, but Mercedes understood that at last, was studying hard for his end of year exams, and sometimes he would forget the time passing ever so much rapidly, as the approaching examinations rushed closer.

This time he was only twenty minutes late, having ran and dodged through the after work crowds in the narrow Old Town streets.

As was normal Café Bilbao was packed; the noise of shouted conversations and friends greetings drowning out the South American soap opera already blaring out from the television mounted in a corner.

Mercedes was sitting in the centre of a group of student friends beneath the television and the pouting lips of a very attractive but bad actress, as she endeavoured to seduce the very rich young Wine Grower in the series.

Iñaki squeezed through to the group, and after salutations all round, managed to extract her outside to a free table out on the Terrace.

As Spanish girls go, she didn´t have the flashing dark eyes of the South. Coming from La Coruña, Mercedes displayed very much the Celtic origins of the Galician people, blue green eyes, dark hair and narrow delicate features washed and smoothed by the tempests of rain and winds off the Atlantic Ocean.

Iñaki himself could have been mistaken for an Irishman, or Scotsman from a distance. He had the small stature, light skin and dark hair Basque features of Northern Europe, rather than the Latin looks of the Spanish in the Central Massif or Mediterranean Coast.

They ordered some *Pintxos*, open sandwiches, and washed them down with generous glasses of Rioja, as they recounted their day to each other.

Replete, they decided to take in a film for rest of the evening and later, who knows, maybe go to a friend´s birthday party over in Las Arenas.

They were both committed ecologists, seriously worried about the effect the expansion of Industry was taking upon the environment. Previously unspoiled and beautiful countryside was being sacrificed to the bulldozer, in the name of economic expansion. Iñaki´s beliefs and active participation in the Basque country´s young street protest movement, the *Kale Borroka*, was a running sore of conflict between him and his father Roberto, who owned a successful and expanding engineering company.

Malevolent Karma

Roberto Anton had started his business from scratch in a lock up garage in Getxo, fabricating precision engineered hydraulic pumps used in the shipbuilding industry. He was not alone in condemning the younger generation of frivolity in their green ecological sustainable ideas.

His beloved Basque country was indeed beautiful, with more than its share of mountains and forests, and a coastline boasting some of the best beaches in Europe, but the people needed work, and industry was the best motor for economic success. A balance was possible, but these damn ecologists, including Iñaki, his very own son, were objecting to every project that endangered a bloody worm or disturbed a meter of soil!

Iñaki and Mercedes had met during an anti nuclear demonstration, and had become members of the university ecological campaign group, frequently taking part in conferences and manifestations all over the Basque country.

It was at one of these demonstrations, against the construction of a nuclear power generating plant that would lead to life changing circumstances for both of them.

ETA, the Basque terrorist group, had infiltrated the *Kale Borroka*, and the demonstrations were becoming increasingly militant. `Commando´ groups were taking to the streets provoking violent clashes with the police, destroying shops and burning buses.

The ecologists and street protesters stopped or disrupted the construction of motorways, oil refineries and in particular, the nuclear powered generation plant in construction at Lemoniz, along the coast.

Spanish Government was forced into abandoning the construction of the Lemoniz Project after ETA terrorists carried out a series of bombings and assassinations that had left five Engineers dead, and consequently, a crackdown on the activities of the militant ecologist movement was ordered.

Chapter 47: The Punishment Squad

In the Nationalist Bars of Getxo, Iñaki and his friends in the *Kalea Borroka* celebrated the closure of the Lemoniz Project a little too enthusiastically, and his name became known to the Guardia Civil Intelligence Unit.

He was not a member of ETA, but his profile came to the attention of the *Grupo Antiterrorista Liberacion*, GAL, a clandestine reprisals organization within the Spanish police services, secretly backed by the Government.

Iñaki and his best friend, Juan Rodriguez, shared a tiny one-bedroom apartment in the narrow streets of the Old Town Barrio Indautxu.

The boys´ had an arrangement; if one was entertaining his *novia*, girlfriend, the other would find a couch in another friend´s flat, or simply go home to mama for the night.

It was only ten o´clock, Juan and his girl Ionea had already come back to the flat. They lay on top of the bed naked, satisfied and happy, having just finished their frantic, lustful lovemaking.

They were enjoying the effects of `puro´ they were sharing, when the door was taken off its hinges, and three hooded men burst into the room.

The girl started screaming, and one of the thugs hit her across the nose with a baton and after dragging her into the bathroom, he battered her again into a whimpering wreck, holding her bloodied, shattered nose and fingers when she had tried to protect herself.

The men were members of a punishment squad from the *Grupo Antiterroristas de Liberacion,* and they were on a mission!

The leader addressed Juan; "Iñaki Anton, you have been found guilty of terrorist acts against the State, now you are to be punished."

Juan screamed, "I´m not Iñaki! *Por favor*! Wait! I´m not Iñaki! *Espera!* Wait!"

"What did you say you little turd?"

"*Por favor*, look at my identity card, I´m not lying!" He pointed to the dresser, and one of the gang checked his photo identity.

"*Jefe*, Boss, it´s true, he´s not the little bastard were after."

The leader raised his pistol and demanded, "Where is he, you little turd? He lives here, right? So where is he?" and crashed the butt of the gun on the headboard right next to Juan´s head.

The boy blurted out, "I don´t know, I think he´s at home tonight. If my *novia* is here, he goes home."

"*Joder*, another fuck-up," breathed the leader, half to himself.

The three held a hurried consultation.

Doors were opening in the stairwell, but everyone knew better than to interfere.

"Okay, young Juan," this time he was almost conciliatory. "We know you´re not Iñaki Anton, but we want you to give him a message, do you understand?"

Juan could only nod his head in fear.

"Tell him to get the fuck out of Spain, if he comes back, he´s a dead man. Repeat the message."

The terrified Juan repeated, "Iñaki has to leave Spain, if he comes back you are going to kill him."

With that said, the third hooded figure brought his baton with a crack across Juan´s left kneecap, shattering it. Juan screamed in agony, and then the other kneecap suffered the same fate. As they passed the bathroom, one of them gave the girl another kick and laughed, "I think our little ecological militant will understand the message."

Someone eventually found the courage to run to a bar and telephone the police and an ambulance. The ambulance arrived twenty minutes before the police. The investigators searching the apartment found the hashish and concluded this was a straightforward drug dispute, and closed the file.

Another young neighbour had been 'phoning around looking for Iñaki, finally locating him at the party in Las Arenas. One hour later, he was on the back of a motorcycle and heading up to a remote Pyrenean mountain hut, belonging to his uncle. Such was the panic to get him out of danger all he had in his rucksack was enough food and water to keep him alive for a few days.

Alone in the cabin for the next three days, Iñaki strained his memory, but was at a loss as to why these men had targeted him. He had been told it was GAL, their reputation was just as terrifying as ETA´s, but why him?

As the Land Rover carefully climbed up through the mountains tracks above Vitoria, Iñaki´s father Roberto accepted that he should never have given him permission to live in Bilbao near the university. His home was just across the river in Las Arenas; he could have easily taken his bicycle over the *Puente Colgante*, the Hanging Bridge, each day. However, Roberto had lived through the suffocating restrictions of the Franco era, and wanted to allow his only son enough freedom to spread his wings.

Maria, his wife had spat her contempt for his decision into his face over the past two days. "You will rue the day you over-ruled me, *carbron!* Only a mother knows what is good for her sons!"

Bouncing over the ruts, Roberto´s mind drifted to the day Iñaki was born. He smiled to himself as he recollected. *Che! What a day that was! Cost me a fortune when I had to pay the Sociedad Gastranomica, the Gourmet Society dinner that night, but they gave generously to Iñaki´s thapela hat; almost two hundred thousand pesetas! Some hatful for a one- day-old baby! Times were good,* he thought, *Franco had invested billions, and business was so good we bought the house for cash!*

Malevolent Karma

He continued with his thoughts, ignoring the splendour of the sun kissed, snow-capped mountains, and lush green meadows full of sheep, and the colourful and distinctive Basque chalet farmhouses dotted around. Reflecting, Roberto smiled to himself, *Iñaki had been a bright, happy-go-lucky boy, almost hyperactive in his search for fun; not that he neglected his school work or the chores he had to do around the house for his mother; ....and then he won his place in the Club de Remo rowing team despite being the smallest in his group! Che! He was an ideal son, any father would have shared the pride he had in him.* Reality checked in and his mood darkened... *now my son's a fugitive from a police assassination squad; how in the hell has it come to this?*

Iñaki was morosely thinking about his predicament when his father arrived with his uncle, and another man, obviously a *pastor*, a shepherd, who would know the mountains.

"*Hijo*," father and son embraced, and kissed, clinging to each other. "What in the hell have you been up to Iñaki?"

Through tears, Iñaki blurted out, "Papa, believe me, I haven't done anything wrong!"

"Iñaki, the Guardia Civil raided our house the day after you left. They had a warrant, issued by a judge specializing in terrorist crimes; they turned the house upside down looking for drugs. They are saying you have connections with ETA. Son, *por favor*, just tell me you are not involved with the fucking ETA."

"Papa, *en mi vida*, on my life, I am not a member of ETA, believe me! I don't know what's happening here!"

"I'll tell you what's happening; You're friend Juan is likely to spend the rest of his life a cripple, and that lovely little girlfriend he has? ...well she'll have a face like a prize fighter to look at in the mirror each morning."

"Papa, listen to me; I haven't done anything wrong. I only went to some anti nuclear and ecological demonstrations, you knew about that."

Angrily, Roberto responded, "I told you not to get involved Iñaki! Are you fucking crazy? Do you think that the government is going to forgive your ecological clowns for murdering five innocent engineers and writing off a seven billion peseta nuclear power generation project?" Furiously he shouted, "You are all fucking mad! Grow up! Ten years ago Franco would have had you all shot!"

There were a few minutes of silence; the noise of the goats´ bells reached them from the valley and calming down somewhat, his father went on, "Mama has packed a bag for you. I don´t need to tell you she´s prostrate with grief over this." Shaking his head sadly, he said, "You have truly ruined your life Iñaki, and your mother will never get over it."

Indicating the shepherd who had been watching the scene with his Tio Andre, "Andoni will take you over the mountains. All the frontier posts are manned and there are guardia patrols all over the place, we were stopped at one coming up here."

He thrust a bundle of French francs into his son´s hand. "This should see you through a month or so until we try and get this mess sorted out. It won´t be easy, Iñaki, you´re in deep shit. GAL is unofficial and no one will admit that it exists, so at this moment in time I haven´t a *puta* idea on how to clear your name." He couldn´t bear to continue looking into his son´s eyes, and inspected the dirt down at his feet,

"Listen Iñaki, don´t telephone the house, phone Tio Andre when you are safe." As his eyes suddenly filled, he continued, "You´d better go now, I don´t think we were followed, but just in case…."

Father and son embraced shoulders and breasts heaving; bitter tears spread over disillusioned and frightened faces, holding on, as if their very lives depended on it.

"Papa, I´m really sorry; tell Mama and Maria I love them."

With that, Iñaki separated from his father, picked up his rucksack and followed his guide up behind the hut, and into the tree line above, watched by his father and Tio Andre, until they disappeared from view

Chapter 48: The Pyrenees

With the necessity to avoid frontier posts and using little known sheep and goat trails and travelling through remote valleys, it took the two men three days to cross the Pyrenees, the massive mountain range that separates Spain from France.

The winter snow had all but disappeared from the lower slopes, but still embedded in the north facing hidden valleys. The higher they climbed the temperature dropped accordingly, freezing the very breathe fogging out from their at times gasping mouths. Andoni knew the mountain refuges, but they had to check carefully for guardia activity before using them for night shelter.

They ate what they had brought with them; bread, cheese and *jamon*, and drank rough red wine from their *bodas*, the wine sack carried by the shepherds in the mountains.

Once they had to lie low in the rocks, after Andoni sensed movement in a Col above them. Sure enough, a guardia patrol passed them by only a hundred meters or so, as they pressed into the rock. Fortunately, the patrol were not being too alert or vigilant, talking among themselves, and they remained undetected.

Sound travels far in the silence of the mountains and few words passed between them. Andoni, being used to solitude, was not interested in passing the time with the young fellow.

Iñaki, therefore had plenty of time to think about what had happened to Juan and Ioana, shivering with fear when he realised it should have been him. By the wisdom and irresponsibility of his youth, he felt that he hadn´t done anything seriously wrong. Anarchist extremists had done some real damage; burning shops and businesses, destroying buses etc. He had to admit to himself that he and his friends had burned some rubbish containers and thrown some rocks, but nothing to warrant the treatment meted out by hooded thugs who were almost certainly police officers.

His sense of injustice gave way to a rage and hatred of the men and the organization that were authorising extrajudicial maiming or killing of innocent people.

At last Andoni and Iñaki, the latter limping and with his feet badly blistered, trekked through a fine mist of rain, unheeded, into a little French Basque country town, well known for its sympathy to the Basque Nationalist cause. They went into a small bar, the proprietor greeting them with a `*Kaixo*´, and ordered the day´s special, `*Potage de Alubias*´ and bread and carafe of red wine, and settled gratefully into a corner table. The few locals, old men playing their daily games of dominos, gave them a curious glance, but no more. No one wanted to interfere with their Spanish brothers who have obviously just walked from over the mountains.

It was their first hot meal in days, so nothing passed between them as they savoured the rich stew, dipping the bread in the sauce.

Finally, Andoni spoke; "Look son, if you want to demonstrate against Big Business, or save the animals that you don´t actually want to eat, go up to one of the big cities like Bordeaux or Nantes, go up to one of the big cities like Bordeaux or Nantes, get a job, and lose yourself. That´s what your papa wants you to do, and probably it´s the best way to get on with your life, but if you seriously want to volunteer and join our war against the Fascist bastards in Madrid, I can give you a name." He went on, "Think very carefully though, because if you make contact and then change your mind, the only way back to papa and mama will be inside a wooden box. Do you understand what I´m saying? You will know too much already."

Desperation entered into Iñakis voice as he answered, "*Claro*, Andoni, but I didn´t do anything. I didn´t bomb or shoot anyone. It´s supposed to be a democracy, we´re allowed to demonstrate for fuck sake!"

"Are you fucking listening to me, Iñaki? If you make contact with these men, you will shoot or bomb and kill a policeman. ETA don´t carry passengers, they will kill you!" Softening a little, he continued, "Look, I won´t give you the name; just go to the Txami bar in old town of Hendaye, and say you know me, Andoni Ortegi. Make damn sure you give the right story, or they might take you for an informant." Softly pounding the table for emphasis he stressed, "I repeat, don´t go into that bar unless you want to join the struggle!"

With that, he stood up and wordlessly embraced Iñaki, threw down some francs and nodding to the barman as he pulled on his *thapela* beret, strode out the door, rucksack swinging.

Chapter 49: St Jean de Luz, France

All at once, a sense of loneliness overcame Iñaki Anton. He was now a refugee in a foreign country, with no friends, and no job. He needed time to think, but here in this bar was not the place. He had been over the border to Hendaye before, and once to St Jean de Luz, a very pretty port near to the border, with as he remembered it, fabulous beaches. That would do; there would be tourists he could melt into as he worked out his next step.

In his passable French, he asked the barman if there was a bus to St Jean de Luz.

"Take the bus to Pau, and then one for Bayonne, it passes through St Jean," came the gruff answer through the cigarette.

"Do you know at what time it leaves?" Iñaki enquired.

One of the domino players answered, "Three o´clock, in front of the Hôtel de Ville; if you hurry you should catch it."

"*Merci, monsieur*;" Iñaki picked up his rucksack, threw down some centimes as a tip, and stuck his *thapela* on his head as he went for the door.

The same domino player said, "A little advice young fellow; don´t go to St Jean with that on your head; the police will mark you as ETA."

"*Merci beaucoup, au revoir*," Iñaki gratefully responded, and went out into the sunshine.

He arrived in St Jean de Luz at half past five, and quickly made his way over to the port now busy with on-lookers and shore-workers awaiting the boats. He found a modest-looking fishermen´s *Pension* off an alleyway, just a few metres from the returning fishing boats with their screaming gulls following on.

In response to his rapping hard on the chipped, wooden reception desk, and his repeated *Bonjour, Bonjour*, an old woman pushed through a dirty, red curtain behind the desk. A curt "*Oui*," and "*Diez franc*," to his enquiry if a room was available finished the reservation process. The `receptionist´ didn´t ask for his identity card, but he had to pay in advance for his first night.

The room, was on the first floor, overlooking the back alleyway, was as he expected, tiny and grubby, but would serve his purpose of a cheap, obscure place to stay until he could figure out what he was going to do next. Iñaki dumped his rucksack on the bed, went out and found a telephone box by the Quay.

His hands were shaking as he dialled, and after an eternity his *Tia,* Aunt Pitou answered. He said "It´s me Tia, Iñaki, I´m safe!"

She began sobbing; "Iñaki, you need to speak to Tio Andre."

The telephone clattered on a table, and in a few seconds his uncle was saying, "Iñaki, is that you?"

"Yes Tio, I'm safe I'm in ……"

"Don't say it!" Andre shouted, "Don't tell me where you are, the guardia are looking for you! Iñaki, they've arrested Maria, your sister!"

"Why?" Iñaki exclaimed, "Maria's only sixteen for fuck sake, what's she got to do with this?"

"Iñaki, they came back and searched your house again and found some propaganda leaflets about the Lemoniz demonstrations in her room."

"Tio, she was never there!" Iñaki was shouting and crying at the same time.

"Listen son, they also found a few grams of hashish, which we know must have been planted by the bastards, but she's being interrogated at Police HQ." He went on; "Roberto is up there with a lawyer right now, he's good, so we're sure he'll get her out on a bond."

Tio Andre didn't sound as confident as his words suggested. Iñaki knew that in a terrorist investigation, there would be no bond. He slumped against the wall of the booth, and, quite unable to speak, tears streaming down his face.

"Iñaki, are you still there?" the telephone asked.

"I'm still here, Tio."

"Listen son, forget about it; they don't have evidence. They want to put pressure on you to give up, and if you do that, you will disappear, so don't even think about it."

"Yes uncle." A defeated and shocked Iñaki managed to respond.

"Good." Andre affirmed, "Listen to me, your father knows your innocent, but this thing with your sister is too much for him. Your father is blaming you for this mess and himself for not controlling you more." He went on, "Iñaki, pay attention; now that we know you're safe, don't phone for a while, understand? Be careful, disappear but look after yourself." Finally he said, "We'll be thinking of you; you'll get back home someday. *Agur,* goodbye Iñaki, take care."

The telephone went dead in Iñaki's ear.

Iñaki dropped the telephone, clutching at the side of the cubicle. He opened the door and wandered, swaying like drunk, thinking of the enormity of the situation. He all but crashed into a tiny fisherman´s bar, ordered a brandy, downed it in one, which left him spluttering and choking, but the fire and warmth in his stomach helped to calm the turmoil in his head.

The woman behind the bar asked him if he was okay; he nodded in return, and asked for a jug of red wine, some olives and *sauccisson* to go with it, and sat in the corner. He had to think!

Going back was not an option. His life, which only a few days ago was so happy and carefree; the reunions with family and friends, the laughter and fun, the games of fronton and rowing races on the River Nervión… all gone!

He thought of his girlfriend Mercedes who had cajoled him into studying harder and playing a little less. He brushed aside the wave of self-pity washing over him; he had to think! The brutality of GAL and the corruption of the police in their vengeance for Lemoniz would continue, but perversely, he felt he was not ready to commit himself to the murderous campaign that ETA was carrying out. He was not ready to kill anyone.

It wasn´t practical, or safe to stay here being so close to the frontier. GAL had assassinated suspected ETA members in France, and the Gendarmerie generally unsympathetic to the Basque cause.

As he was eating his meal, these thoughts were chasing around in his head. Suddenly there was a roar of the crowd from the television, and the half dozen people now in the bar began cheering and clapping.

Iñaki looked up, and saw that a rugby match was on the TV. The French side Biarritz, was at home, playing the Irish side Leinster. The match had only just begun and Biarritz had scored a try, now followed by another roar, as the try was converted.

Suddenly, the solution presented itself. Iñaki had spent two summers in Dublin learning English, and had made some friends there. Gathering his wits together, he formulated a plan that just might work.

He packed the rest of his *sauccisson* and bread into his serviette, and stuffed it into his pocket, hurriedly paid the barmaid, and ran back to the *Pension*. Taking the steps two at a time, he grabbed his rucksack from his room and sprinted to the nearby train station.

Biarritz is only a few kilometres from St Jean de Luz, and on the main line. He was fortunate that he was a little early for the eight-o´clock train north and bought his ticket and waited, mind racing.

Just after a quarter to nine, he was standing in a popular rugby bar in Biarritz, watching the match coming to a close. Leinster had clawed their way back into the game, and had just scored another try to lead 12-16. The game finished shortly after, and within ten minutes, the bar had filled up with boisterous rugby fans.

The Irish are great talkers and hospitable until every penny, or franc in their pockets had been spent, and Iñaki was soon enveloped in the celebrations. As the beer flowed and the party got rowdier, he found himself adopted into group of students.

In answer to their questions on how he spoke such good feckin´ English, he related his story of being in Dublin for two summers. He had also studied English at the British Council in Bilbao. Iñaki casually added that he was planning to visit his friends in Dublin after a spell working in London.

"Oh no you feckin´ well not!" Exclaimed one of his new found, inebriated hosts. "If you´re going to Dublin, you´re coming back with us! We´ve got a bus waitin´, and we´ll be on the bloody ferry at seven in the morning. You´ve got your passport?"

In response to Iñaki's affirmation, his new friend exclaimed, "Well that's it then! A free trip to Wexford for Miguel, or whatever your name is."

"My name is Iñaki, he corrected."

"Pleased to meet you Iñaki, I'm Brendan, that's Sean, and the one that's pissed a fart over there is Roger. Roger, you've got the kitty! Let's get another couple of cases for the road before we go!" Winking at Iñaki, he announced, "If we don't spend the kitty, Roger the dodger will thieve it!"

The journey was long, at times noisy with Irish Republican songs bellowed out, but by the time they got to the Port Customs office at Roscoff, everyone was asleep.

The customs official took one look into the bus, and waved them through.

Chapter 50: Dublin

Sean and Brendan shared a flat in near University College in Dublin, and insisted Iñaki could bed down on the couch until he decided what to do next.

Iñaki refined his story that he had fallen out with his father over his ecological militancy and had dropped out of his course at university, or at least he wanted to take a break; he needed a bit of freedom to breathe. He didn't mention anything about the police and GAL searching for him, but had the feeling that it would not have mattered. His new companions were members of the University Sinn Fein Republican society, campaigning for a United Ireland, and were not slow in voicing their contempt for the English domination of Ireland.

After a few days re-locating his way around Dublin, he found a job in a pub in the lively Temple Bar area. Iñaki was already missing home terribly, but the lively student scene and the hospitality he was receiving from his new friends helped assuage his nostalgia for Bilbao.

Sean and Brendan were at the very heart of the Republican social set, and soon Iñaki was enjoying the continual after hour´s party scene. Unlike his group in the Eco Movement in Bilbao, which at times was too much doom and gloom; the Republicans could be deadly serious and passionate about their United Ireland dedication, but quickly stick `The Cause´ into cupboards in their minds and concentrate on have a good time. It seemed to Iñaki that every night it was obligatory to get pissed, and laugh until you fell down.

After a few weeks, Iñaki moved out from his sofa bed with Sean and Brendan, much to their protests, and found a cheap but pretty, one-bedroom attic to rent in a rundown building near to the famous Guinness Storehouses.

At yet another party, one of his new friends spoke seriously to him. Connor Rafferty was a lecturer in Political Science and although both were more than a little inebriated, he said he was concerned for him.

Breathing high-octane whiskey fumes and spittle into his ear he said, "Iñaki, you can tell me to feck off, and mind my own business, but you are too intelligent to be wasting your time serving in a feckin´ bar. Brendan told me that you gave up on university in Spain to come here, an´ no doubt you have your reasons. But listen, we Irish, the Paddy´s, have always taken pride in education, particularly in literature, and it makes me sad to see someone like you drifting; do you know what I mean?"

Iñaki protested, "Jesus, I´ve only been here for a few months, and I like the bar scene."

More boozy fumes breathed out of Connor, "You´re not trying to tell me that you´re goin´ to make a career of it?"

"No, but right now I need the money Connor, and the bar job´s okay for now," Iñaki replied.

"That´s gob-shite" Connor spat, "listen, I´ve got a friend who has a bookshop near Trinity, he´s looking for an assistant. You could do that and get back into exercising your brain again, instead of destroying it with smoke and drink."

Overnight the idea took root in his mind, and the next day he phoned Connor and arranged to meet him at the shop when he had finished his lectures.

It turned out to be a specialist academic and cultural bookshop, and Iñaki had severe reservations he would be able to cope. However, the owner, a gregarious, bearded homosexual ex-academic convinced him that he would soon pick it up. There were three other staff and Iñaki would not need to deal with the public. Initially his main job would be stacking the shelves and looking after the upstairs storeroom. With a suggestive twinkle in his eye his new boss Joe, assured him that he would personally show him the ropes. The money was more or less the same as the bar, but his hours would be infinitely better.

The bookshop was much busier than he imagined and the other staff much too busy dealing with customers to give him no more than a rudimentary introduction to his duties. Accordingly, he suffered a very nervous first few days at his new job.

A few days later, just before closing at six, he was sorting titles in the Environmental Sciences shelves, when a softly spoken voice asked, from behind him, "Can you point me to the Friends of the Earth reports?"

He turned around to face the enquirer, and found him looking into a startling pair of grey blue eyes, which momentarily stunned his senses.

Gathering his wits he replied, "I'm sorry; I'm not sure, I just started this week."

"Oh, you'll be the new boy then, Connor's Spanish friend." The girl went on, "You'll be no use to me then, you won't know nothing yet."

"Next to nothing," he replied, and pointing across the aisle, "but I think they'll be over there, in Ecology and Bio Science. This time looking closely at her, she seemed familiar. Have I seen you before?" he enquired.

"That's an old line, she laughed; I've seen you at a party, I think in Connor's flat, after a Domhan Glas Iaochra meeting?"

"After what meeting?" he asked.

"Domhan Glas Iaochra, the Green Earth Warrior movement; Connor is the Chairman of the University Chapter. I'll see if I can find this damn Sellafield report, before you close the bloody door. Fancy a drink when you're finished?"

Iñaki was now accustomed to the Irish directness in social affairs. In Spain, it would have been unheard of a girl to invite a boy she had just met to a bar; unthinkable. This girl was attractive, slim and petit; her dark wavy hair was cut short almost to a boy's length. Her humorous dimples on her cheeks suggested mischief, and she was asking him to go for a drink!

"Sure, he said, where will we go?"

"Do you know O'Neil's?" She asked, "Just up from the Bank of Ireland in Oliver Street?"

"Yes, I think so, if I can't find it I'll ask someone. Half past six, then?" Iñaki replied, still a little intrigued.

"That's fine with me, Señor Basque man." She went over to find her Friends of the Earth report, Iñaki stealing glances at her as he finished his work on the Environmental Science shelves.

She gave a quick 'bye wave, "See you later", and hurried to pay for her reports, just as the bell went to clear the shop for closing.

It was Iñaki´s job to collect all the rubbish, and take them to the container in the lane behind the shop. There seemed to be tons this night, and Joe, the owner wanted to ask him how he was enjoying his job. It was twenty past six before he left the premises and sprinted all the way to O´Neil´s and locating it without having to enquire from anyone.

O´Neil´s was busy with shoppers and workers grabbing a pint before going home. It was a traditionally decorated, old established pub, where none of the bar staff, in their white shirts, black trousers and white aprons looked under sixty-five years old. Even though the pub was packed, they had an easy, jovial, and convivial relationship with their customers who in turn forgave the rather slow service, as the Guinness took five minutes to settle.

Iñaki had to search a bit, spirits sinking a little, as he was late, before he found her sitting a tiny table in the far corner of the lounge. "Sorry I´m late, he said, but the boss wanted to talk to me."

"Don´t worry about it; just don´t get caught in the back room with Joe!" Crossly she went on, "I was reading this report. Did you know that the bloody English are polluting the Irish Sea with nuclear waste?"

"No, but I´m sure you are going to inform me. What are you drinking?" Iñaki asked.

"I´m fine for now, maybe later." She replied.

He went to the bar, and came back with a pint of Guinness.

She began again, "I was telling you about Sellafield, that´s one of their Nuclear Power Stations. It´s discharging radioactive contaminated waste directly into the sea, and the currents are bringing it over to us. Not only that, but and the bastards know all about it!" She asked, "Were you not involved with the Green movement in Spain?"

"You seem to know a lot about me," he said, suspicious now. Firstly, you know I´m from the Basque country, and now you know about my eco militancy. Who told you all this? I still don´t even know your name!"

"Keep your hair on Señor! Firstly, Dublin is a small town; secondly, I´m a friend of Roger, who´s a friend of Sean and Brendan and we are all in Sinn Fein." Seeing his still dubious expression, she went on, "We talk, it´s normal gossip and to them it´s a laugh. I know all about you coming over from France with them after the Rugby. Thirdly, there are not that many Spanish student types around here, and I asked Connor about you after the party. Satisfied?" Smiling and holding out her hand, she said, "Oh, and I´m called Siobhan Brennan."

Satisfied to a point, Iñaki had not realised that people, quite naturally would take any notice of him, but after his experience with GAL, he was still a little nervous.

"I´m sorry, I didn´t mean to be rude. Accepting her hand gesture, he continued, "I´m Iñaki Anton. I come from Bilbao and you are correct, I was involved in the Green protests, but I´ve had enough trouble with my father over this without getting involved again."

"Did I ask you to get involved? Jesus Christ!" Angry now, stood up gathering up her papers.

Joder, he was thinking, *this has started all wrong; she´s interested enough in ecology to be a member of this movement and taking the trouble to be studying reports, just as I used to, and I get nervous.....shit!* Getting to his feet, he implored, "Look, I´m sorry, please sit down again......please. There are things that happened back in Bilbao that I cannot talk about now. Here, sit down and have a drink, and we´ll begin again."

Tossing back her hair from her face, the eyes flashed again, "Okay, Señor Iñaki, but no more of your bad moods; I get enough of them from my dad!"

Over the next hour and a half, they drank and talked, mainly about themselves, and their families, but the talk returned to the Sellafield pollution scandal. Iñaki finally relaxed enough to tell her about Lemoniz, and what had happened after ETA had murdered the engineers. He refrained to go into detail of his own problems with GAL, only that Lemoniz had caused a split between him and his father.

Siobhan was completing a degree in Biology and Earth Sciences, impressing him with her knowledge. Her animation and zeal for ecology was forcing his own suppressed fervour for the subject to return. Her almost exaggerated facial expressions, hand movements, and those captivating eyes were convincing enough. He wanted to see more of this alluring creature.

Iñaki realised he was hungry, and decided to risk a bit more. "Are you ready for a something to eat?" he asked.

"I´m famished! I was thinking of eating my left hand in the time it took you to ask me!" she laughed.

He got up from the table, "I´ll get a menu"

"We´ll not be eating here!" She exclaimed. "It´s frozen tourist muck that's served up in here. I know a great pub, it´s not that far, just down behind Trinity, and they serve real food and cheap enough for me to afford."

Chapter 51: The Republicans

They agreed to go Dutch on the drinks, and Iñaki went to the toilet to relieve himself of some of pints of Guinness he had been drinking.

When he came back, she was nowhere to be seen, but looking around on the way out, he saw her talking animatedly to someone on the phone at the bar. She waved and mouthed to him, "I´ll meet you outside."

Iñaki pushed his way outside to find night had closed in, and a fine mist of rain was falling, giving a yellow halo to the streetlights, and a damp swish to the passing traffic.

Just as he was about to go back into the bar to escape the drizzle, she emerged through the doors, her smile melting the surge of annoyance that had begun to creep into his mind.

"Come on," she said, linking her arm through his, "your old Spanish bones won't get cold, it's not very far."

They went up, and around Trinity College and into Docklands turning into an old, run down looking pub called John Flaherty's.

As they entered, the barman called out "Hi Siobhan, how's things?"

She returned the salutation, with "What's the craic Frank?"

Hanging up their dripping jackets, on the rack, Iñaki asked, "What are you having, I can't take any more Guinness, or I'll explode!"

"We'll get a bottle of the house wine," she decided. "I know it looks a dump, but it's class stuff in here. The Fish Pie is great if you like fish; if not, and you want meat, the Irish Hot Pot's the thing for you."

They ordered, and when the wine was poured, clinked glasses.

"Hmm, this is very a good wine!" He inspected the bottle; `Bodegas Marques de Murillo´, Rioja Alta. Appreciatively he added, "It's a *Crianza* as well."

"I told you it was class in here, she laughed, we're not all Paddy's you know!"

As they were awaiting their food, they talked a bit about life in Dublin, when she suddenly asked; "Have you ever been up North?"

"You mean into the British Ulster?" he asked.

"No," she answered, "what I really meant was the country around Sligo, on the West Coast; it's really beautiful up there, and the seafood, is fabulous!"

"Is it not dangerous up there?" Iñaki enquired. "That´s where the IRA and the British are fighting is it not."

"Well, from I´ve read about the Basque country, it´s no more dangerous than that, but the troubles are over the border in Ulster, and mainly in Belfast at that." Siobhan added.

"Why are they fighting?" He asked before explaining, in the Basque country, ETA is trying to get compete independence from Spain, and probably later on, from France as well. The Basque Country, *Euskadi*, straddles both sides of the border. Did you know that my people, the Basque, are among the oldest original inhabitants of Europe?"

"Well that´s just about the same position as we are in," Siobhan interrupted. "There was no Ulster at all; it was a united Ireland until the English invaded and buggered it all up."

"I know that bit," he interjected, "but why are the Protestants and the Catholics killing each other? That sounds medieval; a religious war!"

"Well it´s a bit more complicated than that," she answered, "but basically, the IRA is fighting to re-unite Ireland, and the Protestants want Ulster to remain part of Britain. The root of it all is the injustice. They´ve got the power, the jobs, the best housing. The Catholics are third class citizens in their own country! Furthermore, the Protestants have the police and army on their side. It´s a bloody scandal and the world is doing nothing about it!"

Her eyes were blazing mad, and a flush had appeared on her cheeks; she was really getting steamed up about it; "Sometimes I get so damned angry about it all, I feel maybe I should get involved, and join up and fight, and stop just bloody thinking!" Calming down a little, and with slightly questioning look in her eyes, she reasoned, "I suppose though I´d better wait and finish my degree first."

Iñaki had been taken aback at the ferocity of anger he had just witnessed from this pretty, young and vibrant woman, and a pregnant silence ensued as he thought of something to say.

Finally, heaving a sigh, which broke the moment of awkwardness, she said a little morosely, "Here´s our food, this is all getting too heavy for now."

There wasn´t much more time for conversation, as they wolfed down the steaming, delicious Fish and Potato Pie they had both ordered. They were both mopping up the remains of the sauce, with crusty bread when they heard, "Siobhan Brennan, who is that handsome Latin lover you have there?"

A very attractive, red haired woman, and dark, full bearded man standing over the table, "Fancy you being here tonight," said the red head.

Exasperation in her voice, Siobhan announced, "Iñaki, this here woman is the bane of my life! Meet Shaina, and hairy face there is my brother, Padraig."

"It´s good to know you, I´m Padraig, the man announced, and this woman is Shaina, the bane of my life also!" A firm handshake from the man and a light kiss from the girl completed the introductions. "You are Spanish?" he asked.

"I´m from the Basque country; it´s part of Spain… but I´m spending some time here."

Shaina changed the subject, "Did you know Iaochra Glas were playing here tonight?"

"No I didn´t," Siobhan answered, "as a matter of fact who are they; some sort of Gaelic Choir?"

The three laughed uproariously, leaving Iñaki in the dark until Siobhan explained that the group was actually called Desmond´s Fiddle Band, but as they played at all the Domhan Glas Iaochra´s social events, they were christened with the more salubrious `Green Ireland´ title.

"Sit down and join us," invited Siobhan, indicated the other two seats at the table. We´ve just finished our dinner."

Iñaki was just a bit annoyed at the intrusion. He had been hoping to get to know this girl; but he had no choice but to show some hospitality.

"What's that poncey red wine stuff you're drinking?" asked Shaina, taking the glass from Siobhan's hand and taking a gulp. "Hmm, better than cat's piss; we'll have another bottle!"

Afterwards, he was glad that they had joined with them. They proved to be a very lively, entertaining and fun couple.
Desmond's Fiddlers proved to be a great traditional Irish music band, and the place had soon filled up with an undoubtedly Republican crowd, drinking, singing and dancing to the music.

The night finished at Padraig and Shaina's flat for a coffee, and later Iñaki took Siobhan home near Phoenix Park. In the taxi they had enough desire and lust for passionate kissing and fumbling, but conscious of the driver's amused glances in the mirror, went no further.

Jumping out of the taxi, she blew him a kiss and whispered, "Same time, same place tomorrow, okay?"
Later, in bed, he reflected on his good fortune, smiling with the recollection of the night, but then a worm of thoughts of Bilbao inexplicably entered his head, troubling him. He resolved to telephone his aunt Teresa who lived in Madrid, if she had any news for him, and to send his love to his family.

Next day at lunchtime, he telephoned Tia Teresa in Madrid. She was married to a civil servant in the Justice Department, and her tone of greeting gave Iñaki the impression that she was not at all happy he had telephoned her.

She was surprised to hear from him, but "No there was no more news other than Maria had been released on a Bond until her case was heard in the courts. Your mother is still ill from all the trouble that had befallen the family. You should be ashamed of yourself Iñaki," she added, "we all expected better things from you." However, she promised to pass on a message of love to his mother and Maria, and that he was okay.

The apparent coolness left Iñaki deflated, and he now wished he hadn´t phoned. At least Maria was out of prison!

They met in John Flaherty´s, this time she wore a dark green bomber jacket over red jeans. She looked young and fresh. Looking at her and listening to the animated description of her day, his mood and spirits rose.

Iñaki had been finding it increasingly difficult to conceal his secret story, whilst surrounded by these genuine, open and sincere people. He needed to talk, to get some things off his chest. Although they had only met the day before, he had a confidence in her honest, open-minded intelligence.

Gravely, she listened to his story. She was appalled, but not surprised; she said similar things were happening everyday in Northern Ireland.

"Iñaki, the people have to come off the fence and fight these arrogant bastards, otherwise we´ll be living in a Police State again," all the while emphasizing with her tiny fist on the table. "The ordinary folk will have to resist sometime!"

They had a quieter night, and went back to Iñaki´s, to play some CD´s, and neck a little. Any attempt to go further was gently rebuked by Siobhan; "Iñaki, I´m a good Catholic girl!" whereas he sulked himself into a bad mood when he had to walk her home through the drizzle to Phoenix Park.

They saw each other most nights after this, sometimes for the cinema, others at John Flaherty´s, and other nights at the regular Republican parties. Padraig and Shaina frequently accompanied them, the latter flirting outrageously with her Latin Buoy, much to the embarrassment of Iñaki. Oddly enough, neither Siobhan nor Padraig seemed to mind. They always had a great time with the older couple, usually ending up in their flat afterwards where great Republican victories over the English were predicted in rousing song and verse.

Joe, his boss, had enough confidence in him now to send him on delivery runs to the University, and to various other bookshops that used him as a wholesaler. On returning to work after a delivery, Iñaki was surprised to see Padraig in the shop talking to Joe.

Seeing him, Padraig called out "How´s the craic! I was just telling Joe about last night, a great night! Joe, this Basque man knows a few rebel songs already!"

Joe beamed all over at the thought.

"Hi Padraig," Iñaki returned the greetings, as handshakes and backslaps were exchanged; "what´s up?"

"Nothing´s up, but Siobhan phoned me to tell you she´s got a tutorial between six and seven that she forgot about. She says her brain wasn´t functioning last night, I wonder why?" Padraig was grinning at Iñaki. "She´s normally one hundred percent concentration, someone or something must be on her mind just now. Anyway, can you meet her at the Domhan Glas reunion? Shaina and I will take you to there." Noticing Iñaki hesitating, he added, "Don´t worry, you´ll recognise a few friends there. They´ve got a guest speaker from Greenpeace coming over from England; should be interesting."

A little reluctantly, he agreed, and Padraig arranged to see him in O´Neil´s at six-thirty.

In the afternoon, Joe made some effort to talk a little, and explain the stock system they were using. It was apparent that there was a preponderance of Irish Republican literature on the shelves, as well as the normal academic English literature tomes. Time passed quickly, and before he knew it, it was six o´clock; rubbish to be put out, and up the road to O´Neil´s. The night was fine for a change, just a light, but chilly wind to contend with, as he made his way there.

Shaina was already in the bar. She explained that Padraig would be a little late; something had turned up at the last minute; would he mind if she kept him company, smiling and raising her eyebrows questioningly.

"No, I don´t mind," as he thought, *most of the guys´ in this pub, would fall over themselves to keep her company.*

Iñaki asked her if she wanted another drink, which she declined for the moment; he settled on a half pint of Guinness, but with a Jameson's whiskey chaser to prove his manhood. She was good company, which he already knew from before; no inhibitions in chatting freely, at times placing her hand over his in her closeness. She asked him about Bilbao night life, and what support ETA from the public and so on.

Suddenly, it was half past seven, and she exclaimed, "Where in the hell has he got to?" She excused herself, and went to the bar and used the phone. In a few minutes she was back, and a little annoyed; "We´ve to make our own way to the Student Union, and they´ll meet us there. I shouldn´t say this, but when he gets involved in his Republican Sinn Fein work, there´s no shifting him. Patriot should be his name, not Padraig!"

When they arrived at the Union, there was a small crowd gathered outside. Padraig was standing at the top of the stairs at the entrance addressing them. They caught the last of his words as "…we don´t know anything more at the moment, just that he´s been shot, and he´s in hospital in Belfast."

Someone in the crowd asked, "Is he being guarded?"

He answered, "Some of our people are there, but the police won´t let them near him. I don´t think they would dare let anything happen to him in the hospital!"

Shaina asked someone next to her, "Who is it that´s been shot?"

Angrily the woman replied, "Gerry Adams and three others of our people! The UVF are claiming responsibility! Feckin´ bastards!"

"Shit!" Shaina exclaimed, and turning to Iñaki explained, "Gerry Adams is one of our best commanders in the North, not only military, but politically as well. This really is bad news!"

Just then, Padraig and Siobhan pushed their way through the crowd, both looking agitated and worried. Padraig asked, "You've heard about Gerry Adams?" When Shaina nodded in affirmation, he went on, "You three go on in to the lecture, I'll have to go up to Dundalk and find out what's happening."

"Jesus, do you have to?" asked Shaina.

"Yes, but don't worry, we won't be over the border this time. You'd better maintain a normal routine, don't draw any attention to your-selves." Turning and addressing Iñaki he said, "Look after the girls Iñaki, I'll explain everything to you when I get back." With that, he gave the women a hug, shook Iñaki by the hand and, to Iñaki's surprise left the gathering accompanied with Joe... Iñaki's boss!

Iñaki realised that there was much he didn't know about his friends. He knew they were committed Republican Nationalists, but it now appeared they were much more deeply implicated in the IRA campaign than he imagined. He wasn't concerned about this fact, he himself was a Basque Nationalist; what was bothering him was what he didn't know. He resolved to ask some direct questions after the meeting, when he was alone with Siobhan.

Chapter 52: The Ecology Lecture

The Lecture was a late in starting, due to the commotion outside. It was evident that many of the university Green Earth Warrior movement were also Republican Sinn Fein sympathisers, but they soon settled down to an impressive illustrative lecture from the Liverpool university professor.

Malevolent Karma

Professor Eric McGilvery was a small skinny man, about forty-five years old, dressed in a blue calico smock-like shirt and grey chino´s. His wispy, greying beard and rimless glasses perched on the tip of his nose seemed to accentuate his `green´ credentials.

With his microphone screaming from feedback, he began the meeting with the usual thank you for coming along, as a sound technician scurried around adjusting switches.

Professor McGilvery had irrefutable proof that Sellafield was discharging radioactive contaminated waste directly into the Irish Sea. An independent study, calculated that there was more than two hundred kilograms of plutonium lying on the seabed, making the Irish Sea one of the most polluted sea in the world. A further leakage of radioactive material onto the beaches had resulted in the closing of a ten miles stretch of beach on the Cumbrian coast near Sellafield, and sea-bathing prohibited over a wide area. Using photographic slides he pointed to one of the open air ponds, used to contain radioactive waste was so badly contaminated, that workers were not allowed to spend any more than two minutes at a time around the area.

Angrily he pointed out, "There is no control over wildlife, so birds can land on this radioactive soup, take off freely carrying the plutonium with them." He paused, and continued his talk to his rapt audience, all the time flicking the images forward showing gulls, cormorants sand pipers landing on the contaminated water and taking off again.

He explained, "The official name for this pond is B30, but is widely known in and around Sellafield as Dirty Thirty. We, that is, the Green Party and Friends of the Earth, have raised this complaint in the European Parliament. The European Commission has taken the British Government to court over this issue and the Irish and Norwegian Governments have lodged strong protests, but Great Britain has chosen to ignore the complaints."

The professor concluded, "The British Government seems to be immune to diplomatic protest or intervention

Drawing his small frame up to its fullest, he exhorted, "Comrades it is time for direct action!" Waiting for the applause and clamour to die down, he calmed the audience and pronounced; "I am proposing, and willing to organise a weekend of protest and demonstrations at Sellafield on the May Bank Holiday of this year. We will block that damnable site, and the whole world will be watching!" Finally, he announced, "I am asking for volunteers to come from all over Ireland to demand the closure of this monstrosity, which is poisoning this, and our future generations!"

The Professor received a standing ovation from the audience. When things settled down, Connor Rafferty thanked the Professor on behalf of Domhan Glas Iaochra, and promised full support. He announced that he would be collecting signatures of volunteers to go to Sellafield. Connor told the audience, "On condition of anonymity, we´ve already had been promised ample funding from a group of concerned Irish citizens. Therefore the weekend will be free for the protesters; travel and meals provided, but you have to bring your own tent!"

Iñaki left with the two girls, receiving salutations from friends and acquaintances on the way out. Sean and Brendan were there, and embraced him like a brother.
"Are you going?" asked Sean, and instead of waiting for a reply, insisted, "Of course you are, it will a feckin´ great party!"
Iñaki was thinking that he had been in Dublin for only a few months, but these people had shown great friendship and hospitality since Biarritz!
They made their way to John Flaherty´s pub, along with maybe a hundred others. Iñaki was impatient to question the girls about Padraig, but yet another party was developing and he didn´t want to spoil it by serious discussion.
They had some food, again delicious, and shared a bottle of that Murillo Rioja again. When Siobhan and Shaina

went to the ladies' toilet, Connor came over and asked him what he thought of the lecture, and would he be going to Sellafield with them.

Inaki replied it had been impressive, and he would like to go, providing he knew some of the others.

"That won't be a problem, I'll be going." It was Siobhan, he hadn't noticed the girls had returned. She continued, "Shaina's going home now, she's got a bit of a headache, and she's worried about Padraig."

Connor also excused himself; he had to pick up the professor at his hotel, and show him some Dublin hospitality. He offered to drop Shaina off at her flat and they made their farewells and left.

Iñaki watched them leave, questions in his mind which were interrupted by Siobhan saying, "Let's go to a quieter place Iñaki, I've had a hard day, and I want to talk to you, okay?"

"Fine by me," he replied, thinking *I'll get some answers now.*

Chapter 53: Entanglement

Siobhan took his arm and snuggled in as they walked down by the River Liffey, breathing in the cold night air. They stopped at a trendy business pub, quiet at this time of the night, and sought a table in a corner. They ordered two glasses of Cabernet-Merlot, and then she began to talk.

She began, "Shaina and I think we can trust you, but it's essential that you promise not to divulge anything I tell you to anyone else."

He promised as requested, and she continued.

"Padraig is a high ranking official in the political wing of the Provisional Irish Republican Army Council. He is not involved in the armed struggle, but he recognises that something has to be done to help the Catholic minority in the North, and eventually to force the British into negotiations and accepting that a United Ireland is inevitable."

She was talking in a low, sombre tone. "He was going to talk to you tonight and explain the situation, but the Gerry Adams shooting has meant he has had to go up North for consultations. Padraig doesn´t want reprisals, so he´s gone up to try and calm a few hot heads." She took one of his hands in hers, and looking into his eyes confided, "Iñaki, Padraig was going to ask you for some help. The Political wing of ETA, your own Basque freedom movement has been in contact with him in order to learn from each other´s experience. They want to explore common strategies in public relations, for example, prisoners´ rights, family support and so on. However, the language barrier is proving difficult to overcome."

She went on; "You are the obvious ideal candidate to help both sides. You would not be involved in any way in armed actions, and you would remain outside the membership of both organizations, unless you wished to become a militant. In a sense, you would be a diplomat."

A little bitterly he asked, "So I´ve been targeted Siobhan, is that it? I wondered why the interest in me!"

Angrily she protested, "That´s not true Iñaki! I saw you at one of the Eco parties, and asked about you. Connor told me you had come over with Sean and Brendan, so I asked them about you. I wanted to meet you; we´ve been happy together, is that not true? Please believe me Iñaki, the idea to help us only came today, when Padraig received another letter of communication from ETA; he can´t really understand what they are saying. They are trying to set up a meeting next weekend in France, Nantes, I think, and he doesn´t even talk French!"

"There must be French speakers in your Party", he said. "The Basque negotiators will speak French."

"That's true, but Padraig wants to be able to really understand the Basque mentality." She was being sincere; "Listen, the Protestants in the North are Irish, but their mentality is completely different from ours, and we both speak English; do you understand the point that I'm making?"

Iñaki answered, "Of course I do; but I need to think about this; I can't go back to Bilbao, because I got involved in the demonstrations there. I would like to help, Siobhan, but I don't really need any more trouble."

"Okay Iñaki," she responded, the built up tension had carried into her voice; "it's not your fight here, and it appears that it's not your fight in Spain either. I'm sorry, I had no right to ask you to help." She got up and put on her coat to leave, adding; "Iñaki, please don't say anything to anyone about what I've told you; I'd be in serious trouble, and probably Shaina and Padraig also, if this gets out."

Sighing inwardly, Iñaki said, "Sit down Siobhan, I only said I wanted to think it over. I need to talk to Padraig, about his thoughts, where this is going; you understand that, don't you?"

"Yes, Iñaki, but you don't realise how difficult it is for us. Everyone complains about Thatcher and the rest of the arrogant bastards, but very few have the balls to stand up and fight for their rights! The Brits are slaughtering Catholics in the North; Catholic kids get stoned on the way to school and the IRA is blamed when we fight back!" She sounded and looked deflated, "Look, I don't want to argue, I'm exhausted, can you please take me home?"

Concern was on his face, "Sure, of course, we'll get a Taxi."

Wearily she said, "No, let's walk, I just want to be near you tonight; just take me to your place."

Surprised, Iñaki asked, "What about your father?"

"I'll tell him I'm with Shaina, I often stay with them."

He paid at the bar, almost twice as much as at Flaherty´s and by no means the same quality, but this is a Yuppie bar, he thought.

Walking to his attic, she held on to him, and he realised that she was weeping gently; the stress and pressure of her hidden life was taking its toll.

In the apartment, he poured them both a large Jameson´s, and they sat on the sofa. She snuggled up against his shoulder. She was sleeping before she had finished her whiskey, and he carried her into the bedroom.

She woke up, and began undressing; "Iñaki, please, I need you to hold me tonight, that´s all, just hold me tight."

He hurriedly undressed, and slipped in beside her, and naked together they just held each other, sleeping, co-joined in a lovers embrace.

Chapter 54: Rory Gallagher

An aged looking Padraig was back in Dublin after three days. He came round to the bookshop to speak to Iñaki. He was looking drawn and strained, the tension laying down furrows over his brow; his eyes were dark and sunken sitting over hollow cheeks.

Taking him by the arm he said, "Iñaki, I need to talk to you, but I haven´t got time right now. Can you come by my flat tonight; say nine o´clock? It´s a boy´s night, the girls are going to the pictures."

An inexplicable chill ran down Iñaki´s spine, but he said, "Sure, Padraig, I´ll be there. I assume you´ve said something to Siobhan?"

He smiled for the first time, "Yeah, don't worry, she'll be seeing you later. Sorry, but I've got to go." With that, he was out of the bookshop, as if he had never entered.

Joe appeared in the bookshop in the afternoon, and unlike his normal exuberant self, he was subdued and worried. He snapped at Mrs Murphy, his Assistant Manager, over something she had forgotten to do while he was away. This was completely out of character and left her upset and in tears. There was a tension in the air; everyone seemed to be subdued after Joe's uncharacteristic outburst. That afternoon, time seemed to pass slowly, and Iñaki began to doubt his decision to implicate himself in the PIRA and ETA negotiations, however peaceful they might turn out to be.

He was at Padraig's flat dead on nine, after a convoluted tour making sure he wasn't followed or observed. The door was opened by a big, rough and hard faced individual whom Iñaki hadn't seen before, who checked the street outside before frisking Iñaki thoroughly. He called out "He's clean."

Connor Rafferty came out, looking exhausted and tense, "Glad you could make it Iñaki," showing him into the living room.

Already present and standing around, were Padraig, Joe and a small, ginger haired, wiry framed man of about twenty-five, with icy, piercing grey eyes, who was introduced only as `Rory´.

Iñaki quickly sized `Rory´, as being a dangerous individual, just by the slightly callous, almost contemptuous expression on his mouth, and the disdainful posture of a hard man. He had come across the Basque equivalents in the Nationalist bars of Getxo; a breed of men who had no respect for human feelings and no fear of violence.

Without bothering to shake hands with Iñaki, Rory said, "You're our new translator then?"

Iñaki acknowledged with a quiet "I'm willing to help."

Rory fixed Iñaki with a stare, and with a menace conveyed by his eyes said, "Iñaki, you are now my friend, don´t ever give me cause to be your enemy!"

This brought a cold shiver down Iñaki´s spine, and he felt it prudent not to reply.

Padraig, interrupting, said, "Rory has stayed on to meet you Iñaki, but has to go back up north in few minutes."

Padraig and Rory then went out into the hallway and held a conversation, whilst Connor imparted his appreciation to Iñaki for helping them out. He asserted that he would be protected. He explained, the Provisional Irish Republican Army had infiltrated the Garda Special Branch police, and had sympathisers embedded in the Interior Ministry. They had run a check to ensure that Iñaki was `clean´, and his name has not raised any flags. "We want to keep it that way," he said, "your name will not appear in any documents, and you´ll be provided with a new identity, including an Irish Passport for the France trip. Any contacts between us will be through Joe at the bookshop, or on Domhan Glas Iaochra business." He then produced a membership card for the ecological group in Iñaki´s name, and handed it over.

Iñaki reiterated, "Connor, I am not going to get involved in shooting or bombing anyone."

Connor, somewhat impatiently said, "Iñaki, neither are we; we are a political organization. We are trying to get peace through negotiation, but the Brits won´t respond." Nodding in the direction of the hallway, he went on, "That´s why guys like him are involved."

Just at that moment Padraig returned saying, "That´s him away, thank Christ. If he had his way, he would bomb everything and everyone in Belfast!"

They all sat around the table; Joe opened some beers, and they explained the plans and details of the Nantes meeting to Iñaki, with him asking questions at appropriate times. It was all of political strategy, methods of communication and coordination, to exert pressure on the respective governments.

Iñaki had feared that they were planning some kind of violent action. He felt more at ease by the time the discussions had terminated.

Just in case of questions from nosey people, Connor then explained some of the plans for the Sellafield protest weekend, as tonight's cover was supposed to be a meeting of the Action Planning Committee.

The telephone rang, Padraig answered and said something to the effect that, "Yes, we're finished."

Shaina and Siobhan came in a few minutes afterwards; they must have been close by.

Everyone expressed feeling drained, and the group broke up shortly after. Connor left with Joe, and after a few minutes, Iñaki and Siobhan left to go home.

Once in the street, Siobhan said, "I'll bet you're starving. Let's get a Chinese, and we'll take it home; my dad knows I'm staying at Padraig's again tonight. Is that okay with you, darling?" Her impudent eyes were again flashing a seductive message at him.

Iñaki, of course, felt obliged to go along with the plan; after all, she couldn't go home now that she'd told her father she was at Shaina's.

The Chinese meal was okay, and the bottle of Merlot they consumed relaxed them both enough to stimulate a yearning and desire, only momentarily spoiled when Iñaki couldn't find a condom, it being so long since he'd had the opportunity! It had the benefit of slowing things down though, and they introduced sensuality into their lovemaking, marked up until then by a frenzy of lust.

Naked, with a candle floating in a bowl, it's light dancing shadows on the ceiling, they enjoyed the exploration of each other's bodies, finally reaching the crest of satisfaction, and afterwards the luxury of exhausted sleep.

Chapter 55: Nantes, France

Security for the Nantes meeting with the ETA representatives was thorough. Only Padraig and Iñaki, now `*Fernando Lopez Garcia*´ according to his new passport. They took a ferry to Liverpool, and then flew from Manchester to Paris, and then hiring a small Peugeot to drive down to Nantes.

The two teams met quite casually in a city centre bar, and then made their way to a nondescript apartment, rented by a young newly married Spanish waiter, working in the Grande Palais function suites.

Discussions were productive and ideas exchanged. Iñaki was particularly pleased when one of his suggestions was included in the action plan. Both organizations should set up Welfare Societies, not only to help the poor and prisoners families, but also to stage social events where they could promote a `soft´ Nationalist message. There was no talk about the respective armed conflicts, but letters changed hands between the leaders, presumably messages from their respective military wings.

Most importantly however, a trust was established, and further, regular meetings planned for every three months or so.

Iñaki had prepared an unsigned letter for his mother, which he asked the ETA representatives to post. This caused some consternation, it could be dangerous, but they agreed only after reading the contents.

Security on the return journey was equally tight, this time dropping the car at Orly Airport, then a Metro into Paris, a train to Amsterdam and a flight to Dublin; tiresome, but prudent.

Life returned to normal after the Nantes negotiations. The Provisionals´ had not escalated reprisals in the North, to the relief of Padraig, and the rest of the Political group. However, a worrying issue had surfaced. They were aware that something was brewing; something big being planned by the Army Council, and they were being kept out of the picture.

Chapter 56: 1984 Sellafield

The Sellafield protest went ahead with almost a thousand demonstrators travelling from Ireland in buses, trains, and private cars.

The advance party of the Organizing Committee, which also included Iñaki and the two girls, were lodged at Liverpool University, at the invitation of Professor McGilvery. Liverpool had recently inaugurated the Garden Festival, which the Professor described as "an organic crumb thrown to the peasants who needed real, not illusionary work."
Nevertheless, he, and his volunteers had meticulously planned the protest. It would begin on the Friday with an assembly and social event on a nearby farm field, lent to them by a local farmer. Saturday would see the crowds converging on the main gate, and the plan was to blockade the Power Station for twenty-four hours.

Professor McGilvery was insisting upon a non-violent, passive resistance demonstration, as the national television companies and newspapers had agreed to provide blanket coverage.

The only, but serious problem would be the attitude of the police. They had stated quite clearly, that they considered the blocking of one of the country´s most important Electricity Generating Stations to be illegal, and would forcefully remove any protesters from the access roads, if necessary. Whether they would baton charge peaceful demonstrators in front of the TV cameras was anyone´s guess, but the police were on a high, with their actions against the miners on strike in Lancashire and Yorkshire. McGilvery instructed that all demonstrators should be afore-warned to bring suitable protection, but insisted that the protesters´ resistance must be passive.

After dinner, Padraig, Iñaki and the girls went into the city centre, to take in the music scene, whilst Connor went to visit relatives in Anfield. He returned early next morning with a box of `goodies´.
Connor had brought a large box of firecrackers, flares, and smoke bombs."Just in case the police decided to get rough," he said, "but for God´s sake, don´t tell the Prof!"
      On the morning of Bank Holiday Friday, a huge convoy of buses and cars, decorated with streamers and balloons, threaded it´s way North on the M6.
Over two thousand, mainly but not all were young people. The atmosphere was like a gigantic party; Peace songs sung and with gusto slogans shouted in harmony, the jollity lasting until they reached the campsite.
    The convoy turned off the Motorway onto the A590, and into the narrow winding roads of the Lake District, one of the most beautiful mountainous areas of England. Immediately they picked up a police escort, although no attempt made to impede the progress of the demonstrators´ procession of buses and private cars.
The day was bright and sunny, with just a few clouds hanging around the Peaks and Fells. The protesters were enjoying the scenery; after all they were here trying to preserve the natural environment against the monstrosity of the nuclear industry.
    At Broughton, they took the A595, and received the first interference from the authorities. The police were checking the licenses and vehicle documents of all traffic, causing a huge tailback, which extended through the small town, and inciting fury among the local population. The traffic jam eventually cleared, and eventually the buses reached the

planned farm campsite, about two miles north of the Sellafield complex.

Here, the police were out in force. Dozens of mounted officers, sitting impassively astride their horses, were blocking the entrance to the farm. In their medieval-like armour, they were uncannily like fourteenth century knights.

A river of fear swept through the demonstrators, but the leaders urged calm, and went forward to negotiate with the Chief Inspector in charge.

The Chief Inspector would not negotiate directly with Professor McGilvery, and his party. He insisted that the buses turn back, as the road was too narrow for them.

Calmly, McGilvery pointed out that heavy trucks were using the road every day, taking material into the Power Station.

The Inspector retorted that taking into account of the numbers of civilians in the area, they would have to turn back it. It was simply a matter of public safety.

It looked like an impasse, but the farmer came to the rescue. He took McGilvery to a gate further back along the road, and suggested that the protesters simply leave the buses, collect their gear and walk through the gate. He told the furious Chief Inspector that he was inviting all of these people to stay the weekend. It was his private property, and the police had absolutely no jurisdiction on his land.

A huge cheer went up, and the crowds began singing, "For he´s a jolly good farmer, for he´s a jolly good farmer!"

They poured onto the field, which had been prepared beforehand with a marquee canteen and kitchen in the centre of the field, and latrines dug in each corner. Probably in the region of three or four hundred protesters were already camped, and quite soon a small tented town had sprung up, and campfires lit to provide a barbecue party ambience.

Professor McGilvery called a council of war in the marquee. He was extremely worried about the attitude of the Police, their inflexibility and aggressive stance.

The TV and Press crews had arrived, and a decision made that the Prof and his team go back down to the police lines to negotiate some kind of peaceful demonstration agreement under the glare of the TV cameras.

Again the initiative failed; cameras or not, the demonstrators would not be allowed anywhere near the main gate to the Sellafield complex, and if they attempted to do so, they would be arrested. Frustrated, the negotiators went back to the campsite, to report to their followers.

McGilvery repeated that this had to be a peaceful, non-violent demonstration. "We must stand by our principles, he said, `Give Peace a Chance´, and get rid of this monstrous abomination on our doorstep!"

The mood turned ugly, with quite a few voices raised to charge the police lines now, without waiting for the morning. Many of the protesters had travelled from Scotland and Ireland, and they were not prepared to let the `Pigs´ treat them in this manner. The leaders again calmed the crowd, promising that nobody would be going back home without a protest blockage of some sort.

Later, Connor gathered a group of about twenty of the Domhan Glas militants, and he and Padraig outline a plan to disperse the police barricading the road by means of guerrilla tactics. "We didn´t come all this feckin´ way for a bunch of Police thugs to bash our heads in for no reason. We´ll block that feckin´ gate whether they like it or not!"

If the march was hindered, they would position themselves behind, and to the far side of the Police, using the hedges of the fields as cover. Firecrackers would frighten the horses, and then the smoke bombs would add enough confusion for the protesters to break through.

Professor McGilvery could not be informed of this action, as this would compromise his stance on non-violence. Connor then appointed a dozen militants who´s responsibility would be to rally the crowd into a united charge when the order came.

Chapter 57: The Battle of Sellafield

Next morning, Saturday, it had turned cold with heavy rain threatening later. The demonstrators were reinforced by a few hundred `independents´ who were there on their own violation.

They all lined up behind the Professor and advanced in order, with their banners and slogans held high, until they were about one hundred metres from the police lines. There they sat down in the road in defiance of the police. Professor McGilvery again went forward to try to convince the police inspector-in-charge to let them go through to the main gate.

Once again, he was rebuffed, and warned that the police would arrest anyone not obeying the order to disperse, which would be given in five minutes time.

Wearily, he and his team retreated to the front line of the demonstrators.

Five tense minutes went by, the TV reporters, with their cameras mounted, in the field to the right of the police ranks.

The chief inspector at last began to talk through his megaphone. "You have been told to evacuate the public highway, and now, in the interest of public safety, my officers will arrest anyone who refuses to disperse in five more minutes."

Again a ripple of apprehension ran through the four thousand strong crowd, but was quickly replaced by a communal belief that they would prevail. They had not travelled so far to be thwarted by this arrogant bastard and his minions, mounted or not.

At last, a whistle went up from the police lines, and the mounted officers began to move slowly forward.

The first firecrackers fell among the horses, and mayhem broke out. The police were unable to control the terrified animals; a few mounted officers were thrown from their saddles at the unexpected fury of the explosions. Some horses bolted towards the crowd, now on their feet and beginning to break in panic.

The majority of the mounted police, that is, those who were still in the saddle, were wheeling their terrified animals around looking for a way out of the trap. Many drove back down the road towards the Power Station, trampling and scattering the lines of police that had been following on foot.

Smoke bombs then added to the chaos, as Eco-warriors with Connor and Iñaki at the head, screamed at the crowd to charge.

Four thousand protesters, from all ages and backgrounds including pensioners, all at once terrified, but also exhilarated and united in common cause, charged down on the broken police lines.

Absolute chaos reigned, with screaming Eco-warriors hacking at terrified, whinnying horses. Hysterical shouts, screams of pain, smoke and explosions added to the pandemonium, until the sheer numbers of the eco protesters forced the police to give ground at first, and then a full scale retreat began, with them running down the road to the safety behind the gates of Sellafield.

Being unable to run in their armour, some of the now unhorsed officers received some rough treatment at the hands of the militants. The chief inspector had lost his hat, which was now on the head of an ecstatic Siobhan; Shaina having captured a mounted police helmet.

Finally, it was over; a jeering four thousand crowd sat down in front of the gates singing, `We shall not be moved´, whilst the disheartened police reformed behind the gates. The mood in front of the gates continued to be exultant; it was a victory party!

Behind the gates of Sellafield, it was a different disposition. The Sellafield Ministry of Defence Police force could hardly suppress their mirth at the inept performance of their counterparts in the Cumbrian Police, who´s `foot soldiers´ were furious and humiliated. They were blaming their officers for the tactical disaster.

Their chief inspector in turn was berating his mounted force for failing to control their horses at the crucial moment.

In the middle of his rant, he was called away to take an urgent call in the Security Centre from the Home Secretary.

"What the hell is going on up there?" The Minister demanded. "I'm at Chequers this weekend, guest of the Prime Minister, and I have been watching an absolute shambles on live television. The Prime minister will be arriving this afternoon for the weekend, so you tell me what in the hell went wrong here!" He went on, "The Police have been disgraced and humiliated by a bunch of sandal wearing ecologists! What do you think is going to happen in the mining areas next week, never mind Northern Ireland! I want it terminated and I want to inform the PM that this fracas has been brought to an end!" He roared on, "I'm sending the Assistant Chief Constable of Lancashire up there to take over. He will bring reinforcements. He's got the experience with the miners to deal with this. I will clear this action with your own Chief Constable. Ensure your full cooperation Chief Inspector!"

Professor McGilvery was furious. He was in great pain having had received a baton strike on his shoulder. As he berated the Irish contingent for the action, Connor replied, "If it wasn't for us, there would have been a few split heads back up there, and nothing achieved!"

The casualties were being ferried away in a fleet of ambulances to the hospitals in Whitehaven and Barrow-in-Furness for treatment. Some had quite serious wounds caused by the trampling, terrified horses, baton injuries and there was one heart attack victim.

McGilvery also had to go off for treatment, and Connor took over the leadership, using the same 'leaders' and shock troops as before to gain control of the crowd. He sent for a tent from the camp to be used as a forward HQ. Without doubt, the police would be responding with reinforcements.

Connor advised Padraig that he had to get out of the area. Padraig, however unwillingly, had to accept Connor's reasoning; the situation had changed radically. He was a political commander in the Provisional IRA and the situation was going to get very serious. They had to assume that the police would be putting up roadblocks all over the area; the chances of arrest had suddenly increased to a critical level.

They talked to Shaina and Siobhan, advising them to go with Padraig, but they were having none of it; they were having too much fun! Iñaki and Connor promised to look after them.

It went completely against all Padraig's character, but it was the correct thing to do before they tightened up the security checks at the ports. Making a hasty farewell to his friends, he drove away alone, taking a route down to Holyhead to catch a ferry back to Dublin.

The afternoon wore on with the protesters, still exhilarated by their victory, taking turns to go back to the camp for food and refreshment. The sky was turning black in the West, the weather was changing and it would almost certainly be a long, damp night's vigil.

When it was their turn to return to the camp, Iñaki, Shaina and Siobhan fell in with a group of protesters from Scotland. They instantly hit it off with the Scots.

The Scottish protesters were in the main from the peace camp at the Clyde Nuclear Submarine Base north of Glasgow. Over their tea and sandwiches, they talked about what the police would do now. An attractive Japanese-American woman was leading the Scots.

She introduced herself as Meryl Heston, and explained the different tactics adopted by the Scottish police in their dealings with the miners in Scotland. They had adopted a non-confrontational tactic by an agreement with the miners to avoid violence, whilst in England it had been direct confrontation regardless of the circumstances. She was of the opinion that the eco-protesters had to expect a tough line and violent response from the police, but hopefully it would be tempered by the presence of the TV cameras.

Most agreed that if nothing happened by seven o'clock tonight, it would be in the morning of Sunday when the police attacked. This was fine, the protesters' target of a twenty-four hour blockage, would have been achieved, and they could all go home satisfied.

Before going back to the front line, Meryl invited the Irish to visit them at Faslane, promising them a good time as well as a chance to demonstrate against the Polaris nuclear missiles.

They finished their tea, took their turns in the lines for the latrines, and then just as the rain started to come on, they walked back down to the protest

A police helicopter and two others, hired by the television companies, were circling overhead. A local resident reported that the Police were reinforcing from the Seascale side of the Sellafield Complex.

By six o'clock, the rain was falling steadily, and conditions were becoming miserable in front of the gates. A steady leakage of demonstrators began; as first, the older and the less committed ecologists began to drift back to the camp, and then more and more of the `freelance independents' also walked away. Finally, there were only about five or six hundred dedicated militants remaining, sitting huddled in blankets or below umbrellas. Now and again, they would burst into song, and shout their slogans at the watching police, protected in their wet weather gear, behind the gates.

The Assistant Chief Constable of Lancashire had arrived by helicopter, and was observing the scene with the Chief Inspector from the top of the Security Building.

After listening to the reports of the morning Police rout, he commented, "You made a complete arse of it Henry. Never put your calvary at the head of the attack. They are best chasing and mopping up the enemy flanks in the fields."

The Cumbrian Chief Inspector was advising him to attack now, before dark, but his superior with a look at the TV helicopters and the reporters on the ground, ruled against it. Besides, his reinforcements from the Lancashire coalfields were still arriving.

"Patience Henry," the ACC Lancashire counselled, "never rush an attack in a war. I want a complete rout of these bastards. That way they´ll have second thoughts before trying this again. Nope, we´ll wait until first light, when they´ll still be groggy. Meanwhile I want the whole area floodlit with the lights beaming directly into their eyes and get some oil drums or something down here, and a relay of your boys banging on them. That will drain their energy for singing!"

The Communications Centre called the Assistant Chief away to take a telephone call from the Home Office.

MI5 had received information from their Irish counterparts, that elements of the Provisional IRA Political wing had infiltrated the Domhan Glas militant group, and have travelled to Sellafield. There were rumours in that Provisional IRA is planning something big for the mainland; therefore an attack on Sellafield could not be discounted. In view of the organised violence today, it is possible that the Provo´s military wing had also arrived in the area, security would be stepped up.

The Minister of Defence, had ordered a platoon of SAS to arrive by Chinook from Northern Ireland. That was less than a half hour´s flying time. They would be there to prevent any attacks on the Nuclear Reactor or storage areas. Deadly force had been authorised if necessary. A list of PIRA militants suspected of being at Sellafield would be sent up later; they should be detained immediately.

"Jesus Christ, the Assistant Chief Constable commented to his deputy, we´ve been upgraded to Red Alert! These buggers out there are going to answer for this!"

Connor was analyzing the situation, and knew that the police would be attacking in overwhelming force. They would be seeking revenge, so rough treatment was to be expected. He decided that the flares and smoke bombs would only inflame the police into greater brutality.

They had achieved their purpose; therefore, it was prudent to retain them for another day. He retained about half of them, and gave the other half to Iñaki to look after.

The police would not risk a dangerous night battle, but the protestors would have to maintain their positions all night just in case. Connor thought that they would attack at about seven o´clock, just as the protesters were awakening. He had the additional anxiety that he or Iñaki could be arrested because of their PIRA involvement. That was too serious to contemplate. The ecological cause was one thing, but the possibility of serious trouble was now a real possibility.

The sound of the big military Chinook helicopter arriving overhead chilled his bones. The authorities had upped the stakes, and now he worried if the army had been called in to clear the demonstrators.

Connor called Iñaki and the girls together and outlined his disquiet, particularly as the army was now involved. He proposed that they should take the first night guard duty, twelve until four, and when relieved they should make their way back to the camp. When, and if they were attacked, the four of them should make for the latrine area nearest to the farm buildings. He stressed that the four of them could not make any difference this time, as the police and perhaps the army too, would be in a brutal and overwhelming strength.

Iñaki understood at once and secretly he was relieved, if arrested he could be deported back to Spain!

The two women were furious however; they saw it as an act of betrayal to the other Domhan Glas supporters. They accepted that the two men had to avoid capture at all cost, but they weren´t going anywhere!

Connor and Iñaki argued vehemently that they needed to stick together, and they were not going to leave the girls behind! Shaina and Siobhan argued that they were grown up, and didn´t need any feckin´ nanny to watch over them.

A compromise was reached; the captured police hats were attracting too much attention, so they would take them off or give them away, and when the fighting began, they would try and get away from the area. In the event of a rout, and separation, they would meet up in the Scots in the public bar of the George Hotel in Whitehaven on Sunday evening. They should not return with the Irish group; it was obviously too dangerous now.

Chapter 58: Strike back!

In the Security Centre, Assistant Chief Constable Jennings was describing his plan to the assembled reinforced police and Sellafield security top brass. They had been joined by a captain from the SAS Regiment, who had flown in with a platoon from their operating base in Portadown, near Belfast.

The Sellafield MOD police were sticking to their well rehearsed plans, and the SAS captain was liaising with them over the dispersal of his troops, around the `Hot Zones´.

The final placing of the SAS, was directly his responsibility; he stressed the importance that the police should stay clear of his troops, and in case of a fire fight, they must go to ground immediately and stay there until ordered to move. On no account were they to attempt to help whatever the circumstances; His boys would take care of any threat to the nuclear installations.

On this sobering thought, Jennings, outlined his plan to disperse the eco warriors. He stressed the need to teach them a lesson to respect the Police and the Law, otherwise

Sellafield, and other nuclear generating plants would be targeted by the week.

He was going to use classic military tactics of attack from front and rear, and use his mounted officers in the fields alongside to outflank the demonstrators. Meanwhile, and throughout the night, he would disorientate the protesters by the use of floodlighting and drum noise, whilst his police officers would take up positions well back from the front.

"The lights will be switched off and noise stopped at four o´clock in the morning, giving them time to relax and maybe sleep a little, that´s if the buggers can, with this rain still falling," he added with a smile. "I am assured first light will be around six o´clock, the men will take up their attack positions under strict silence, fifteen minutes early. Three blasts of a whistle will signal the attack. Hold your men at the ready for the signal, I want complete surprise."

In response to a question from the SAS captain, he stated with firmness in his tone, "There will be no new warning given. As far as I´m concerned the warning to disperse that was given at eleven this morning, will stand until eleven tomorrow. Finally, pay particular attention to the Irish contingent. They are organised around the front of the protesters next to the gates. They were the one´s responsible for initiating the violence today. The Home Office believes that there may be certain members of the IRA present in this group; I am awaiting identification details from London. The captain here is going to infiltrate some of his SAS boys in there to neutralise any terrorists embedded there, but be careful!"

Looking around, he asked, "Any questions?"

"What´s the engagement rules regarding applied force, Sir?" An inspector from Yorkshire asked.

Jennings set his jaw and ordered, "Apply as much force as you need to uphold the Law, Inspector." He elaborated, "I have a dozen officers in hospital in Kendal with serious injuries, and another twenty or thirty sufficiently injured to be out of action. The demonstrators began the violence, but by God, we will end it!"

A murmur of approval ran around the room.

Holding up his hands he finished, "Well gentlemen, you know what to do, do it well." He turned to the chief inspector beside him, and said, "Henry, make bloody sure that you recover your hat! If that gets into IRA hands...! Now, I´ve got a bloody press conference to do!"

Public relations advisors from the Home Office now met with the chief constable. Their job was to assist him determine last minute strategy for the live TV press conference in half an hour. The hacks from the tabloids just love the chance to criticise the Establishment, and particular the police who were in the spotlight on a daily basis with the miners´ strike. The TV front men also would be keen to humiliate the assistant chief constable in front of their audiences of millions, so Jennings knew he could be in for a rough time.

The general strategy agreed would be to emphasise the importance of protecting the Sellafield complex from any perceived threat. The protesters were breaking the Law in their blockage of essential supplies into, and from the Plant. The Eco-militants should be blamed for provoking the violence this morning by throwing the firecrackers and smoke bombs, causing serious injuries to civilians and police alike. This type of behaviour could not be tolerated in a civil society, or anarchy would reign!"

The Press Briefing began promptly at ten, to correspond with the main evening news.

ACC Jennings read out a prepared statement, outlining the events and the situation according to the strategy agreed with his advisors. He was an accomplished professional in his dealings with the Media, and spoke confidently and seriously, particularly on the subject of public order and safety.

The Press listened quietly, taking notes; he began to believe he had carried it off. He finished his address on the theme of anarchy, using the miners' strike and the publicly stated ambition of their leader, Arthur Scargill was to topple the elected government of Margaret Thatcher.

Looking around the gathered Press corps, and with added steel to his voice he emphasised, "The miners' strategy of intimidation and violence, imitated here by these so-called peaceful demonstrators, will not be allowed to succeed."

He almost expected a round of applause, when he asked if there were any questions.

At once, a forest of hands shot up; he ignored the known troublemakers of the gutter press, and chose the attractive young reporter from ITV.

The Chief Constable fielded her and the subsequent BBC reporter easily, answering their bland, general questions as if swatting flies. He was about to wrap up the conference when an unknown young woman reporter stood up.

"Yes Miss, your question?"

She identified herself, "Mary Rowantree, Wigton Press; "Is it true, that the SAS have been called in to protect Sellafield from these ecological protesters? Are we facing a possible IRA terrorist attack? If so the public have a right to know, and have a chance to evacuate the area."

Jennings was taken off guard, almost panicking; *"How in the hell does she know about the SAS?"* Recovering quickly he answered; "We have no knowledge of a terrorist threat Miss Rowantree." Gathering his papers, he hastily said, "Thank you all for coming."

The Press Corps were now baying for more information, but ACC Jennings was already half way out of the door heading for a well-earned cup of tea.

The rain had eased a little but a strong wind was blowing in from the Irish Sea and conditions in front of the main gate remained miserable. By midnight, half of the remaining Eco-Warriors had silently abandoned the vigil, returning to the camp for some warmth and sustenance. Only a diehard two to three hundred or so were still huddled together trying to keep dry and warm; nay impossible in the circumstances. The floodlights, the noise from the drums and the bone chilling cold was taking its toll, but the Eco-warriors pride and determination kept their spirits intact.

As the first relief shift was coming back down the road at four in the morning, the rain had stopped although it was still bitterly cold and damp. Suddenly, the lights went out, and the incessant noise of the drumming stopped. The abrupt darkness and silence at once assaulted the senses of the protesters. Nerves jangling, they braced themselves for something to happen.

A further nervous ten minutes passed, they sat, disorientated, taut, and motionless. Nothing was happening; there were no sounds or movements from inside the gates.

Finally, Connor concluded that the floodlights and drum beating was causing just as much pain to the police and that they, also needed some respite. He decided that the second shift badly needed some food and sleep, and gave the order for them to retire. Reluctantly, but as they had agreed, Shaina and Siobhan passed over the trophy police hats to two of their Domhan Glas friends, and they all wearily made their way back up to the camp.

The Faslane group joined them in the Canteen, and over mugs of hot tea and sandwiches, Connor talked to Meryl, the leader of the Faslane Peace Campers about his idea if things got out of hand. He confided that he thought that he and Iñaki would be a target for the Police as they were leading the Irish contingent. "Do you mind if we used your base at the George in Whitehaven as a meeting point, if things get chaotic?"

Meryl readily agreed; there was no sense in them spending time between English prison bars, as many would be, after this demo. "Our minibuses are meeting us there, so you´re welcome to come with us. I´ll bet you didn´t know our local council has provided our transport."

She explained, "One of the councillors is an active peace campaigner and would have been here with us, but he's at a CND conference in Germany this weekend."

Connor addressed his group.
"Right, I think the police will attack us just after dawn, probably about seven. We've got to be back in position by six thirty. Wake up everyone you can, so we get as many bodies in front of the gates as possible. Everyone should hold each other's hands and remain sitting so the police have to drag us away one by one." A murmur of agreement went round the group and he held up his hand for attention again, "Listen guys, no violence this time round, unless the pigs start it. If they do start cracking heads, feel free to crack theirs! Right now, let's try and get some sleep."

At precisely a quarter past five in the morning, a column of police mini buses, two abreast, silently glided past the sleeping campsite. Light was just beginning to invade the darkness and the mist was gently lifting in the false dawn. The first birdsongs and cocks crowing were welcoming the brand new day, now mingling with the odd soft whiney, and clink of the harnesses of the mounted police taking up their positions.

Down at Sellafield, the police operation in front of the gates was a comprehensive success.
The eco-warriors were either sleeping in the pre-dawn, or were completely off guard as the gates were swung open. A whistle blasted out and they before anyone could respond, they were attacked from the front and rear by a wall of police in riot gear.
    The protesters didn't stand a chance.
The police swung into action, batons flailing left and right. A burly sergeant went straight for his chief's hat, snatched it off, and crunched his baton over the girl's right ear, almost ripping it off. The screams of pain and terror from the trapped crowd only abated after twenty minutes, when the

watching assistant chief constable signalled for the carnage to end.

The rout was complete; even the most experienced police officers recognised that the brutality had gone too far. Thank the Lord that the press had not seen the horror of the action, and it had been too dark for the TV cameras.

At the camp, surprise was also complete. They were too far away from the gates to hear the mayhem going on down there.

The first the protesters in the camp knew anything was happening was when two women went up to the latrines and noticed the mounted police patrolling along the hedges of the field. They immediately ran through the camp shouting a warning, but before anyone could react, four lines of police in riot gear had blocked the entrances to the field and farm.

Down in front of the Sellafield complex, fleet of ambulances began to arrive to treat and ferry the wounded to the hospitals. More than one hundred protesters needed treatment, fifteen with serious head wounds and twenty-four with fractures of fingers or limbs as they blocked blows from police batons. The rest were to be bussed to Kendal Police HQ, for interrogation, but a high-level order came through from the Home Office to release all but the Irish citizens without charge, after their identities were established and fingerprints taken. The Irish were to be interviewed individually.

Siobhan and Shaina reacted with fury; it took all of the persuasive power of Iñaki, Connor and Meryl from the Scots contingent, to calm them down and prevent them hurling themselves against the police barricades.

As it was, Connor and Iñaki had to escape from the trap they were in. Gathering their gear together, they made their way back up the field to the latrine he had earmarked earlier. This was in the far corner away from Sellafield, and had a steep bank with a stream running at the bottom. The near darkness and general panic in the camp would help cover-up their escape.

Iñaki, crept through the hedge to scout the land, and immediately received a tremendous blow on his shoulder. He tried to reverse back through the hedge, and at the same time tried to protect his head with his hand. He received a kick in the face and another baton blow struck his wrist.

The noise of the bone cracking could be heard by the others, who dragged him back through by his feet. He could hardly bear the pain. His friends launched a barrage of stones and clods of earth over the hedge at whoever was on the other side accompanied by a stream of oaths.

They were answered by a voice saying, "Do you want some more of this, scumbag? Just show your fucking head again, and I´ll oblige!"

Siobhan and Shaina took Iñaki down to the camp First Aid station, where a young Scottish doctor looked at his injuries.

He cleaned up his face, commenting, "You´re going to be wearing a real shiner on that eye," but could do nothing but put a temporary, but effective splint on his wrist, and advised him to surrender to the police to get transport to the hospital.

Shaina answered, "That´s not on the menu Doctor, can you give him something to kill the pain until he gets home?"

Glancing at Iñaki he asked, "Where´s home then, Madrid?"

Siobhan spoke up for Iñaki, who was still in a great deal of pain, and visibly shaken. "He´s living in Dublin just now doctor. Please, we´d be very grateful, he just can´t go to a hospital around here."

Looking at them curiously, the doctor said "I´ll see what I can do; here´s some strong analgesics which should keep him going twenty four hours, but he really needs to get hospital attention." He continued, "If he stays behind, I can get him taken to Carlisle, or to Dumfries. He´ll be safer up there, away from of these sadistic thugs."

They held a brief discussion, and Meryl, who had just joined them, suggested that she would accompany Iñaki. Later they could work out how he would travel back to Dublin. This seemed the sensible option, and Iñaki lay down on one of the camp beds in the tent.

Connor was seriously worried now. He recognised that he had made a grave error of judgment on police tactics, and that he had run an irresponsible risk in remaining at the protest after the violence of the day before. He was in grave danger of arrest if he was to be recognised and identified. He decided to stay put, and hope that he would be lost in the crowd. After all, the police couldn´t arrest the almost two thousand protesters still trapped in the camp area!

The remaining protesters in the campground were interned in the camp for a further three hours, but the police did not attempt to enter. Eventually they allowed the demonstrators to leave in groups of one hundred, and led away from the direction of Sellafield. The protesters had to pass lines of grinning police in their riot gear as they exited the narrow entrance to the campsite.

Connor saw the danger! They were going to have to pass a knot of senior police officers. He tried to turn away, but the press of the crowd coming behind was forcing those in front forward. It was too late to get away.

Professor McGilvery was standing beside an inspector. He caught sight of Connor and the girls, and immediately identified Connor to the officer, pointing and shouting, "That´s him! That´s Connor Rafferty, the one who threw the firecrackers!"

The police immediately moved in to arrest Connor.

Siobhan and Shaina, and some other of the Domhan Glas Iaochra contingent began screaming and shouting abuse. They were quickly surrounded by the now hard-faced officers.

Shaina went up to the inspector and asked, "Why is this man being arrested?"

Angrily he answered, "This is no business of yours Miss. Move on, and take these people with you, or you will all be heading into the cells. Is that clear?"

She persisted. "Where is he being taken? He is an Irish citizen and his family and the Irish Embassy will need to be informed."

"That is our job, now Miss; if you don´t move on, you will be arrested for impeding a police officer carrying out his lawful duty!"

Dejectedly, they could do nothing as Connor was led away.

Fortunately, Iñaki was lagging well behind at this time with Meryl and the young doctor from Glasgow and escaped detection. Siobhan explained what had happened to Connor. "Shaina and I will have to stay around and make sure he´s alright. I don´t trust the pigs. We´ll have to get in touch with Padraig, he´ll know what to do."

"I don´t think he´ll be home yet," Shaina put in.

"Well, we´ll have to hang around," Siobhan reasoned, "we just can´t abandon him!"

In the Press Centre, Chief Constable Jennings was in his element. He stated that the eco warriors had again attacked the gates, but the police had been vigilant, and prevented them entering the Nuclear Installations. With a genuinely sympathetic face, he announced that it was to be regretted that there had been so many injuries, but this was due to the excessive violence of the mob.

Pulling himself up to his full height, he proclaimed, "My Officers are to be congratulated on their restraint and sheer professionalism under difficult circumstances. I commend them all, for preventing an extremely dangerous situation from developing by standing firm, and preventing these anarchists form gaining access to Sellafield."

There was no live television report of the police operation in front of the gates. It had been exemplary. The public at large praised the police on the operational efficiency.

Connor was taken to a nearby police bus, where he was searched. To his dismay, he realised that he still had some of the flares in his rucksack. *Jesus Christ, how could I have been so feckin' stupid.*

Inevitably, the flares were discovered, and the mood of the police sergeant in charge suddenly turned ugly.

"You fucking Irish bastard! One of my mates is in hospital because of you!" He racked up the handcuffs until they embedded into Connor's wrists, and for good measure gave him a knee in the genitals, knocking the breath from him and leaving him writhing in agony.

The sergeant explained the find to the inspector, who in turn radioed ACC Jennings with the news of the arrest. Jennings was still in the Press Centre talking to some of the journalists, and listened intently to the report. He ordered that Connor should be brought down to the Security Centre immediately, and announced to the Press that there had been an important development in the police operation.

Beaming with importance, he announced, "We have arrested a senior member of the Domhan Glas Iaochra organization, that's the Irish Green Warrior movement to you. He has been positively identified as the instigator of the violence against the police yesterday." Softening his tone, and taking a conspiring pose, he continued, "That's all I can give you now, but off the record for now, he has been found to have explosives in his possession."

A host of hands shot up from the Press, clamouring attention. Holding his hands up for calm Jennings continued, "As I said, I cannot take any questions at this time; a press conference will be convened at one o'clock at Cumbrian Police HQ, in Penrith."

Chapter 59: Connor

Jennings called a meeting of all the senior police commanders. The SAS captain, who had been preparing his men to return to Belfast, was also requested to attend. In view of the explosives having been found on his person, Connor was to be held under the Prevention of Terrorism Act.

Jennings put a telephone call through to the PPS of the Home Secretary at Chequers, and gave him an update on the situation. The Home Secretary was at Chequers this weekend, and they would advise him immediately; meanwhile, the PPS insisted, the terrorist must be held under extreme security.

The PPS ordered, "No one, but no one is to be allowed to see him. He is to be denied access to a lawyer, family member or friend, and for God´s sake certainly not the Press! We´ve been correct in assessing a potential terrorist attack; MI5 and the Special Branch will have to be involved in this, so do nothing, Mr Jennings until you hear directly from Home Secretary."

Connor was in deep trouble. His only hope was to maintain absolute silence. He understood that he was in for a very rough time of it in the coming hours and days. All of his strengths; resolve and discipline would be tested to the limit before help could be organised.

The five-minute journey down to the Security Centre had been a taste to come with the police escort taking turns to beat him in the kidneys and buttocks with truncheons wrapped in towels. He had vomited in the shock of the beatings. Now he was a secure cell with two guards outside, and absolutely no hope of escape.

"I am not damn well standing for this!" Assistant Chief Constable Jennings, white with anger was venting his fury at the special branch chief inspector standing before him. "If you arseholes had been doing your job properly, this fucking animal would not have got anywhere near to Sellafield, and I would have been enjoying my bloody Sunday roast at home!"

The special branch officer replied, "Sir, the decision has come from the Prime minister herself, so if you have a complaint, I suggest you phone her at her country house, that´s Chequers, by the way. She´s entertaining your boss, the Home Secretary over the weekend."

Mike Reid, the SB Inspector had arrived by helicopter from Scotland Yard SO13 Anti-Terrorist branch. He was in no mood to take a verbal lashing from a plonker of a County Assistant Chief Constable, whose only claim to fame was riding down striking miners.

He went on, "The orders are written, some bloke from MI5 is going to join us here for the initial interrogation of Rafferty, and then we are going on a little jaunt over to Belfast, where they assure me, the real experts in terrorism are based. One other thing, if I may remind you, that you haven´t charged him with anything yet; his alleged offences were carried out in Cumbria which is not your patch of the woods …and, another minor point, Chief; he is being held here in a Nuclear Facility, therefore comes under the jurisdiction of the MOD Police. I know they will not object if the bastard is removed from under their feet; after all they have missed watching the football on the tele all weekend!"

Angrily Jennings intervened; "You bastards are all the same. Big City cops; half of your lives spent in posh wine bars, but if there´s a hint of fucking glory, you´re shoving your arses in to grab it! I want to see this in writing before he gets shifted from here."

Reid shrugged his shoulders, "Suit yourself Chief, I think that´s MI5 coming in now."

The two men watched another helicopter swooping in, to land beside the big army Chinook out in the helipad.

A small figure, carrying a briefcase and rucksack jumped out, and keeping his head down, ran towards the SAS soldiers guarding the Chinook. Over the racket from the rotors, he shouted something to the men, and one of them pointed in the direction of Jennings and Reid. He looked over, shouted his thanks, and squelched his way over the grass to where they were waiting.

Recognising the special branch man he said, "Oh it´s yourself Mike; they didn´t get you off your golf course for a wee insignificant Dubliner did you." Turning to the ACC, he smiled, "You must be Mr Jennings?" He shook hands with the two men.

"Assistant Chief Constable Jennings, Lancashire, thank you," replied Jennings, drawing up to his full height.

The newcomer added, "I recognise you from the television Sir; by Christ did you give it to these miners last week ... impressive!"

"We don´t pussy around up here, Mr...? Jennings queried.

"Just call me Jock, if that´s alright with you, Sir. I´ve got some paperwork for you here somewhere. Had to do a bloody tour around; ended up at bloody Chequers! First time there; maybe next time I´ll get to stay the weekend, although I´m told Mrs T was blistering the hair of anyone in range yesterday."

A seriously miffed assistant chief constable interrupted, "Well the situation has changed somewhat since I got here. Now I´ve been informed that you two experts are about to take the credit." he added as he studied the documents `Jock´ had just passed to him.

"No Sir, we never like to get our pictures on the tele," the MI5 man responded, "unlike my friend Mike here, who is becoming more famous than Mick Jagger!" He asked innocently, "Any chance of a cuppa? Mrs T has forgotten her manners today otherwise I would have stayed for afternoon tea and maybe a round of croquet on the lawn."

Sighing noisily, Jennings led them into the Security Centre and into the office he had requisitioned. He ordered tea and sandwiches, and the briefing session began with the participation of various police top brass, MOD police and the SAS captain in attendance.

"Okay; Mr Connor Rafferty of James Joyce Street, Dublin, what are you doing here in England trying to blow up a nuclear power station, the property of the Crown?"
Connor was sitting at a table in what was obviously an interview room in the basement of the Security Centre. Sitting opposite him, across a fixed desk, were two civilians. He had no doubt that there were other watchers behind the large mirror attached to the wall.

He looked, felt and smelled terrible. There were no visible marks on his face, but he had vomit stains down his jumper. His kidneys had calmed down to a persistent throbbing ache, but when he had urinated, his penis flushed with fire.

Looking direct into `Jock´s´ eyes he answered; "I am an Irish citizen, and I want to see a lawyer of my choosing. I will not answer any questions from you, or anyone else, until the lawyer of my choosing is sitting here beside me."

Jock persisted, "Listen Mr Rafferty, I´m your best friend here at this moment in time. It´s definitely in your interest to talk to us here; to try, let me say, remove the explosives out of the equation before others get their tackity boots into you, if you get my meaning. Now, just confirm something for me; has this been an official action? Or have you been buggering around without permission."

Connor did not flinch, or blink, or changed his expression of indifference in any way, except to repeat, "I want my lawyer by my side."

They kept at him for a further three hours, without getting another word out of him. They threatened, cajoled, explained the consequences of terrorism charges, after all, he had explosives in his bag, and without any doubt faced thirty years hard labour. The interrogators received not a word in return.

Jock was not unduly worried; they had twenty-eight days to work on him, and he knew full well that marine flares would not be classed as explosives before a Cumbrian magistrate. He also knew background that the Scotland Yard man didn´t know, and was not about to educate them just yet.

Mike however, was getting anxious; he was aware that once Connor was on the flight to Belfast, his link and credit in the capture would be lost. At one point he lost his temper, and looked as if he was going to slap the prisoner, but was held back by a restraining hand from Jock. Frustrated, they went back to the office to confer, and have another cup of tea. Jock arranged for tea and a sandwich to be taken downstairs to the prisoner, as they discussed the situation.

Finally, Mike had to concede that they were getting nowhere and the transfer to Belfast, where they could work on him away from the Press was the best option. He grumpily demanded a daily report on the interrogation be sent direct to him at Scotland Yard.

Connor felt the first, terrifying sensation of fear when a hood put over his head for the flight. When he complained, a gruff Scottish SAS Sergeant said, "Hold yer tongue laddie… or ye might find the hood gettin´ a bit too tight fur yer health. We don´t want ye tellin´ yer pals wee MacLean wis´ beatin´ ye, dae we?

Chapter 60: Castlereagh Barracks, Belfast

The Military took Connor directly to Castlereagh RUC Barracks, where he was taken to the IRA suspects Holding Centre.

He was stripped naked, and then body searched, issued with a white boiler suit and then roughly escorted to a white tiled, eight by four foot cell, completely bare except for a bunk and a blanket, and a slop bucket in the corner. The cell stank of old piss, sweat and disinfectant, but more menacingly, an all-pervading sense of fear lay thick in the fetid air. His escorts, two red faced RUC uniformed police constables literally threw him in, one giving him shove with his boot.

One announced, "Welcome to Castlereagh, tea and biccies will be served shortly," and to their inane laughter slammed the cell door, Connor wincing with the explosion of sound closing off his freedom.

Connor was dead tired; he only had one hour's sleep last night, and the stress of Sunday's events lay on his skull like an anvil. He sat, shivering on the concrete hard bunk, wrapped the blanket around his shoulders, and mustering all his remaining strength, fought to concentrate his mind. He began to contemplate his options.

He reckoned it would take at least three, maybe four days for the contacts and command wheels to engage, but he was sure they would connect. He mentally thought through the training he had undergone to endure interrogation. They would play hard and soft, enjoy the hard, suffer the soft his instructor had drummed into him. He had learned how to meditate; to go into a higher plane as they beat you.

His old ex-military intelligence instructor had drummed into him, "The harder they slap and kick, the more you are winning! Each hour that passes and you don't give them nothing, think, *I'm beating the bastards!* You have something, information, they are desperate to know; get your rocks off from keeping it from the bastards."

In his tests he hadn't succumbed, much to their frustration. He was a mild mannered man on the outside, but hard as nails inside. However, they didn't want him damaged; after all, he was a volunteer and this was only a training exercise!

Four days passed. Despite the slaps and insults, (His sister was giving blow-jobs to the local priest etc), sleep deprivation and strip lights blaring in his cell; cold showers, enforced standing for hours and hours; he would not cooperate. He would not even confirm his name. His interrogators were gentle, understanding his position, and then they would turn brutal. Tea was offered, and tea thrown over him.

The RUC E4 Special Branch, had some time with him; Military Intelligence and the MI5 Northern Ireland Section Head had their turns, but nothing; not a cheep from this bird.

Chapter 61: West End of Glasgow

After leaving Sellafield, the young doctor and Meryl had decided that Iñaki should have his broken wrist and other injuries treated at Western Infirmary in Glasgow where he worked. Glasgow was only a couple of hours drive further on from Cumbria, and there would not be the same awkward questioning on how he came about these injuries.

Iñaki's journey north to Glasgow passed in a confused blur of half consciousness, brought about by his physical and mental exhaustion and the strong analgesics the doctor had given him. The orthopaedic surgeon had diagnosed a compound fracture, and inserted some pins in the wrist, which kept him in the hospital overnight. The surgeon ordered him to return for a further examination after a week or so to have the pins removed and avoid possible complications.

Next morning, Meryl was back at the hospital to collect him. She looked fresh and rested, although she would not have had much time for sleep after having left him at midnight. She explained that she had stayed with a friend in Glasgow overnight.

Before he left the hospital, he attempted to telephone Siohban and Padraig, and finally his own flat in Dublin, but there was no reply to any of the numbers. Meryl was not surprised as the girls were going to stay close to Connor in Cumbria, and would be out of touch at least for a day or two.

Iñaki still wasn't feeling well after the anaesthesia. His arm was aching badly, but he agreed to go for a coffee, as she had not had breakfast.

This was his first proper look at Glasgow, and he looked around with interest as they walked to a nearby coffee shop. It had been raining earlier in the morning, but now a weak sun was piercing through the clouds, highlighting the red sandstone tenements of Byres Road. The streets were busy, and had a lively atmosphere. He commented that this was a city quite unlike Dublin, or London.

Iñaki questioned the high number of young people around, until Meryl explained that Glasgow University was just around the corner, and that the Western Infirmary was a teaching hospital. It was likely that a young medic had practiced on him!

Entering the coffee shop, the smell of appetising freshly baked cakes mixed with the aroma of the coffee assailed his senses, and he suddenly found a hunger, which had not been present a few minutes previously. He wolfed down bacon and egg in a breakfast roll, several scones and butter, and a gum sucking sweet caramel fudge cake, washed down with two cups of black coffee, whilst Meryl settled for toast with scrambled egg, and lemon tea accompanied by a small French cake.

To his surprise, she began, haltingly at first, speaking to him in Spanish. "*¿Como esta tu muñeca, ahora?* How is your wrist now?"

Smiling he replied, "*Mucho mejor ahora, gracias; ¿Hablais español?* It´s much better now, do you speak Spanish?"

She smiled, "I come from California, and our home help, gardener and pool guys were all Mexicans. I also took a Spanish language course in case I got a job in a Spanish speaking area."

Iñaki commented a little wistfully, "*Interesante, echo de menos mi idioma.* Interesting, I miss speaking in my language," He thought, "This is an interesting woman, kind and helpful, not bad looking and obviously intelligent ... and she speaks my language. Perhaps my stay in Scotland will not turn out to be all that bad."

They spent a very pleasant half hour talking in Spanish about his life in Dublin; Iñaki being careful to relate his story without mentioning any connections to the Republican groups. Finally, Meryl asked him if he would like a short tour around this part of Glasgow.

After he said he would love to, they collected the Minibus, which had a parking fine stuck on the window. She simply laughed; "Dumbarton District Council will pay this; it´s their bus!"

Iñaki was surprised; Glasgow, similar to Bilbao, had a reputation of being a big industrial city with little to commend it, but the half hour tour opened his eyes to the rich heritage that the Victorian merchants had left. He was particularly interested in the university, founded in 1451 AD, with its imposing spires on Gilmore Hill.

Meryl was a good guide, explaining she often stayed with friends in Glasgow, and gave frequent lectures at the universities and colleges, as well as CND meetings.

Chapter 62: Meryl Heston

On the face of it, Meryl Heston would only stand out from the crowd by her smallness, her slightly musky, but attractive Oriental looks she had inherited from her Japanese mother; from her diplomat father's genes, she had the strikingly blue Grant family eyes, usually hidden behind John Lennon glasses. Her father had also given her a propensity to study and ability to reason, and win, an argument with a stubbornness, which would wear down the most verbal or muscular opponent.

She had studied Politics, and her almost religious fervour for human rights brought her into focus when she took a leading organizational role in the anti-Vietnam War demonstrations at University of California. After graduating in Political Science, she landed a job as a Political Research Assistant at CAL, and among her dates was Alex Heston, a respected English Literature professor at Berkeley.

Alex was ten years older, but she fell for his charisma of intelligence, which complemented his obvious good looks and confident, easy manner. Meryl moved in, and quickly adapted to her new responsibilities of entertaining and semi domestic routines.

At first, Meryl enjoyed the circle of intellectual friends she had eased into, through Alex's literary reputation, but after a couple of years began to realise that this rather small scholastic clique were jarring on her nerves with their petty bourgeois debates and opinions. She became discontented and depressed; their lovemaking seemed to have become a routine for Saturday nights after the gang had left.

She was always in Alex's shadow; no one was phoning to speak with her. The calls were always for Alex.

During these past few years, Meryl had become distant from her own family, but when one day her Mother phoned and asked her if she would accompany her to visit her family in Japan, Meryl seized the opportunity to take a break from Berkeley.

The visit to her grandparents turned out to be a life changing experience for her. They lived in a small town near to Hiroshima, and her grandfather had survived, but had suffered terrible disfiguring burns in the atomic bomb attack in nineteen forty five. Their description of the event, and the terrible suffering experienced by the people after the Bomb, moved Meryl to tears. Meryl had always had a deeply held hatred for the Bomb, and now, talking about the attack to the victims, it boiled into a fury.

On her return to Berkeley, it became apparent that Alex had been playing the field while she had been away, a fact he did not deny or attempt to hide. The blatant exhibitionism from Alex, as he paraded around the campus with his latest conquests, became too much for her. Rows were frequent and abusive, and finally Meryl moved out.

It was the gnawing feeling of loneliness and the dead end feeling that she was in the wrong place at the wrong time. A radical change was needed and three months later, she was in London as Visiting Professor of Political Science at the London School of Economics.

Meryl revelled in the open, liberal environment of LSE, and became an active member of the CND chapter at the university. At one of the CND demonstrations in London, she recognised one of her students. Excitedly they teamed up, shouting their slogans and generally enjoying each other´s company. After the demo, they decided to have dinner together in a new vegetarian restaurant in Soho.

Lesley, no longer thought of as being Meryl´s student, but now her new friend and companion, suggested going on to a nightclub, which turned out to be for gays and lesbians. This did not provide any problem for Meryl, after all, San Francisco is the gay capital of the world, and being honest with herself, she felt a frisson of sexual excitement with her young friend.

They had a wild time, drinking monstrous cocktails, dancing free and liberated to the thumping resonance of the discotheque, and surrounded by equally free couples, released from the straitjacket of their normal everyday lives.

They went back to Meryl´s flat, and after initial hesitation, made love, inhibitions forgotten, uncontrolled lust being the only game in town.

They became a couple, but clandestinely. LSE did not have a policy of discrimination against gay couples, but teacher and student relationships were prohibited by the Administration. They kept their affair discrete, but everyone in their LSE CND left wing bohemian circle suspected. Theirs was not the only gay relationship, but the lecturer and student relationship produced a few frowns of approbation.

One weekend, they travelled down to Greenham Common Airbase, to protest at the deployment of American Cruise Missiles on English soil. The protests turned violent, and unfortunately, Meryl and Lesley were among those arrested.

The News of the World identified Meryl as a professor at LSE, and her lesbian relationship with her student was publicised on the front page.

Lesley´s parents were appalled and enraged by this turn of events. She was only nineteen years old, and they demanded action from the LSE.

The University invited Meryl to resign, with a modest payment in lieu of her contract. Knowing she would be hung out to dry if she refused to resign, she immediately accepted the pay-off and left her post. However, Lesley´s parents bid to control their daughter backfired when she also left the university and went to live with Meryl.

They both took a job in a veggie sandwich bar to tide things over, but shortly afterwards decided to adopt a more radical position in their anti-nuclear beliefs and they joined the Greenham Common protest camp. Almost two years later, they decided a change of scene was required, and after attending a protest rally at Faslane Polaris submarine base, they decided to stay on and become involved in the Peace Camp.

That first winter was one of the worst in fifty years. Incessant rain and gales lashed the area, and the few peace campers huddled in the caravans and shelters. The camp facilities were no worse than at Greenham Common, but Lesley contracted pleurisy and spent several weeks in the Vale of Leven hospital. Lesley had had enough of the peace camp, and when she was discharged from hospital, decided to abandon the camp and move back down South to live with her forgiving parents.

Meryl stayed on, and with her demonstrable intelligence, commitment and organizational ability, became a leading figure in the Glasgow branch of CND.
She took on the role of the peace camp's leader a few months later.

Chapter 63: Peace Camp, Faslane, Scotland

Iñaki had no idea what to expect in respect of his new temporary home at the peace camp.

On a lovely May afternoon, they drove up from Glasgow, passing through the pretty village of Cardross, the town of Helensburgh and then Rhu.

Meryl had described the camp as being primitive, but liveable, which in all honesty it was; but in the warming May sunshine, the views from the camp across the Gareloch to the

Roseneath Peninsula and the mountains beyond were quite stunning to his first impressionable eyes. The light was sparkling on a rippling loch, and seemed to illuminate the dark purple heather covered mountains.

Then there was reality, as a monstrous, ugly black Polaris submarine, with its grey Royal Navy warship escorts sailed into view from behind the trees. It all seemed be as out of place as a scab on the face of a pretty woman.

The peace camp was well organised, and Meryl treated him as an honoured guest, ensuring he was made comfortable in one of the newer caravans.

He found her good company, vibrant and not without humour, and although much older than he, very attractive with her petit Oriental looks.

The day after coming down from Glasgow, she gave him and another young protester called Jono, a tour around the area in her old psychedelic painted Volkswagen campervan.

They drove up the Glen Fruin road to see the Faslane submarine base from the hills above, and then back down and round the peninsula to Coulport, to stand at the entrance of the enormous Nuclear Warhead Storage facilities.

The MOD Sergeant at the gate approached and recognising Meryl exchanged pleasantries and politely asked them to park off to the side of the road.

Meryl declined, smiled, and turned the VW around, driving back towards Cove, the way they had just come.

The British Government had ordered the new, much bigger Ballistic Missile Trident submarines. The expansion and upgrading of the Faslane Base, and Coulport Missile Storage areas to accommodate them, resulted in the whole area converting into a huge construction site. There was a constant roar of heavy construction work, and the occasional explosion from the hillside above as the new roads were blasted out of forty million year old granite.

Meryl kept up a running commentary on the costs involved. "Fourteen million pounds for a new security fence which I guarantee can be breached any time we want. Sixty million for a Ship-lift, whatever that is, and meanwhile there´s no money for keeping the local hospital open!" She laughed as she pointed to a group of bored looking MOD policemen, "Security? We have contacts inside the base, who keep us informed on what´s going on." Addressing Iñaki, she asked, "Did you know Jono´s stepfather is the man-in-charge, Commodore Clyde, no less?"

Jonathan mumbled something that his stepfather was an arrogant prick and that he almost never saw him, and looked away.

Meryl went on, "We know that one of the Polaris submarines, Revenge, is leaving on a patrol in a few days time. We also know when a submarine is coming back from a patrol, the taxi drivers tell us!"

Expanding on her observations she continued, "Remember, we are only thirty miles from more or less half of the population of Scotland. If there was an accident, and one of the damn nuclear missiles exploded, it would be goodbye to half of Scotland."

They drove into the local town, Helensburgh, and did some shopping in the local Coop, which produced a small tinge of homesickness in him. The old Victorian villas, tree lined streets and the proximity of the sea reminding him of Las Arenas, his home in the Basque country.

They continued with the tour, driving up the hill past the old mansions in the upper part of the town. Iñaki knew nothing of this area, and, his eyes widened when they came over the hill to look upon the breathtakingly beautiful Loch Lomond with Ben Lomond over the other side. Meryl kept up the commentary, pointing out the various historical sites on the way up the side of the Loch, until they stopped at the Inn at Inverbeg for a beer.

She got chatting to the big jovial, kilt wearing owner of the Inn, and explained Iñaki came from Spain, she was

American, and indicating Jonathan, "this young man is English."

"You are most welcome Ma'am," before jokingly adding, "but the Englishman stays outside. I'm James MacGregor, and over there on the other side of the Loch, one of my antecedents, Rob Roy MacGregor used to slit English throats, so you'd better watch out my lad!"

Jonathan only scowled; he was fed-up to the teeth of these anti- English jokes.

MacGregor regaled them of the area, and invited them down to see, in his opinion the most beautiful view in the world. They all drank up, and he led the way, past his own bungalow, to be greeted by two boisterous black Labradors, who generally made a nuisance of themselves until the big man got them under control.

MacGregor led them out onto his private jetty. Loch Lomond was flat calm, sheltered by the mountains above Inverbeg; the trees and mountains mirrored off the water by the sun. A flight of ducks flew overhead, and the only sound came from a small launch chugging at the far side, close to Rowardennan. "What do you think of that then?" a proud MacGregor asked.

"Breathtaking," Meryl replied, "so beautiful; I could stand here all day." After a few minutes taking in the ambience, and promising to come back, Meryl suggested they had better be on their way. They thanked their host, and carried on up the road to Tarbet, taking the left fork and leaving Loch Lomond to reach Arrochar, and then down the fiord like Loch Long.

Once more, there were ample signs of military activity. On the far side of the sea loch, a Royal Navy torpedo testing facility sat directly below Cobbler peak, stark against a clear blue sky, snow still in a few Corries. Two small naval patrol craft were keeping station offshore, but again the stillness, the calm on the water, and only the odd sound of a tractor, or a man's voice carried across the water.

In answer to Iñaki's query, Meryl confirmed that practically the whole area was a military zone. Not only Royal Navy, but the Army also had a training base above Garelochhead, and the RAF frequently flew training missions around the mountains.

Chapter 64: Life-paths converge.

They were almost back in the Faslane area when she asked if they were hungry. Receiving the expected affirmations, she turned off the road and stopped at a small Swiss lodge style hotel, sat on a hillside above the confluence of two sea lochs.

Going round the front of the hotel, they took a seat on a bench in the beer garden. There was still a sizeable lunch trade going on, and the proprietor was helping the waitress on duty. Recognizing Meryl, he came over to their table with the menu, giving her friendly recognised greeting.

After the usual pleasantries, he asked her how her Sellafield demo had gone, to which she simply said, "Don't you ever watch television Hamish? We took a beating from a crowd of thugs calling themselves policemen."

Hamish only laughed, and looking directly at Iñaki said, "I take it he's one of your shock troops then? Looks like he was front line infantry, eh?"

"It did get out of hand a bit," she admitted, "but the police were way out of order; they are animals down there."

"Not like our nice plods then," Hamish replied. "Look Meryl, can you do me a favour? Next time you block the bloody road, how about letting me know in advance? It's a pain in the arse to spend half an hour gazing at your layabouts sitting in the road, you know!"

She laughed and said, "How else are we going to make our point, Hamish? A half hour delay is nothing to getting a bloody great Soviet nuclear strike over your head, is it?"

"Let´s not get into this again, Meryl. I personally think Trident is a good idea….look at the business I´m getting!"

A young chef, immaculate in his whites approached their table. "Dad, there´s a phone call for you, it´s Loch Fyne Oysters."

"Christ, don´t tell me they can´t deliver again!" Hamish excused himself, and hurried away.

The newcomer recognised Jonathan who was sitting quietly beside Iñaki. "Hi Jono, what are you doing here? I haven´t seen you for years; is it true you told old Kennedy to shove his school up his….backside?"

Blushing to the roots, Jonathan replied, "Well, not in so many words Sandy, but yes, I had enough of that bloody awful school." Brightening up Jonathan asked, "Are you a chef now? Were you not going to be an accountant or something?"

"No; well yes, that was the plan my mother had worked out for me, but she finally accepted that I can´t count the fingers on my hand, and finally gave in …and here I am!"

Meryl intervened, "Do you like cooking Sandy?"

"Well I´ve being doing it since I was three years old, so my dad tells me, so it´s kind of grown on me I guess. No, that´s not true, I love it, especially when it´s busy….hard work though." He apologised, "Excuse me, I´d better get back. I´ve just come on duty and we´ve got a big party in the restaurant tonight, one of the Navy jobs. He came round the table and shook Iñaki´s hand …"It was nice to meet you Iñaki. Good to see you again Jonathan, we´ll catch up sometime, okay?" He gave a final wave of his hand and left to get on with his work.

"Yeah, okay we´ll do that," replied an unenthusiastic Jonathan.

Meryl commentated, "What a nice young man; I take it you knew him at school, Jono?"

"Yes, he was in the same year as me, but we weren´t really friends, he was a day pupil, and they tended to stick together."

Iñaki had been listening and observing the exchange, and couldn´t help comparing the two. The young chef, clean image, confident and outgoing, and Jonathan; introverted, unemotional and seemingly nursing some kind of resentment from deep within him. He was also obviously at a loose end despite his education, with no ambition to do anything other than protest.

Shrugging his thoughts aside, he asked, "Meryl, I´ll have to phone Siobhan and see what´s going on. Can we stop at a phone box?"

"You´re better to go into Helensburgh, if it´s anything private," she advised. "The public telephones in around here are monitored by the security services as part of their so-called security blanket!"

Chapter 65: Siobhan

It was Thursday; four days after leaving Sellafield, that Siobhan finally answered the telephone in his flat.

He was in Helensburgh; Meryl had driven in her Volkswagen bus with three other peace campers, who were collecting their social benefit Giro cheques from the post office. Meryl had things to attend to and dropped them off, with the proviso if she was not back in an hour, they should make their own way back to the camp.

Pulling up the collar of his anorak, and braving the brisk, almost gale force wind, Iñaki took in the vistas around; the tide was roaring in on the wind, white caps upon a grey blue heavy sea, clouds racing above in the direction of the hills above the pretty town. The seagulls screaming on the wind, and the taste and smell of the salt, again gave him a pang of homesickness.

He found a telephone box outside a pub by the pier. It was full of old fish and chip wrappings, and stank of urine, but turning up his nose, he decided to persevere. He was on the point of giving up, when she answered.

As soon as he began to speak, she interrupted him, with "What´s your number, I´ll phone you in ten minutes!"

Iñaki had a problem making out the number amidst the graffiti, but at last gave her the number. He was reluctant to leave the box, in case someone wanted to use it, and, put up with the ordure, pretending to speak into the receiver when anyone came by.

The phone rang, and he picked it up on the first ring.

"Siobhan?" he enquired.

"Who else would it be?" she brushed him off; "Listen Iñaki, the shit has hit the fan here, so don´t phone or try to come back just now."

Iñaki tried to interrupt, but was told to listen, and listen carefully.

"Connor was taken to Castlereagh Barracks in Belfast on Sunday. That´s where they take suspected terrorists for interrogation! Padraig was taken in for questioning by the Garda Special Branch, but he´s out now; he told them nothing. The Army Council are incandescent over this. They are saying that Padraig and Conner should never have gone near Sellafield. I think they are going to censure them in some way for endangering our security.

"What about Connor?" he asked.

"They´ve got a human rights lawyer fighting the Brits to get Connor released, but we´re really worried about him." She added, "He´ll be going through hell up there. Iñaki, Padraig has asked me to tell you not to come back right now; he's wants to keep you clean. He says he's got some translation work for you again."

Iñaki told her that he would be back after he was given the all clear at the hospital, but she was firm in her instruction that he was to stay where he was, until Padraig gave him further orders.

"What about my job, though? Joe will be furious if I don't come back."

"Don't worry about Joe, you're job's safe and Padraig will sort it out," she answered. "Phone me on Monday at seven, you got a pen?"

"Wait a minute," as he found an old biro in an inside pocket, but no paper. "Okay give me the number," writing it on his plaster cast."

She repeated the number twice, and said it was John Flaherty's Bar. He was to keep trying if the line was engaged. "By the way, how's your arm?" she asked as an afterthought.

He explained the operation, and before he had a chance to say anything else, she abruptly interrupted and said, "Look sorry, I've got to go."

The telephone went dead, leaving Iñaki with a flood of unanswered questions in his head. Looking down at his feet, he said to himself, "Jesus, what people piss in telephone boxes?"

The answer came faster than he imagined, when, exiting, a group of drunken sailors fell out of the pub singing and bawling obscenities. It was only mid-day!

Later, when he related his news to Meryl, omitting the PIRA connection, she expressed surprise and indignation at Connor's plight.

"I think that our governments are getting more and more dictatorial, Iñaki. If you protest, they crush you; look at the way they treated us, right from the beginning. They don't even allow any criticism, they see themselves as always being in the right, and we, the people must accept their orders." She went on, "That Castlereagh place has a bad reputation for torture; there´s been several unexplained deaths and suicides there. My God, poor Connor, he´s in for a bad time of it." Finally, she said, "I hope he gets some good legal representation quickly."

Chapter 66: The Assassination

The bombshell broke on the fifth day.
A Top Priority instruction from the Terrorism Coordination Group in London, and signed by the NI Secretary of State. Connor Rafferty was to be released without charge, and placed into the custody of the Irish Garda, at the border of Northern Ireland and Eire. Details of timing, and arrangements were to follow. The Home Office declined to give any explanations or reasons for his release.

"What in the fuck is going on?" demanded a superintendent at the barracks. "This guys big in the organisation, no doubt about it; nobody sits and takes all this punishment without saying something, even if it´s just *Fuck you!* It just doesn´t make any sense!" Angrily he shouted at the room, "These desk jockeys in London don´t know their arses from their elbows! We are the ones who are being fucking bombed and shot; it´s us who have to fucking check our cars every time we get into them! The nearest these bastards come to danger is when a fucking secretary passes on the clap!"

"Orders are orders Bill," his Chief Superintendent sympathised, "this is signed by our very own Secretary of State, so that's the story."

"Well George, I not one bit fucking amused; if they would leave it to us, this fucking war would be over in three months, and a whole lot of Fenian trash buried up in Milltown Cemetery!"

The chief superintendent advised, "Just follow the instructions when they come in Bill; the Irish have obviously rattled some one's cage over in London."

The Irish had indeed rattled cages over the arrest of Connor Rafferty, although the deals struck for his release known only to a very close circle. The Head of G-2, the Military Intelligence Unit of the Irish Defence Force, had consulted his Home Office Minister; they then had an urgent meeting with the Taoiseach, Dr. Garret FitzGerald. He personally telephoned Mrs Thatcher in London and she then ordered her Home Secretary and RUC to cooperate fully with the Irish Authorities.

Connor Rafferty was the most secret mole inside the Sinn Fein/Provisional Irish Republican Army Council!

Details and the arrangements for the transfer of the prisoner arrived later that day, and Connor advised of the situation.
He still had nothing to say, but requested a shower and a change of clothes.

At seven thirty next morning, two RUC constables drove him in handcuffs to the Central Station in Belfast. They were too early for the Dublin train, and went into the station buffet to have some breakfast. Handcuffing Connor to a chair, as one of his escorts went to the buffet counter. After a few minutes, the other constable said he was desperate for a pee, and left Connor to go to the toilet.

Witnesses testified later, that two men casually walked in from the station concourse, and drew automatic pistols. One stood at the door, whilst the other walked up behind the prisoner and shot him twice in the head. The gunman then threatened the RUC policeman who was at the cash desk, took his firearm, and ran out of the station to a waiting black taxi, which sped off. The officer who had been in the toilet rushed after them, but was too late to stop them escaping. The assassination of Connor Rafferty had taken less than thirty seconds to carry out.

Later that day, the Belfast Courier received an anonymous telephone call claiming UVF responsibility for the execution of a well-known IRA commander.

Chapter 67: The News

Saturday arrived; five days since Iñaki arrived at the Peace Camp. Meryl was going in to Glasgow for a meeting, saying that she might well stay overnight, but would be back on Sunday.

Iñaki felt a strange tinge of disappointment about not being asked to accompany her, but accepted that he couldn´t follow her around like a pet dog. He decided to walk into Garelochhead. Jono volunteered to show him around, which irked him. He had wanted some time to himself, but felt unable to refuse the rather strange character´s offer.

The village was a disappointment; other than a few older private villas and bungalows, it was grey and really quite unattractive, with a large council house estate for MOD and other base workers. Even the shoreline was littered with debris and oil. After a wander around, they went for a beer in one of the local hotels.

Iñaki had a pint of Tenants lager, whilst Jonathan had a cider. They both ordered *Stovies* to eat; a traditional potato and mutton mash, and they sat back observing two distinct groups of football supporters, at opposite ends of the bar.

Jono explained that those wearing the blue scarves were Rangers supporters, and Protestant, whilst the green outfits belonged to the Celtic fans, the Catholics.

Now and again, the two rival groups would end up fighting; but now not so often, as they would all be barred from the bar! It was not a derby today, and the rival groups were exchanging good-natured banter.

Today Jonathan was being more communicative, and was quizzing Iñaki about life in Spain.

Iñaki was explaining the heavy boat rowing races held in the Basque country, when his eye caught the News on the television above the bar, just as it was describing another assassination in Belfast. The rest of the bar carried their noise as normal, but Iñaki suddenly felt an unexplained chill running up his spine.

The announcer detailed how two men had walked into the Central Station in Belfast, and shot dead a Republican prisoner being escorted by two RUC policemen.

"The victim, believed to be a citizen of the Irish Republic has now been identified as a Mr Connor Rafferty, who had, according to sources, been arrested at the anti-nuclear protests at Sellafield on the May holiday weekend. More details are still coming in, and will be announced during the program."

Iñaki was staring at the television in disbelief. He sat frozen and immobile for several minutes, until he registered Jonathan saying something he couldn´t hear. He felt the bile and the recently consumed lunch rising in his throat, and just made it to the door where he threw up in the car park, much to the merriment of a group of supporters waiting on their bus.

"Can ye´ no haud yer drink, Manolo?" one shouted, as the rest guffawed.

He stumbled down the car park, with Jonathan running after him. "Where´s the telephone box Jonathan," he managed to blurt out. "I need to phone Siobhan"

"Iñaki, remember the phone here is bugged," Jonathan replied.

"Just show me where the fucking phone is, it´s an emergency."

They had to go to the other end of the village, and then discovered that the telephone box had been vandalised out of action. Beside him-self with rage and frustration, Iñaki fought hard to control his breathing and calm down.

Jonathan said he thought that he saw the bus coming on the other side of the Loch, it would be here in a few minutes, and they could go back to the peace camp, or on to Helensburgh. They decided Helensburgh was the best option as there were telephones all over the place.

The box by the pier stank even more than yesterday, but at least was still in a working condition. Iñaki tried his apartment, and got no answer. He was reluctant to telephone Padraig, but he desperately needed to talk to someone.

Shaina answered, he was careful not to give his name, simply saying he was a friend.

Shaina, sounding angry and shaken, simply said, in answer to his question, "Yes, the feckin´ Protestants have killed him. They´ve got the information from the feckin´ army or pigs, that´s how they knew he was in the station." She added, "Siobhan´s not here; there´s no one else here, and you´d better hang up now; the pigs are listening in."

Meryl had seen the television news; it was big news. Connor had been alongside Professor McGilvery on TV at Sellafield, and then he had been in police custody. The Press and politicians were demanding answers on how this could have happened, without some kind of security breach.

Meryl cancelled her plans to stay in Glasgow and hurried back down to Faslane. She knew Iñaki would be upset, and she wanted to be there for him.

Iñaki and Jonathan had brought back several cases of beer and wine to the peace camp to hold a wake in honour of Connor.

They all drank, and drank to a nice Irishman, who cared for his country and the environment. He had been cruelly murdered; shot down in cold blood, by gangsters dressed up as Policemen. Meryl led the homage for Connor. Most of the people there had come to know Connor at Sellafield, and all had admired his commitment and organizational skills. He was simply a nice guy. They laughed at the way he had outwitted the police on the first day of the protest, and bitterly condemned the police brutality and subsequent murder of Connor in Belfast. We were all living under a dictatorship! The capitalist establishment was determined to crush the people under their jackboots again.

Meryl launched into a tirade against the ultra-right wing armaments industrialists who now controlled the governments of the USA and Britain. They continued to escalate the nuclear arms race; it was making them into billionaires but putting the rest of humanity in grave peril of nuclear annihilation.

Iñaki tearfully recounted his arrival in Dublin, and the friendship he had received there. He thanked Connor for pointing him in the right direction again, to rediscover what really matters in this life and *joder*, fuck, he was going to fight these bastards!

Connor Rafferty had been well liked and respected in Sinn Fein circles and Dublin's green movement. He didn't have a reputation as a firebrand troublemaker. It was a bit of a mystery why he had taken the firecrackers to Sellafield. He was heavily committed to the Domhan Glas Iaochra cause, of which he was a founder member and president; he had never been known to provoke violence in the protests he helped organise.

Although his Republicanism was well known, only a handful knew of his Provisional IRA involvement, and this was political, not active service.

Connor Rafferty´s Service of Remembrance in Dublin attracted thousands. They came from his university and ecological connections; representation from Sinn Fein, CND, Friends of the Earth, Green Peace and the like. They came from the all over Ireland, the United Kingdom and the Continent.

After the Cortege left for a private family funeral in his hometown of Kinsale, and despite pleas for calm from the family, a march was organised to protest in front of the British Embassy in Dublin.

In anticipation of trouble, a large force of Garda had cordoned off the British Embassy. Inevitably, the demonstration quickly turned ugly, the Union Jack burned, and bricks thrown at the windows.

The Garda struggled to maintain control, but it was the sudden downpour of storm proportions, which finally cooled the anger of the crowd. They left the area bedraggled, disgruntled but satisfied they had made their point to the arrogant English!

The Irish government was outraged, and demanded an explanation from the British government. How an innocent man, the President of Domhan Glas Iaochra, could be arrested at a demonstration at Sellafield in England, be transported to Northern Ireland without any charges being lodged against him, and then be assassinated whilst in the custody of the Royal Ulster Constabulary.

The Irish withdrew all inter-governmental cooperation on security issues, until Britain issued satisfactory legal explanations and apologies, and the perpetrators brought to justice.

Mrs Thatcher was equally outraged, and summoned the Heads of all the security organizations involved. She made the shamed Heads aware of her embarrassment and displeasure.

An Assistant Chief Constable from a large County Police Force went over to Belfast, to carry out an independent investigation into the circumstances of Connor Rafferty's assassination.

Almost as soon as his plane touched down at Aldergrove Airport, he was ostracised from any real cooperation from the RUC, running up against brick walls in his investigation, including at times threats to his well-being.

The investigation never established who had leaked the details of Connor's release to the Ulster Volunteer Force, but it certainly came from a select few group of senior officers based at Castlereagh Barracks. The two RUC police constable escorts were severely reprimanded for their role in the affair, and suspended from duty for a month.

Chapter 68: The volunteer

Meryl drove Iñaki back to the Western Infirmary, for his appointment with the consultant. A new light plaster cast put on, with instructions to come back or go to another hospital in four weeks to have it removed. It still ached a bit, but it was the discomfort and itch of the cast, which had bothered him more than the actual wound.

Meryl was staying on in Glasgow for another meeting at the university. She gave him the option of waiting for her, or catching a train back to Helensburgh. He took the latter option. Meryl pointed him in the direction of the subway, to take him in to the centre of the city.

The subway itself was a Victorian relic, and Iñaki almost had to travel with his head bent in the clattering antique carriages. Meryl had instructed him to get off at Buchanan Street, which was also near to Queen Street railway station for his train back to Helensburgh.

Coming up back into the sunshine of Buchanan Street he found himself wandering about the city centre for a couple of hours, drinking in the atmosphere of the business and shopping streets. Suddenly feeling hungry, he turned into the Horseshoe Bar, in Drury Lane, attracted by the traditional stained glass windows and the smell of delicious food emanating from the doors.

The place was packed, noise and laughter from dozens of competing conversations filled the smoke laden bar, and Iñaki had to struggle through to ask for a beer. Most of the men around seemed to eating the Scotch Pie, so he ordered likewise, and found a seat in the corner besides two old men, nursing their half pints and shots of whisky. Although the food was as far away as you could get from Bilbao's `Pintxos´, similarities abounded; men drinking shots of whisky with their beer, and a few Lawyer or Banker types downing gin and tonics and talking football or business deals. Two old men, bearing the same pale, sharp features he was accustomed to in the Basque country, but here wearing typical *bunnets* instead of *xapelas* engaged him in conversation.

"Whe´re ye´ frae son?" This was repeated several times, as Iñaki couldn´t make out what they were asking.

He told them Bilbao, but they kept getting confused with Barcelona.

"Wee Stevie Archibald plays fur ye, an´ that English arsehole, Terry Venables is the manager isn´t he?"

"No, I´m from Bilbao, that´s at the other side of Spain from Barcelona." Iñaki responded, amused.

Screwing his eyes against the smoke from his cigarette, the old man asked, "Is that near Benidorm? Ma daughter´s been tae Benidorm, ye know."

"I´ve been to Benidorm for my vacation as well, but no, it´s quite far away. Did she enjoy it?" Iñaki asked conversationally.

"Aye, she said it wis magic; this year she´s goin´ tae Majorca!"

He passed a pleasant hour, educating the old Glaswegians, who insisted in buying him a `dram´, and went out into the warm Mayday, with a glow of contentment; a respite from his recent tragedy.

Iñaki caught the six-o´clock train for Helensburgh, which was full of commuters going home. He was tired now, and avoided looking at anybody. He also had a telephone call to make to Dublin at seven o´clock; a call he was not looking forward to making.

This time he telephoned from the station. The cubicle was only a little less repugnant than the one at the Pier, leading him to the opinion this was the normal in Scotland. The line was engaged, and he had to vacate to allow a woman to use the phone. She took her time looking for change, then dropping a coin before her ten-minute call to her daughter finished.

Iñaki felt his nerves stringing, he was late with his call, but it wasn´t *his* fault.

Eventually, the woman left, giving him a tight smile as she held the door open for him.

Dialling as fast as he could, the ringing tone had just begun, when the phone answered by the barman at John Flaherty´s. Iñaki asked for Siobhan, and was told to hold on. It was seven fifteen now, and he could hear the buzz of the bar in the background, giving him a yearning to be back in Dublin. A voice he did not recognise came on the line.

"John Flaherty´s."

"Can I speak to Padraig? Iñaki asked.

The voice, suddenly angry, answered, "You´re feckin´ late in phoning! Padraig can´t make it tonight, so I´ve to tell you what to do."

Iñaki asked, "What´s wrong with Shaina or Siobhan then? Who am I talking to?"

That´s no business o´ yours," the voice retorted. "Yer girlfriend has volunteered for active duty and she´s no´ here now. Padraig has said you´ve tae trust me, an´ he´ll speak with you later. Are ye still listenin´?"

Iñaki had been shocked into speechlessness. Siobhan had often talked about volunteering for active service, but Connor´s murder must have pushed her into the decision. "Yes I´m still listening," he replied.

The voice continued, "Right then, you´re away on a trip again." You still got the plaster on your arm?"

Iñaki responded, "Yes, I was at the hospital today, and it will be on for another few weeks."

"Look son, I didn´t ask ye for a medical report; can ye still drive?"

An annoyed Iñaki replied, "Yes, I can drive!"

"Well just listen to me and concentrate. Go to the Royal Bar, that´s on the front in Helensburgh, Friday at five o´clock. It will be packed wi´ workers from the base. Sit down near to the toilet at the back and make sure your plaster is visible. Buy a Helensburgh Advertiser and hold it in your good hand. Make feckin´ sure that my man can see the headline, got it?"

Iñaki responded, "Yes, Friday at five, at the Royal Bar, toilet seat, and Helensburgh Advertiser. What´s your man look like?"

"Big man, red faced, and he´ll be wearing blue overalls and boots. He´ll say he´s a friend of Siobhan's, and he´ll give you an envelope from her. You understood al that," the voice rasped.

"Okay I´ve got all that, what´s in the envelope?" Iñaki was wondering what he was getting into.

"I don´t know that son, but when you get it, open it in private and then phone me at the bar at seven again. Have ye´ got all that?"

"I understand, but what´s your name?" Iñaki asked.

"Just ask for Siobhan again." The line went dead.

Chapter 69: Paddy

The week passed slowly, the weather was ideal, cold fresh mornings, slowly heating up under crystal-clear, blue skies.
Iñaki took his turn of watching and studying the pattern of life and work at the Base. The idea was to discover chinks in the security systems and find ways of gaining entry into the Faslane complex, more to embarrass the MOD police than to present any kind of threat to the nuclear submarines sitting at their berths like huge black mechanical whales. The evenings were pleasant enough, but if it wasn´t for Meryl´s presence, he would have been bored out of his wits by the limitations of his surroundings and fellow peace campers. She seemed to take a particular interest in him, talking to him in Spanish

about how her visit to Hiroshima had made such a profound change to her life.
Iñaki was a little uncomfortable by the exclusion of the others from their talks; he was aware that Jonathan in particularly resented his favoured status, but frankly he found him strangely uncommunicative, nursing some deep scarred chip on his shoulder. His forthcoming meeting in the Royal Bar was always on his mind.
Meryl treated them to a night at the cinema in Dumbarton on the Thursday. The film was A Passage to India, which afterwards they all agreed underscored an English arrogance still held true to this very day!

The day after, his nerves taught, Iñaki made excuses at the camp, and walked all the way into Helensburgh, enjoying the brisk breeze coming in from the sea. Despite walking out on the pier and up and down the Clyde Street to kill time, he was early for his meeting at the Royal Bar.
It was almost empty, so he bought a lager, and sat down as instructed near to the foul smelling toilet doors. He felt conspicuous, and strived to pretend to read the paper, whilst keeping the Helensburgh Advertiser banner showing.
At five to five, the doors to the bar burst open, and a mass of construction workers surged in. Soon the bar was crowded with according to the accents, what seemed to be half of Belfast, downing Jameson whiskey and pints of Murphy´s.
Ten minutes went by, and he was beginning to panic he had made a mistake, when he was startled by a big, rough looking man squeezing in beside him.
  Iñaki had been looking out for him, but hadn´t noticed him in the crowd.
The big man asked him "What´s the craic, son? How´s that girlfriend o´ yours… what´s her name?"
"Siobhan," Inaki answered dry mouthed, and received a wide gap toothed smile in return. He was aware of the

shrewdness of the eyes boring into him, searching his conscious.

"Well lad, Siobhan has given me a wee present for you. Relax son, and ye can put the paper down now. I´m Paddy, pleased to meet you," as he offered a hand crushing handshake. "So you were a friend o´ Connor Rafferty? Ah´ only met him a couple of times, but he was a good man, was Connor, eh?" He continued without waiting for a comment from Iñaki, "A bad business that was; the bloody Prods run the show over there, but you mark my words, we´ll find the bastards that did it!"

Paddy went on, "Business now; you´ve to phone Siobhan at seven tonight to confirm we´ve had our little meeting." He downed the last of his pint, bent down and fished into his tool bag, and using his bulk as cover, passed a thick brown envelope. "Stick that in yer bag, but read it before you phone yer girlfriend. Good tae meet ye son," and he was up and out into the street before Iñaki could ask any questions.

Suddenly Iñaki felt claustrophobic, picked up his bag, and pushed through the throng along the bar, and out into daylight.
There was no sign of `Paddy´ and he debated where to go to read his letter from Siobhan. He decided to walk along the sea front, but remembering the public library, Jonathan had shown him, he diverted into the centre of the town.
The library was housed in a purpose built Victorian edifice and the matronly librarian gave him a smile as he entered.

Keeping his voice low, he asked her if there was a study room. She pointed over to a separate room, with a large Quiet Please, Reading Room sign over the door.

Iñaki had the room to him-self, and picking up a Glasgow Herald newspaper to use as cover if necessary, sat down and pulled the brown envelope from his bag.

It had been sealed with tape, and he struggled to open it without destroying the contents. Inside there were two more envelopes, one, the slimmest, he recognised was in Siobhan's handwriting, and addressed to him.

He opened this one, his heart beating a little faster, although he sensed what was inside. It was brief, and to the point. In the letter, she said she was sorry not to have had a chance to speak to him direct, but her feelings for him had changed. She thought that she had been in love with him, but realised her feelings fell short of what her idea of love should be. She had been going to end their relationship after they got back from Sellafield, but the circumstances had intervened.

Connor's assassination has been the final provocation for her to make the decision to fight for a United Ireland. The Brits would never negotiate seriously, and would have to be forced by armed struggle to give up the Six Counties.

She continued, *"I hope you will be able to continue to help us in our revolt against the people who ordered Connor to be murdered in cold blood.*
Finally Iñaki, my Basque man, you have suffered the injustice that a State can heap upon you; please understand my reasons for saying goodbye.
You will always be special in my heart, and I will think of you often.
We will meet again, until then `Saor in Aisce Ireland`!"
Siobhan.

Iñaki read through her letter three times, before putting it down and sighing in resignation. She was right; what they had between them had been brief, and wonderful, but had retreated to being agreeable and nice. Connor's murder had also awoken in him a sense of outrage against the same type of arrogance and authoritarianism that had made him flee from his family and homeland. He, like Siobhan, was now ready to commit to actively resisting the yoke of State Imperialism!

He opened the bulky envelope, to find it full of English twenty-pound notes. Surreptitiously counting, there appeared to be about two thousand pounds in total.

The letter accompanying, was from Padraig.

He eulogised his dead friend Connor. *"He was a thoroughly decent Irishman, a patriot to the Republican Cause."*

He then went on to explain that another international conference had been organised, and in about ten days time Iñaki would be travelling again, details to follow. He himself would not be present as he was under constant surveillance, but he could trust with his life the people who would be representing our Cause. The money enclosed was to cover expenses for the time being. Until things settled down, he should not attempt to return, or phone Padraig in Dublin. `Paddy´ would be his main contact, and he could always phone John Flaherty´s Bar, if he urgently needed to get in touch.

"Good luck, and thanks for your help. You can be sure that Connor will be avenged! The Loyalist killers and the bastards who gave them the information would face Irish justice!"

Padraig.

PS. *"Don´t forget to telephone Siobhan!"*

Iñaki checked the time, and realised that he only had twenty minutes to spare before phoning Siobhan again. Gathering his papers together, he replaced the Glasgow Herald into the rack.

He asked the librarian if she could direct him to the nearest telephone and responding with her customary smile, she directed him back down to Colquhoun Square; if they were out of order, he could try the station.

He was five minutes early, but decided to phone John Flaherty´s bar anyway, just in case the line was busy. This time, telephone was picked up on the first ring, startling Iñaki into stuttering, "Can I speak to Siobhan?"

"Speaking," answered the same rough masculine Dublin voice. "Ye´ met Paddy, and he´s given you the packet, that right?"

"Yes, I´ve got the money," answered Iñaki. "What´s next?" he asked.

"You´re goin´ on holiday next Thursday. Meet Paddy at nine in the Anchor Bar in Garelochhead on Tuesday night; he´ll give you another letter from Siobhan wi´ instructions on your travel plans. Dae ye still have your Irish passport for foreign travel?" `Siobhan´ asked.

"Yes," answered Iñaki.

"Well, use it; the tickets will be in that name, understand?"

Iñaki repeated, "I meet Paddy at nine, Anchor Bar, Tuesday and the tickets are in my passport name. Do I sit near the toilets again?"

`Siobhan´ rudely replied, "Ye can sit on the feckin´ toilet, just as long as you wait fur Paddy, and he see´s you! Now here´s another number fur ye, got a pen?"

Iñaki had anticipated this, and had his ballpoint and a slip of paper ready. "Yes, I´m ready," and was given a local area telephone number.

"You got that?" `Siobhan´ asked.

When Iñaki affirmed, the voice instructed, "That´s Paddy´s digs, ye´ can phone ´phone him there, but only in emergencies. No phoning fur a wee chat about the weather, understood?"

"I understand, but do you want me to phone you on this number as well?" Iñaki asked.

He was sharply admonished: "Are ye thick or something? This is a bar. Ah´ can´t be chattin´ to you all night. Paddy is yer contact now and he´s in touch wi´ the Chiefs. Ah´m only the messenger, an´ ah´ve passed ye´ the message, right?"

"Jesus," thought Iñaki, "this guys a real bad tempered *Tio*. I understand and thanks for passing on the message; can you get a message to Siobhan for me?"

"No, she's no' in Dublin now, an' ah' don't know where she is."

"Thanks anyway," Iñaki said as the telephone went click in his ear.

Chapter 70: Shaina

The following Wednesday, Iñaki was now travelling as Fernando Lopez Garcia, a student at the University of Dublin. His cover said that he was studying Environment and Bio-diversity.

He bought a ticket from Glasgow Central to Birmingham New Street station, changing at Crewe Junction. He would not complete the journey, getting off the train and stopping his journey at Crewe, where he would meet a fellow student, his girlfriend Marie Maguire. She would be easily recognizable in a white casual outfit, and wearing a red bandana around her neck.

The train was almost full, with few seats free, and he was lucky to have found a corner seat where he could observe his fellow passengers without being obliged to engage in conversation.

Iñaki had borrowed a CND Nuclear Warfare book from Meryl to get to know the subject better and pass the time, but his mind kept returning to his mission, and what he still didn't know about it.

As the express sped south, he was largely unaware of the country-side flashing by the windows. `Paddy´ hadn't told him anything other than he was going to France for another ETA meeting of extreme importance to the Cause, and he would be accompanied by a girl as part of the cover. His `girlfriend´ was a member of the organization; she would brief him on the details of the journey from there on.

Iñaki would meet this girl in the buffet at Crewe Station, and they would be joined in France by two other Provo volunteers, one of them Paddy had hinted was *Top Level*.

Paddy had emphasised, "Be careful! No fuckups, this guy is taking a big risk going over there!"

The clickety-clack of the train was lulling him into a trance as he ruminated on who this `girlfriend´ might be, "Could it be Siobhan? ... If so how would they relate? Would it be as if nothing had happened, as if she had not broken with him? Then he thought, maybe it would be one of these hard faced Belfast women, who lured young Brit soldiers into honey traps, then walking away without any conscience, as the boys were executed on the very bed they had been fucking on when the Death Squad burst in?" This thought did not lie well on his mind.

He had dozed a little, and sooner than he expected they were leaving Warrington Station and the guard was announcing, "Next stop Crewe Junction. Change here for Birmingham and North Wales."

Soon after, the train began slowing down, and, looking out of the window, he could see the brown brick workshop buildings, and that rail tracks were branching out as an indication of a major junction on the network.

The train glided to a halt, and grabbing his rucksack and alighting along with several dozen other passengers, Iñaki passed the ticket barrier and asked a porter where the buffet was located He was told sharply that he didn´t have time for a cuppa, as the Birmingham connection was waiting for the Glasgow passengers to arrive.

Iñaki appeared to be the only one not travelling on to Birmingham, and separating himself from the other passengers, he made his way onto the concourse and found the buffet. He decided to reconnoitre before going into the Buffet, perhaps subconsciously thinking of the trap that ended with Connor's death. Looking through a grimy window, there were other few customers seated. He found the girl with the white outfit and red bandana sitting with her back to him. There was no mistaking that red hair....it was Shaina!

She sensed his eyes on her and turned, giving him her widest smile; her green eyes alight with obvious pleasure.

As he entered the cafeteria, she ran towards him, happiness all over her face; "Fernando, darling, you're here at last," enveloping him in an obvious lover's kiss and embrace for the benefit of the onlookers.

Aware of the attention this was receiving, and taken aback with the intensity of the theatrical performance, he found himself tongue tied, forgetting his `girlfriend's` name, and blushing to the roots. He recovered enough to say, "It's great to be here, I've missed you!"

`Marie` asked, "Is your arm hurting still? It looks so painful!"

Iñaki answered, "No, not really, it's awkward, but I'm getting used to it."

"Are you hungry darling?" she enquired, concern on her face.

Iñaki responded, "I could do with a sandwich and a coffee, have you eaten?"

"No, I've been waiting for you, but let's go to the pub down the road."

She went back to her table, and picked up her own rucksack, which he immediately offered to carry, much to her amusement. They left the Buffet returning smiles from several older women admiring the handsome young couple obviously so much in love.

Once outside, and away from the Station, Shaina got more serious saying, "The sandwich will have to wait a bit, we've got to pick up our transport first." She explained that they were taking a campervan down to Bayonne in France. They would be given further orders when they arrived in Bayonne.

They walked towards the town centre against a stiff breeze, strong enough to keep their heads down and exchanging superficial news mainly about the Sellafield demonstration. The wind prevented any talk of Connor, still too painful in their minds for casual comment.

They arrived at the Brunswick Hotel after a ten-minute walk and went into the bar. No one was paying them attention, so they assumed that their contact hadn´t arrived yet. They ordered two half pints of cask ale, and toasted cheese sandwiches and sat down near the door. Talking in low tones, Shaina grimly filled in the details of what had happened to Connor, and the resultant upheaval in Dublin.

They had almost finished their sandwiches when a young fellow, dressed in oily mechanics overalls entered, and looked around.

Satisfied he had the right couple he came over and asked them, "Are you the people with the campervan?"

Iñaki looked askance, but Shaina quickly said, "Yes, has it been fixed?"

"I´m Mick by the way; yes missus it was the carburettor, but it´s going great now. It´s outside in the car park, do you want to see it working?"

Leaving their half-finished beers behind, they picked up their rucksacks and followed the mechanic outside to a battered looking blue coloured Volkswagen Camper with a rust covered spare wheel affixed on the front.

"It´s not as bad as it looks," the mechanic assured them. "We´ve completely overhauled the engine; it´s got new tyres and brake pads on it ... and there´s a new MOT certificate to go with it. Incidentally, don´t try to raise the roof, it´s been fixed in place."

He opened the passenger door, and opened the glove compartment and drew out a folder. "The Log Book, Hire Papers, Insurance Certificate and Green Card are all in order,

Malevolent Karma

and it´s registered in the name of Tommy´s Garage in Anfield, so you shouldn´t get any trouble with the Law. There´s also a map inside just in case you get lost.

He added, "You´re heading for Ramsgate, and you have a reservation on the seven o´clock Hovercraft over to Calais tomorrow morning, so you don´t have to thrash it down the road. After that, it´s up to you as long as you are around Bayonne on the twenty eighth."

Mick drew another envelope from under the seat. "In here you´ll find a map of France, and a phone number for a rendezvous on the twenty eighth, so you´ve got four days to get there, okay?"

Iñaki and Shaina nodded their affirmation.

He asked, "Have you driven one of these before?"

Iñaki nodded, and looking at Shaina, explained, "Meryl has one of these at the peace camp."

Pointing to Iñaki´s plaster cast, Mick offered, "I can adjust the angle of the steering wheel if you like."

Iñaki responded, "No, it´ll be fine, I´ve been driving one all week."

"Well then, if you´ve no questions here´s two sets of keys. You can drop me off at the station, I´m going back to Liverpool."

They stowed their rucksacks, and Mick jumped into the back seat. Iñaki got behind the wheel and adjusted the seat and interior mirror, then checked the controls and the gear action before starting up the engine. The motor fired first time with that peculiar air-cooled Volkswagen grumble.

Feeling the push from the rear slung engine, he crept out of the car park and took a left into the flow of traffic, turning back the way they came. On the way to the station, Mick gave them instructions on how to get to the M6 Motorway. Amidst parting `good lucks´, they left him at the entrance.

They exited the Station concourse and turned in the direction of the M6 Motorway south. Almost immediately, blue lights were coming up behind them and a police car, siren wailing and lights flashing raced by, almost causing the campervan occupants to empty their bowels, but the police were followed by an ambulance with its emergency lights flashing.

"*Dios mio*", Iñaki heaved a sigh of relief.

"Look man," Shaina assured him, and herself at the same time, "we are just a young couple going to France for a week´s holiday for feck´s sake; let´s relax and enjoy it. We´ve got business to attend to but in between times we can have some fun….no?"

She leaned over smiled and kissed him affectionately on the side of his cheek, adding, "You know, I´m really glad you and me are going on this mission. I volunteered for it as soon as I knew you were going. They were going to send some bitch from up North, but I pointed out that her accent would give her away."

He felt the cool of her lips and smelled her perfume, immediately recalling the same sexual frisson he had experienced with her in Dublin, but then she was with Padraig, and he was with Siobhan.

"What did Padraig have to say about it?" Iñaki cautiously asked.

She turned serious. "Nothing; Padraig is a shite. He doesn´t give a toss for me. I am of no importance to him, other than someone to fuck, cook, and clear up after him. Besides he was off to some Command Conference up North somewhere and I wasn´t invited." Scornfully she added, "He aims to become the President of an All Ireland you know." She continued, "It´s all about using people, manipulation, manoeuvring and getting the Armed Wing of the Provos to do the dirty work. Sure he wants a negotiated settlement with the Brits, don´t we all, but for him it´s all ambition." Sarcastic this time she added, "My Padraig buoy sees himself as another Michael Collins, only he doesn´t want blood on his hands."

Malevolent Karma

The sign for the M6 came up, and they took the slip road indicating Birmingham and the South.

Iñaki observed, "You always seemed to be happy Shaina. Anytime we were out with you we always had a fun, what happened between you two?"

Angrily she replied, "Nothing has happened! It's bloody great charade! Iñaki, there's a power struggle going on between Dublin, and the Provos in the North, so personal relationships take second place! Christ, we have not had sex for over six months!"

Shaina was a very sexy woman, and being unable to believe her statement but thinking about the possibility, Iñaki felt a stir in his loins. He mildly asked, "Why have you stayed with him then?"

She shook her head, a lock of her rust coloured hair fell over her eye, but she didn't bother to push it out of the way. She looked despondent and depressed as she replied, "I've been with him five years Iñaki, and you don't know how difficult it is for a woman to walk away from her life with the man she once loved....even when she realises that she's become no more than an accessory for his image. What would I do? Where would I go; back home to my parents?" A gloomy cloud passed over her as she said, "it's not that simple, Iñaki."

They had reached a tail back on the Motorway, which needed his concentration, both of them reflecting on what had just been said. The stop-start traffic continued for about twenty minutes, neither of them conversing, Shaina fiddling with the radio and studying the map on her knees. Finally, the traffic cleared around the accident, and as if the clouds had cleared from their heads, they began talking naturally again.

She looked directly at him, her eyes imploring, "Iñaki, let's enjoy this trip; we're adults, free and on holiday. If anything happens, it happens ...no hang-ups okay?"

Lightening the mood, Iñaki used her cover name, "That´s okay with me my Marie; ...*Maria, I once had a girl called Maria; and suddenly I found......*"
They were laughing and singing, the questions and tensions had passed, and they were damn well going to enjoy the trip, come what may.

Shaina found BBC Radio 2´s afternoon show with David Hamilton, and sang along with the Stones, Queen and laughed like hell as she belted out Madonna´s `Like a Virgin.´

Iñaki took time off from concentrating to join in the chorus, but soon the traffic slowed again on yet another traffic tail back.

They progressed fitfully in the rush hour traffic just north of Birmingham. Maria was studying the map, and keeping an eye out for signs for London and the South. She need not have bothered. The motorway traffic came to a standstill before `Spaghetti Junction´, and they had more than enough time to look out for the orbital route around Birmingham.

The sun was glaring in from through the windscreen, and they were stuck alongside a six-wheeler lorry belching out diesel fumes, which kept pace as they crawled forward a few yards and stopped. They had to wind up the windows, which made the interior of the cabin even more oppressive.

Iñaki's wrist was aching with the constant changing of the gears in the traffic, and the need to concentrate precluded conversation between them.

Shaina now content to make the occasional comment about the awfulness of living around here, "Jesus, can you imagine going to work in this every day?"
It took them an hour to negotiate around Birmingham and get into a clear stretch of road again.

Iñaki was exhausted; he had been up since seven o´clock and was completely unused to driving in this traffic. His head was throbbing and piercing pains were shooting up his injured arm. They decided to stop at the next service station for a bite to eat, and a break from the Midlands traffic inferno.

He turned off the motorway into a Little Chef and found a parking space quite close to the cafeteria. Wearily they climbed down from the VW cabin. They separated to use the toilets, *No need to ask where they were,* thought Iñaki, as the smell wafted out almost to the entrance to the restaurant.

He beat a retreat from the overflowing urinal, grabbed a pile of paper towels and washed his face and neck as thoroughly as he could, a task he still had difficulty in achieving with his wrist in plaster. Checking himself in the mirror, he looked and felt only marginally better, the train journey and driving leaving their mark on his face.

Thinking of Shaina …*well you never know!* He took the trouble to buy a packet of condoms.

She was waiting for him at the entrance to the cafeteria. She looked stunningly refreshed, the red hair and makeup impeccable, and good enough to be attracting the lewd comments and propositions from the lorry drivers coming in and out of the cafeteria.

"Jesus, I thought you were never coming out, I was about to come in get you; it´s bloody dangerous for a woman to be here alone with these creeps!"

"I was only in there ten minutes," he protested.

"I was in and out of there before I could catch anything. I can´t feckin´ stand these places where a girl has to stand up to pee; the standard of hygiene is feckin´ abysmal. Hah! Great Britain at its greatest! Well let´s go and eat; hopefully we can eat something here that´s not going to result in illness, unlike the bloody bogs!"

After picking up their trays and cutlery, and perusing the tired and stale looking food in the hot displays, they both decided on ordering the `Special Aberdeen Angus Burgers, freshly prepared and cooked over charcoal, and topped with a generous thick slice of mature Cheddar cheese.´

They both had cokes to drink, Shaina opting for the light variety, whilst Iñaki felt he needed all the caffeine he could get! He popped a couple of his analgesics, praying to him-self he wouldn´t fall asleep at the wheel! He paid with a twenty-pound note, and was shocked only to receive a few pence as change, stimulating him to think of Bilbao, where he would have had a serious meal for two and wine included! The Burgers were to their surprise, excellent, with fresh, thick cut chips, and a more than adequate side salad included, the best choice after all!

Shaina brought the map out of her bag, and they both took time to check over the route to Ramsgate; on the face of it not so very far, but they had to negotiate around London! They calculated more or less three and a half hours, plus a bit more for traffic around London…..maybe four hours in total.

Iñaki´s face fell; it was now seven o´clock, and the thought of driving for another four hours dismayed him.

Shaina saw the look and volunteered to do some of the driving, an offer Iñaki gratefully accepted.

"I didn´t know you could drive, you didn´t say anything when Mick asked us," Iñaki observed. "I´m the one with the broken wrist," he complained.

"There´s a lot you don´t know about me sonny boy," she laughed at him, "my daddy´s a farmer and I´ve been driving since I was five years old!"

"Well in that case we´d better get going then," he said just a little churlishly; just a little put down. "You take the first leg down to London, and I´ll take the last part." He immediately regretted his tone of voice, but couldn´t bring himself to correct his mistake. He realised that he would have to be careful if he was to get where he wanted to go with this woman.

Shaina refrained from a riposte of "Aye, Aye Sir!" but only in the interest of maintaining the cordiality they were now enjoying, *Jesus, why do these bloody men think they must be in charge all of the time?*

He handed over the keys, and she climbed up behind the wheel and expertly adjusted the seat position and the mirrors, before starting up and driving over to the petrol pumps to top up the tank.

The traffic flow had subsided considerably and the road was now clear enough to drive at more or less the seventy per hour limit. The sun was still strong enough to pierce the inevitable Midlands pall of pollution, which turns the passing fields into a greyish green haze. They were making good progress, now on the M1, and again had found the spirit of fun, laughing at Iñaki´s attempts to sing along to the latest hits.

In a lull Shaina asked; "Why haven´t you asked about Siobhan? Don´t you want to talk about her?"

Questions about Siobhan had been racing around Iñaki head, but he hadn´t wanted to return to the serious conversation they had before.

"I didn´t want to spoil the journey with any more talk about her and Dublin, but I´m curious why she volunteered for active service so quickly." He added hurriedly, "I knew that we were about to split....no real reasons, except we were not so close anymore. We both knew it was time to move on, but neither of us had the guts to say it. I just hope that I was not the reason for her decision."

"No, you were not that important to her Iñaki. Remember she is Padraig´s sister, and she is just as committed to getting the Brits out of Ireland." Shaina continued, "Siobhan told me a while back ...before Sellafield; she felt too restricted, but it was not that she wasn´t fond of you or anything like that. She just needed space to do what she wants to do, and at the moment she wants to do something concrete against the Brits." She went on, "Connor was the decisive factor; he was like a brother to her, and the killing has triggered her into action." She looked over at him, smiled a little sadly and softened, "We are orphans on this trip Iñaki let´s forget the past and have a good time."

They made it to Ramsgate at just after ten, exhausted, and decided to take a room above a small hotel near the Hovercraft Terminal. Sleeping in the campervan could wait until they were over in France, when they could stock up and work out the sleeping arrangements in the VW.

After checking in, and asking for a six-o´clock wake up call, they dumped their beds in the cramped bedroom. Both noted, but neither commented, on the old fashioned, double bed, which took up most of the space. The only other furniture was a chair and a shelf on which sat the ubiquitous tea and coffee making kit with its panoply of instant coffee, tea and digestive biscuits.

Looking out of the window, they had a panorama of the parking area and piles of beer crates and barrels from the paint-stuck sash window, however they weren´t here for the view.

Shaina pointedly suggested Iñaki should go downstairs to the bar, as she needed a pee and a wash. "Get me a large Jameson´s and a ham and cheese sandwich," she shouted as she closed the door on him.

Iñaki did as he was told, and smiling inwardly, descended the stairs to use the toilets just off the reception area.

The bar was buzzing; Country music was belting out of the speakers and there appeared to have been some kind of mixed bar skittles competition, which had just finished by the sounds of derision and laughter between the teams and their supporters.

When she appeared at the entrance to the bar, raucous conversations stopped. Women instinctively edged closer to their men-folk, recognising competition with a capital `C´; whilst the men stared appreciatively if not longingly, until their partner´s yanked them by the arm.

It was not as if Shaina had dressed in a bikini, or an expensive Dior cocktail dress, she had simply changed into a light cotton shirt, tide at the waist over black sequined jeans.

The only concession to decoration was an emerald green silk scarf around her neck drawing even more attention to her startlingly expressive eyes, her flame red hair contrasting a confident and smiling face.

In the twenty odd minutes she had been upstairs alone in the room, she had showered away a million miles of travel grime, and replaced it with an allure that only naturally beautiful women can do, seemingly effortlessly, and without the gimmickry of expensive make-up pampery.

Iñaki in contrast still looked and felt grimy, despite his best efforts to clean up a bit in the toilets. His plaster cast had travel smudges, and he still had on the blue jeans and T-shirt he had been wearing since leaving Glasgow at seven in the morning. He stood and waved her over to the table he had managed to stand guard over.

She pushed her way through the throng around the bar, drawing further questioning commentary and upon reaching Iñaki, she drew him to her and kissed him passionately, whispering in his ear, "That´s for getting us here safely, and for the benefit of the crowd."

They sipped on their whiskies as they waited for their food. When it arrived, the kitchen had produced excellent crunchy toasted sandwiches accompanied by a bowl of chips, which they consumed ravenously. They ordered a couple of pints of Kentish Stout to wash down the food.

Replenished, they nursed their beers as they relaxed, not saying much, winding down and watching the good-natured crowd at the bar. Shaina suggested an early night as they were up at dawn for the ferry. Whilst paying at the bar, Iñaki bought two more Jameson´s for the room.

There were no inhibitions or moments of shyness. She laughingly turned up her nose and suggested he showered, which had been his intention in any case.

She sat on the bed watching him, and sipping her whiskey, as he somewhat self-consciously stripped to his boxers.

Taping and wrapping his cast in a plastic bag, he stepped into the cubicle, adjusted the temperature to a nice hot, but not too hot temperature, and began as best as he could soaping his hair, and enjoying the warmth of the water cascading over his head and shoulders.

He became aware of her presence when she began caressing him from behind, kneading the days´ tension from his shoulders and back, relaxing blissfully, not quite believing his good fortune. He felt her breasts, her nipples pressing into the small of his back, her tongue licking away the cascading water, her left hand travelling around his trunk to find his erection, turning him around, pleasuring, biting at his neck, guiding him into her.

Later, in bed she again dominated, until they both fell into an exhausted sleep.

Chapter 71: The Crossing.

The shrill ringing of their wake-up call jolted them awake.
She gave him a good morning peck and a playful tug on his now flaccid penis as she got out of bed. He responded with a groan and bleary smile, and *"Dios Mio,* it´s not that time already."
    "You make the coffee and I´ll go first" she replied entering the bathroom and closing the door.

They made the Hovercraft Ferry with plenty of time. Most of the fellow travellers were truckers going over to the Continent, but there also was a fare sprinkling of private cars and a couple of other campervans. Neither Iñaki nor Shaina had ever seen one of these ugly and ungainly looking craft before, looking at it curiously.

The morning was cloudy but fine; they could see France in the distance; a fair wind was making the Channel grey and choppy with white caps on the waves.

. They had been revising on their Fernando/Marie identities on the way to the terminal. Iñaki still felt a shiver of nervousness travelling on his false passport, but Shaina looked as cool as ever. Two sleepy looking customs officials were half-heartedly looking over the trucks, paying no attention whatsoever to the campervan as they drove up the ramp into the cavernous interior. Quite quickly, the engines started up and after a few warming up minutes, they felt themselves being lifted up on the curtain of air, as the engine noise increased. It was a strange sensation of vibration, speeding, suspended above the sea, only shuddering and bouncing when they hit the big waves out in mid-channel.

They had brought the map, and plotted their course down south, deciding to take in a couple of French resorts on the way down to Bayonne.

In less than an hour they were disembarking, and other than flashing their Passports at the French Custom Officer, they were rapidly on their way south.

Chapter 72: Guéthary, South West France.

They had two gloriously free days camping at a surfers campsite on the cliff top overlooking the beach just north of St Jean de Luz. `Fernando´ and `Marie´ had quickly and easily integrated in the young surfers´ weekend crowd.

Iñaki had surfed before at Algorta, close to his home in Las Arenas, but Shaina just couldn´t get the balance right and spent more time immersed in the still very cold Bay of Biscay than on the surfboard, but she still managed to laugh and enjoyed the fun.

When dusk fell, they went down to the beach watching the wonderful romantic golden, red ball sunsets over the now calm sea. Later there were parties at the bar, and afterwards two nights of unadulterated sex in the campervan.

On the morning of the twenty-eighth, real life caught up with them and regretfully, but as instructed, they made contact by telephone to the agent in Bayonne.

A Spanish voice commanded them to go to the Bar Vasca, in front of Hotel Madrid in nearby Guéthary, one o´clock sharp. They would be met by the other two Provo representatives. It was already eleven and they needed to find the place, so they hurriedly packed up, made their farewells to their friends already down on the beach, and took the D911 coast road to Guéthary.

In less than twenty minutes, Iñaki drove the VW into the little fishing village, leaving them plenty of time to scout around and find the Bar Vasca.

They then decided to go down to the pretty port for a beer and wonder about their mission, which had taken a back seat in their minds over the previous three days.

They found a table outside a little bar/bistro overlooking the harbour. Ordering a carafe of Rosé wine instead of beer, they sat quietly, taking in the scene set out before them.

The sounds and smells drifting up from the Port as deeply weather beaten and unshaven fishermen sloshed water over decks, and manhandled their gear around the little boats.

Harsh Basque accents filtered through Gauloises mixed with the caw caw´s of the seagulls, ever watchful for the odd scrap discarded, when they would rise up as one and swoop down screaming in competition for the prize. A perfect blue sky, with just the occasional white cloud scudding across completed the picture postcard scene.

Iñaki was still in a relaxed, switched off mode. It was Shaina, who brought him back down to earth. Her face became serious as she looked directly at him, her normally sparkling eyes now unsmiling. "Iñaki, our little idyll is over now. We've had a fantastic time, and I've loved every damn minute of it, but it's time for business now. These guys' don't mess around, so as far as they are concerned we've been as celibate as nuns in a convent. No looks, touches or anything, do you understand?"

Quizzically, he looked at her.

"Iñaki, wake up! Concentrate! We're here on IRA business, and there's no more fun, right?"

Seeing how serious she was, he replied, "I understand Shaina, but what happens afterwards?"

"Nothing happens, Iñaki, it's just too dangerous. Padraig is a shite, but he's a proud shite, and he won't take kindly to us having an affair, understand?"

A touch of panic entered his head, "Shaina, this can't just end like this, for Christ sake, you know how I feel about you."

Softening a little she said, "Yeah, Iñaki, I have feelings too, but we've got to be realistic. He would kill you, and probably me as well."

She pulled his head around so he could look directly into her eyes. "Iñaki, look and listen to me ...Concentrate! Grow up! These people will report back to him, don't give them any reason to make him jealous."

Downcast and smarting from her words he said, "You're right of course, but don't shut the door just yet... *por favor*?"

His look of desolation and sincerity made her smile. "Listen, my boy, next week is next week, just you keep focused for the next couple of days; do the business that we are here for and later on... who knows?"

Relaxing now, and smiling, they clinked glasses in salute, and received a shocking return to reality when a voice they well recognised interrupted.

"Well then, what a sight for sore eyes…young lovers toasting their happiness in a romantic French fishing village."

They hadn´t noticed, anyone approaching, or expected Rory Gallagher to be in France.

Rory was with by the same thug that Iñaki met at the meeting at Padraig´s house. They were both dressed as fishermen, although any reasonable inspection would have aroused suspicion due to their pale complexions.

"Ye don´t mind if we join you, we´re starving." This was said as he was drawing a chair from another table, adding with a leer, and his head tilted provokingly to one side, "But we don´t want to be interrupting anything, do we Jonnie?"

"What could possibly be amiss here boss, she´s Padraig´s woman isn´t she? Naw, they´re just a little surprised to see us, that´s all."

Shaina´s face had turned white, a mixture of embarrassment, fear and anger, but managed to say, "Sit down, it´s a free country; nothing´s being interrupted here."

Still smiling Rory said, "Aye, I believe you colleen… I truly believe you. Shaina me´ darlin´, do you think I could get a good old fashioned Irish bacon roll here?"

The waitress came over, and much to Iñaki and Shaina´s surprise, Jonnie ordered *"Deux oeuf frits, bacon et tatin; avec café au lait aussi,"* in near perfectly accented French.

"That surprised you, didn´t it?" laughed Rory. "My big friend here was in the Legion for ten years, weren´t you Jonnie?"

Jonnie just smiled and nodded, leaving the two others still a bit taken aback.

Rory enquired, "How was your trip down, have any problems with the customs? Of course not, otherwise you wouldn´t be here." Again, the slightly mocking tone, and the same menacing smirk directed at Iñaki.

Shaina answered, "None whatsoever, we got waved through in England, and the French didn´t even ask to see the passports." Catching the mood, she asked, "Were we carrying anything?"

Rory was having fun, "Well you don´t think we´re going to give your boy here, a couple of thousand quid and a lovemobile, and send him on a holiday to France without us getting a little something in return, do you?"

Shaina demanded, "What´s in the van, Rory? I think we should have been told we had something on board, you know."

"Nothing important and anyway you would have got all sweaty at customs. You see, we really do look after you, Shaina."

Just then, their breakfast arrived, and as the two wolfed it down, a kind of nervous tension pervaded the table.

Iñaki stole a glance at Shaina, both wondering just what they had smuggled into France, sharing an icy dread at the possibilities of discovery.

Finally, as he gulped the last of the coffee, Rory announced, "Okay, down to business, do you know where the meet is… the Bar Vasco?"

"Yes, we checked it out before coming down here," replied Shaina.

Rory´s mood had darkened, "Good girl but look, I don´t want to be bolshie, we´re here on an operation, but has your fuckin´ boyfriend lost his tongue? He hasn´t uttered one fuckin´ word all morning and it´s getting´ to me! Where have you parked the van?" He directed this directly into Iñaki´s face. Iñaki took a few seconds to respond, resulting in another expletive from Rory.

"W…w…we´ve parked it in a side road about two hundred meters from the Hotel Madrid." Iñaki managed to get out.

"It talks, fuckin´ hell it talks Jonnie! Right then, we´re meeting a couple of Spanish guys there so lover boy will be in his element; after all that´s his job, to help us talk to these heathens."

At last, Iñaki found the courage to snap back. "You might find these Basque heathens, as you describe them, are intellectually more than capable in looking after themselves!"

This time Rory laughed, but the hardness in his eyes didn´t reflect his mirth. "Only kidding Fernando, you´ll soon get used to my sense of humour." Rising, he continued, "Fine, you pay the breakfast out of the kitty fund, give us twenty minutes and watch for anyone following us; if so, clear out and phone your contact at three o´clock, got that?"

"Okay, I think we can handle that," answered a now more sure of himself Iñaki, receiving a warning raised finger from Jonnie.

No one appeared to be taking the slightest interest when Rory and Jonnie left, walking purposely up the little cobbled road leading up into Guéthary, passed the quaint whitewashed and black timbered houses and shops. Twenty minutes passed with Iñaki and Shaina quite casually looking around checking if anyone was paying them any attention.

Satisfied with their security, Iñaki paid the bill, and they set off up the hill to the meeting. Almost comedy-like, they would stop at a shop window, and surreptitiously checking no one was shadowing them. Ten minutes later, they entered the heavily timbered Bar Vasco.

They were immediately accosted by a young casually dressed Spaniard, who greeted them effusively, "Fernando, primo!" *"Como va, hombre!"* all the time embracing and kissing Iñaki. Turning his attention to Shaina he continued, "This is Maria? *que guapa! cojones!"* Embracing and kissing her on both cheeks. "Gloria is dying to meet you...she´s preparing lunch already!"

Minds racing, and nerves jangling on the possibilities of a trap, they allowed themselves to be steered back through the door before they had time to react.

Once outside, he assuaged their fear by explaining he was Roberto, their contact in Bayonne. Rory had left already and they were to follow on to the farm. As he led them round the back to where a battered, old, and rusting Renault 18 was parked, he asked, "Where is your car?"

They explained it was just around the corner, but he insisted in giving them a lift to the Volkswagen. Sighing noisily he said, "Hombre, man, I´ve always wanted one of these love-mobiles."

Shaina said under her breath, "Jesus Christ, have we got to put up with this crap all day?"

Roberto turned serious, "Listen, you must follow me carefully, the farm is not easy to find; if you get lost, go to the Supermarche Champion on the A63 outside Bayonne, and I´ll meet you there at three o´clock, okay? Don´t get lost though; important people from Spain will be waiting, and your boss won´t like it, *compende*?"

Roberto drove fast out of the village, with Iñaki almost tailgating to maintain contact, until they met the lunchtime rush on the A63 going towards Bayonne. The traffic was slow, and finally they were crawling along. As they rounded a bend, Iñaki´s stomach gave a lurch. From his elevated driving position, he could see a police roadblock about three hundred meters away.

Heart pounding, he quickly risked a flash of his lights to warn Roberto in front, as Shaina laid a cool hand over his on the wheel.

"Calm down, come on, breathe deeply; you are Fernando, I´m Maria, we are students at Trinity, and on a tour with the ´van."

As they crept forward, she rehearsed their cover story with him, all the papers were in order, her uncle Charlie in Liverpool had lent them the campervan, and they were having a great time at St Jean de Luz. She opened up her blouse another button, and lazily put her feet up on the dashboard in front of her, showing a good deal of thigh.

At about one hundred metres, the first pair of gendarmes, machine pistols at the ready were scrutinising the occupants of the cars. As they passed them, Shaina gave them a smile, but their stony expressions failed to register any eye contact, intent on their search for suspects. A further hundred meters with the sweat pouring down Iñaki´s back, almost there, at the entrance to the lay-by. Fuck! The gendarme has signalled Roberto in for a check! Iñaki got such a fright he almost followed him in, when the gendarme blew his whistle and irritably waved the campervan on!

As they accelerated away from the alligator stop chains and another pair of machine gun toting Gendarmes, Iñaki exhaled the pent up breath and straining nerves. "*Madre de Dios*, that was close!"

"You did well there Fernando boy," counselled Shaina, "We´d better stop at the next lay-by to see what´s happened to Roberto, otherwise we´re lost!"

They were both were watching the rear view mirrors and wishing for a lay-by, when in the distance loomed the Supermarche Champion that was to be their emergency contact place. Iñaki turned into the supermarket and selected a parking bay next to the entrance, where they could be seen from the road, and where they could watch out for Roberto´s Renault.

Shaina began throwing their gear into their rucksacks as they discussed the situation. They had lost their contact; they had no idea where the farm was located, and if the police had in fact arrested Roberto, they were in a very precarious position if he talked to the gendarmes. There would be no option but to abort the operation, dump the Volkswagen, and get out of the area.

They agreed a plan. If Roberto didn´t appear within ten minutes, they would move the van to a less conspicuous position, split up, Shaina to the supermarket cafeteria, which fronted on to the parking area, and Iñaki would observe from the bar across the road. It was now after two, and they felt that they could maintain their surveillance until at the latest, a quarter past three, and then abort if no one contacted them.

The minutes passed, the sun was glaring hot through the windscreen, making it difficult to concentrate on the traffic passing. Iñaki visibly sweating, was unconsciously ticking of the seconds with his index finger on the steering wheel, until Shaina snapped at him to "Stop that bloody racket," showing for the first time her unease.

Finally, looking at each other for confirmation, he started up the motor, but just as he was engaging gear, the red Renault suddenly drove into the parking area flashing his lights as he passed them by, and heading over to the furthest corner.

Iñaki waited a minute to ensure Roberto had not been tailed by the police, before following him and parking a little distance from him.

Roberto passed the van, nodding in the direction of the cafeteria, and again they delayed before following him inside.

He was talking to someone on the telephone just inside the entrance, so they continued into the self-service, selected two filled baguettes and cola´s, paying before selecting a table by the windows overlooking the car park. Five minutes went by as they nervously kept checking the road and the car park before a worried looking Roberto appeared, bought a coffee and sat down beside them.

"*Joder!* That was an escape. The bastards checked the whole fucking car; thank God it was legitimate, but even then I´ve got a bloody fine for my tyres!"

"Jesus Christ, we thought you´d been arrested," Shaina exclaimed, "you´re our only contact here!"

Tensely, Roberto replied, "I know, it´s a cock up, I´ve no idea why you weren´t given a back up contact... probably security I suppose. Look, I phoned ahead, and they want me to clear off, in case I´ve aroused suspicions. You´ve got a map?"

Iñaki nodded affirmative.

Roberto continued, writing on a paper napkin as he spoke. "Follow on this route, A63 north to St Pierre and then A64 going south as far as Briscous. You then take the D21 and you will come to a Relais Routier; it´s only about fifteen kilometres. A dark blue Citroen will be sitting in front of the restaurant. The man´s name is Eugene, he´ll take you to the farm, is that all clear?"

Shaina interjected, "Don´t you have another phone number to give us if he´s not there?"

"He´ll be there alright, but no, it´s a top level reunion, and they are all getting nervous. The Basque people have been delayed also, if you have a problem, you must phone me at the Bayonne number." Looking around, he added, "You´d better go now, we´ve wasted enough time already … good luck."

The traffic had thinned out now, and in a surprisingly short time, they made the meeting with `Eugene´, who turned out to be one of the ETA negotiators that Iñaki had met earlier in the year in Nantes.

After the customary embraces and salutations, Iñaki introduced Shaina, prompting a "*Coño, su novia?* Fuck, this is your girlfriend?"

Iñaki flashed a grin, "*No, es mi compañera.* No, she´s only my cover."

"Si, Señor," an unbelieving Eugene smiled back. "We must go, it´s not far, but the farm is difficult to find if you don´t know where you are going."

Chapter 73: The Farm, Basque Country, France

Eugene led them through the pleasant, typical Basque region village, passing the towering church spire, before turning off onto a gravel agricultural road, first going south, and then turning east for a few kilometres. Several junctions and turns later, they stopped at a padlocked gate, waited for Eugene to open it, wave them through, and replace the chain and lock. They entered and drove through a wooded area to exit into fields of lush meadow grass.

On one side of the road a flock of sheep grazed with their lambs bleating and gambolling alongside their mothers, whilst, on the other, a herd of white, heavy, Charolais cows munched noisily through their field, pausing only to lift their heads and gaze curiously after the intruders.

The farm buildings were still about a kilometer away, and set on a small promontory, giving a clear view over the fields and to what turned out to be a forest at the rear. As they got closer, they could see that the buildings were connected in a square quadrangle style, almost like a miniature Basque castle, and were accessed through an archway, the doors of which opened as they drove up.

As Eugene did a U-turn, and sped back out of the compound, the doors closed again and one of the armed guards directed Iñaki into a barn to one side. Again, the door was closed behind them, and as they jumped down from the van, their eyes adjusting to the gloom, another small door opened at the far end.

"Where in the fuck have you been!" shouted Rory as he and Jonnie strode into the barn.

Shaina replied heatedly, "Roberto got caught up in a police control. He got out of it, but he had to get someone else to meet us. Didn´t you know? He telephoned someone."

An agitated Rory responded, "I know fuck all, no one´s phoned me, the ETA guys were supposed to be here by now as well. What the hell´s going on?"

"Roberto said that they were having problems getting here. I think the gendarmes have been checking cars and documents all over the region."

"Well that´s just fucking handy," Rory complained, "We´re supposed to be back on that stinking fishing boat by midnight!"

Jonnie intervened, "It´s okay Boss, we´ve still got plenty of time."

Rory still fuming, grumbled, "I fucking well hope you´re right Jonnie. Let´s get the gear off this van, in the hope these cunts get here today! You two, get your gear into the house, you´ll be staying here tonight. The old French fart will give you something to eat and show you a room."

They crossed the courtyard to enter into the farmhouse itself closely watched by the two shotgun carrying guards at the archway. An old Pyrenean Mountain Dog came out of its kennel to snuffle at their feet, as the earthy pungent smells of the farm assaulted their senses.

The door to the farmhouse itself was directly opposite the archway entrance, protected from the elements by a shallow angled inverted vee porch, which stood on solid, black-painted wooden pillars. Two old established vines twisted up and over the porch and along above the lintels. Three sets of windows framed by traditional wooden shutters on each side ran the length of the building. A dozen or so halved wine barrels containing a selection of flowers and herbs, stood against the white-painted walls giving a pleasing colour contrast.

Iñaki knocked hard on the door but, after waiting a few minutes, he opened the door and shouted, "*Bonjour.*" No one appeared, so they crossed the threshold directly into a large traditional farmhouse kitchen. A huge, old-fashioned wood or coal fired stove took up the centre of one wall. An enormous pot of what appeared to be some kind of soup, simmered on the centre plate. Marble tops ran from the stove onto a double sink at one end, and a series of what appeared to be slaughterhouse blocks with hooks hung from a running rail above.

The old grey, slate floor was scrubbed clean, but showed years of wear and tear at the stove and around the enormous bleached deal table that along with the chairs, dominated the room. The other side of the kitchen was taken up with traditional, plain-wood cupboards and dressers.

The adornments in this room were the herbs, garlic, peppers, and gleaming copper pans strung above the cooker but at the far end, on either side of an interior door were an enormous crucifix and a faded picture of Mary with her baby son. A speckled mirror was hung on one of the cupboards beside the door they had just entered.

Despite the heat from the stove, the temperature was remarkably cool inside and, as they looked around, the interior door opened allowing a tiny, wiry, white-haired old woman, dressed completely in black, to enter.

"*Bonjour monsieur, mademoiselle*, you are expected, come with me," as she led them through the door into a large hall and up one of the narrow staircases leading off from the vestibule.

They were led up two flights of stairs, which left the old lady gasping for breath. She showed them along a narrow corridor, stopping to indicate the door of the bathroom, and into a small attic room, with two narrow beds with iron headboards. The only other furniture was a small dresser with a three-panelled mirror, a bentwood chair, and an old-fashioned ceramic bowl on a stand alongside a large jug of water. A threadbare woven rug of indiscriminate colour complemented the greyish-white curtains.

It was basic, sterile but clean, and with the obligatory crucifix adorning the wall. If it wasn´t for the fact that there were two beds, the overall effect was that of a monk´s cell.

The old woman was still waiting at the door as they looked around, until Iñaki, remembering his manners, smiled and spoke, "*Merci beaucoup* madam, the room is lovely."

He was answered by a tight smile, and a slight nod of the head as her shrewd little eyes passed from one to the other in appraisal. As she turned away, she said, "You will meet my son later, and dinner will be served at eight o´clock but, if you want some cheese and wine beforehand, I will be in the kitchen or the dining room downstairs."

"How many other people are staying here tonight?" Iñaki asked.

Again, the eyes glittered as she replied, before closing the door on them. "You must speak to the Boss or my son, *monsieur.*"

"Security is tight enough here," Shaina asserted, "Look down there."

The window looked out onto the rear of the farm, to a series of paddocks and corrals and more fields, this time with some horses grazing. The forest lay about five hundred metres away.

Over to the right, two men were working at the back of a silage pit. Close by, another man stood astride a paddock fence, looking over in the direction of the forest with what appeared from this distance, to be a rifle. A muzzled Rottweiler lay at his feet, chained to the post.

Iñaki calculated that this would be at the end of the barn where they had left the campervan.

As Iñaki and Shaina watched, the men strained to haul a large plastic drum from the mess of the pit, and rolled it carefully over to a tap, before washing off the silage sticking to it. One of them shouted something to the guard, who acknowledged with a wave, as they disappeared from view. As they looked at each other questions unvoiced, the door opened, and Rory walked in, Jonnie in tow behind.

Shaina angrily protested, "Don´t you think to knock?"

Malevolent Karma

"Why? You´re not up to anything naughty, are you?" came the instant repost. Rory continued, "You sweethearts may have gathered by now, this is a big meeting we´ve got here. It´s not political shite, this is military, and I don´t want any more fuck-ups springing out on me. Get it, Shaina?"

"Christ, it wasn´t our fault Rory, the fucking gendarmes don´t ask us where to run their road blocks."

"Okay, that´s clear, but you will be running home with some important goodies for us, so I want to clear something up with lover-boy before the other guys get here." Looking at Iñaki, with his snide smile, he added, "That alright with you, son?"

Iñaki felt his stomach contracting again, but managed a fairly normal, "Sure Rory, what do you want to know?"

"Not in front of the folks´ son, just a wee chat, you and me in private. We´re not going far… just across the way."

Iñaki caught a fleeting look of alarm crossing Shaina´s face, before she regained her composure and gave him a reassuring smile.

As he entered what appeared to be bed-sitting room, a tremble of fear and apprehension ran down his back. He didn´t trust the man and he knew Rory was a very dangerous individual; someone to be wary of, and to be avoided if possible. The room was identical in size and style to the one they had just left, but there was only a single bed, and this room also had a table and a bentwood chair over by the window.

Rory closed the door behind him, pulled a straight back chair out from the table, and placed it in the centre of the room.

Iñaki asked, "What´s going on, Rory?"

"Relax, nothing´s going on sonny boy; just plank your arse on the chair; we´re only going to have a wee talk… just you and me."

"What do you want to talk about?" Iñaki´s trembling voice asked. Iñaki knew all about PIRA interrogation methods; he was almost lightheaded with fear now.

Rory sat on the table, swinging his legs slightly and asked, "Tell me about Connor, how you met, how exactly he became your best friend, son." The ice eyes were boring into him, a rigid smile on his face as the words were spoken calmly, and almost sociably.

Surprised, Iñaki could only say, "What do you mean? I don´t think I was his best friend, Rory."

"Okay let´s begin again; tell me how you met Connor Rafferty." This time there was a hardening of tone and the smile had vanished.

Concentrating, and searching his memory, Inaki replied, "I think some friends introduced us at a party; you know, after one of the Domhan Glas meetings.... or it could have been a Sinn Fein party for that matter."

"....and how did you end up working in that queer Joe´s bookshop?"

Iñaki explained, "I was working in a bar, and Connor suggested it. The hours were better and I could get the weekend, or at least Sunday off....I remember; he also suggested that I restart studying at the university, so the bookshop was a better environment. Look Rory... why all the interest in Connor and I. What´s this all about?"

Rory eased himself off the table and came over to stand over him. He wasn´t a tall or big man in the physical sense, but his aura of violence seemed to give him an added dimension of danger. "We´ve been hearing rumours son, not very nice rumours, that your friend Connor, High Priest of your pansy Domhan green shite whatever; this respected member of our shit useless Sinn Fein Party was a tout.....do you know what a tout is, Eenyakee?" Increasing the menace in his voice he grated, "He´s the lowest of the low, a fucking spy, a traitor; that´s what he is. I want to find out if your friend Connor was a fucking tout, and more importantly at this moment....are you a fucking tout?"

Visibly shocked, Iñaki could only gasp, "Are you *loco*? He´s just been killed for you! The Protestants shot him! Why would they kill their own spy? Why in the hell would I spy for the Protestants......you´re all fucking *loco*!"

Menacingly Rory shot back, "Watch your mouth sonny boy, or you might get a dose of fives in it." He gave Iñaki a hard stare to back up his threat, and then eased himself back onto the table.

Looking up at the ceiling, he reflected aloud, "Why are we wondering about friend Connor? Well, we… that is the Active Service, have our own sources of intelligence in Dublin and Belfast, and we´ve been getting feedback that someone very close to Army Council has been passing information to the other side."

He continued in the same vein, "Let´s look at the coincidences." Holding his forefinger up, "One; friend Connor was in such a position, and he was best friends with Padraig our illustrious freedom fighter… that is as long as it doesn´t need any actual fighting, if you know what I mean." This spat out with such scorn, Iñaki that involuntarily shuddered.

"Two; Despite being arrested with `explosive devices´ at one of the biggest Nuclear Plants in the world, and then interrogated for five days at Castlereagh Barracks….Pouf! The fucking Brit Home Secretary, no less, signs an order for his release without any charges, and he´s free to go home to his tart Joe. A wee bit strange, no?"

"Three; now we come to you, Eenyakee, or whatever you´re called. Suddenly you appear on the scene, as the expert who can help us negotiate with ETA, who as it turns out knew fuck all about you; and then they tell me, you passed a letter through them to Spain after the meeting. What was in this letter Eenyakee?"

Iñaki intervened then, "*Joder*! Fuck! It was Padraig who asked me for help in negotiations; he said it was to help establish good relationships with ETA; he said that I knew how they thought, and it was going to help the political exchanges."

"Well sonny boy," he had pushed himself off the table again, the eyes were flaming ice, index finger pointed like a pistol directly into Iñaki´s face, "can you explain to me, why we need a fucking Basque interpreter, when we have managed to negotiate pretty well with the fucking Libyan Arabs for the past ten years?"

Suddenly Iñaki grasped the realities of the power struggle between the factions in Dublin and the North. The anger rose in his chest, he overcame his terror of his interrogator, and stood up, "I don´t know why I was asked, but I was fucking asked to help. The letter was for my *jodida madre!*"

It came so fast he had no time to avoid it. A solid punch sent him sprawling back over the chair, and as he struggled to regain his feet, pain shooting through his broken wrist, he was looking into the barrel of a small, but deadly looking Berretta automatic pistol.

The door burst open and Shaina threw herself in front of Iñaki, followed by Jonnie. "He´s innocent, he´s on our side!" she was shouting, "Leave him alone!"

Johnnie had come between Rory also. "Calm down for fuck´s sake Rory, the guy´s only here to help us!"

White with fury, Rory grated, "Just tell him that if there is one fucking word of this, or any other operation that he´s involved in get´s to the Brits, I´ll cut his balls off before I cut his throat!" Pointing his Berretta at Iñaki´s face hissed, "You…I´ll be watching every fucking move you make!"

He stormed out, slamming the door as he went, his boots clacking on the wooden steps as he ran down the stairs and outside into the farmyard.

"Jesus Christ!" Jonnie expelled his tension. "That bastard see´s touts in every cupboard."

Iñaki had sat down in the chair, white faced and shaken; for a minute before the others had burst into the room, he had thought he was going to be shot. He almost lost control of his bladder, as Shaina cradled his face in her hands.

She said, "That man's a psycho, Jonnie, he's absolutely crazy!"

Looking around, as if to check if Rory was still in the room, Jonnie replied, "For fuck sake, watch what you're saying Shaina, he'd kill you if he heard that! You've got to understand the pressure he's under. The fuckin' super-grasses are playing havoc with our Brigades up North. Nobody can trust anybody now, and this Connor thing's got his mind spinnin' around. He never sleeps in the same place two nights running; he can't have any form of normal life, the Brits have a ten grand reward out on him."

Warming to the theme, he continued, "You know, he can't just book first class and fly over here for the weekend. Just to get here, took three fucking days on a manky fishing boat, and we were downstairs for most of the time among the stinking fish! Then we've got this problem of a tout in Dublin... aye, there is one; another operation was shot to bit's last week from information that only could have come from the South; so it's no surprise his nerves are a bit taut just now." He went over to Iñaki, and clapped him on the back. "Sorry lad, you're okay; I know him, he wouldn't have pulled the trigger!"

Iñaki, trembling, just stared into space, wondering how he was going to survive this trip.

Chapter 74: The Academic

Jonnie left, and Shaina slopped some water into the basin, and using the end of a towel, bathed Iñaki's face. Rory had landed the punch just on the side of his chin, so there wasn't much damage other than a slight grazing on his lip, rapidly swelling bruising and of course his injured pride. His wrist was throbbing, but not agonizingly, therefore he hadn´t broken it again.

They were too busy with their own thoughts for conversation, other than Shaina repeating that he needs to avoid provoking Rory at all cost.

They lay down on their separate beds. Shaina felt enough sympathy to go and lie with him, but could not risk another compromising situation if Rory or Jonnie came back in the room.

Iñaki must have dozed off; for the next thing he knew, Shaina was shaking him awake.

"Iñaki, wake up, they want you downstairs! The Spanish have been here for over an hour!"

Groggily, he got to his feet and tried to focus; he had a thumping headache, and his jaw ached. As he staggered through the door to the bathroom he said, "I need to pee and clear my head first, who´s there?"

"I don´t know. I was in the kitchen and Eugene came in looking for you; they are all in the dining room downstairs. C´mon Iñaki, you´d better hurry!"

After relieving himself, he quickly splashed some cold water over his face, wincing as he dried his swollen jaw, all the time thinking what a psycho Rory was. He would have to tread carefully in his contact with this guy, avoiding him wherever possible. With these thoughts, they went downstairs to be met by Eugene standing outside the dining room door.

Eugene stopped Shaina from entering, "This is only for you, *la chica* is not invited."

Shaina shrugged her shoulders, and went through the door to the kitchen.

Taking him aside for a moment, Eugene said, "I heard what happened today; you must be very careful with these people Iñaki; they are not political, they are all on Active Service… killers!"

"*Joder*, I know Eugene, but this guy hates me for some reason."

Eugene knocked on the door and entered, leaving Iñaki outside. After a few minutes, he came back out, and motioned Iñaki inside.

Four men, obviously Basque origin, were seated at the far side of the big oval table. There was no sign of Rory or Jonnie in the room. They were all smoking a particularly pungent French cigarette, and pall of thick smoke hung in the air. Iñaki recognised two of them as being the men working outside at the silage pit; they had obviously changed their clothes for casual shirts and jeans, both with *txapela's* on their heads. The other two men sat grim faced, studying Iñaki intently, as Eugene introduced him.

One was balding, very pale and sallow faced for a Spaniard, wearing thick lenses glasses over heavy black eyebrows. He appeared to be in his late thirties or early forties. He had an air of intelligence about him; Iñaki thought he might have been, or was possibly still, a teacher or an academic.

The other was obviously a country type; almost a head taller than the academic, and had a ruddy, deeply tanned windswept face with a thick mane of brown hair sprouting out of his *txapela*. No one offered introductions; the academic seemed to in charge, as he motioned for Iñaki to sit down.

Eugene stood over at the door, arms folded, watching.

The academic began. "I want to clarify something for you Iñaki. This is not a political reunion…..this meeting is for the military command of both our revolutionary organizations, ETA and the IRA. You have not been brought here as an interpreter, we have managed to communicate effectively without your services in this respect."

He paused as if gathering his thoughts together.

"As you may know, you have brought a valuable cargo for our military campaign, and you will be taking our contribution to the Irish struggle when you return. The Irish have been very generous in their negotiations; as well as the goods you have brought over; they are going to share the next Libyan shipload of arms with us; and at a very favourable price to us. They will give us the coordinates, and we will meet with the ship in the Bay of Biscay… a very generous gesture I think, don´t you?"

Iñaki feared he was way over his head in this company, but nodded his agreement anyway.

The academic continued; "They of course want some of our new Goma2-C4 military explosive to make much smaller, but ten times more potent bombs for the war against the British. We are going to provide other material also, but you need not worry about that."

He stood up; Iñaki was now looking at a man of below average height, but above average power. "Now we must address the issue of why you are here, and not some other courier." Iñaki felt the tension in the room escalate, eyes boring into him from around the table as he continued, "The Irishman, Rory, has transmitted to us some doubts about your loyalty to the revolution in Ireland, and also to Euskadi, the Basque country."

Iñaki protested, "He has no reason to think this, I haven´t done anything… "

The academic held up his hand and interrupted, "This is not a trial Iñaki, but I´m here to advise you of certain realities that you are probably not aware of." He put his hand into his pocket, and brought out an envelope. "This is a letter from your sister Maria; you can read it later."

Iñaki´s eyes widened in surprise, but the letter remained on the other side of the table.

The academic had sat down again, "More seriously, we have invested much time and effort in seeking retribution for the police inspector, and his *compañero*, who violated your young sister at the detention centre."

Iñaki gasped, "*Dios Mio*; violated her?" This was the first time he had been informed that Maria, his innocent fifteen-year old sister, had been raped in the detention centre.

The academic continued, "Ah, I see you didn't know of this disgrace; but as you know GAL do what they like with impunity from the Government…it's a dirty war, you see. Your *Tio* Andre brought it to our attention, and we exacted some retribution on behalf of your family." He went on, "The inspector was eliminated, and his *compañero* would have extreme difficulty in violating any more young Basque girls, as he had no legs or balls left on his miserable body."

Iñaki, still reeling at the thoughts racing round his head "Is Maria alright," he asked.

"Yes, she's fine. Your sister has more spunk in her than some others in your family it seems. She has joined the *Kalea Borroka*, the youth wing of the struggle." Patting the envelope, he said, "She has written this letter to you, no doubt explaining a few things."

"My mother; is there news of her? How is… "

Impatiently, the academic cut him off. "This is not a social services interview!" Suddenly his mood darkened, and angrily he shouted, "It's not your mother, sister, or fucking dog that's giving us a problem; it's your fucking father!"

Shocked, Iñaki could only gasp, "*Mi Padre*? What's he got to do with this? He has always supported the nationalist cause."

His anger mounting, the academic jumped back up to his feet, and banged his fist on the table. "Your father, this gentleman industrialist, this proud Basque nationalist, has shown absolutely no gratitude for our retribution against the *cucarachas*, the cockroaches that raped his daughter!" The pallid face had turned red in his fury. "As if this was not enough, he has made a public statement that he did not agree with our action…he called it barbaric! Can you imagine that? The Fascists bastards first try to kill you, his son; then they plant drugs on his daughter in order to violate her… and this son of a bitch accuses the Movement of being barbaric?"

Iñaki looked down at the table, and murmured, "I'm sorry, I had no idea …I haven't spoken to my family for over a year now."

Actually, Iñaki was not surprised by this news; his father had principles of non-violence, and always had been an opponent of ETA´s bloody campaign, but had never voiced this opinion in public... a very dangerous thing to do in the Basque country.

The academic sat down, as if an immense weariness had overtaken him. He took off his glasses, and rubbing his eyes added, "Your father is also refusing to pay the *Impuesto Revolucionario*, the Revolutionary Tax. *Camarada*, comrade, you are well aware that this action by itself would condemn him for retribution against his business, or he can even be executed. However, your sister has shown herself to be a loyal and useful member of the Youth Wing, and of course you have been helping coordinate political cooperation between us and the IRA." Pointing his finger directly at Iñaki´s face, he announced, "We are prepared to suspend action on your father upon your guarantee of loyalty to the armed struggles in Euskadi and Ireland."

Iñaki was trapped, he was aware he had been enmeshed for a long time now; but Iñaki knew now there was no going back; no return to any semblance of a normal life. There was no time to think, collect thoughts or try to negotiate; the academic, and the three others were all watching his reactions. He couldn´t see Eugene, but sensed he was right behind him.

Sweat had beaded on his brow, his voice began to break with nerves: "You have my word. I´ll do whatever you want me to do, but I don´t think I could kill anyone in cold blood. I think you should remember this, in case I mess up an operation."

The tension that had hung in the air like electricity abated. The Academic smiled, the others visibly relaxed.

Iñaki suddenly realised he might have been killed there and then if he´d refused in some way.

"Don't worry, Iñaki, you won't be put in the front line, we have commandos for that job. No, you are more valuable as a liaison officer between our two armies… that's if we can convince the mad Irishman not to kill you!"

They all burst out laughing at Iñaki's discomfort. Eugene appearing beside him and clapping him on the shoulder, sending a jolt down his arm and making him wince with pain.

. The academic rose from the table, the others following; "Come now, and we'll show you what trade we've been doing. Don't forget your letter," as he threw it across the table at Iñaki.

They all trooped out, through the kitchen and out across the courtyard under the watchful eyes of the two guards at the door of the archway. There was no sign of Shaina. Iñaki assumed she had gone back upstairs.

Chapter 75: Compañeros

Inside the barn, Rory and Jonnie, now dressed in mechanic's overalls, were leaning up against the campervan smoking a cigarette. The pop-up roof had been raised, and the van had been jacked up to stand on four blocks; the wheels were off and lying to one side.

Arrayed over plastic sheeting on the floor of the barn, sat two American Barrett 82 50BMG 29´´ long barrelled sniper automatic rifles, mounted on bi-pods; each with telescopic sites affixed. Beside each one, lay five ten round magazines. This weapon had a range of almost two kilometres and could penetrate light armour. A little off to the left, a RPG Launcher with four anti tank rockets added to the display of armaments. Even to the inexperienced eyes of Iñaki, these weapons looked formidable and deadly.

The academic said, "This is what my friends in Ireland have given in exchange for our little contribution over here." With a wave of his hand, he indicated four brick like objects wrapped in wax cloth sitting amongst a collection of timing devices, and detonators.

He went on, "A good trade for both of our organizations; we get very valuable new tactical weapons, and the IRA acquires the latest in bomb technology." Now in a jovial mood, the academic, announced in good English, "Our little problem has been resolved my friends; our young *compañero* is be trusted, he knows who´s side he is on."

Rory only scowled and answered, as he unconsciously flicked his cigarette away, "He fucking well knows what will happen to him if he screws up."

"That´s all very well," the academic retorted, as he stooped down to pick up the still lit butt, "but we are allies in the struggle, and I am personally going to vouch his allegiance. It´s better this way; and maybe on the next trip I can bring his sister over the mountains to meet her brother again and keep the family safe and happy so to speak."

The meaning of the reference to Maria did not escape Iñaki´s attention. She was the carrot, and a very big stick was being held over his father´s head if he did not cooperate fully with the two organizations. His father´s principles and obstinacy in refusing to at least pay the `Impuesto Revolucionario,´` had placed him in great danger.

Iñaki´s thoughts wandered. Maria´s letter was burning a hole in his pocket; he had been out of touch for over a year now, and he was desperate to read news of his family. His mind was wandering, the other´s were talking among themselves, suddenly he was aware of silence, and everyone looking at him.

"Did you understand that?" the academic asked.

"...I'm sorry, I missed what you said," stuttered Iñaki.

"*Joder! Pagar atencion*, Iñaki, this is important! Jonnie was describing how he is going to hide the explosives."

"Awake now son?" Rory asked, snide smile on his face.

Jonnie began again; he had an old car battery in front of him. Bending down he twisted the terminals between his thumb and forefinger, and lifted off the top. The space where the acid and terminals would have been was empty. "I'll pack the plastic in here, and the top will be remounted, along with fake connections to the left of the engine." He went on, "You already have a battery on the right hand side; remember the right hand one is the real car battery. The fake one on the left will have a small booby trap on it if anybody interferes with the lid. Don't worry though, the bomb won't go off, but the guy will get one helluva shock!" He continued, "I'm going to give you a small bottle of battery acid; just before you get to Calais, spray some around the fake battery; this will confuse the dogs at the customs if you are stopped. By the way, make sure you buy some cigarettes and booze before you go into the port. Anyone travelling without Duty Free would arouse suspicion. Okay Iñaki, repeat back what I have just said."

Iñaki, once again feeling and sounding nervous as he thought about the explosives, repeated his instructions word for word, including the buying of the Duty Free.

Jonnie declared, "Right now that's settled, can you all fuck off and let me get on with my work? Rory and I have got to be out of here by eleven latest, and we have a shit load of work to do on this thing!"

The academic turned to Iñaki and almost paternal in tone said, "We'll talk over dinner; we've got to leave tonight also. You've still got your letter to read and you'd better get back to that lovely *novia* you've got."

This brought a glare from Rory, but nothing more was said.

Chapter 76: Maria

Out in the still warm and peaceful courtyard, Iñaki sat down on the edge of one of the herb barrels outside the kitchen door. There was still no sign of Shaina, but in any case, he desperately wanted to read the news from home. As he tore open the envelope, he recognised at once Maria´s neat girlish handwriting, her face and smile instantly springing into his mind.

Querido Hermano,
I have only a few minutes to write this letter as `Txoti´ has just called in to our peña to tell me someone is meeting you soon.
I am fine now. I was in the detention centre for three months before papa could get me out on bond. Terrible things happened in there to get me to testify that you were part of a terrorist cell, but I resisted all their cruelties.
I am now back at college, but have lost all interest in studying.
The Madrid Fascists are intending to destroy our freedom and culture just like it was in Franco´s time.
Things are bad at home. Mama has not recovered her old spirit after what happened to you and me. She lay weeping in her bed the whole time I was in detention. She blames papa for everything, and they have terrible rows. Oh how I wish we could turn back the clock to when we all had these wonderful barbecues down on the shore.
I don´t understand papa. He seems to be more angry at you for causing all this trouble, than the bastards who violated me and crippled your friend Juan. He gave a press interview and criticised ETA as barbarians after they killed the Fascist inspector.
The militants have been furious with him for giving the interview. Tio Andres has tried to reason with him to pay the Impuesto Revoulcionario, but you know how stubborn he is.
I´m afraid, that the militant command will lose patience and punish him.
Querido hermano, it is very dangerous for you to come back to Bilbao. We´ll meet again soon I hope, but wherever you are, I am with you.

I must stop now, the courier is waiting.
Muchos besos y abrazos,
Maria.

Iñaki blinked back the sudden tears that had sprung in his eyes in his fit of self-pity and longing for his family. Reading the letter for the third time, the self-pity had changed into a fury and loathing for the people who had targeted him and his family for no reason. He sat there for almost twenty minutes mulling over in his mind his options for revenge.

Under the stony gaze of the two guards, he re-crossed the courtyard and went back into the barn, now a hive of activity. Jonnie was half inside the engine compartment drilling mounts for the false battery, which lay beside his feet. It looked completely authentic, down to the layer of dust and dirt to match the real one. Rory and Eugene were remounting the wheels, Rory cursing as the wheel wrench bounced off his shin.

The academic and the two Basques were stripping, oiling and wrapping the two sniper rifles, and packing them into a blue plastic agricultural chemical drum. The academic looked up. "You have read your letter, yes?"

Iñaki answered, "Yes, and thanks for bringing it. Can I write a reply?"

"No problem, but I must read it, so nothing too personal, understand? …we must maintain security."

"Yes, of course," a grateful Iñaki added, "thanks again."

As he turned for the door, the farmer looked up from his work and said, "Call mama if she´s not already in the kitchen; we eat in one hour….is that okay with you Rory?"

"Jonnie, will we be finished in an hour?" Rory shouted at Jonnie, who grazed his skull as he exited the engine compartment.

"Fuck!" He exclaimed, "If you two finish with the wheels and the detonator compartment, we can then all fix the roof back on."

"There's no more stuff going back is there?" Eugene asked.

"No," Rory replied, "too dangerous, we can't take the chance of some fucking smart sniffer dog detecting the hashish... next trip for that."

Jonnie laughed, "Well some poor cunts in Belfast will have to wait a while yet for their fix."

"It's a tough life out there," Rory replied... what in the fuck are *you* staring at?"

"Nothing," Iñaki replied, "when am I going back up the road?"

"Tomorrow; I want this bus back in two days max."

A little dejectedly, Iñaki replied, "Fine, have you decided the route?"

"Yeah, but we'll talk about it later, once I've finished with this fucking job."

The old woman was in the kitchen setting places at the big table as Iñaki passed through. He related the message from her son, and received the barest nod in return. He asked the old woman if she had a pen and paper to write a letter. Again, there was almost no response that she had heard him, except that she opened a drawer in one of the dressers, took out a school notepad and a biro pen, and placed them at one end of the table.

He thanked her, and complimented her on the rich odour of baking bread, and a stew or soup bubbling on the stove.

A perfunctorily nod of the head greeted his compliment, leaving Iñaki to wonder what circumstances, dramas, or tragedies had turned what must have been an attractive young Frenchwoman, with all her dreams, love and desires into a bitter cynical old crone.

He sat down at the end of the table, under the unspoken disapproving stare of the old woman.

Malevolent Karma

Querida hermanita,
It was so good to hear from you, I miss you all so much. The past year has been so different from my life in Bilbao....it seems so long ago now.
I am angry and disgusted about what these animals did to you, my little innocent sister, always so full of life and fun. I feel ashamed that I may have been responsible for such calamity to you and our family. I didn't do anything illegal; we are supposed to be allowed to demonstrate for a better world for God's sake, without having to fear violation or murder from the State.
I feel very sorry for mama y papa, they did not deserve this to befall upon them, and neither do we, querida hermanita.
Recently, good friend of mine was murdered in Ireland by the same extra-judicial killers as we have in the Basque Country.
Ecological issues, so important to me in the past, pale in to insignificance compared to State terrorism....we have to fight it with all our resources!
Your letter has made me stronger in resolve to fight the Fascists.
You are always in my heart; if possible tell Mama and Papa I love them. Muchos besos,
  Iñaki.
`Euskadi Libre´!

He re-read the text, and decided that although he could easily write more, but he'd better go and look for Shaina.

Chapter 77: Home truths

Thinking she had gone for a walk, he went back outside and asked one of the guards at the archway if she had gone out.

The cold look given almost answered the question. "*No monsieur,* no one is allowed to leave the farm until the Chief has left."

"*Strange, she must be upstairs then,*" he said to himself turning on his heel and walking back through the kitchen, past the old woman, and upstairs to their bedroom.

As he entered, Shaina was lying in her bed facing the wall away from him. She didn´t stir, so he assumed that she was sleeping and tiptoed over to the bed.

Leaning over, he saw her eyes were open, staring expressionless at the wall. Gently touching her shoulder, he asked, "Are you all right?"

She gave no response to his touch.

"Shaina, are you okay?"

Still no response, her eyes still fixed at some spot on the wall in front.

"What´s wrong Shaina? What´s happened? Just tell me." All kinds of horrific ideas came flooding into his head; did Rory or Jonnie do something to her when he was with the ETA group?

He sat down on the edge of the narrow bed, leaning over gently, trying to catch her eyes; those beautiful emerald green eyes, normally bright as life, but now dull and still fixed on the wall. "Look Shaina, you need to tell me what has happened, you´re …"

"I don´t have to tell you shit, came the vicious reply; nothing´s happened, just leave me alone."

Iñaki persisted, "It´s obvious something has happened, you are never like this! Just tell me."

Suddenly she sat up, forcing him off the bed and to stand up. "Listen, just fuck off and leave me alone... go back downstairs and play commandos with your mates."

Iñaki couldn´t understand what she was talking about, "What are you talking about? I don´t understand what you are saying."

The answer came right back, and with venom, "No, because none of you fucking revolutionary heroes have any clue about how we feel. All we are there for is to cook the fucking dinner, serve it, wash up, clean the kitchen and service our soldier boy with a quick blow job, or a proper fuck if he has the time!" Screwing up her face into an ugly tight smile, she mocked... "Otherwise stay out of our way and do some knitting or something!"

"Jesus Christ Shaina," Iñaki protested, "It was like a bloody court martial down there."

Sneering again, she poked a finger at him, "You just don´t get it at all, do you? You are just a wee boy trying to play in a big man´s game. Well, I´m sick of mothering you... I´m fucking well sick of waiting around for the big man to come home; that is if he doesn´t have more important business to attend to."

"Shaina, listen..."

"No you listen!" ...but suddenly she lowered her tone. "Look, this has been festering inside me for a while in Dublin with Big Chief Padraig. I thought, "a wee trip to France with the fit Latin lover might do me some good; lighten up my fucking boring life." Then today, when I was in the kitchen trying to talk to that old woman, I had another thought; "this is crazy, if I stay around these guys, I´m going to end up like this old crone....or in fucking jail!" Deflated now she said, "Listen Iñaki, it´s not you; don´t take this personally... just leave me alone."

She fell back down on the bed again, eyes once again averted to the wall.

"Shaina, I... "

"Can´t you fucking hear me? .... Fuck Off!"

Dejectedly and mystified, he turned away and lay down on his bed. Lying, staring at the ceiling he was thinking, "What else can go wrong?" This was a new worrying development; he had hoped for a continuing relationship with Shaina; he was fond, verging on love with her; she was beautiful, intelligent and amusing. They´d had a great time on the journey down; not just the sex, which had been spectacular, and the two days they had spent with the surfers had been great fun, almost recapturing his student days in Bilbao.

He had to admit though, she had changed; there was a calculating hardness about her he hadn´t noticed before which had nothing to with the fact that she was older than he was.

He had no option but to drive the Volkswagen with its cargo back to England; if he didn´t comply, then he and undoubtedly his father would be in grave danger. Reflecting further, the naked truth was, that after all that had happened to him, his family and friends, he wanted to be part of the fight against the Fascists who had targeted him.

His voice carried across the gulf between the beds. "Are you coming back to England with me?"

"Do you think I´m going to stay here? ...of course I´m going back, you stupid prick!"

They lay in silence for a while. Boots sounded on the stairs and light banter came from Rory and Jonnie as they came into the corridor outside their room. Shaina didn´t move, but Iñaki tensed and sat up expecting them to enter, but they went into the room opposite.

A little while later, they listened to the sounds of the bathroom, until Jonnie shouted, "Will you hurry up, Rory, I need a crap."

"Do it in the washbasin!" was the laughing response.

"I´ll just use your bag instead!" laughed Jonnie.

"Okay, I give up," as the bathroom door opened, "remember and pull the plug."

"Jesus, they have a sense of humour after all," thought Iñaki.

Jonnie went in, and a few seconds later, and enormous fart rocked the building, followed by a loud guffaw from the bathroom.

"Bejesus, Jonnie, you should have kept that one for Belfast!" shouted Rory.

"Fucking animals," came from the still prone Shaina.

Shaina had refused to come down for dinner; Iñaki making the excuse she was feeling unwell, probably her periods or something.

The farmer brusquely instructed his mother to go up and check on her. She came back in a few minutes and whispered something in his ear in Basque French; he shrugged his shoulders and she prepared a tray of bread and cheese and a carafe of wine, and took it upstairs.

After the tension and stress of the day, Inaki had too much on his mind to get into the now relaxed, almost exultant mood of the group as they firstly toasted each other, then freedom from Fascists everywhere, with some robust local wine.

The old woman moved like a phantom, shuffling around the table expressionless and saying nothing, as she piled the food onto the now ravenously hungry men-folk. They gorged on the delicious beef *daube*, mopping up the rich sauce with the newly baked bread; no time now for talk. Afterwards there was a platter of regional cheeses to choose from, and a flagon of very potent but smooth brandy to go with it.

Although the mood was much lighter, the conversation moved to last minute exchanges of information and questions. No one was over drinking, aware of their need to go on their respective journeys.

The academic asked Iñaki if he had written a letter to his sister. Iñaki handed it over, and watched as he quickly skimmed through the contents, finally approving with a "Good, I will have it delivered." He then took him aside and reaffirmed the faith he had in Iñaki and his sister Maria, but countered the praise with "It´s a pity about your father, but I will protect him for now."

In return, Iñaki expressed his gratitude and loyalty to the cause.

It was time for the group to split up and go their ways.

Eugene was taking Rory and Jonnie back to Guéthary, and as they were going outside, Rory, almost as an afterthought, turned Iñaki into the now dark Barn.

Gripping his arm, he instructed, "Be at the same hotel in Crewe by three in the afternoon the day after tomorrow. The same guy will be there to meet you. Catch the half past three night ferry, from Calais to Dover; that way the customs on duty at Dover will be in the land of nod." Finally, tightening his arm and pointing into the darkness at the Volkswagen he impressed, "This load is special; I´m depending on you to get it over there so don´t let me down ...oh, and by the way someone will be keeping an eye on you all the way."

"What if I have a problem with the van?" queried Iñaki.

"This side of the water, phone Roberto, the other side phone Liverpool, and they will sort it out."

Much to Iñaki´s surprise, Rory turned, put his arm around his shoulders and said, "Look son, I might have been a bit too hard on you; now is the time to show me how good you are."

Walking out to the car, Jonnie shook his hand and said "Good luck son, just do a good job! Give Shaina a good one from me!" said with a broad wink.

The archway door opened, and in the twilight, a motorcycle was kicked into action to act as a guide, or kind of outrider for them as they sped away down the farm track.

Twenty minutes later, the motorcycle was back, leading a dark blue BMW Seven series saloon.

The academic and his *compañero*, his Spanish Basque country-man came out, having briefly held a last minute conference with the French Basques. He went around everyone, including Iñaki, embracing and saying *Euskadi at Askatasuna*, Basque liberty.

Giving Iñaki a kiss on both cheeks he said *"buena suerte, amigo.* I will look after your family; don´t worry, we will meet again soon." Finally, with their fists raised in salute, they were away, the motorcycle roaring away in front of the BMW.

Suddenly feeling claustrophobic, Iñaki began walking out of the compound, only to be stopped in his tracks by the guard.

The farmer came up and advised, "No one can leave until morning now... a necessary security precaution I´m afraid."

"Oh I´m sorry, I only wanted to stretch my legs a bit." Iñaki explained.

"You will have to walk around the courtyard then *Señor*," was the less than sympathetic reply, and you must be away from here before seven in the morning before the police set up their school patrols; your campervan is unusual around here." He continued, "Mama will have a breakfast for you and your companion at six o´clock, and the motorcyclist will be here at quarter to seven, to guide you back to Bayonne."

Iñaki said in reply, "Thanks for your hospitality, shall I see you tomorrow?"

"I don´t think so, we have much work to do with the lambs; it´s market day on Wednesday, and I have many to sell."

"Well, I will say goodnight then, *et au revoir."*

The farmer responded raising his hand in salute *"Au revoir Monsieur.... bon voyage!"*

Dejectedly, and unhurriedly, he passed through the kitchen, now empty but with about ten places set for breakfast, perplexing him a little until he realised that there must have been more men or guards around the farm that he hadn´t noticed before. Reluctantly he climbed the stairs; he was not looking forward to another confrontation with Shaina, and diverted into the bathroom for his ablutions giving himself a little more respite.

He stripped down to the waist, and checking the mirror, firstly a little annoyed that his once powerful frame was showing the neglect that lack of training has brought on; his chin still displayed an angry looking bruise, but his stubble had begun to disguise it a little. He would not shave until it had disappeared, he thought. He had not noticed his arm hurting, so his wrist was okay. He thought of the drive back up tomorrow, of almost the whole of France, more than a thousand kilometres, and shuddered. Shaina would have to take her turn of driving whether she liked it or not.

Suddenly, there was a quiet knock on the door, and Shaina was saying, "Open the door please, Iñaki."

Surprised and wary he unlocked the door.

Entering and looking a little contrite she said, "I´m sorry Iñaki, I was a bit out of order today, but you´ve got to get into your head nothing can happen with us again."

Changing the subject before he could answer, she continued, "I´ve checked the map, and we have over a thousand kilometres to drive up to Calais, so we have to away early. I´ve had my shower; I thought it better tonight than delay our departure tomorrow."

Seeing him still uncomfortably washing with his good arm, she said, "Here, give me that cloth," and she proceeded to give him a thorough wash down, but noticeably this time avoiding his genitalia.

Iñaki explained, "Our departure is already organised; breakfast is at six, and the motorcyclist is coming at a quarter to seven to escort us as far as Bayonne. Rory has told me that someone will be keeping an eye on us all the way in case of trouble, but didn´t say who he was. I was thinking that it can´t be Roberto, because we have to phone him if we have any problems with the van. I suppose it could be Eugene, but I think he would have said something and arranged a route."

"Well I´m sure they have people all over France," Shaina closed the conversation and changed the subject. "I´ve mapped out a route, more or less directly north on the N10, we can be at Le Mans at lunchtime."

Iñaki said, "It´s the same route except our diversion into Deauville is it not? ...anyway I´m knackered, we can talk on the journey."

He was secretly pleased that at least they were back talking together, albeit with a tension in the air between them. He permitted an ironic thought to pass through his head, *Even if there was an opportunity, sex was the last thing he needed tonight!*

There was an aura of awkwardness between them as they prepared for bed. Iñaki took the initiative and quickly undressed to his shorts and slipped under the covers.

She watched him reflectively, and in a quiet voice said, "It´s for the best Iñaki; it´s impossible for us to be together." He didn´t reply, and when she turned out the light, nothing passed between them.

Chapter 78: The Return journey

The sound of the early dawn chorus of birds singing and a cock crowing awoke them. Shortly after, they heard the rough Basque voices of the farmer and his workers. A tractor started up beneath their window, and the clunk of a trailer being attached, precluded the roar, as it left the corral.
It was still in the grey-white pre-dawn with a few stars still displaying a weakening light. Looking out Iñaki saw it would be a good clear day; nothing in the sky to threaten rain; a positive start.

He was surprisingly alert; first into the bathroom, quickly emptied his bladder, brushed his teeth and then a quick splash under the cold tap over his head and face. Towelled dry, his stubble gave him a not unpleasant ruffian look he thought, and it was hiding the bruising. He was now anxious to be away from the farm and on the road as soon as possible.

Shaina too was impatient to leave; she needed to put a bad experience behind her. She was sitting on the bed in her shorts, her breasts barely being contained in a lacy white bra, her long tanned legs and carelessly brushed hair causing a quickly suppressed stir of desire in Iñaki´s loins.

His rucksack was lying opened on the bed, and a clean Tee shirt and casual jumper waiting on the bed besides his jeans. "Thanks" he mumbled, afraid to look into the emerald eyes, the ones he had loved only yesterday.

"...and good morning to you also," she snapped, picking up her toilet bag she added, "I´ll just be a minute if you want to check on the van."

He had a look around the room, thought about taking his bag downstairs, then dropped the idea and ran downstairs into the kitchen.

Two Basques he didn´t recognise were sitting at the table finishing their coffee and talking in the strange Euskadi language of the Basque country. They both looked up as he passed and greeted him with *Kaixo*!

Iñaki returned the greeting, went outside and crossed the yard into the barn, watched by a shotgun carrying guard at the still closed archway door.

The VW sat where it had been the night before; he jumped up into the driver´s seat and turned the key in the ignition, to hear the familiar grumbling roar from the rear engine. He checked the fuel gauge, almost full, so no need to top up around Bayonne. He shut off the power, climbed out, and went round the back to have a look at the engine. The fake battery on the left, with it´s appropriate gouges and dirt exactly matched the real one on the right. Satisfied, he checked the oil level; ...perfect. *We're ready to roll*, he thought.

He opened the barn door wide intending to drive out into the courtyard when the two Basques entered.

One said, "You are too early son, the escort will not be here until after half past six."

"I know, I was just testing the motor, and bringing it out into the yard." Iñaki replied, *Dios Mio the security around here is extreme!*

"You cannot do that; the police have helicopters around here!" The other one interjected angrily.

"Of course, I wasn't thinking," apologised Iñaki.

"You must always think, and be alert son, or you will be dead very quickly."

Sheepishly Iñaki walked back over the yard into the kitchen, aware of their disproval.

Shaina was standing at the table trying to help the old woman, who was having none of it. She had brought the rucksacks down, and they were sitting by the door. Seeing Iñaki, she just shrugged her shoulders, and sat down at one of the two remaining place settings.

She was looking great; how she could transform herself into a form of such beauty in so short a time was, to Iñaki's opinion, miraculous. *Jesus, this is going to be a hard day's travel.* He need not have worried, Shaina was completely in control of her emotions, and there was no way he was going anywhere she didn't want him too.

As they munched down a delicious breakfast of ham, cheeses, fruit, jams and honey, with still more freshly baked baguette, they studied the map. Shaina had it unfolded on the table, plotting stops. They agreed two hours each on the wheel for each changeover. Calculating twelve or thirteen hours driving, they should be around Calais at about nine or ten that night allowing for two stops.

Just after half past six, they heard the rumble of a big motor cycle engine, and greetings shouted above the noise.

They went outside to look, and one of the Basques came over, "It´s time; the roads are clear, you go now!"

They exchanged glances, went in and picked up their rucksacks. Shaina turned around to say goodbye to the old woman, who only nodded back, but pressed a package of bread and cheese into her hand for the journey.

Shaina smiled at her small act of kindness, closed the door behind her and followed Iñaki across the yard and into the barn.

One of the Basques noticed the food parcel, and confiscated it. "Sorry, but that could be traced back here."

Again, Iñaki had to marvel at the detail of the security, whilst Shaina contented herself with a "Shit, fucking little boys playing commandos everywhere!"

They stowed the rucksacks, and Shaina brought out the sleeping bags, roughing them up to give the impression of having been slept-in.

The Basques were talking to the motorcyclist, who looked over and waved, revving his engine. One of the guards directed Iñaki out of the barn; he gave a wave in salute, and slowly followed the motorcycle out of the compound.

Suddenly, after the confines of the farm courtyard, the sky and vistas of the beautiful countryside opened up before them.

The sun was up, the grass greener than they remembered only sixteen hours before. They drove down the farm road observing the farmer and one of his workers separating lambs from their mothers using a Bouvier farm dog they hadn´t seen before. The old Pyrenean hound was keeping close to his master, trying its best by worrying at the legs of the sheep.

Man and nature was in harmony. An unseen tractor started up its engine with a roar, disturbing for a moment the plaintive bleating of the lambs and their mothers echoing

Malevolent Karma

over the farm. The cows in the next field paused in their chewing to stare at the spectacle. An early falcon circled lazily on the thermals looking for an unsuspecting vole or rabbit, over-viewing the work of man in the fields.

Back in the compound, the men were already wiping out traces of the campervan having ever been there. Hay was now being spread all over the floor, ready to receive a few calves to spread some manure where the van had stood only a few minutes before.

After a long, tiring and traffic frustrated journey, Iñaki drove into the car park of the huge all night Carrefour beside the ferry terminal at Calais. It was after eleven, and both of them were exhausted. They eased down from the front seats of the campervan, and stretching, looking wanly at each other, decided that firstly it was to the restrooms to freshen up, and then something to eat and a strong coffee to help keep them alert.

They had maintained a curiously detached relationship on the journey, both accepting the need to avoid any issue that might spark an altercation. Iñaki at first had been on the lookout for the mysterious car or motorcycle whom Rory had said would be keeping an eye on them; a relatively simple exercise as the Volkswagen was slower than most of the other traffic.

Shaina had just laughed the whole thing off as Iñaki being neurotic; which he admitted to himself was probably true.

At one of the stops, he had a sudden thought; *"How did Shaina know we were going by Calais this time, and not Zeebrugge?"* She had worked out the route before he had a chance to tell her which ferry Rory had specified. Reflecting further, he dismissed it as probably being a chance guess on her part.

Now they were about to enter the danger zone, so it was time for another rehearsal of the Fernando and Marie characters. They had elaborated a simple engagement party as part of the cover story, and bought some crates of beer, cigarettes and wine, and six bottles of vodka, all just within their joint duty free limits. *They had a light meal of Moules Frits for* `Fernando´, *and Croque Monsieur* for `Marie´. They agreed that they should buy the tickets for the ferry at the Bureau in the supermarket, saving a direct contact with officials at the port itself.

It was now midnight, and after they stowed the duty free in the campervan, Iñaki drove over to a quieter zone and parked.
They lay down in the back for a couple of hours sleep, but oddly, now Iñaki had no desire to seek, or enforce the love and affection he had craved only yesterday. He imagined a kind of woolly barrier had come down between them, and intriguingly, it was okay by him. She was still beautiful, but the charismatic sparkle had vanished from her; she appeared older, certainly too old for him now.

Their mini alarm clock shrilled at two thirty; they got up but left the sleeping bags untidily on the bed.
Iñaki took out the little bottle of acid, opened the engine compartment and sprayed the false battery as Jonnie had instructed to fool the sniffer dogs. Then it was over to the restrooms for a quick wash. They were then moving out of the car park and within a few minutes, in a small line going through the *Duanes* at the ferry terminal.

This time they had to show their passports, but instead of a bout of nerves, Iñaki had entered a state of professional calm, handing over the documents with a bored indifference. Shaina flicked on the cabin light, and gave the official one of her radiant smiles, this time getting nil reaction but a simple *"Bon Voyage,"* as he passed the passports back through the driver´s window.

Boarding the ferry, they were directed into a line of caravans at the side of the big container trucks. Iñaki killed the engine, and as instructed, climbed the gangway stairs to the passenger deck.

The ferry shook and shuddered as it continued to load trucks from all over Europe. The night ferries were popular for truckers as the fares were much cheaper than daytime, and they could be in depots all around London before the rush hour began.

`Fernando´ and `Marie´ although alert, were still physically tired and they found a table well away from the bar area. She asked what were his plans after they had dropped the Volkswagen at Crewe. He replied that he would be going back up to Glasgow to get this damn plaster cast removed, and then probably on to the peace camp until he was given another job to do.

"What about you," he asked, "are you going back to Padraig?"

She answered, "Just to pick up my things; I think I´ll give London a chance; my cousin lives there, and she can give me a bed for a while."

"Will he let you go, I mean without a fight?" He asked.

Irritably she snapped, "I told you before he´s not interested in me... listen, I don´t want to talk about it."

Almost before they knew it, the announcement came for drivers to return to their vehicles.

"Here we go," she said, "are you okay?"

He grinned at her, replying, "I feel good!" leaned over and gave her a light kiss on the cheek.

She smiled a little sadly, squeezed his arm, and said, "It´s now or never."

Back on the vehicle deck, they rehearsed their engagement story, where they had been on holiday and their family backgrounds. Iñaki was surprised by his own sense of calm; he was in control. Glancing across at Shaina, she showed absolutely no trace of nerves.

The campervan, and the cargo of high explosives and detonators, were waved through Passport Control, and again at the customs area, and were out of Dover on the A2 for Canterbury within fifteen minutes of leaving the ship.

Unlike their journey down to the Ramsgate just over a week ago, they cleared the London conurbation in record time, the still dark, pre-dawn traffic light and moving freely. They reached Watford Gap services, before Iñaki, his adrenalin diminishing, felt a heavy wave of tiredness descending over his entire body.

Chapter 79: The Long Goodbye

They drove in and as Iñaki filled up at the pumps. Shaina went into the bathroom to freshen up. Coming out, she went to the bank of telephones and dialled a number in Anfield in Liverpool. It took a few minutes for a rough, Irish-Liverpudlian voice to answer.

She identified herself, and asked if the meeting could be brought forward to mid-day, as they were running ahead of schedule.

The voice told her to phone back in half an hour.

She encountered Iñaki outside the cafeteria and after briefing him on her proposal, he nodded in agreement; the sooner the handover and its cargo was made, the better as far as he was concerned. Hunger overtook them and they stood in line for an English breakfast; not that it looked appealing, but calories were required to top up lost energy.

Iñaki bought a newspaper to catch up on events. The headline story was about another battle between the miners and the police, this time 64 people were injured, which brought a tinge of regret to his mind as he thought about Sellafield and Connor, only a few weeks ago. He turned the pages, and spotted an article by a well-known Dublin journalist he had spoken to at a Sinn Fein party.

The journalist was reporting the escalating tensions and internal feuds going on at the highest levels of the Republican movement. Sources indicated a serious split occurring, with the Moderates calling for direct negotiations with Britain, and the Hardliners, who wanted an all out war on the British mainland.

He showed the article to Shaina, who just shrugged, "What's new, Rory would bomb the place to rubble, whilst Padraig would talk them into dust."

Shaina left to telephone Liverpool again, as he continued reading and finished his tea.

She returned after five minutes or so, and sat down. "Right, it's been okayed. We have to meet the same mechanic at twelve at the station car park." She paused a little and went on, "I'm going back with him to Liverpool; I can get a ferry and be in Dublin tonight; will you be getting the train to Glasgow?"

"I suppose so, I've still got my return ticket, and there's no point in hanging around." Lifting up his plaster cast, he continued, "... and I want this damn thing off!"

Shaina got to her feet, "Well, we'd better be away then, now that I've changed the time, all hell would break loose if we were late in getting there."

She drove, and he dozed a bit, turning things over in his head. He had almost completed his assignment. Four powerful bombs were sitting behind him in a fake battery. He did not feel bad about that. He had no issues of conscious other that he hoped no women and children would suffer, but then he reasoned, this was a guerrilla war, and innocent causalities were inevitable. They called it collateral damage

He took over the driving as the traffic choked up south of Birmingham; they would make it to Crewe in plenty of time, so they weren´t unduly worried.

Silence had again pervaded the space between them, each with their own thoughts, as they motored on to their destination.

Iñaki was perplexed at his own feelings of ambivalence; the lack of emotion he was feeling for her; he wanted it over, and done with now. She would be disappearing into the vastness of London, while he was heading back to a little seaside town in Scotland. He was sure he wouldn´t see her again. "I must be getting used to it," he smiled grimly to himself.

They turned into Crewe Central Station car park at eleven-fifteen, and found a parking space near to the entrance. Giving a long sigh of relief, as he switched off the engine, he said *"Dios mio,* we made it," looking over as she unfastened her seat belt.

She commented, "You did well Iñaki, despite what I said the other night. Look, we´ve got plenty of time, let´s have a beer."

"Fine by me, and I can check on the train times. We´d better get a parking ticket though, it would be funny if the van got towed away."

Unsmilingly she reposted, "Not so funny I think! I´ll get the ticket, while you gather up your things; make sure you don´t leave anything."

Ticket affixed, and his rucksack packed, they entered the cafeteria where they had met up just over a week ago. So much had happened in that one week; so much, he thought that it would be imprinted on his brain forever.

They ordered two beers and a packet of crisps, and sat next to the door, where they had a clear view of the Volkswagen.

That awkward silence descended again; out of the corner of his eye, lines had appeared on her previously flawless pale skin; serious black pouches sat under her eyes, and the red painted mouth that he had loved, had weakened and dropped down at the corners. She looked, and was, desperately tired, but it was more than that; a weariness of life had invaded. He saw her face practically age before his eyes.

Suddenly a tear appeared, and she turned to him with desolation in her eyes; "Iñaki, you´re too nice for this game, understand what you´ve got into; there´s so much double dealing it makes me dizzy at times. You don´t belong!"

"What do you mean," suddenly concerned for her distress and attempting to take her hand.

She brushed him off, and wiped her eyes; hard again. "You were manipulated and recruited into the Organisation right from the very beginning. You were virgin; fresh meat that nobody knew or cared about. It was your good buddies, Brendan and Sean that suggested we could use you, and Siobhan did the rest."

"Well I guessed that before, but why me?" he asked.

"Why you?" she repeated, "You were fresh, unknown, and Padraig had this dream of internationalising the struggle; a bigger audience, more fame." She carried on, "I told you I had volunteered to go with you. That was untrue; the meeting with the Basques was supposed to be political again, but the military wing hijacked it for their own reasons, the exchange of the weapons. Padraig was shut out of the negotiations; he has been sidelined, kept out of the picture."

She went on, staring into space, "the Army Council is planning something special on the mainland, and he´s desperate to know what it is, but Rory and his gang are obsessive about touts now."

Iñaki turned to meet her eyes, "Now I understand; you did know of the route and meetings in advance; you knew we were coming via Calais and not Zeebrugge."

She confessed, "I´ve had the timetable from the beginning. I had to watch you didn´t do anything silly on the way back. There never was supposed to be anyone following us." Taking a deep breath she resumed, "Listen Iñaki, I only agreed to do this after Padraig promised I could go my own way after the mission." Bitterly she continued, "It was almost a relief for him to get rid of me." She pleaded, "Listen to me Iñaki, you´re too nice to get involved in all of this shit; catch a train, get on a plane or whatever, but disappear for your own good."

Iñaki hardened also, "Well thanks anyway for the confession and advice Shaina, but you´ve forgotten something. I have been driven out of my homeland; my little sister was raped, my mother is one step away from the lunatic asylum, and my father is going to be killed if I don´t stay in....but the truth is I want to stay in. I´ll take your advice though and watch my back."

"Hello, are you the couple that phoned the garage?" The mechanic was standing over their table. They didn´t know how long he had been there, and how much he had heard.

Recovering, she replied, "Yes, that´s our Volkswagen Camper out there."

"Well, we´d better have a look at it then, by the way I´m Mick."

They trooped outside, Mick asked for the keys. Jumping in he started and gunned the engine, making it cough and stutter. "I think it´s the carb, they get dirty on this bus; let´s have a look." He got down and unlocked the engine cover at the back, checking there were two batteries and making several adjustments for any spectators around.

"Yep, it´s sticking a bit, I´ll take it down to the garage and have it sorted in half an hour, are you coming?"

"Yes," she said ... but he´s staying."

Iñaki reached in the side door, and brought out his rucksack and stood back as she climbed up into the passenger seat. She would not meet his eyes.

"OK, let's go!" The engine roared, and Mick steered the VW past the two Policemen who had just walked out of the station.

She didn't wave, the last he of saw of her was the red hair blowing in the wind framing a pale face staring straight ahead.

Chapter 80: Glasgow June 1984

Iñaki was in a kind of limbo. He had no other instructions from the Provos, other than to check-in with Paddy on the Friday after he got back from France. He had not attempted to contact Siobhan or Padraig in Dublin after Shaina's `confession´, which had over the days left a lingering, unpleasant taste in his mouth.

He had spent a couple of days in a B&B in the West End of Glasgow, and had his plaster cast off and the titanium pins removed from his wrist. It was still painful after the operation, but now at least he only had to contend with a dozen stitches and a light bandage; a local doctor could remove the stitches in a week's time.

He liked the area; it was cosmopolitan and lively; the cafes and bars hummed with an eclectic mix of academics, students, doctors and nurses from the nearby Western Infirmary, as well as the Diaspora of locals who melded easily with the `university´ types. On his third night there, Iñaki bumped into Jamie Peacock, a friend of Meryl's in the Rubaiyat Bar in Byres Road, who asked him if he had seen her. Over a pint of McEwan's, Iñaki explained that he had been in France visiting friends for a week, but would be seeing her in a day or two when he got back to the Faslane Peace Camp.

"She's here, in Glasgow, Jamie informed, "She's been waiting to hear from you; I think she's got a job for you, well ... that's if you're interested."

"What kind of job?" asked Iñaki, a little warily.

"She's directing a Summer School at the university, and I think she wants you to run a Spanish course; but it starts in two weeks, so she needs to know right away."

"She didn't mention anything about this before," Iñaki complained.

"She probably didn't know. It's all just come out of the blue; the guy who was going to do it has resigned or something."

As he was taking all this in, Jamie interrupted his thoughts by saying, "Look, there's a party tonight at Sam Boyle's place, I'm sure you'll remember him, he's very keen on the CND. Meryl will probably be there; if not someone will know where she is staying and we can find her."

Meryl was, indeed at the party; she appeared to be a little drunk and after smothering him in welcome back kisses; demanding to know why he had not told her he was back.

Over the clamour of the other hundred or so guests, all talking over the big stereo belting out Charlie Parker, he explained a little peevishly that he was only back three days, and had been in the hospital to get his wrist attended to.

"But darling, where did you stay?" She asked, "I have a university flat for the summer; you could have stayed there."

"Look Meryl, I didn't know you were in Glasgow, and I wanted to get the hospital out of the way before going back to Faslane."

Smiling into his eyes she said, "Well I'm just so happy to see you ...I have got a job for you, that's if you want it."

"Let's get some drinks first and find a quieter corner." He suggested, looking around.

They found a space on the landing leading up to the bedrooms as a steady stream of people squeezed past them going up and down the stairs. He assumed there must be a bathroom up there as well as bedrooms.

In the Rubaiyat with Jamie, Iñaki had thrown back a couple of Grouse whisky's, enhancing his spirit for having a good time. He was aware of their crammed intimacy and the scent of her perfume accentuated her petit femininity.

Getting back to the subject he voiced, "Jamie mentioned something about a summer school; but what about the peace camp?"

She smiled and answered, "Don´t worry about the peace camp. The work at the Faslane closes for the holidays, and any demos will be at the weekend. The others can look after it and besides, the midges are intolerable in the summer down there."

Before he could ask, she explained; "Midges are Scotland´s version of the torture rack; they are a type of tiny mosquito and they breed in warm damp conditions and they swarm. They can literally drive you crazy... just take my word for it!"

"Tell me about the job then," he asked.

"Every summer the university either mounts, or promotes their own Summer School courses in a host of subjects as a way of gaining more income. The one I´m in charge of is European Literature and Languages, and I´m short of a Spanish teacher. You are ideal, Iñaki; you could even do some lectures on Basque Culture and Literature if you wanted to."

Iñaki had been thinking about the summer; he couldn´t hang about the peace camp all summer; he´d go crazy listening to Jonathan and some of the others. This could be ideal!

"… and, you can share the flat with me, it´s just around the corner ...are you listening?" she laughed.

"Sorry my mind wandered a bit ...no, it sounds great, but you´ll have to help me with the syllabus and things like that," he added.

Meryl replied, "Don´t worry about that, it´s pretty basic stuff, not graduate level. The majority of the people are mature students, looking for something interesting to do during the holidays. I suspect at least fifty percent are there reliving lost youth; you should see the amount of bonking that goes on! We´ll talk about it tomorrow, okay?" She shouted over a particularly noisy crowd pressing past, "Let´s get back down into the party, can you get us some more drinks while I go up for a pee?"

Waking up next morning, someone seemed to be hammering on his skull, and the thick sour taste of smoked weed still stuck on his tongue as he tried to figure out where he was.

Meryl was snoring quietly, mouth open and lying sprawled and naked across the bed, one arm stretched over his chest, a small breast pressed flat against his ribs.

Iñaki didn´t want to disturb her, and lay for a while, staring at the old Art Deco light on the ceiling, marvelling at the metamorphosis that he had experienced. He was a different person, as if he had just emerged from a suffocating shell. He now felt in charge of his future, his destiny. He was in control of his emotions; he could evaluate a situation dispassionately and respond equally dispassionately...and this had happened overnight it seemed! Dublin, Shaina, Siobhan, Padraig, and even Connor were a part of his past, they were over there...he was here! He felt freer than he had been since Bilbao.

Eventually, she stirred, and asked sleepily "what time is it darling?"

He moved her arm and climbed out of the bed, eventually finding his watch in the bathroom, "It´s eleven thirty," he shouted as he closed the door.

"Oh my head," she groaned to no one in particular, "Jesus I need a very strong coffee! Hurry up in there, I´m desperate!"

After they had showered and dressed, she suggested coffee in a little Italian Trattoria, up on Woodlands Road; it wasn´t far and the walk up and over Kelvingrove Park would be refreshing.

It was a fine, clear but cool June day, as they climbed the steep side of the hill up over to Park Circus, admiring the classical old terrace mansions, and passing by Queens College to go down through Park Gardens to Pino´s Trattoria.

They both ordered espressos and Ciabattas Napolitano's giving them the necessary shot of caffeine and carbohydrates to jolt them awake.

Meryl then explained in more detail the temporary job he would be doing, and assured him that the syllabus was simple enough, the majority of the students would be starting from the very beginning, and the accent was on basic grammar and verbal communication. There was no question of the students sitting external examinations, but the Summer School would be issuing a Certificate of Study at the end of the course. She felt that he could also provide one or two lectures on Basque culture, and he would be paid extra for this.

"So how about it then," she smiled, already guessing the answer, "Are you interested?"

Instead of affirming immediately, he qualified by telling her he had family business to attend to at odd times in France. He didn´t think anything would happen until after the summer, and if it did, he could be back in a day or two. Was this a problem?

She frowned as he spoke and answered, "I really want you take this job, Iñaki, but it does complicate things a bit," but more brightly she added, "I could cover for you as long as it´s not more than a day or two."

"Sounds good then; when do I start?" he asked.

"We´ll do the documentation tomorrow, I want to register you as a student; that way you won´t need to apply for a work permit. I don´t want you deported, well, not just yet," she laughed. "We can go down to Faslane this afternoon, pick up your things and leave Jake Robinson in charge of the camp."

Iñaki was quite enjoying the Summer School routine. It wasn´t taxing, but he had to study and prepare his lessons. The students ranged in age from an eighteen-year old Glasgow girl with a punk hairstyle, who´s dress and appearance belayed an extremely intelligent brain, to an elderly couple from Aberdeen who intended retiring to the Costa Blanca. They took the lessons most seriously, but their accents almost made it impossible for Iñaki to understand them in English, never mind Spanish.

Living with Meryl was okay. They lived mostly independent lives. At the Summer School, she was business like, administering efficiently. In their private lives, she didn´t demand constant attention from him, nor insist he accompany her to her reunions with her friends, although he did do so often enough. They had an open and free relationship; sex was frequent, important and good, but neither felt the need to complicate it by a deep romantic relationship. Faslane, as Meryl had said, was quiet, and merited only one weekend all summer, which was more of a fiesta than a demonstration.

Nationally 1984 was the summer of discontent, with the Miners and Police battling it out on the picket lines.

It was late August. Iñaki was in the Curler´s Tavern in Byres Road having a lunchtime drink when he picked up a discarded newspaper. He fought to control his emotions as he read the front-page story in the Scottish Herald.

Breaking News!
Republican feud erupts in blood-bath!

Last night Dublin saw the acrimonious feud between the Moderate Political wing, and the radical Militants of the Provisional IRA boil over into violence and bloodshed between the rival factions.

The discovery of two bodies in a burning flat belonging to Padraig Brennan, the Republican Political Activist, heralded
the start of a grim night of brutality and bloodshed in the City, not witnessed since the dark days of Partition in the twenties.

The quick response of the Fire Brigade to an emergency call, and a passing Garda Patrol prevented the fire getting out of hand, but alas, unable to save the lives of the occupants of the apartment. There are unconfirmed reports, that the bodies had gunshot wounds.

The Garda are refusing to verify this, or to confirm that the bodies are that of Padraig Brennan and his long-term girlfriend Shaina McDonal; however neighbours have confirmed seeing the two entering the flat earlier in the evening with two unidentified men.

The violence continued with the firebombing of the High College Bookshop in Clarendon Street, owned by Joseph Tynedale, a former academic and prominent member of the Sinn Fein Political Executive, resulting in the complete destruction of this well-known bookshop. Neighbouring flats had to evacuated, but there are no reports of injuries other than by smoke inhalation as the affected residents were led to safety by the fire brigade.

Neighbours reported that they thought they had heard gunshots and someone screaming as the fire erupted, but as yet the Fire Brigade refuse to confirm if any bodies were found on the burned out premises, citing that the building was in a dangerous state, and a thorough search would not be possible until later today.

Earlier in the evening, there were reports of a shooting in a Republican Bar in Docklands, with one man dead, and another seriously wounded. At the time, this was thought to be an isolated incident.

Other well-known members of the Sinn Fein Political structure have disappeared into hiding following death threats from a dissident faction within PIRA.

The reason for this sudden purge and bloodbath are not clear, but in the internecine warfare within the Republican ranks, as well as the fundamental arguments of the peace through negotiation stance of the Politicals, the Armed Wing have been demanding to take the War to the British mainland.

The Militants have long been suspicious of a Mole in the Dublin Brigade, pointing a finger at security leaks in the Political hierarchy as being responsible for several failed attacks in the North resulting in the death of active commandos and the capture of weaponry.

There are other twists in this unfolding drama and tragedy.

Shaina McDonal, Padraig Brennan's long term girlfriend, shot to fame five years ago when she was exposed as the lover of the then Secretary for Security in the Home Office.

The scandal enforced a thorough review of security procedures and resulted in his resignation and retirement from politics altogether.

Just over two months ago, Connor Rafferty, a close friend of Padraig Brennan, was assassinated in the Central Station in Belfast whilst under Police guard. This killing was claimed by the UVF, but now as a result of last night's shootings, doubts may be raised as to the authenticity of these claims.

JMcM. Dublin.

The article was framed by lurid coloured pictures of the fire fighters spraying water from their hoses into the burning bookshop, and one of the police and fire brigade conferring outside Padraig's flat amidst the chaos of vehicles, hoses and water flooded street.

Iñaki's hands began shaking violently enough for him to grasp the table as he re-read the news from Dublin. He knew immediately what it was all about; Rory and his active service group have won the power struggle, but why kill them? ...then he thought again, *Because there is no other way; Padraig would never have given up his power in Dublin and the militants in the North wanted undisputed control of the war.*

He ordered and quickly downed a whisky to calm his nerves. After a few minutes, he realised he was quite dispassionate, quite detached from the thought of Shaina being dead; it was almost as if he had expected it to happen. He thought back on his last meeting with Paddy in the Royal Bar. It had been one week after he had come back from the Basque country with the bombs. Paddy had congratulated him. The `Commander´ had finally been impressed that Iñaki was for real. He had instructed that Iñaki lie low for a while; he would be sent for if they needed him; meanwhile he could keep his eyes and ears open for a fault in the security at Faslane, but he should enjoy his time out.

His final bit of advice had been break off ties with Dublin for the moment, "You don´t want to get involved over there; things are getting hot."

"What things?" Iñaki asked, thinking that it was something to do with Shaina, Padraig and himself.

"Look boyo, don´t ask, just don´t go there, understand?"

Iñaki nodded meekly as Paddy drained his pint. He got to his feet "I´ve got a ferry to catch and my wife is heating up her pussy, so I´d better not be late or O´Sullivan next door will be stroking it in my place, heh, heh, heh."

He fished in his bag, gave him an envelope and departed with a "See you boyo!"

Opening the envelope in the toilet, Iñaki found another five hundred pounds, and another emergency contact, this time in Glasgow.

Now, here he was, comfortable in Glasgow and re-reading the details of the assassinations again, he was disturbed that he didn´t feel more emotion for his former friends.

Sure, he knew he had been used by the Dublin group. He accepted that Siobhan must have had an ice-cold heart to seduce, and stay with him over the past months. They had some wonderful times, but at the heart of it was her and her brother Padraig´s dedication to the Republican cause.

He still could not accept that Padraig was a traitor; he put so much effort into the struggle for a United Ireland...no, it was definitely a power struggle. He assumed that the other body in the flat was Shaina, but then again, it could be Siobhan. She had not been mentioned in the article.

Chapter 81: McManus

Iñaki risked a call to his new contact in Glasgow.

A broad Glasgow accent answered, "Aye!"

Iñaki asked if that was McManus, and the voice said, "Who´s askin´ fur him?"

"I´m a friend of Paddy´s."

"Well he´s no´ here the noo´; gie´s yer number, an´ he´ll call you back in ten minutes."

Iñaki gave him the number, he was in a group of telephone boxes at the top of Byres Road, so he added, it might be engaged, it´s a busy place."

"McManus will phone ya´, just wait."

Iñaki sat on the wall of the Botanical Gardens watching the phone, but had to wait twenty minutes before the phone rang, and got to it just before a passing woman was about to lift it.

"It's for me", he explained to the rather alarmed woman, and spoke into the telephone, "Hello, is this McManus?"

"Aye, this is McManus," another Glasgow voice said, "… and this had better be important!"

Iñaki spoke, "I´ve just read the papers; what´s going on?"

"What´s going on is that a nest of vipers are being eliminated; these bastards have been selling us out to the Brits for far too long, but we've got them in the end."

"What about me?" he asked, "it was Padraig Brennan who brought me in."

"Well son, if you´d been fingered, you wouldn´t be speaking to me the noo´, you would be lying peacefully wi´ a bullet in yer brain."

"What do you want me to do now then?" Inaki asked.

"Just do as you've been told, and keep your head down; don't fur Christ's sake contact Dublin. The polis over there will be lookin' fur ye, bein' sae close tae the family so tae speak. Paddy will get in touch wi' ye if anythin' turns up, so don't phone me again unless it's a real emergency, understood?"

Iñaki said, "I'm not at Faslane just now, how will you contact me?"

McManus laughed, "We know where ye are son, so don't worry, we'll get a message tae ye." The telephone went dead in Iñaki's ear.

Iñaki stood looking at the telephone in his hand, wondering how they knew where he was, when he had no idea who or where they were. Other than Paddy, who he could only connect with in the Royal Bar in Helensburgh, he had no contacts. Replacing the receiver, he walked away thinking. He marvelled at the cell system of security they were employing; no one knew or could connect with anyone outside the cell. He was just a messenger, a go-fur, and therefore was not privy to any secrets, so he couldn't finger anyone else, other than Paddy.

He looked around, wondering if he was being followed, but dismissing the thought as being unlikely. Shrugging his shoulders, he decided to do as Paddy advised him, and take it easy. Checking the time, he realised he had to run to get back for his afternoon class.

They returned to Faslane in late September, but the weather was so bad that they decided to rent a mobile home over the Gareloch at Rosneath.

From their new home, they could just about make out the peace camp across the Gareloch, and the periodical demonstrations blocking off the access to the nuclear submarine base resumed.

Iñaki, under his guise as peace activist, spent many hours observing the security systems, but could not work out an effective way of inflicting major damage on a Polaris submarine without mounting a suicide mission from the sea. Dedicated as they were, he doubted that the Provos were up to suicide missions. His only contact with the Provos had been in Glasgow at the start of September, when a man had suddenly sidled up to him in the Curler´s Tavern, asked him for a light, at the same time handing him an envelope. Afterwards he could not even think of a proper description of the man, as the exchange had been so fast. Inside was another five hundred pounds and a note to keep his head down, the garda in Dublin were still making enquiries about him.

It was October and Meryl and Iñaki were having breakfast at home. Meryl turned on the television for the news.

The shocking bombing of the Grand Hotel in Brighton took up the whole of the programme, including an interview with Mrs Thatcher on her way to the Conservative Party Conference. Margaret Thatcher and most of the British Cabinet had almost been assassinated by a massive explosion, which blew out the front of the Grand Hotel.

A bomb warning had not been given, and the Provisional IRA had claimed responsibility and issued a statement;

"Mrs. Thatcher will now realise that Britain cannot occupy our country and torture our prisoners and shoot our people in their own streets and get away with it. Today, we were unlucky, but remember we only have to be lucky once. You will have to be lucky always. Give Ireland peace and there will be no more war."

Meryl was appalled at the loss of life, which went against her pacifist beliefs. She was absolutely anti-Thatcher and her policies, but felt that this attack on a democratically elected Government was akin to a declaration of War on Britain.

Iñaki had almost failed to hide his excitement; he was certain that the explosive he had smuggled back from

Bayonne had been used in the attack. The rumours had been correct, and his organisation had struck a massive blow against the Establishment.

He instead simply argued with her that there was in fact a war going on in Northern Ireland; normal people were being killed every day, therefore why should politicians be considered an exception. This sparked an argument, which continued over to the peace camp with the majority in favour of the IRA!

The bombing activated an immediate surge in Security at the Base. There were noticeably more police patrolling the perimeter, and the security on the access gates was both increased and uncompromising, resulting in long queues snaking down the A812 from Helensburgh.

Out on the Gareloch, the Special Boat Service in their Zodiacs were visible buzzing up and down, supplementing the MOD Marine Police who had been required to turn off their portable televisions.

Meryl thought it prudent to suspend the weekly protest, as without doubt, the MOD police would not be so lenient with the protesters at this time.

Book 4

Convergence

"Making peace, I have found, is much harder than making war." - Gerry Adams

Chapter 82: Polaris

The American Nuclear Submarine Fleet first arrived in the Holy Loch in March 1961. They were met by an angry demonstration of CND marchers, who did not seem to appreciate that SUBRON was there to protect the Scots from Soviet nuclear attack.

As a result of the Nassau Agreement of 1962, between the old, experienced Harold Macmillan, and the new, young charismatic American President John Kennedy, the Americans agreed to supply the Polaris ballistic missiles for Britain´s own nuclear defence strategy.

In order to minimise risks, it was desirable that these submarines and their related nuclear missiles should be based and stored, in a relatively lightly populated area in case of accidents, or a war situation.

There had been a Royal Navy Submarine Base at Faslane on the Gareloch, since before World War 2, with the required easy access to the Atlantic through the Clyde Estuary. Therefore, the good citizens around the scenic sea lochs found themselves probably the first target for the Soviet side in, what was described as the M.A.D war strategy that is Mutually Assured Destruction.

If this was the downside, there was also an upside in that the huge influx of American Navy personnel into the attractive little seaside town of Dunoon, spending their mighty dollars in what had become a rundown depressed area.

On Fridays, the trains and ferries to Dunoon were packed to the gunwales with Glasgow girls, in their quest to hook an American husband.

Over the other side of the Firth of Clyde, the mainly English navy personnel, and support services, provided a much needed stimulus to the local economy, and in the minds of most, a job or money in the cash drawer outweighed the risk of nuclear annihilation.

The subject was the main conversation topic at the dinner parties of the time. Some wag pointed out that in the event of war, with the Holy Loch over there on the left, and Faslane on the right, the good citizens of Port Glasgow and Greenock would be evenly toasted to a crisp.

However the main discussion was; "How will you spend the last sixteen minutes of your life after the incoming missile sirens go off?"

The women would mainly respond by rushing off to the school, to die alongside their children, but one or two would rush out to do some shopping! Almost to a man, the men would find the nearest woman to have sex with, and go out with a Bang so to speak.

One of the ladies made a scathing comment; "Henry, you would have time to have sex with at least four of them if your usual performance is to be relied on" Another cruel attack on manly attributes was; "Roger it would take you fifteen minutes to find your willy, so maybe you should think of doing something else to do!"

Chapter 83: Faslane Peace Camp

The Peace Camp at Faslane was established after the Thatcher government´s decision was made to upgrade the Navy´s Polaris submarines and missiles to the much more powerful Trident system in 1982.

There was uproar in the CND circles, and one weekend found a pensioner couple from Glasgow camping out in protest opposite the main gate to the Faslane Royal Navy Base complex.

The idea caught on, and within weeks a sizable protest peace camp had been founded, and populated that summer by disparate groups of clergy, academics, social workers, anarchists, trade unionists, CND activists and socialist groups, including a local Councillor.

The `Ricos´... the residents on the privately owned high-end estate above, were not so at peace with the Peace Camp. The Shandon residents had to put up with the disruption of traffic, the noise, the smells of campfires, cooking and hastily built latrines. They watched the value of their main wealth asset diminishing daily as new arrivals joined the demonstrations. Neighbours, who had not looked in each other´s direction for years, suddenly had a common cause, convened a meeting and called the police. The police judged that they were unable to interfere, as the peace demonstrators were, in fact, peaceful, and not causing a `breach of the peace." The camp was on public land therefore local council would have to make an official trespass complaint.

Protests and complaints to the council, the local MP, and all the way to Downing Street, brought no relief except that the council granted planning permission, installed mains water, and toilet facilities for the campers.

The irony was not lost on many commentators, that, still in the throes of the Cold War, and after the Cuban Missile Crisis, the `Ricos´ were more concerned about the value of their houses than the risk of instant annihilation by some crazy Russian president.

Unlike the `Rico´s above them, (who could not sell up and move out), the peace camp resident numbers fluctuated by the season, the freezing, rain drenching winter being particularly hellish, so diminishing the fervour for Peace, or increasing, if there were important CND demonstrations planned.

The peace camp was attracting national TV and press coverage, the result being that the campers were reinforced each weekend by a medley of aspiring and established political VIP´s, TV and theatre celebrities, brought by the free publicity. Thursday was the day to avoid going into Helensburgh however, as the bus would be full of pensioners and peace campers going in to collect their benefits.

The queue at the post office would snake out the door, and the refined, genteel pensioners of Helensburgh would all but throw up with the smell of unkempt and unwashed camper residents. They would be forgoing their tea and scones at the Oxfam Café, to go rushing home afterwards to shower and wash, or even burn their clothes.

Chapter 84: Hamish

It was a fine early September day, clear, blue sky, a little crisp fresh feel to the morning, a welcome relief after the usual unstable summer holiday weather, ranging from hot and steamy, fine soaking through drizzle. The Scots have a great word *dreich*, and within the hour a squall would blow in from the loch with horizontal rain, just to reassure you that this is the west coast of Scotland and over there is the Atlantic, and then a bit further out is our `Special Relationship Friend´, The United States of America.

The unwary and unprepared tourists would alternate between marvelling at the magnificence of the mountains and lochs, the extraordinary colours, and scurrying for the nearest bar or restaurant, often to find that last orders were two-o´clock and the kitchen was closed!

In the summer, when dusk fell upon this silent and wild landscape, the local midge hordes would inflict anguish and suffering upon the demented campers and fishers for mackerel, who would strive in vain to ward them off with smoky fires the effect of which only left the victims bitten, and with streaming eyes looking out of blackened faces. Some would resort to wrapping their heads Bedouin Nomad style as they came up to the bar for respite and refreshment. Out in the beer garden, no one would be excused the torment of *Midgemus monstrous´* as they would fly in like a sandstorm and cover the pint, or glass of Cabernet with a quarter-inch of living crust in the time that the thirsty tourist could lift it to his, or her mouth.

This morning however, all this was in the past as nature was on it´s very best behaviour. The high cumulus clouds and dramatic mountains mirrored on a flat calm loch, with a silence of nature that you can almost feel. As we waited on the school bus with Kirsty, this spectacular Nature show was rudely disturbed by a Special Boat Services training exercise out of Faslane.

Two SBS Fastcraft came hurtling round the point, to be reinforced by another group who were jumping out of a helicopter into the sea-loch over towards Carrick Castle. The incongruence of the scene unfolded as the two military groups attacked up the mountain, which in turn seem to darken and glower at the puny little men and their war machines.

Lochview always gets busy on days like this, as we get lots of Ladies who Lunch from Rhu and Helensburgh, as well as our usual Faslane and passing crowd. We have long worked out that it´s pub grub that´s wanted, and we don´t open the main restaurant downstairs during the day, unless we have a group booking of VIP´s from the Faslane Base.

As we expected, we had a good lunch trade, the usual crowd were going for the Soup and Specials Lunch, and the ladies were, in the main, taking the `Delice of Salmon in Filo Pastry, with the Minted and Buttered New Potatoes with Hollandaise.´

Almost to a woman they would continue with, "a bottle of that nice Chardonnay, Hamish, please. How is Lorna coping in the kitchen? ...we have no idea how she does it, poor thing."

I reply, "Poor Lorna will do as she´s damn well told, or she´ll be out the door and a nice young French Cordon Bleu installed in her place."

"You´re such a tease Hamish, give Lorna our love and ask her to join us later for a drink, will you?"

Entering the kitchen, I shouted, "Check on! Lorna, if you´ve got time, Hannah, and Penny Smith want you to join them for a glass of wine later."

"And do you think I´m going to have the time to sit with them?" was the rather grumpy, `I am a victim´ reply.

"Public relations Lorna, very important," I rejoin.

"There´s only one us here got the time to stand and gossip to a couple of bored housewives, and it´s definitely not me."

"For Christ sake, Lorna, they like you, and only want to tell you how wonderful you are."

"Hamish, get out of my bloody kitchen and leave me in peace....is that bloody bread still lying there? Table six ... now! ... and don´t forget the butter!"

With that reminder that I had work to do, I served the bread and the butter, even though it is Helen´s duty, or Ronald´s, the useless college trainee we have agreed to provide work experience. He would have been back, wasting his time, and taxpayers money, in college long ago, except that it´s a favour we´re doing for his dad, who just happens to be Chief of Operations at the Base, as well as being a good friend and customer. We can only hope that Ronnie senior is more capable than his boy …or we are all doomed!

In my state of high alert and tension, I didn´t notice the two men until I heard:
"D´ ye have Guinness on tap?"
. The voice, which must have been forged in a Belfast shipyard, came from behind me, and when I turned around, two well dressed business types had entered the bar, but the voice did not associate bankers, or the Rotary that meet every first Tuesday of the month in the restaurant.
"Hello there gents, I´m sorry, I didn´t see you coming in …what did you ask for?
"Dae ye have any Guinness on tap", said the smaller of the two. The other, older, man was what can only be described as Big. Big head, big shoulders, big in the chest, big in stature, big shoes…a BIG man, and he maintained a penetrating silence, which unnerved me a little for some reason.
"No, but we´ve got Murphy´s, I replied, but I´ve got bottled Guinness."
The small one, who I realised looked a lot like Michael Flaherty of Riverdance fame, said "Murphy´s shite; give us two pints o´ Tartan Special and two Black Bushmills."
I knew I was in trouble but had to admit "Jameson's, no Bushmills."
"Just make it two Grouse." This was said with a look of absolute disgust.
"Would you like to see the menu gentlemen?" I asked.
"What´s that Special you´ve got on there….Sligo Fish Pie? Have you ever been to Sligo?" he asked.
"Of course I´ve been to Sligo, otherwise how could I bring one back for the menu?" A weak joke in an attempt to cover the lie, and instantly recognised. "It´s A bit of smoked

haddock and fresh salmon poached in milk with onion, cabbage and mashed potato, very delicious."

"Ok, we'll have one of these, and one of that haggis shite."

In my best Glasgow accent I replied, "Oh, Oh, your entering dangerous ground here Sur, the Haggis is Scotland's national dish, an' ah'll no be staun' here havin' it insulted."

"Calm down Braveheart, ma friend here is well acquainted with yer Haggis an' Neeps, jus' you make sure it comes wi' a free dram o' whisky"

I like a bit of banter with the customers, but the Big man was saying nothing but observing everything and making me nervous; a man from the Tax Office? My apprehension increased when spreadsheets appeared all over the table.

We got another rush on, and tempers in the kitchen were fraying, not especially helped when Ronald dropped a steak pie over his shoes, which both put him out of action for a while, and inflamed Lorna's blood pressure to exploding point.

I wisely kept clear as much as I could, but suffered the abuse only a woman can unleash upon a helpless male just doing his best, when I reminded Lorna that Hannah and Penny were waiting to see her. As I retreated backwards out of the kitchen, I stood on Michael Flaherty's doppelganger's toes, as he came out the toilet.

"Having a hard time Jimmy?" he asked.

"Chef's a little excited; just daily lunchtime repartee, nothing to worry about. How was the fish? Was the haggis up to gourmet inspection?"

"Ye surpassed yerself, or was it the missus in the kitchen? Aye, it would be the missus, you can't even serve a decent Guinness or malt. Dae ye have time tae sit with us for wee talk?"

I almost unloaded my bowels when he said that, "Shit, I thought, it's the VAT Inspectors!" …famous for stripping naked their victims. "I'll be free in about ten minutes, if that's okay", out came a squeaky voice I didn't recognise, drawing a funny look between Mr Big and the famous Riverdancer.

"That's fine, can you get us two espressos and two more Grouse"

I shot down the stairs and into my cubbyhole office, had a good check around there was nothing incriminating on my desk, had a quick wee, and freshened up, ready for an inquisition. Now I was ready for them; "How can I help you gentlemen?"

"By sitting your arse down here beside us for a moment," the dancer replied.

I thought, "Jesus Christ, how the hell can they be VAT inspectors?"

"Get a drink for yourself, first, and put it on our Bill; not one of your feckin' overpriced whiskies though!"

I asked Helen, who was passing, to bring me a beer, as he continued. "Do you know a Margaret Geddes in the village?"

"The Darlandhuie? Margaret's a good friend of ours."

"That's the one, she speaks very highly of you; you're Hamish, right?"

"That's me, and can I ask who you are?"

"Sure, I'm Michael Comyn, and this is my boss, Patrick McTier.

We exchanged handshakes as he continued; Mr McTier here is the owner of McTier Construction. We've won some construction contracts, for the Faslane and Coulport Trident expansion plan."

So far the big man hadn't spoken a word, I was beginning to think he had a speech problem.

Michael carried on, "We will have about three hundred men on site, and we are looking for accommodation for about one hundred of these. Are you interested?"

"I'm always interested in filling rooms Mr Comyn, but with respect, I don't think I can mix your lad's with my normal clients," flicking my eyes over in the direction of Penny and Hannah.

"Look Hamish, call me Michael; listen I think I would want to take one of your rooms for myself, I take it you have a room with a bath for me?"

"They're all en-suite," I said, still a little doubtful, but the lucre of pound notes was melting my objections.

"Well you can be sure my lads' won't cause any problems; I'll be living here and you'll get 'la crème de la crème' of my boys, and with your feckin' prices, they'll drink in the village!"

Yes, we were very interested, and for two lucrative years, we housed twenty of these rough, but impeccably behaved (in our hotel) Irish labourers.

Chapter 85: The Not-So-Peaceful Camper

Meryl had been spending more and more time in Glasgow. She had secured a visiting professorship at the university, and only came down to Faslane every other weekend.

Iñaki and Meryl's relationship had always been liberal with no demands of undying love on either side, but more than just a physical distance now separated them.

In her absence, he was now the de-facto leader of the peace campers in favour of more direct action, which angered her to no end. Meryl had maintained a respectful relationship with the MOD and local police. They allowed the demonstrations and in fact kept order, as long as the protesters maintained a posture of non-violence.

She had no idea of his active IRA links, although she suspected his trips down to the Basque Region were for more than visiting family.

Iñaki borrowed Meryl's Volkswagen campervan to go down to Liverpool on a job for the Provos. He had telephoned her with the excuse that he was meeting his old Dublin friend Roger, in Liverpool. He had picked up a two-man assassination squad with their weapons and dropped them off in the east end of Glasgow. A few days later, he drove them overnight to Felixstowe. Another volunteer would then take the assassination team over to the Continent in his lorry. It was to be an attack on soldiers in a pub in Germany, as part of the internationalisation of the war, in agreement with the ETA command in the Basque country.

One of the volunteers, a baby faced individual, seemed to the one in charge. He looked no more than eighteen years old, Iñaki thought, and talked incessantly in the strange accent of the Dublin slums. He described some of the bloody operations he had been on and questioned Iñaki about mounting an operation against the Brits at Faslane.

Iñaki explained that a direct attack would be suicidal; there was too much security about the place, and you couldn't get anywhere near a nuclear submarine. However, he outlined an idea that had been festering in his head for some time. Actually, it was Jonathan's idea, that a group of protesters could ambush the officers of a submarine at their Ladies' Dinner, held just before they went out on patrol.

Jonathan had proposed that they thrown flares and smoke bombs into the restaurant as they were having dinner, "It would scare the shit out of the bastards, just like Sellafield," he had claimed. Iñaki added that he had been at a hotel one day as they were preparing a navy dinner, and there was absolutely no security.

"Sounds a possibility," Fergal, the young guy, mused; "Could you produce some details, a Plan, on how it would work and I'll put it to the Army Council." He added, "The

AC want to attack the Brits all over the place, and this sounds good. The Navy don´t get any attention from us; might shake them up a bit!"

Iñaki thought, "How can this young guy, younger than me I think, get access to the PIRA Army Council?"

They were in the middle of the transfer at the meeting place in a lay by, when they were surprised by a passing police patrol car with its lights flashing and siren wailing. In the panic, they left a bag containing a pistol and four grenades in a corner of the bedding cupboard.

Iñaki was sitting at the kitchen table at home reading the Sunday paper. Meryl had gone to Helensburgh for some shopping and she said she might clean out the Volkswagen in the self service car wash, as "Nobody else seemed to notice how bloody filthy the interior was!"

He heard the roar of the Volkswagen come back, but didn´t make a move; she was in a foul mood today, he thought.

The door burst open and she screamed at him, "I want a fucking explanation for this," holding a black cloth bag in front of his eyes. He had never seen her like this; her hair dishevelled, face red with fury, eyes bulging with rage, "…and it better be a fucking good one."

Completely taken off guard Iñaki shouted back, "Explanation for what?"

"For this you fucker!" she screamed, pulling the Berretta out of the bag, and pointing it at his head.

Iñaki froze, at last registering what had happened; a chill ran down his spine, as he put up his hands in supplication. "Meryl, put it down, I can explain, just put it down."

She didn´t relax, or put the gun down; she just said menacingly; "You are a lying, cheating bastard, I know what ᴇse are for, and you´re not going to get away with it. I´ve ᴍy whole life as a Peace Activist and now you are using ᴋing murder people at the Base!"

"No, Meryl, that´s not true! Please! Just give me the gun; I´ll explain!"

"No, you can do your explaining to the fucking people you were intending to murder!"

She made for the telephone on the wall, Iñaki realised she was serious and threw himself across the kitchen grabbing at her; they both fell to the floor, he landing on top of her. There was an almighty bang in his ear, and she was jerking, blood spurting from a gaping hole in her head.

Horrified, he managed to pull a towel from the rack. Cradling her head in his arm, he tried to stem the flow of brain matter and blood from her head, but as he pressed into the hole, he knew she was dead.

He was deaf in his right ear, and he could smell that his hair had been singed by the blast from the Berretta. Still holding the towel to her head, he was shaking his head, trying to clear the ringing in his brain. *"Dios Mio,"* suddenly he slumped, as the adrenalin left him.

He must have lain in that position for a five minutes before his strength returned, and thinking more clearly now, he thought, *"Someone must have heard the shot."* He laid her head gently on the floor, still cushioned with the towel. Shakily he struggled to his feet, picked up the gun and the grenades that had spilled from the bag. He put the grenades in a kitchen cupboard, but hid the Berretta under a cushion on the sofa.

No one came near. The Park had very few residents at this time of year, and perhaps if anyone had heard the shot, they would have put it down to the local farmers shooting rabbits.

Iñaki found the strength to pick Meryl´s body up and carry her through to the bathroom, where he laid her in the bath. He didn´t want to look at her face, but he found his eyes drawn to the hole where her eye had been. There was no expression on her face; nothing; no fear, anger, wonderment, she had died instantly.

Once again, Iñaki was curiously aware of his feeling of detachment from death; this corpse, Meryl, used to be his friend, his lover, but now it could have been a carcass of meat on a butcher's slab. He covered the body with a towel, and sluiced his head and face with cold water, trying to think straight. Looking in the mirror, he wondered who he was; no feelings, no emotion, no nerves.... *Strange*

Iñaki began clearing up the mess of brain and blood on the wall and floor by the phone, surprisingly little he was thinking, and found the bullet hole in the wall. There was no sign of the bullet though, it had passed through the flimsy wooden walls of the mobile home, and he didn't dare go outside to look for it. He had to dispose of the body though, and decided to phone his emergency contact in Glasgow for assistance. Locking the caravan, he got into the Volkswagen and drove through the autumn rain, round the Gareloch to Helensburgh, slowing as he passed the peace camp but there was no sign of life. The pier was deserted, the rain was now pouring down, and gusts of wind from the sea were soaking the legs of the few foolhardy people around.

He went through the usual motions of security, awaiting the call back from McManus.

The telephone rang and he answered; having confirmed the code names, he explained what had happened.

McManus whistled, "Jesus Christ, how in the fuck did they manage to lose a pistol and grenades? I'll bet the fucking Army Council don't know about this ...but don't you be tellin' them, you keep out of it."

Iñaki replied, "I'd like to, but I've got her fucking body lying in my bath, and people are going to be wondering why she isn't at work tomorrow."

McManus interrupted, "Don't panic, we'll work something out." He paused and asked, "She was American she not, small, dark haired, Japanese type, is that right?"

"How do you know that," asked Iñaki.

"en son, I'm not Chief of Staff in Scotland for now everythin' about you; everythin', okay?"

Continuing, he said, "Listen; I've got a niece who would pass for her at a distance, I'll bring her down and then you'll put her on a train. You'll book the ticket with a connection to London; your ex-girlfriend is going back to America because her mammy's dying or something, understand?"

"Yes, I think I understand...and I phone the university in the morning to inform them of this."

"You got it boyo, and my wee Mary can get off the London train at Motherwell, when it makes a stop."

"What about the body though?" Iñaki asked.

"Well you've got a big deep sea in front of you, have you not? She's goin' fur a swim! I'll be down there in an hour an' a bit wi' some help; meet us in the Commodore public bar, okay?"

"Okay, Iñaki said, as the line went dead.

The shock of the killing was now affecting him. He went over the details in his head a dozen times; it could easily have been him lying with a bullet through his head. It was an accident; he hadn't pulled the trigger; perhaps Meryl had, but no one would ever know.

The effort would now be on getting rid of the body, and covering up her death, at least for a while. He was confident that the university personnel office would accept the story about her mother, but her friends would be asking questions after a week or two.

At just after four o'clock, the three men walked into the bar, looked around, and fixed on Iñaki nursing a beer.

Iñaki recognised McManus from the pick-up he had made in Glasgow. He was with Fergal O'Brien, the volunteer he had taken down to Ipswich, and another guy, who's face seemed familiar.

They sat around the table and McManus opened the conversation, "Well boyo, you've given us a wee problem ...but don' you worry about it, we'll get it sorted alright. Wee Mary is sittin' outside in the car; it's the Cherokee wi' the

Zodiac on the trailer. You take her tae the station, and dae as ah´ telt ye. Here´s a few quid, keep her in the background and buy her a ticket tae London; stay there until she gets on the train; she knows what tae dae, an´ then you get back hame." He asked, "You´re still livin´ in the Holiday Park at Rosneath, aren´t ye?"

Iñaki nodded in affirmation.

"Okay, we´ll moor the boat next to Silver´s yard, and meet you over there."

Iñaki went outside out and easily found the Cherokee Jeep parked up the road a bit. A pale faced, girl with short, dark hair was inside, and he rattled the window to attract her attention. He realised she would pass for Meryl at a distance as she got out of the Jeep. She was wearing a black cagoule over black jeans, and had a sports-bag in her hand.

A trace of a smile, and "Hi, I´m Mary, you must be Fernando or whatever yer name is," as she held out a small thin hand to him.

He took her hand, and her bag, and simply said, "Thanks for doing this; we´d better go."

Mary bought a magazine and some chocolate over at the kiosk for her journey, as Iñaki bought the through ticket to London, asking if the connection was from Queen Street station or Central?

"Central," came the gruff reply, "should be on time for the six o´clock. That´ll be twenty six pounds and forty pence."

Iñaki pushed over thirty pounds, and got the change and tickets pushed back under the window at him.

Mary boarded the train, giving him a peck on the cheek as a goodbye, and whispered in his ear, "I hope we meet again, ʾandsome."

"Not if I can help it," Iñaki thought, *"I´m too dangerous!"*

⊤ Meryl´s body didn´t pose any problems; no one ɑnd the Jeep was backed up to the door of the caravan. McManus had organised everything. He and the other two manipulated the body into a brown sleeping bag, whilst Iñaki stayed in the kitchen, and began the washing down of the whole area with a strong disinfectant.

The rain had eased off to a foggy drizzle, and the wind had dropped; visibility was down to about one hundred yards. Meryl´s body was stowed in the Cherokee. McManus joked "I just love fishing on a night like this, we might even catch something tonight boys," which brought chuckles from the other two.

Iñaki was left to clean up the bathroom with plenty of bleach to remove any trace of blood. As he scrubbed away, once more he was somewhat unsettled by his lack of conscience and remorse. Meryl had ceased to exist; *it was her own fault, she had the gun, not me*, he reasoned.

Two hours later they were back complaining, "We nearly got run down by a fucking police boat! Thank fuck your missus was already crabbin´ on the bottom! You owe us one now boyo. Phone me on Friday, about twelve, we want to talk about your plan."

Chapter 86: Fergal O´Brien

Early October and we were sitting in my `office´; that is the table beside the full length window in the Lobster Pot Bar that looks out over the car park and down the road towards Garelochhead. The other advantage to this `office´, and not of my official one where our bookkeeper works, is that the old fashioned log stove is right beside it. As I do my paperwork, menus, work rotas etc, my backside is snug and warm, even on a day like this where the wind and rain is lashing against the window two feet from the aforementioned bum.

Lorna and I were working on the menus for the coming Office Party Christmas campaign, which normally she would acquiesce to my judgment on these matters, but this time she was digging her heels in over our image.

I wanted normal, simple menus with the usual Christmassy selections , roast turkey, duck, steak, a fish dish etc, but she was making a point that our reputation for Progressive Cuisine should be reflected at Christmas also, otherwise the base crowd will go to the Carvery in Helensburgh.

I took a bite out of my treacle scone and a sip of my coffee,….we were very proud of our Gaggia and Italian blend , the local Italian was still using a Cona coffee percolator! "Lorna," I said, "do you think the wee lassies in the offices will know what a capon is? Okay, there´s room for more flamboyant starters and sweets, but people expect turkey!"

We finally agreed, she got her Sole and Salmon Plaits in Crayfish Sauce, but not the capon, and I retained the Roast Tom Turkey with all the trimmings.

"Who´s that coming up the road?" asked Lorna.

"You mean getting blown around the road …it can´t be one of Michael´s bunch, they don´t finish until 7 o´clock. It´s a bloody awful day to be walking up from the village."

We continued to stare out into the weather sweeping off the moor, trying to fathom this rarity of a human being exposed to full ferocity of our famous tempests, when even the meagre traffic on the way to Arrochar had more or less curtailed for the day. As he came nearer, buffeted almost horizontal, we could see it was a young boy, about seventeen or so, dressed only in black anorak and jeans. He had a small rucksack, which he was vainly using as a shield for his face against the driving rain.

"It must be one of the new boys, it's a bit strange they haven't sent him up in the van."
He disappeared for about five minutes as he negotiated the bit of the road we couldn't see and down to our entrance.

The boy had to struggle against the force of the wind to open the door to the Lobster Pot Bar, entered and stood drenching water all over the carpet. His black hair was plastered over his brow, the dripping, red nose contrasted starkly on a surprisingly young, chalk white face, he was an ideal example of a baby-faced adult.

"Look son, You're flooding the bar! Can you stand over there on the mat?"

"Oi'm very sorry Sur", a very Irish voice replied, as he almost leaped the six feet back to the Welcome mat at the entrance.

"Did Michael Comyn send you up? ...are you up from McTier Construction?"

"Oh no Sur, I was asking fur any work at the hotel in the village and it was the lady who thought you might need a hand."

"You're just about six weeks too soon, son, we won't need anyone until the middle of November."

Lorna, with her at times, infuriating mothering instinct now intervened. "Let the boy in Hamish, come on over here by the fire, and take your jacket off...and these shoes as well. You look frozen, here heat yourself up...do you want a cup of tea?"

Lorna gave that look that said, tea is a bar job, not kitchen, and I clamped my jaws tight and prepared the tea for our guest.

"What's your name son?" she asked.

"Fergal O'Brien missus....it's awfie guid o' ye... this tea an' that."

"That's no trouble Fergal, but I don't think we can help with a job right now. Have you worked in a hotel or restaurant before?"

"Aye sure missus, I've worked in Sligo, an' Dublin, and when I came over, in Liverpool as well."

"And what did you do? You look very young for all this work, when did you leave school?"

"Ah've been out o' school nearly four years missus. Ah've done kitchen work, like helpin' the Chef, washin' up, but ah had a stint at servin' in a Wimpy Bar in Liverpool."

I had by this time served the tea, with a scone, but no butter, and asked him, "Where are you going now Fergus, it's going to be dark in half an hour."

"Ah don't know Sur, probably back down to the village."

The Mother hen again butted in… "Do you know anyone in the village Fergal?"
You could see it coming; the open door….Fergus was in!

"Naw missus, ah only came up today, but don' worry yersel' ah'm used tae luckin' efter myself."

"Hamish, he can stay overnight in the staff caravan, couldn't he, it's such a terrible day, and he's absolutely soaked through."

Defeat stared me in the face, I could see Nature's maternal impulses had left me situated like Scrooge if I turned this poor wee soul out into the terrors of a moorland nightstorm …"Ok then, just overnight though, there's just no work until mid November."

"Ah'll be no bother, Sur, an' thanks very much missus, if I can help wi' the dishes or anythin', just to pay ma way, ye know."

Lorna took charge of the `poor wee soul´, and showed him to our live-in staff quarters, two mobile homes, one in principal for females, and the other for males, although there was a great deal of movement between the two, especially when we had girls from the Islands on the staff.

I finished the menu and publicity plans, had a look around, and left Helen to mind the bar while I went down to our cottage to have a shower and a break.

Lorna was already in the shower, and I waited until she had towelled herself dry. "Lorna, I know you mean well, but sometimes you let your heart get in the way of common sense. We know absolutely nothing about this boy, and for all we know he can be robbing the other staff right now."

"Oh come off it, Hamish, how many times have we taken staff off the road during the summer? Did we run any checks on that idiot Robbie, who just managed to screw us in the bar? If I remember that was one of your beauties, right?"

"Christ, Lorna, at least he looked and sounded the part, this guy talks and looks like a tramp!"

"So would you if you were out on a day like today; and don´t give me the hard-man bit; if that was a wee, bedraggled lassie from Skye with a big chest, we wouldn´t be having this conversation!"

"Give it a break Lorna, this is a figure of your imagination, just make sure it´s just an overnight …this wee guy´s story is a bit too Irish! I´m going for a shower, are you making the tea?"

"Get Helen to make your damn tea, the way she is ogling you just now, I´m pretty sure she´ll give you more than a biscuit with it!"

Two doors slammed simultaneously as we retreated to our own thoughts, as always stressed by living, loving and running a high-pressure business together, day after day as well as trying to bring up a family, which admittedly was not my priority, Lorna, being the mother.

Our routine was well established. When Kirsty, our thirteen year old, was dropped off by the school bus, Lorna would be there, and over a cup of tea, chat to her, find out the school gossip, and help, or at least supervise the homework chore, which was not all that pleasurable all of the time.

Kirsty was a very pretty, normal teenage girl, with a great personality and sense of humour taken from her mother, but with no great academic achievements or ambitions. When we had suggested to her that she should go to a private school to improve her results, she suffered a genuine attack of nerves and childhood depression, which extended to a period of bed-wetting. We dropped the idea after she promised to put more effort in class, and restrict her romantic notions on the school´s pin-up boy, Gregor Murray, who also just happened to travel on the lochside school bus. Despite this daily distraction, she did in fact perk up in her school reports, but we accepted that this child would not turn out to be a hot shot lawyer or doctor.

Kirsty just loved helping out in the restaurant at the weekends, she loved the buzz and the repartee with the customers, and could charm the dourest client out of a hefty tip. "A wee something, only for you Kirsty," as they folded a fiver into her hand.

You would have needed a chainsaw to cut the atmosphere when my wife, deigned to report for her duty as Head Chef that night. Immediately, points were scored, as she at last, met my eyes.

"I´ve just been speaking to Andrew (our kitchen porter), and he tells me that tramp I´ve allowed to spend the night is busy cleaning the caravan. Andrew´s worried that he´s going to lose his job, but I´ve assured him that his job is safe, but his accommodation isn´t, given the state of the caravan."

"Jesus Christ Lorna, Andrew´s been with us for four years, and we have known about his pigsty for all of this time, so why all of a sudden, tonight, just before service, we have to talk about his living conditions? Let´s forget about it, the first table is coming in." I retreated into the bar.

"Evening George, what a bloody awful night, you deserve a medal for coming up here tonight."

"Stuff your medal Hamish, but I´ll take a dram to heat me up."

"Melanie, how in the hell can you live with this crabby old despot? Here, give me your coat and come down to the fire."

"Hamish, if only we were free, we could go to the Caribbean and live the simple passions of life," Melanie gushed in our ritual game.

"That all sounds wonderful," George interceded between the thoughts of a seventy year old, well used, jolly wife, and the forty two year old silver tongued, professional smoothy, to add, "Is this fire only for her, or can I heat my arse as well as drink your malt?"

"Lorna! I shouted into the kitchen, George and Melanie have arrived."

Lorna came out of the kitchen with her usual delightful smile, that extended into her eyes for our best customers, and passed a moment in the welcoming `our friends to our home´ mode, before excusing herself to kitchen duties. As she passed, her eyes-smile turned to ice in my direction, and I knew, with a sinking feeling, that this was going to be a long war.
The professional in me kicked into action again, and I situated George and Melanie's backsides in front of the fire, George with an Oban Malt in his hand, and Melanie with my special-for-you explosive Martini cocktail.

The restaurant quickly filled, and I had no time for interpersonal warfare with my wife, concentrating instead on the physical and mental happiness, and wellbeing of our clients in time-honoured fashion, with great food, great service and a wonderful warm ambience. We all took our jobs seriously, and our customers would travel long distances, past innumerable restaurant competitors to spend an evening with us, and then rewarding us with a fat bill, and a generous tip for the staff in appreciation of our efforts.

It came as no great surprise, when I eventually had time to notice, the little Irish shite was washing down the walls of our cold preparation room. I knew better than to make any comment the Gorgon in the kitchen, but he appeared to making a good job of it, much to the disgust of Andrew, who´s negligence was becoming more exposed by the moment.

The wee shite spotted me and said, "It´s aw right Sur, the missus said a´ could dae it if a ´stayed oot o´ the way. Ah´ only want tae help Sur."

`Sur´ only wanted to throw the little fucking con artist out of the window, but realised this strategy would not work in the quest to get my marital rights restored anytime soon, so I muttered a "Don´t worry about it" and left the room.

I damn well knew it! This little bastard was sliding his way into a non-existing job, and there was not a lot I could do about it without a major war breaking out on the home front. The frost continued long after the last guests had gone, and continued throughout the staff dinner, with no one saying much but everyone knowing that Hamish was in trouble again.

Lorna went to bed as soon as we went home, after looking in on Kirsty, who was sound asleep in her room. Alistair and I watched a late night movie to wind down a bit, and chatted a bit about the night´s business.

When the subject of the Irish leprechaun arose, he assumed his usual neutral position of non-participation in other people´s wars, but commented that the little Irish guy was a really good worker, a condition pretty rare in our particular area. He suggested we could find some odd jobs for him to do around the place, and maybe give him some training until we got busy.

That was an opinion I did not particularly want to here, and went to bed, back to back with an iceberg.

Next morning, the rain was still lashing the windows when we were having our family breakfast. My porridge tasted and felt like ground glass under the frigid looks from Lorna, but no one else seemed to be suffering the same treatment. Lorna was fussing over Kristy's hair and school uniform, and Alistair half reading his Rangers FC News magazine with that kind of amused half smile on his face

. I finally broke the tension, and at the same time left my masculinity on the floor; "Okay, let´s do a proper interview on him and see if we can keep him busy on something."

Was there a smile of gratitude or relief on her face? No, of course not, it was a `told you I´d win´ look and a comment, "I think he could be a good worker."

We didn´t need to waste time on an interview, and to be fair, he scrubbed up fine and looked reasonably normal, except for his bleached looking complexion, but in any case, he was in, and proved to be a good conscientious hard worker at the odd jobs we found for him.

When, eventually Michael Comyn met our new boy, there appeared to be a kind of coolness I hadn´t seen before in Michael. I put this down to the `Troubles´ in Ireland, and the fact that Fergal was from the Catholic South, whilst Michael and most of his crew were from the mainly Protestant North. At the bar, Michael questioned me about the boy, and after I had related his story gave me a bit of advice. "Hamish, don´t trust that little bastard, get rid of him, or he´ll rob you blind. I wouldn´t touch him with a bargepole, so if you keep him, make sure he stays well away from our rooms."

When I related this story to Lorna, she simply dismissed his comments as being the usual bigoted Belfast rubbish. She added, "You´ve forgotten our own family bigots. If they´d got their way, we´d never have got married ….mind you, I could have found a good Catholic man, who would have treated me like a Queen; instead I ended up a Proddy´s bloody kitchen slave!" This was said with a toss of her head, but lacking the warmth that would have accompanied the humour.

I thought, *I´ll need to get a holiday booked or I´ll be looking out for a new Chef!*

Chapter 87: Meeting of Joint Intelligence Committee, Downing Street, October 26 1985.

Cabinet Secretary, Sir Myles Conrad, brought the meeting to order.

"First on the Agenda, `National Security implications appertaining to the NATO War Games due to commence on Saturday 23rd November 0100 hours."

He looked over his half-moon glasses, "Major General Smythe-Jones, your views first, as it´s a Military matter on and around British soil."

Smythe-Jones was a career Intelligence Officer, and represented DIF, the Defence Intelligence Force on the JIC meetings.

Clearing his throat noisily, the bespectacled and normally unfazed Major General began his presentation, "Thank you Sir Myles. We have not detected any undue threat to the exercises from the Soviet Bloc, other than the normal diplomatic sabre rattling which the Foreign Office is handling." He went on: "There have been no abnormal troop or tank movements across the Polish and Hungarian Plains, but we can expect extra vigilance on their part by their long range reconnaissance aircraft, and there has been an increase of the Russian monitoring trawlers operating in the North Atlantic, Irish and North Seas. We, of course are taking measures to ensure that vigilance does not escalate to interference, but the Services are taking a discrete posture to avoid provoking a confrontation."

Sir Myles then asked the Chief of MI5 to address the Committee.

"We´ve had reports from multiple sources in Northern Ireland that the Provisional IRA are planning something spectacular, however none of the sources, RUC Special Branch, Scotland Yard Terrorist Unit or our own units in situ, have come up with any details. Whoever, and whatever they are planning is being kept to a very tight circle; one of which none of our informants have access to." He finished with; "We are recommending that the prime minister orders a Imminent Threat emergency order, and appropriate security measures."

The Cabinet Secretary exploded, "Good God man, you are expecting the PM to order a full scale alert when no one knows what, where, when or even *if* the IRA is going to plant a bomb or whatever. That would be politically inacceptable as well as being impractical. The sight of armed police and soldiers guarding Central London and the other major cities, the airports, the train stations, public buildings; it would cause panic amongst the population, and can you imagine the cost of overtime payments? The police are already stretched with the bloody rioters in Tottenham; I´m afraid you will have to come up with something more specific."

The Director of GCHQ, the British Government´s telephonic monitoring service intervened; "We´ve detected a considerable amount of `chatter ´consummate with a big PIRA operation in the offing, but nothing specific either I´m sorry to say."

Exasperated, Sir Myles intervened again, "So what do I tell the prime minister; the IRA are going to launch an attack, but we don´t know where or when ...she´ll go ballistic!"

MI5 proposed that they prepare a list of possible targets and added "Although PIRA are currently favouring civilian, easy, unguarded installations, we´ve been studying the situation closely, and believe an attack on a military installation during the War Games, would provide the type of spectacular headlines they are looking for, as well as giving us a bloody humiliation. We are recommending that all military installations be put on High Alert status."

The Major General expressed irritation, "They will already be on high alert with Bonanza; the IRA would be suicidal if they attempted an attack on the military at this time."

MI5, annoyed, broke in on him, "Well maybe it would be a good idea if you suspend marching up and down in Hyde Park banging on your drums, at least for a while, until things become clearer."

"Gentlemen, gentlemen," the Cabinet Secretary tried to calm the arguments; "let´s concentrate on providing a briefing that I can present to the prime minister, one that she can rely on to answer questions in the House if it arises in Question Time."

After several more hours, the Joint Intelligence Council came up with a Security Risk Assessment report, detailing the perceived threats to National Security with particular references to the War Games schedule.

The Report included a list in order of priority, potential targets for an IRA attack. In the Military section, Army installations were placed well above RAF and Royal Navy Bases, as they had never featured in any previous attack before.

Chapter 88: Suspicions

The weeks had passed as normal, business was slow as was normal for the time of year, and Lorna and I managed to get a few days away to London, at the beginning of November.

This was Lorna´s idea of winding down before the Christmas Party season. Personally, it was my idea of burning in Hell, as we trekked around the shops, doing our Christmas shopping.

It had some consolations though, Lorna relaxed back to her old self, and we met up with some London based friends, enjoying good company, restaurants and saw Phantom of the Opera, which had just opened in the West End. We finished our break with two nights at the Prince of Wales Hotel at Grasmere, in the Lake District; the place where we had spent our honeymoon all these years ago.

Nothing much had changed in the twenty years; certainly the weather hadn´t; it was as miserable as before, but we didn´t care. The mountains hidden under sodden clouds, and the water streamed down the slate stone of the houses.

We went walking, visiting the tea and souvenir shops, interspersed with the bars to keep warm and to dry out a little.

Relaxed and away from our demanding business, we rediscovered our love, which had been buried too long in the background of our busy, high-pressure lives. I swear our lovemaking now, was better than the first time in this hotel!

Refreshed and happy we loaded up the trusty old Volvo, and headed back home early on Saturday morning. We had been in daily contact, and everything had gone smoothly since we had left on the Sunday, but we both felt that it was asking too much of Alistair, to run the kitchen on our busiest night. Good sense as it turned out, as we were fully booked in the restaurant, and a rugby crowd were coming into the Lobster Pot Bar later on.

We were back in Lochview Lodge at lunchtime, changed and ready for action within ten minutes. Lorna went straight into the kitchen, much to a tired looking, and hard pressed Alistair´s relief.

I recognised one of our young navy officer customer´s and his wife eating in the bar, and went across to say hello. It turned out he was waiting for me, to discuss reserving the restaurant for a Ladies Dinner. His submarine, HMS Resolution was leaving on an extended patrol in two weeks, could we fit them in?

I was more than happy to oblige. These farewell dinners were a real profit maker; the officers did not stint on food or drink. Although full dress affairs, and with Navy traditions adhered to, the accent was on fun and entertainment, and I personally enjoyed the night. I admired these young officers immensely, their professionalism, discipline and good heartedness impressed me, and to host these events made me very proud.

We agreed Thursday twenty-first of November; ideal as they were sailing on the following Sunday, and we could close the restaurant exclusively for them. Menu, numbers and details, we would agree the next week, over a complimentary dinner.

Alistair had a surprise on the following Tuesday evening, when John Buchan and Tommy Gannet, came up for dinner with their glamorous wives. John was the captain of Glasgow Rangers, and was a regular customer along with Tommy. They lived in Helensburgh, and the Lochview was sufficiently out of the way, without being too far. The Rennie´s was intimate, the food good, and mine host discrete enough that they could enjoy their evening in peace without being ogled, and pestered by fans. They also knew Alistair was a red-hot Rangers fan, and had given him a tour of Ibrox Park, some time before. This time they gave him VIP tickets for the upcoming Rangers versus Borussia Monchengladbach EUFA Cup game, the week after next. It was the night of his birthday and needless to say, he was over the moon, and when they invited him to sit with them at dinner later, he was in football fan heaven. I thought, *what a pair of really nice guys, to take time to entertain a young fan in this way*…so I treated them to one of my best malts; only a tot though, they were playing next evening!

Michael Comyn had not been around, although some of his boys had been hitting the Black Bushmills in the bar. I got caught up with them one night we were quiet, and very much regretted it next day. At one point, I had five Bushmills Malt Whiskey´s in front of me. Thank the Lord, Andy the barman that night looked after my health. Three of them were ginger ale, or I would never have woken up.

A good, ebullient, hard working, hard drinking crowd they were, jokes flying all of the time. Curiously, not one of them would give Fergal, our tame Southern Irish boy, the time of day, which still disturbed me. It was not only the Catholic/Protestant argument. Eamon Mulligan, who was Michael´s Comyn´s brother-in-law, was also Catholic, and he despised Fergal. However, I was not going to allow anybody, (except my wife), to tell me who I should, or should not employ. I did not want any more discussions, so I just kept him out of the way, whenever possible.

The said Fergal had been working extra hours in the kitchen when we had been away on our break, and was due some time off. When he asked for three days off, to go down to his sister in Liverpool, I told him to take four, which evened us up with his entitlement.

Mid to late November is probably the worse period in the year for business, and the weather is normally awful, as it was all this week. It was after lunch on the Friday, and Lorna and I were occupying our seats beside the fire.

Staring, mesmerised by the amount of water streaming off the hills, we decided that next year, we would take two or three weeks, and drive down to Spain. We haven´t done anything like that since nineteen seventy-four, when we took a campervan through Europe on a Gourmet Tour, during which we very quickly found out, we could not afford! We had one gourmet experience, in a very, very overpriced restaurant near Rheims in France, which scalded the wallet sufficiently enough to call off the gourmet bit of the holiday. As we were reminiscing, still smarting over the Michelin inflated bill, Michael came into the bar, as was usual on a Friday, to have a drink with me and pay the week´s lodging for his boys.

"Hamish, did ye know, yer wee tyke is also a peace camper?" he asked.

"What wee tyke are you talking about?" I asked.

"The wee Fergal guy," he replied, a grin on his face.

"Michael, what in the hell are you talking about?"

"Jimmy, our van driver, picked him and a foreign looking guy up in Helensburgh yesterday, and dropped them off at the peace camp. Normally Jimmy doesn´t pick anybody up, but he recognised the wee shite, and thought he was coming up here."

"Well it's definitely news to me, but he's been away to see his sister, so he might have met the other guy, or whatever. Michael, I don't check up on their private lives you know."

"Hamish, calm down, I'm only telling you a bit of news you obviously didn't know about."

"...and I don't really want to know about, Michael; here drink up, Lorna's got a bit of shortbread for your wife."

"Well she'll get something not so short, when I get home alright!" He laughed; "Thanks Lorna, you're the only decent one around here!"

A quick knock back of his glass, and he was out of the door, for the weekly trip down to Stranraer and the ferry back to Belfast for the weekend.

Lorna added, "My God, he really has a bee in his bonnet over Fergal. I wonder what's the problem? Michael has always been a fair minded guy in the past."

"Probably nothing more than Ulster hating the South, I replied; a bit like how some of the locals hate the English, even though the Royal Navy is the biggest employer in the area."

Annoyed she added, "Yes, but this Fergal thing goes deeper than that, I just wished I knew what it was."

The peace campers hardly ever appeared up at Whistlefield. Garelochhead was much closer, and our bar was too expensive, and out of the way. I don't particularly want them here, it's not in keeping with the image of the place, but they had never misbehaved, unlike some other's from the village. I knew Meryl, their leader; she'd been up several times with various councillors and CND types in the past. However, the Fergal thing had started a buzzing in my head, and I resolved to ask him about it.

"It was nuthin' Sur," was his response when I tackled him about the peace camp that night. "Ah met him on the train from Glasgow; he's from Spain ye know, an' says he's an eco-warrior, or somethin' like that. He invited me intae the camp for a cup o' tea, an' ah ended up stayin' the night. It's no bad, the caravans look worse than they are."

"So what do they do?" I asked, "when they're not sitting down on the road."

"Well, last night they had a cook in, where everyone brings some food an' drink to the big caravan, an' we had a bit o' a party. It was good fun, lot's o' singing an' that."

"Was Meryl, the American woman there," I asked, a bit intrigued, "she's the leader?"

"No, 'seems she's back in America, or somethin' like that. There was only about ten of us, although they're expecting a big crowd to come next weekend for a big demonstration. They were talking about a big NATO exercise they want to demonstrate against."

"Shit! They will block the bloody road again, buggering up our Saturday lunch business. Who's in charge of now?"

"The Spanish guy seemed to be in charge, which is a bit funny, ah suppose; a Spanish eco-warrior in a Scottish peace camp?" He laughed again, "Dae ye know, one of the guys in the camp is the son of some high heid officer in the base? Imagine that; an' the guy's had a private school education as well; talks like he's the duke or somethin'."

"That will be Jonathan; he went to school with Alistair."

"Yeah but Alistair disnae' talk like that," he intervened. "He's a bit weird, doesn't say much."

"Some of our wealthy customers are CND activists," I said "but I don't think they sleep at the camp. That's enough talk of the peace camp. Look, that end wall, next to the gas tank, needs a touch of paint before we put up the outside Christmas lights. That's your job on Monday; you can also stack the logs and tidy up that whole area."

"Ah'll do that Sur, anything else?"

"Monday's the day you tidy the cellar as well," I reminded him; that should keep you busy enough."

Saturday, and at last the downpours had stopped during the night. There were still plenty of clouds about on the mountains, but at least we could go outside and tidy up without getting soaked through.

The firewood supplier arrived to our relief; we had been going through so much over the past couple of weeks with the bad weather, we were in danger of running out. I had to separate Andrew and Fergal from an argument, which was almost coming to blows; Fergal accused Andrew of going into his room in the staff caravan, which Andrew had vehemently denied. I'm still uneasy with Fergal, there's something about him that I can't put my finger on; however Lorna reminds me all of the time, that he's a good worker, and he's a lost soul, whatever that means.

The bar was quiet for a Saturday; people were in Glasgow doing their Christmas shopping I suppose, but the restaurant that night was okay, considering we were now entering the pre-Christmas party season. One of the part-time waitresses phoned in sick, but this didn't cause any problems as the bookings were well spaced, and we didn't get any casuals coming in. Alistair reminded me that it was his birthday the following Wednesday, (as if I would forget!), and he had VIP tickets for the European Cup match at Ibrox. In response to my suggestion that I go with him, he laughed and said he would rather take Fergal, who was a committed Celtic supporter! "No I'm taking Fiona, she's suddenly interested in football!"

Chapter 89: Sunday 17th November 1985

Vice Admiral Harry Wellesley had been away all week at high-level meetings at the NATO HQ in Brussels, and later at Northwood, the HQ of Commander in Chief, Fleet.

Tension was rising and nerves were fraying in the run up to `Bonanza´, as the War Games were entitled. The result of three years of executive planning, negotiation and coordination of the military capability of sixteen NATO countries was going to be tested in a Europe wide scenario.

President Reagan was demanding a first class professional performance, ahead of next year´s scheduled Summit with the new Soviet leader Mikhail Gorbachov; therefore, the pressure was intensifying down through the levels of command.

Harry Wellesley had hoped to spend the weekend in Scotland, working from his home in Helensburgh, where he had an office complete with secure communication facilities, but the exigencies of last minute adjustments to the overall plans had held him back. He told Alicia that he would definitely at Faslane on Wednesday, and they would be attending the HMS Resolution Ladies dinner on Thursday evening, so could she get his dress uniform looked out?

Alicia spent Sunday with her mother, accompanying her to church and then lunch at The Queen´s Hotel. It was a fine cold but sunny morning and she left her car at home, walking through the park, colourless except for a few evergreens and still with last night´s frost on the ground.

Mrs Vickery, her mother, was still, in her seventies very fit, and the two enjoyed the walk down Sinclair Street to the church. St. Columbus boasted a good and regular congregation, mainly from the upper, and wealthy part of Helensburgh. Entering, they smiled and acknowledged the greetings of acquaintances and took their place near to the front in the pew that her mother normally occupied. Alicia wasn't a regular church goer, but attended when it was necessary as part of her role as the wife of the Vice Admiral to keep up appearances.

The minister was a committed anti-nuclear pacifist, and was to be seen at the front of many of the peace camp protests at Faslane, but retained his decorum and decency in avoiding fire and brimstone sermons. He did not refer directly to the coming War Games, but asked the congregation to pray for the young men and women, who would be in peril the following Sunday, the beginning of Advent, and the Joy of Christmas.

Alicia could feel dozens of eyes on her as he spoke his sermon, and could almost feel her cheeks colouring, but controlled herself as her mother gave her the slightest of nudges.

Leaving the church, the minister shook her hand and enquired of the admiral, hoping to see him at Christmas.

Alicia murmured her thanks for a lovely service, and wished him, and his shrew of a wife, well.

They walked down the hill, the view over the estuary opening out before them and for the first time in many weeks, the sea had relinquished its angry grey, white capped waves, replaced by and almost gentle, rolling not-quite-blue shade. The sun was dazzling of the houses of Greenock on the other side of the Clyde. They were strolling at an easy leisurely pace, arm in arm, like sisters.

Alicia, since her marriage to Harry, had at last found a peace in her life. He was dominant and exuded power, and she rather enjoyed his authority over her. She felt safe, protected from harm by his sureness and conviction. She enjoyed the residual respect and entitlements that came with her position, and in consequence worked hard at being a good wife, one that Harry had often commentated, he was proud. This new confidence and stability, had helped to mend fences with her mother, and the two women now had a much closer relationship than ever before.

Arriving at the Queen's, the proprietor, Neil Drummond, personally welcomed them, fussing over them as the good friends they were, and sat them down at a window table overlooking the estuary. Drummond suggested Dry Martinis, and the two women succumbed to the idea, still discussing who was who, at church, and what they were doing to whom.

Both now had appetites, and ordered a light Seafood Cocktail to begin with, and Roast Rack of Lamb, done pink as main courses. Drummond suggested a ten-year old Premier Cru St Julian Bordeaux, to complement the lamb, and again the ladies concurred. He hurried away to get it opened to let it breathe a bit.

They were served with a complimentary glass of Riesling with the starter, and Alicia ordered some Perrier to offset some of the alcohol.

Throughout lunch mother and daughter exchanged stories and Navy gossip. Alicia passed on the various scandals circulating at the top end of the Royal Navy Command, her mother interrupting with "I knew it, he was useless when he was under your father at Devonport," as they were discussing another Admiral.

The lamb was exceptional, and the wine historic. Declining a dessert, they retired to the lounge for coffee and petit fours. Finally, the talk turned a little more serious, when Mrs Vickery brought up the subject of Jonathan.

"Can we not do something for him, Alicia; I feel so sorry for him. He came to see me last week, the first time for ages, and I had to insist he takes a bath. After he bathed, he looked and smelled a lot better, but he was on edge. He asked about you; I said you were fine and suggested he comes here to see you, but he wouldn't listen." She continued, a worried expression on her now lined, but handsome face, "To get some conversation, I asked him about the peace camp, what do they do, and things like that. The poor boy went on and on about defeating the establishment, and getting rid of nuclear weapons; he said they were planning a big demonstration when the NATO exercises begin. I said, "I hope you are not going to do anything silly. Your mother and the admiral have some important engagements next week before it starts; I don´t want you to be embarrassing them, Jonathan."

Alicia intervened grimly, I hope to hell they don´t do anything to embarrass Harry... the whole world will be watching what goes on in the War Games."

"No, Alicia, he actually asked when you would be at Faslane so he would avoid protesting on that day." I told him, "I think they have a lunch at Faslane on Wednesday; that´s your birthday Jonathan, is it not? They are also going to the Resolution Ladies Dinner up at the Lochview Lodge on Thursday. Promise me you won´t do any protesting when they are there, Jonathan, promise me."

"I promise Grandmother, but everyone will be demonstrating on the Saturday, whether the admiral is there or not."

Mrs Vickery, looking pensive continued, "I had a birthday card I was going to post to him, and I gave him twenty pounds from me, and thirty pounds from you for his birthday. I asked him if he wanted to have a birthday dinner with me, but he said they were going to have a party at the camp; another boy, a Spanish boy he said, had his birthday on the same day. That´s a coincidence, is it not?"

The old lady sighed, her face creasing into a frown of sadness, "I do wish he would get away from that bloody Peace Camp."

Alicia leaned forward placing her hand on her mother´s knee. "I´m sorry Mother, there´s nothing I can do about Jonathan. Harry has done his best for him; first the Outward Bound School, which he ran away from, and then when he offered to sponsor him at Greenwich to prepare him for officer training. Jonathan wouldn´t even hear him out." Creasing her brow with frustration, she continued, "You have no idea what he said to Harry. It was the vilest language and hatred that he spat at him. It was most embarrassing; Harry lost his temper and told him not to come back. The Flag Lieutenant was working next door, and I think he was about to have an apoplexy also! We really can´t be doing with this up at the Official Residence."

Sadly, the old lady concurred, "I know, I know, Alicia, I just feel he is a lost soul."

On the Taxi home, after dropping her mother at her cottage, Alicia bitterly thought of Jonathan. "Why is he still causing me all this trouble? Every time I see him, or talk about him, we all end up depressed!"

Chapter 90: Sunday at Lochview Lodge

Sunday awoke to a beautiful cloudless sky; a touch of frost still spiked the grass and scarred the puddles in the car park.

It never failed to energise me, looking over the flat calm of the converging Loch Long and Loch Goil, with the pretty lighthouse on its little island. The overhanging mountains, lost, seemingly for weeks in the rain and clouds, now topped in a brilliant snow covering; they were shouting out their magnificence to all who looked upon them.

People love to drive out to the country on a day like this, so we knew we´d get a good Sunday lunch; the telephone´s incessant ringing for bookings confirmed it. By ten-o´clock it was all hands on deck. Mrs McGowan, our cleaning lady, was busy vacuuming and polishing, whilst Hugh, our weekend barman had the fires lit in the bar and down in the restaurant.

Lorna and Alistair were already well advanced in the kitchen; the joints of beef, legs of lamb and loins of pork just about to be popped into the ovens, and soups and vegetables prepared. In the cold kitchen, the gruesome twosome, as I liked to call Andrew and Fergal, had settled on an uneasy truce, and were busy preparing salads and sweets for the buffet. Helen, Mary and daughter Kirsty, were setting up the tables in the restaurant, and I was organizing the table plan, making sure our regulars got the best tables with the loch views. Hugh came down and asked if it was worthwhile opening up the beer garden; we both went outside and although the grass was still a bit soggy, we agreed that a few hardy souls would appreciate the sun, soaking up the views as well as their beers.

Later, after cashing-up, I was puffing my breast in pride and satisfaction. We´d had a record breaking November day. Everyone had enjoyed themselves; the place had been buzzing, the atmosphere electric with conversations and laughter. We were all exhausted with the running around, but this was part of the exhilaration of our trade. The cash register was full, and the staff tips bell had been chiming out all day, with generous gratuities from satisfied, happy customers.

Opening up the beer garden had been a masterstroke. We´d had a crowd of about thirty of what I call Charlie´s Hells Angels; rich young banker and lawyer types, out on their gleaming chrome, gadget adorned Harley Davidson´s. I´m certain they would not have risked getting their treasures wet on a rain filled day.

Hugh had persuaded them all to order the Special Stovies, which eased the burden on a very stressed and overworked kitchen. He came down to the restaurant towards the end of service to say that there were some peace camp types asking for Fergal.

I managed to steal a minute to have a look at them. I recognised a couple of them, including Jonathan, who´d been to school with Alistair, and the Spanish guy, who according to Fergal, was now in charge. They were behaving normally, and

I didn´t think any more about it, other than thinking they must have got extra in their dole benefits this week,

Sunday evenings are special to our family. We close the restaurant, and the only food available in the bar is a selection of toasted sandwiches, which are handled by the bar staff.

It´s the only real time of the week, when we can sit down for a proper family meal together, which invariably comes from the leftovers from the Carvery buffet! We´d been so busy today, there was hardly anything left, and we were all tired, so I phoned my friend, Mr Chow in Helensburgh. He sent up an excellent Cantonese meal for us, which was practically demolished in minutes by a hungry family.

How can a restaurant family go hungry? Easy, the food is there for selling, not eating, and to be honest we are too busy at times to think of food!

After our dinner, Lorna busied herself with Kirsty, getting her things ready for school on Monday, and rehearsing her part in the school Christmas play.
I contented myself with a glass of Highland Park, and half watched a re-run of Ski Sunday on the television, and reading the Sunday papers at the same time.

Alistair was meeting Fiona, and they planned to drive round to Lochgoilhead in the MGB for a game of curling at the ice rink there. I suggested he takes the Volvo as there was likely to be ice or snow up on the Rest and Be Thankful stretch of the road, but he reminded me he had just fitted his winter tyres on the MGB the week before.

Gathering his curling gear together, and with a wave of his hand, he was off, only come back in a few minutes with a grin on his face. "Dad, you´ve forgotten something."

"What?" I asked.

He laughed with his customary not-a-care-in-the-world manner, "The *money* sonny! How do you suppose I buy everyone in the bar a drink without my wages?"

"Sorry Alistair, you know times are hard," as I fished in my pocket for his wage packet. I added an extra ten pounds in his hand.

In response to his big smile and thanks, I said, "You deserve it, and more. Have a good time," as he kissed his mum, and disappeared out the door again.

Lorna worried her head off, as he, like all of us young bucks, drove too fast on the narrow, curving `B´ roads around the lochs. I had to remind her, we were doing the same ourselves until fairly recently, and we had survived.
Kirsty went to bed, and Lorna and I sat up quite late. I poured her a good measure of her Kalhua liqueur, and another generous Highland Park for me.

We relaxed, talking about the business; we had good prospects of a great Christmas trade, bookings were well up on last year, and our staff at last had stabilised into an efficient, professional team. The subject of Alistair´s birthday present surfaced again, although we had agreed previously to give him an envelope of money. Lorna thought that that was too impersonal, and wanted to buy him a nice watch. As usual, she won the day, and we agreed on a Gucci, not too expensive but still with cache.
At midnight, we went to bed, contented and satisfied, but much too tired to make love.

Chapter 91: Monday 18th November 1985

I slept in a bit next morning, awakened by the ringing of the phone. Still groggy, I heard Lorna talking or rather shouting at Alistair, which registered as a bit odd, it only being seven thirty on the clock!

When I staggered through to the kitchen, she saw me, gave me one of her acerbic looks, and passing the phone to me, "Talk to your son!"

"Alistair? Where are you?" I asked, knowing he was still in his bed.

"Dad, we´re still in Lochgoilhead, the road was blocked by snow when we were coming back last night."

"Why didn´t you phone last night then?"

"What was the point? It was two in the morning, and the police had stopped all traffic going over the Rest and Be Thankful, so you couldn´t have come and get us anyway."

"Where did you sleep then?"

"In the lounge of the hotel, along with about thirty others, so before you ask....nothing happened!"

That would have been the last of my questions, although I suspect his mother might have had that one up very near the top of the list.

"Has Fiona phoned her mother yet?" I asked.

"Yes, she phoned before I did, and before you say anything, she was okay about it."

I thought that was probably stretching the truth a bit, but I knew I had a discussion on parental responsibilities with my own wife to face yet.

"What´s happening about the road then...Is it clear now?" I enquired.

"The police expect it to be open again by lunchtime, the `ploughs have been working all night, so I should be home by about tea time. Look dad, I´ll need to get off, there´s a queue for the phone, see you later, ´bye!"

I said `bye son, into a crackling telephone, and turned to face the gathering storm about to be unleashed over my head.

"That´s your bloody fault!" she hissed, "you encouraged him to go up there!"

I could feel the blood pumping up in my temples, on the way to turning my mild malt whisky headache into something much more horrible.

Wearily I responded, "Lorna, he´s twenty years old on Wednesday, he´s not a child anymore. I didn´t encourage him to go anywhere, I offered him the Volvo, which wouldn´t have made any difference in any case… the police closed the bloody road!"

Narrowing her eyes like cat, and pointing the index finger like a Magnum 357, she accused, "That boy´s got you wrapped around his little finger; he gets off with everything. Fiona´s parents are going to blame us for this!"

"Fiona´s parents are quite used to them being late, he doesn´t normally finish his work until eleven at night."

"You´d better phone them then!" she ordered.

"I will, as soon as you stop bloody shouting at me!" as I picked up the phone. "Do you know the number?"

Kirsty, who had been keeping her head down at the table, eating her cereal, and reading a Jackie girls magazine piped in; "It´s in the directory, dad."

"Kirsty, just read it to me will you, I can´t see the damn directory this morning."

"Oh dad …I´m busy!"

"God Almighty!" The alcohol had finally collided with my blood pressure melding into a bloody explosion of pain and rage in my head. "Give me the damn directory!"

"Its 014*****3," the caustic advice came from behind me, as Lorna read it out from her diary.

Garry, Fiona´s dad was already at work, and it was Fiona´s mother Sue, who answered the phone. As I explained the situation, she interrupted; "Don´t worry Hamish, they´re both responsible adults, we didn't even know she wasn't home until she phoned!"

What a wonderful understanding woman this is, picturing Sue, a more mature, extremely attractive version of her daughter, but guiltily looking away as Lorna caught my eye. "They should be back sometime this afternoon," I assured her, adding, "We'll be seeing you around about Christmas?"

"Only if my daughter returns by then," she laughed.

"Yes, we'll make a point of it Hamish, love to Lorna, `bye."

For the second time that morning, I said "`bye," into a crackling telephone line.

"What did she say?" asked the mother of my children.

"She was alright about it, she wasn't worried at all."

"Some mother she is," humped Lorna, as she began organizing her daughter for going out into the snow lying around outside.

We were going in to Glasgow. Lorna was visiting her sister Shona, who had, at last, dumped her useless, now ex-husband Norman.

I would do the cash and carry run, linking up later with Henri Pascual for a game or two of snooker.

Lorna had literally been `cast out' of her family twenty years ago, when we got married. The only `family' she had was her Aunt Theresa, now retired and living in Spain, and Shona, for whom she now felt a little guilty, although she couldn't really fathom out why she should.

She would drop off the Christmas presents for Shona and the kids, and suggest they all come up to Whistlefield for Christmas. Lorna was grateful that her sister would almost certainly decline the invitation. We would be too busy to give them any attention, and gaggle of council house kids running amok around Lochview Lodge would not go down well with the genteel folk expected over the Festive season. Later on, Lorna would be meeting up with her best friend, Ana for last minute Christmas shopping.

Ana and Henri Pascual had been our friends since before we were married. We would all be meeting up later for drinks and dinner, our last social event before the frenetic Christmas season.

Alistair had, at last, got back from Lochgoilhead at three o´clock, dropped off his girlfriend Fiona at her house, and after offering profuse apologies to her mother, jumped back in the MGB to go into Helensburgh for a haircut. An hour later, he had put the car through the car wash and headed back up towards Whistlefield. Just as he was passing the Sailing Club, he saw in the gloom his old schoolmate Jonathan Amersbey hitching a lift. He hesitated about stopping, but changed his mind and reversed back to him.

Jonathan had not recognised the car, and when he pulled open the door he exclaimed, "Jesus Sandy, you´re doing all right!"

Alistair replied, just a little irritably, "Well you could do alright as well Jono, if you would work like I do, and not sit about on your arse on the road protesting!"

Jonathan began with his well-prepared ideological statements, "I am not prepared to be a slave to the bourgeois capitalist establishment enriching themselves on the backs of the workers."

"No, but you don´t have a problem in cashing the bourgeois capitalists benefit cheques, do you?" retorted Alistair. "Are you going to the peace camp now?" he asked, already regretting he had stopped the car.

Jonathan answered, "If you don´t mind Sandy, I appreciate it."

They drove in silence for a few minutes until Alistair, relenting asked him, "Jono, Don´t you ever think of your future? You can´t be a peace camper all of your life."

"Sandy, nobody, not even you are going to have a future if these Trident missiles come here."

Malevolent Karma

"Aw, let´s not go down that road again, Jono." Changing the subject he asked, "What are you doing for your birthday on Wednesday, got anything planned?"

A little happier, Jonathan replied, "We´re having a party at the camp; it´s Iñaki´s birthday on the same day; isn´t that a real coincidence Sandy, you, me and Iñaki are all twenty on the twentieth!"

"That´s the Spanish guy, isn´t it; I thought he was older than us... it is a bit weird right enough; just shows you, ...our parent´s all shagging at the same time! Changing tack he asked, "So what´s the story on him, why is he a peace camper? They don´t have nukes in Spain, do they?"

"The Americans do, and they accidently dropped four nukes in Almeria, but none exploded; Iñaki told me all about it."

"Well I suppose that would give him some reason to be anti-nukes, but he just doesn´t seem the type; mind you I don´t know the guy." Alistair signalled, and drove into the lay by at the peace camp.

Jonathan cracked his head off the soft-top supports as he was reaching in for his rucksack, "Shit, you´re car is too fucking small," he complained. "Look it´s going to be a great night on Wednesday, why don´t you come down; there´s a crowd coming from Glasgow; just bring some booze."

"No thanks Jono, I´m off to Ibrox, but have a good time; incidentally I think your mother is up for a dinner on Thursday; are you still out of favour with the admiral?"

Jonathan´s face fell, "I´m barred from the official residence it seems; the admiral doesn´t like my company around there, so I don´t really see her that often... mind you, I have never really seen her that often, so what´s the difference now? See you!" as he slammed the door shut.

Reflecting upon his memory of his days at Castle School, Alistair thought, "Poor bugger, thank God my family´s normal!" He shifted into first, and roared away, beaming satisfaction as the acceleration forced him back in his seat.

Chapter 92: Monday 18th, 8pm, Dumbarton

As a precaution, Iñaki had parked the Volkswagen in the car park on the pier in Helensburgh, and then took a train to Dumbarton. He was early but needed time to find the Bridge Bar for the meet.

Fergal had taken the seven twenty bus from Garelochhead, and got into the High Street just before eight; he knew where to go. He entered the lounge bar and took a table away from the half dozen other customers dotted about the place.

McManus had come down from Glasgow, and parked his car down by the river. He met Iñaki outside the pub, putting his arm around his shoulder, saying "You´ve done good with this son" as he pushed the swing door open.

They both ordered pint´s of McEwan's, and the Glaswegian asked the barman for the domino set, before sitting at Fergal´s table. They emptied the dominos out of the box, and began cracking the tiles on the table. Anyone looking would think it was a normal game between three friends, although the Glaswegian, in his brown bomber jacket and leather *bunnet*, looked a lot older than the other two.

Under the noise of the blaring TV showing Coronation Street, they discussed the bombing of the Lochview Hotel. Iñaki voiced his doubts that it was necessary to destroy the hotel. McManus quite forcefully reminded him, that it was he, who suggested it as a possible target. His suggestion had gone to the Army Council in South Armagh, who controlled the bombs, and the hotel confirmed as being a legitimate target, as it was housing a bunch of fucking Belfast Prods building a military installation for the Brits.

McManus, pointing his finger at Iñaki said, "They had put a lot of time, effort and money into this plan, so tough shite, too late to back off now! So, remind this old reprobate of how you are going to do this."

Fergal said that the bomb was in place, and just needed to be primed, which he would do the night before. He was going to go sick after lunch on Thursday, and get to Glasgow Airport by seven for the Dublin flight at eight.

Iñaki detailed his plans for the peace campers to mount their demo at the hotel, adding that this by itself would be a serious embarrassment for the Royal Navy. He would make an excuse he had forgotten some rockets, and have to go back down to the peace camp, just a few minutes away. Instead, he would drive over to a disused factory in Alexandria, and dump and burn the Volkswagen. A volunteer would be there to collect him, and drive him to Edinburgh by the country route via Stirling for a flight to Amsterdam. He would then make his own way to Bayonne to join up and fight with ETA in their war of liberation against the Spanish Fascists. Again, Iñaki asked for assurance that the warning would be given on time to evacuate the hotel.

The Glaswegian angrily retorted the IRA was not in the business of blowing up innocent people in hotels, apparently forgetting the bloody excesses of the past. Looking him in the eye, he gave his solemn oath that they would get thirty minutes to clear the area. Iñaki was again reminded that this was a highest-level attack; he had better not think of backing away now; these people are unforgiving.

After discussing a few more details, he reached into his pocket, and handed Iñaki and Fergal their new identities, passports and plane tickets, as well as the envelope of money they had earned.

McManus went back to the bar, and bought three large Jameson's Irish malts, returning to toast to the success of the operation, and to a Free Ireland.

Chapter 93: Rennie's at the Lochview Lodge Hotel.

**The Officers' Mess of HMS Resolution.
The Ladies Dinner: Lochview Lodge Hotel
Thursday, 21st November 1985. 7.30 for 8pm**

"Don't talk to me about Navy tradition; it's nothing but rum, sodomy and the lash!" ~Winston Churchill.

M C: Lieutenant Commander John Robinson.

"……..and it gives me the greatest honour to introduce our principle guest, one of us, a submariner, whose illustrious career has extended from entering as a cadet at Dartmouth College, a truly magnificent campaign in the Falklands War, to the highest echelons of the Joint Chiefs of Staff at Norwood.

He has made a nuisance of himself by his uncompromising defence of the submarine service." Looking along the table at his distinguished guest, he continued, "This man was responsible for a change in MOD policy at a time when the government was contemplating major cut's to our Service."

He continued, "Our guest has, until a few months ago, been responsible for the coordination of NATO Maritime Forces at NATO Headquarters in Brussels, and has taken a leading role in the planning of the NATO Joint Command War Games exercise in which we, HMS Resolution, are about to play a pivotal role." Drawing himself up, and taking in a deep breath to reinforce his delivery, he announced, "Ladies and gentlemen, please be upstanding, and welcome ....Vice-Admiral Sir Harold Rupert Wellesley, GCB. CB: Flag Officer Scotland and Northern Ireland."

The entire company rose, cheered, and applauded the Hero of the Falkland Island submarine war, who now was the most senior Royal Navy officer commanding the North British Region.
The Officers of HMS Resolution were celebrating the traditional Ladies Dinner, before they went out on an extended patrol in the North Atlantic Ocean. They would be submerged and maintaining a silent vigil deep underneath the GIUP Gap in the North Atlantic, in their role as Britain's ballistic nuclear deterrent.

The Cold War was still very much alive, and the combined army, air and naval forces of NATO were, in five days time, beginning a ten-day war simulation exercise, during which HMS Resolution was to play a key role.

Dress was formal. At the Top Table this evening was the Captain of Resolution, Commander Andrew Randolph with his wife Audrey; Admiral Sir Harold Wellesley and his wife Lady Alicia; Lieutenant Commander John Robinson, who was acting as the Master of Ceremonies for this evening with his wife Felicity; a visiting American admiral, and two very high level MOD officials and their wives.

The Reception and Dinner had passed smoothly and enjoyably.
The Lochview Lodge Hotel staff were as ever professional, and discrete in their service; and the food, cooked by the owner Lorna MacLeod and her son Alistair, mouth-watering and satisfying. Hamish, Lorna's husband, was 'out on the floor', supervising the service and hospitality, paying particular attention to the Top Table.

Coffee had been poured, and Cigars distributed; a 1945 Grahams Fine Old Vintage Port had being passed around, whilst the ladies had mainly opted for a variety of liqueurs.

As tradition demanded, the speeches would be light-hearted and funny; it was an evening of enjoyment before the long, enforced separation endured by submariners and their loved ones.

Sir Harry had asked for his speech to be moved up in the programme, as he had to fly down to London afterwards. His Flag Lieutenant would be collecting him at half past ten.

The applause died down. Admiral Sir Harry Wellesley slowly rose to his feet. He was just under six feet tall but his broad, powerful shoulders, greying short cut hair capping a bull like head and rugby torn features, said this was a physical man to be reckoned with.

He exuded authority as he passed his penetrating gaze around the room, taking in his officers, a half smile played at his mouth as he enveloped his audience in his personality. Seconds, seemingly minutes, passed in complete silence, and just as the ambience was turning a little uncomfortable, he began his speech.

"Well, first of all, I must thank Lieutenant Commander Robinson for his Hollywood Star description of me, of which modest as I am, will have to say he´s looked up the wrong man in the Navy List!"

The ice was broken, and the audience laughed accordingly.

"However, I must say, I was flattered enough to be impressed, and this young man can look forward to early and rapid promotion"

More laughter, as he changed the tone and continued;

"Si vis pacem, para bellum."
"If you wish for peace, prepare for war."

Malevolent Karma

He paused, and looked around the room, enveloping all in his presence, expectant silence hanging in the air. "This, as you all know, is the motto of the Royal Navy. The Royal Navy is the Senior Service of the Realm; the submarine service is called the Silent Service; but my officers should never doubt that in fighting the cause of our magnificent submarine fleet, and the outstanding submariners who man them, I will not ever be the *silent* in their service!"

Wild applause, and a cacophony of hear, hears´!

"You are all aware of the importance of this mission. The eyes of the World, including our adversaries in the Soviet Union, are going to be focussed on the success of these war exercises. I am not going to ask that you do not let me down; I know you will not fail in your duty, because you love your duty!"

The audience showed their appreciation with more wide applause and thumping on the tables.

Holding his hand up for silence, Wellesley went on, "I am, frankly envious of you, the Officers of HMS Resolution. As you know, I served on Resolution, on her first Operational Tour, back in 1966, and as you patrol around the GIUP, you may come across some of the hairs and skin from my head, which I left on board as I got to know my way around!"

More laughter erupted from the listeners.

"Now I will be submerged under a sea of paper, whilst my thoughts are with you on your mission."

Taking a more serious tone, he continued: "The submarine service is a family; HMS Resolution may be out of normal communication for months, but my experience is that we are bonded to our wives and sweethearts all of the time. I swear that this connection between us is telepathic at times." A smile passed over his craggy visage, "If Commander Randolph pops the periscope up under a Soviet Bomber, he will instantly be aware of my thoughts!"

The laughing Officers turned their attention to their Captain, who smiled, but had begun to flush red.

"Now I must turn my attention to the Ladies, beautiful in their evening wear, a pleasure to my eyes. You are the ones, who really ought to get the medals. We men, out on our missions, are isolated from the day-to-day problems of family life. We can be professional in our work, but it is you who bear th...............

Chapter 94: The Aftermath.

The explosion had lit up the night sky, an orange-red ball of fire reflecting of the clouds, illuminating the snow covered fern and heather covered hills and mountains.

The first reaction came from a guard tower at Faslane Submarine Base, when a MOD policeman screamed into his radio, "There´s a huge explosion over at Finnart!"
This mistake was understandable, as the Finnart Oil Terminal was in a direct line over the hill from his tower.

The Control Room immediately alerted the Strathclyde emergency services, and authorised the base´s own fire brigade into action. This was going to be a major fire, therefore every available fire brigade unit from north Glasgow to Dumbarton asked to assist.

Confusion erupted in the Fire Brigade Control headquarters at Johnstone, when they received an emergency call from the Finnart Oil Terminal to report a major explosion and fire to the south of them. They thought the explosion was connected to the Faslane Navy Base!

When the first response units from the part-time Garelochhead volunteer fire and rescue service breasted the hill at Whistlefield, they witnessed a scene out of Dante's Inferno. The few timbers left that had once been the Lochview Lodge Hotel were still in flames, as were the trees and some unrecognizable cars in the car park.

Bodies and bit´s of bodies, were spread over a wide area. Survivors, some lying prone on the ground moaning softly, others still screaming in agony or running around in shock and pain. The emergency teams set about their work with a grim resolve. Arc lights were set up to illuminate the scene of devastation, the flames doused and the injured given first aid until the ambulances with wailing sirens could get them to hospital for proper medical and intensive treatment.

Many of the victims appeared to be Royal Navy officers, and someone had the presence of mind to radio the Royal Navy Command Centre at the Base.

The full horror at what was unfolding became apparent when they checked the whereabouts of the Flag Officer and the officers of HMS Resolution. The Joint Services Command in Norwood was immediately informed, as was Prime Minister Thatcher. She called an emergency meeting of her National Security Committee.

The first indications as to what had happened when one badly injured but conscious Peace Camper was found more than thirty yards from the building, in a clump of gorse bushes. He babbled incoherently about fireworks had exploded or something; there was a huge flash and explosion which blew him over some cars into the bushes.

Dawn broke, and the first rays of winter sun broke over a scene of complete and utter devastation.
The blast and fire had completely levelled the Lochview Lodge Hotel to the ground; the trees and vegetation over a hundred square metre area were blackened stumps, and charred bodies and body parts were still being located in the undergrowth.

There was still no accurate count of the dead and injured; no one knew for sure who, or how many people had been in the hotel at the time of the explosion.

A badly injured and unconscious young man wearing a chef's uniform, had been found among the wreckage of the MacLeod's family home, fifty yards from the hotel. An onlooking neighbour identified him as being Alistair MacLeod, but so far, there was no sign of his sister Kirsty, who, according to the same neighbour would normally have been in the house at the time of the explosion.

Many of the victims in the hotel had disappeared, blasted to pieces or consumed by the three thousand degree heat of the explosion, others charred beyond recognition. The assumption was that the owners, Hamish and Lorna MacLeod were among the victims.

When the Fire Brigade Forensic Investigation team arrived on the site, they realised at once that it was improbable that a gas tank explosion could not have caused carnage on this scale. In view of the military importance of the victims, they were joined by a specialist Home Office Forensic team, who cordoned off the whole area. Top-level orders were issued, that this investigation would be conducted under strict conditions according to the Official Secrets Act statutes.

The National Security Committee had discussed the situation during the night. The testimony of the surviving peace protester and the few witnesses who had survived the explosion and fire presented and discussed.

There was still no evidence this had been an IRA attack, although this theory had not yet been discounted.

The issue of the Bonanza War Games was number one priority. There was no question that they be cancelled. Mrs Thatcher insisted that the War Games must go ahead, as planned; "We would look fools in the eyes of the world; after all," she pointed out, "Ships and submarines are sunk during a real war, and the war does not stop!"

Despite vociferous protests from the press and various church leaders, the War Games went on as planned. A Nuclear Attack submarine, already on patrol in the North Atlantic took the place of the ill-fated HMS Resolution.

By the time the Fire Brigade and Home Office forensic teams finally found the residue evidence of bomb explosive in some pieces of shrapnel from the gas tank, Fergal O'Brien was at a safe house in South Armagh, and Iñaki Anton in Amsterdam. The forensic findings were reported direct to the National Security Council in Downing Street, which was then faced with a public relations dilemma.

The government did not want the humiliation of admitting that military security had been breached so easily, especially in such a highly militarised zone.

"There must be two thousand troops, the SAS and SBS as well as the MOD police all within a ten mile radius of the place," a Major General (Intel.) admitted to the National Security Committee.

Many around the table were thinking, but not voicing "Where in the hell was your military intelligence then?"

Another opinion was that while it was naturally tempting to blame the Provos as callous murderers of innocent civilians, but that would raise questions of our security at the HMNB Clyde.

The Prime Minister decided that it would be prudent to wait until the IRA issued a statement of culpability; meanwhile a tight lid on secrecy would be maintained over the disaster.

The Provisional IRA had not given a warning. It was as simple a reason of vandalised phone boxes in the east end of Glasgow, and not enough time to find a secure alternative.

The Army Council was concerned and surprised at the number of civilian casualties. The building had literally exploded consuming almost everyone inside. No one had explained to the normally callous capos, that the Lochview Lodge Hotel had been constructed, almost entirely, in wood.

Their American fund-raisers, NORAID, had been critical of collateral damage, and had threatened to stop funding unless there was more effort invoked to avoid civilian casualties.

With this in mind, the Army Council decided that they would not claim responsibility. Thatcher would know that it was an IRA operation, and they had demonstrated that they could launch an attack anywhere on the British mainland at will.

An official Accident and Sudden Death enquiry would be set up under the jurisdiction of the Sheriff of Dumbarton at a later date after the conclusion of police investigations were concluded.

The sole survivor of the protesters, Jonathan Amersbey, was to admit his and his companions' accidental culpability, in setting off flares just before the explosion.

Experts were to testify that the placing of the high pressure propane gas tank in a depression of the slope, and being so close to the building, had accelerated the blast straight into the wooden building. An explosive expert likened it to the explosion of gunpowder inside of a cannon. The wooden fabric of the hotel in turn disintegrated into wooden shrapnel, and this, in conjunction with the superheated gas flame caused instant death to most of the people inside the hotel.

The Sheriff was to reserve judgement for a later date.

Norman MacRitchie Reeley

Epilogue

"I know not death, I live in the winds."~Anonymous

The mountains around, they still look the same, as are the skerries on the surface of the sea at the confluence of the lochs down there in front of the visitor. Even the little lighthouse on its rocky island is where it always was; and Carrick Castle, over on the other side is also in its usual place.

The Lochside Lodge Hotel and the little family cottage is no more; a cleared flattened grassy area with a little remembrance Cairn to those who died. The benches arrayed around for visitors to sit in contemplative meditation are long gone, destroyed by vandals or stolen to adorn someone's semi-detached garden.

Nevertheless it's more than this though. Something fundamentally natural, or ethereal, is different about this place. There's a brooding silence; a grey shadow on the clouds even though the sun is shining, there's a silence. The mountains are glowering more than before, and the sea looks black hostile and colder these days. The very land has become embittered. Even on a warm spring day, when lambs are gambolling, and buttercups are pushing through the grass, this chill in the air that can produce a shiver down one's spine reeks of the daunting sadness that stalks this place, and in Glencoe, where the Campbells put the MacDonalds to the sword in their homes in the winter of 1692.

On this very spot on the earth's surface, these wailing winds of fate laid down the lives of seventy-eight human beings, the same death bell toll as rang in Glencoe. In Glencoe that terrible winter's night, one of these unfortunates was a visiting cousin from the Hebrides. His name was *Seumas Mhic Leòid*... Hamish MacLeod.

Ask yourself the question: A tragic twist of fate? Destiny? or **Malevolent Karma?**

Norman MacRitchie Reeley

About the author:

Norman MacRitchie Reeley

Following family tradition, he was originally destined to be an engineer in the shipyards of the River Clyde in Scotland. A chance meeting on a rain filled winter´s evening with an old school friend changed the direction of his life forever. He defied his father; quit his `secure´ engineering apprenticeship to train to become a chef.

As well as enjoying the creative but high-pressure world of the kitchen, he re-discovered the joys and satisfaction of education, and became a Senior Lecturer in a college of further education. His underlying ambition however, was to open a family-run bistro-style restaurant in the manner of the French or Italian model. He quit his job in the college and opened his dream bistro-restaurant near to HMNB Clyde at Faslane on the Gareloch, which quickly obtained a reputation far beyond the local area.

In nineteen-ninety, the family moved to Spain, buying a Hotel and Restaurant in the beautiful seaside town of Javea, on the Costa Blanca.

After retiring, Norman has enjoyed travelling around Europe in his old campervan, written travel articles, dabbled in local politics and amateur sculpture.

Norman MacRitchie Reeley

Praise for Malevolent Karma (Unfortunately no star national press critics yet!)

Three innocent boys, born on the same day, thousands of miles apart who's paths are ultimately destined to cross resulting in carnage and destruction beyond belief. A dramatic ending, that I didn't anticipate left me initially in a state of shock, followed by a confused mixture of outrage, anger and eventual sadness about the seemingly inevitability of our lives on this planet. An excellent, thought provoking read that had me mentally shouting, "Don't do it," and "Look behind you," from beginning to end. Benny Davis, Freelance Journalist

By the way, just finished your book and have to say that it was brilliant, I couldn't put it down. You have an exceptional talent for writing. Well done! Hurry up with that next book please. Marie Smith, Javea, Alicante.

You are a born story-teller, and that is a real gift. It´s quite rare to start a book and just have to continue on until you reach the end. Well done! Nina Davies, Javea Book Circle, Alicante.

A fantastic can't put down novel with everything you could want from a book! Raunchy sex scenes; sabotage, teen dramas, politics, naval exploits, happy families to suicide! Truly well written and based in the most beautiful scenery ʰat is the West of Scotland with many landmarks that are ˑy well known to the local reader! Highly Recommend! ˑrley Burns, Loch Lomond, Scotland.

Malevolent Karma

At last I've gone in to face book to write a comment on 'Malevolent Karma' - It was one of those books I couldn't put down once I started to read. The many twists and turn in peoples' lives amazed me, I was surprised at the intricacy of the plot(s) and was equally surprised as to whom would survive!! (Enough said - you need to read it yourself to find out what happens!!!) **Glyn Griffiths, Barry, Wales.**

An excellent page turner... The author has written with an obvious passion for where he has travelled and weaved a tale that keeps the reader entertained. I will look for more from this author! **Bobby Bowers, Rutherglen, Scotland**

Took time to bed in to reading this book as writing style is a bit different from my usual bestsellers but once the storyline got under my skin it was unputdownable! I look forward to a sequel, prequel or even a movie. **Eveline Howels, Toronto Canada**

Just finished the book. I must say I was surprised, what a well written and enjoyable read. Could not believe I was not reading a best-selling author. Perhaps I was! **Mark Bell, Surrey, UK.**

Set in the '70s and '80s this novel hooks you from the start, as, chapter by chapter, it introduces us to three separate and non-connected lads raised in different countries and whose destinies and fates are inevitably to cross, not always in the happiest of circumstances. It's a long and bumpy ride, and not always with travel companions whose company you'd enjoy, but at the end, worth the time spent getting there. **RG Cowley, Glasgow, Scotland**

Norman MacRitchie Reeley

You really feel connected to the characters in this book. They are manipulated by many of the people they come into contact with, including family. They appear to be unrelated, but are drawn together in a way that ties them up in an inescapable way. Be careful what you say or do as it will catch up with you, not always in the way you expect! Plenty of twists, turns and shocks in this story. Who gets caught up in the crossfire? You will need to read it to find out. Ann Pryce, Dumbarton, Scotland

Malevolent Karma by Norman MacRitchie Reeley, This is an excellent book, brilliantly written and very well researched. A non-stop page -turner, Once I had started I couldn't put it down "riveting plot with many twists and turns" I look forward to reading more from this Author. For my friends and contacts back in the UK, it's a must buy. Ken Laidlaw, Lisbon, Portugal

My husband Bruce and I loved this book. When is the sequel coming out? Trudi, van Dorf, Holland.

They say that there is a book in everyone, but then there are books that shine above others.
Malevolent Karma is one of those books! I cannot recommend this book enough. THIS IS A BOOK YOU REMEMBER! Beverley Harper, Bookworld España.

Malevolent Karma

460

Printed in Great Britain
by Amazon.co.uk, Ltd.,
Marston Gate.